The Twelve Chairs

》》》》》》》》》》 《《《《《《《《《《《

Ilf & Petrov

The Twelve Chairs

TRANSLATED FROM THE RUSSIAN BY
JOHN H. C. RICHARDSON

INTRODUCTION BY MAURICE FRIEDBERG

NORTHWESTERN UNIVERSITY PRESS
EVANSTON, ILLINOIS

》》》》》》》》》》》 《《《《《《《《《《《

Northwestern University Press
Evanston, Illinois 60208-4210

Copyright © 1961 by Random House, Inc. Northwestern University Press
edition published 1997 by arrangement with Random House, Inc.
All rights reserved.

Printed in the United States of America

ISBN 0-8101-1484-4

Library of Congress Cataloging-in-Publication Data

Il'f, Il'ia Arnol'dovich, 1897–1937.
    [Dvenadtsat' stul'ev. English]
    The twelve chairs / by Ilf & Petrov ; translated from
the Russian by John H. C. Richardson ; introduction by
Maurice Friedberg.
        p. cm. — (European classics)
    English translation originally published: New York :
Random House, 1961.
    ISBN 0-8101-1484-4
    I. Petrov, Evgenii, 1903–1942. II. Richardson, John
H. C. III. Title. IV. Series: European classics (Evanston,
Ill.)
PG3476.I44D913 1997
891.73'42—dc21   96-29783
                                       CIP

The translator wishes to express his appreciation to Mr. and Mrs. N. Nikolenko
for their assistance and valuable advice.

Introduction

IT HAS LONG BEEN my considered opinion that strains in Russo-American relations are inevitable as long as the average American persists in picturing the Russian as a gloomy, moody, unpredictable individual, and the average Russian in seeing the American as childish, cheerful and, on the whole, rather primitive. Naturally, we each resent the other side's unjust opinions and ascribe them, respectively, to the malice of capitalist or Communist propaganda. What is to blame for this? Our national literatures; or, more exactly, those portions of them which are read. Since few Americans know people of the Soviet Union from personal experience, and vice versa, we both depend to a great extent on information gathered from the printed page. The Russians know us—let us forget for a moment about *Pravda*—from the works of Jack London, James Fenimore Cooper, Mark Twain, and O. Henry. We know the Russians—let us temporarily disregard the United Nations—as we have seen them depicted in certain novels of Tolstoy and Dostoyevsky and in the later dramas of Chekhov.

There are two ways to correct these misconceptions. One would be to import into Russia a considerable number of sober, serious-minded, Russian-speaking American tourists, in exchange for an identical number of cheerful, logical, English-speaking Russians who would visit America. The other, less costly form of cultural exchange would be for the Russians to read more of Hawthorne, Melville, Faulkner, and Tennessee Williams, and for us to become better acquainted with the less solemn—though not at all less profound —Russians. We would do well to read more of Gogol, Saltykov-Shchedrin, Chekhov (the short stories and the one-act plays) and—among Soviet authors—to read Mikhail Zoshchenko and Ilf and Petrov. Thus, in its modest way, the present volume—though outwardly not very "serious"—should contribute to our better understanding of Russia and the Russians and aid us in facing the perils of peaceful coexistence.

If writers were to be judged not by the reception accorded to them by literary critics but by their popularity with the reading public, there could be no doubt that the late team of Ilf and Petrov would have few peers among Soviet men of letters. Together with another humorist, the recently deceased Mikhail Zoshchenko, for many years they baffled and outraged Soviet editors and delighted Soviet readers. Yet even while their works were officially criticized in the literary journals for a variety of sins (the chief among them being insufficient ideological militancy and, *ipso facto*, inferior educational value), the available copies of earlier editions were literally read to shreds by millions of Soviet citizens. Russian readers loved Ilf and Petrov because these two writers provided them with a form of catharsis rarely available to the Soviet citizen—the opportunity to laugh at the sad and ridiculous aspects of Soviet existence.

Anyone familiar with Soviet press and literature knows one of their most depressing features—the emphasis on the pompous and the weighty, and the almost total absence of the light touch. The USSR has a single Russian journal of humor and satire, *Krokodil*, which is seldom amusing. There is a very funny man in the Soviet circus, Oleg Popov, but he is a clown and seldom talks. At the present time, among the 4,801 full-time Soviet writers there is not a single talented humorist. And yet the thirst for humor is so great in Russia that it was recognized as a state problem by Malenkov, who, during his short career as Prime Minister after Stalin's death, appealed to Soviet writers to become modern Gogols and Saltykov-Shchedrins. The writers, however, seem to have remembered only too well the risks of producing humor and satire in a totalitarian state (irreverent laughter can easily provoke accusations of political disloyalty, as was the case with Zoshchenko in 1946), and the appeal did not bring about desired results. Hence, during the "liberal" years of 1953-7 the Soviet Government made available, as a concession to its humor-starved subjects, new editions of the *old* works of Soviet humorists, including 200,000 copies of Ilf and Petrov's *The Twelve Chairs* and *The Little Golden Calf*.

Muscovites and Leningraders might disagree, but there is strong evidence to indicate that during the first decades of this century the capital of Russian humor was Odessa, a bustling, multilingual, cosmopolitan city on the Black Sea. In his recently published memoirs, the veteran Soviet novelist Konstantin Paustovsky fondly recalls the sophisticated and iconoclastic Odessa of the early postrevolutionary years. Among the famous sons of Odessa were Isaac Babel, the writer of brilliant, sardonic short stories; Yurii Olesha, the creator of modernistic, ironic tales; Valentin Katayev, author of *Squaring the Circle*, perhaps the best comedy in the Soviet repertory; and both members of the team of Ilf and Petrov.

Ilya Ilf (pseudonym of Fainzilberg) was born in 1897; Yevgenii Petrov (pseudonym of Katayev, a younger brother of Valentin) in 1903. The two men met in Moscow, where they both worked on the railwaymen's newspaper, *Gudok* (*Train Whistle*). Their "specialty" was reading letters to the editor, which is a traditional Soviet means for voicing grievances about bureaucracy, injustices, and shortages. Such letters would sometimes get published as *feuilletons*, short humorous stories somewhat reminiscent of Chekhov's early output. In 1927 Ilf and Petrov formed a literary partnership, publishing at first under a variety of names, including some whimsical ones, like Fyodor Tolstoyevsky. In their joint "autobiography" Ilf and Petrov wrote:

> It is very difficult to write together. It was easier for the Goncourts, we suppose. After all, they were brothers, while we are not even related to each other. We are not even of the same age. And even of different nationalities: while one is a Russian (the enigmatic Russian soul), the other is a Jew (the enigmatic Jewish soul).

The literary partnership lasted for ten years, until 1937, when Ilya Ilf died of tuberculosis. Yevgenii Petrov was killed in 1942 during the siege of Sebastopol.

The two writers are famed chiefly for three books— *The Twelve Chairs* (1928; known in a British translation as *Diamonds to Sit On*); *The Little Golden Calf* (1931), a tale of the tribulations of a Soviet millionaire who is afraid to spend any money lest he be discovered by the police; and *One-Storey High America* (1936; known in a British translation as *Little Golden America*), an amusing and, on the whole, friendly account of the two writers' adventures in the land of Wall Street, the Empire State Building, automobiles, and aspiring capitalists.

The plot of *The Twelve Chairs* is very simple. The mother-in-law of a former nobleman named Vorobyaninov discloses on her deathbed a secret: she hid her diamonds in one of the family's chairs that subsequently had been appropriated by the Soviet authorities. Vorobyaninov is joined by a young crook named Ostap Bender with whom he forms a partnership, and together they proceed to locate these chairs. The partners have a competitor in the priest Vostrikov, who has also learned of the secret from his dying parishioner. The competing treasure-hunters travel throughout Russia, which enables the authors to show us glimpses of little towns, Moscow, and Caucasian resorts, and also have the three central characters meet a wide variety of people—Soviet bureaucrats, newspapermen, survivors of the prerevolutionary propertied classes, provincials, and Muscovites.

The events described in the novel are set in 1927, that is, toward the end of the period of the New Economic Policy, which was characterized by a temporary truce between the Soviet regime's Communist ideology and limited private enterprise in commerce, industry, and agriculture. The coffin-making and bagel-baking businesses referred to in the novel have long since been nationalized; the former noblemen masquerading as petty Soviet employees and many of the colleagues of the priest described by Ilf and Petrov are no longer alive; and it is impossible to imagine the existence today of an anti-Soviet "conspiracy" similar to the humorists' "Alliance of the Sword and the Plowshare."

Other than that, however, the Soviet Union described in the novel is very much like the Soviet Union of 1960, industrial progress and the Sputniks notwithstanding. The standard of living in 1927 was relatively *high;* it subsequently declined. Now it is just slightly higher than it was thirty years ago. The present grotesquely overcrowded and poor-quality housing (there is not even a Russian word for "privacy"!) is not much different from the conditions Ilf and Petrov knew. There are now, as there were then, people to whom sausage is a luxury, as it was to the newlyweds in *The Twelve Chairs*.

Embezzlers of state property, though denounced as "survivals of the capitalist past," are found by the thousands among young men in their thirties and forties. The ominous door signs protecting Communist bureaucrats from unwanted visitors still adorn Soviet offices. Nor has the species of Ellochka the Cannibal, the vulgar and greedy wife of a hard-working engineer, become extinct. And there are still multitudes of Muscovites who flock to museums to see how prosperously the bourgeoisie lived before the Revolution —Muscovites who are mistaken for art lovers by unsuspecting Western tourists who then report at home a tremendous Soviet interest in the fine arts. Why, even the ZAGS remains unchanged; only a few months ago *Komsomolskaya Pravda*, a youth newspaper, demanded that something be done about it, because brides and grooms are embarrassed when the indifferent clerk inquires whether they came to register a birth, a death, or wish to get married—just as Ippolit Matveyevich Vorobyaninov did over thirty years ago in the little Soviet town deep in the provinces.

Similarly, the "poet" Lapis who peddled nearly identical verse to various trade publications—providing his hero Gavrila with different professions such as druggist, mailman, hunter, etc., to give the poem a *couleur local* suitable for each of the journals—enjoys excellent health to this day. There are hundreds of recent Soviet novels, poems, and dramas written by as many Soviet writers which differ only in the professions of their protagonists; in their character delineations and conflicts they are all very much alike. And, finally, the custom of delivering formal political speeches, all of them long, boring, and terribly repetitious, persists to our times. These speeches are still a regular feature at all public events in the USSR.

Thus the Western reader, in addition to being entertained, is likely to profit from the reading of *The Twelve Chairs* by getting a glimpse of certain aspects

of daily life in the Soviet Union which are not normally included in Intourist itineraries.

The hero of *The Twelve Chairs* (and also, it might
be added, of *The Little Golden Calf*) is Ostap Bender,
"the smooth operator," a resourceful rogue and confidence man. Unlike the nobleman Vorobyaninov and
the priest Vostrikov, Bender is not a representative of
the *ancien régime*. Only twenty-odd years old, he does
not even remember prerevolutionary Russia: at the
first meeting of the "Alliance of the Sword and the
Plowshare" Bender has some difficulty playing the role
of a tsarist officer. Ostap Bender is a Soviet crook, born
of Soviet conditions and quite willing to coexist with
the Soviet system to which he has no ideological or
even economic objections. Ostap Bender's inimitable
slangy Russian is heavily spiced with clichés of the
Communist jargon. Bender knows the vulnerabilities
of Soviet state functionaries and exploits them for his
own purposes. He also knows that the Soviet Man is
not very different from the Capitalist Man—that he is
just as greedy, lazy, snobbish, cowardly, and gullible
—and uses these weaknesses to his, Ostap Bender's, advantage. And yet, in spite of Ostap Bender's dishonesty
and lack of scruples, we somehow get to like him.
Bender is gay, carefree, and clever, and when we see
him matching his wits with those of Soviet bureaucrats, we hope that he wins.

In the end Ostap Bender and his accomplices lose;
yet, strangely enough, the end of the novel seems
forced, much like the cliché happy ending of a medi-
ocre Hollywood film. One must understand, however,
that even in the comparatively "liberal" 1920's it was
difficult for a Soviet author not to supply a happy
Soviet ending to a book otherwise as aloof from Soviet
ideology as *The Twelve Chairs*. And so, at the end of
the novel, one of the greedy fortune-hunters is killed
by his partner, while the other two end up in a psy-

chiatric ward. But at least Ilf and Petrov have spared
us from seeing Ostap Bender contrasted with a virtuous
upright Soviet hero, and for this we should be grateful.
Much as in Gogol's *Inspector General* and *Dead Souls*
and in the satires of Saltykov-Shchedrin, we observe
with fascination a Russia of embezzlers, knaves, and
stupid government officials. We understand their weaknesses and vices, for they are common to all men. Indeed, we can even get to like these people, as we could
not like the stuffy embodiments of Communist virtues
who inhabit the great majority of Soviet novels.

Inevitably, some of the humor must get lost in the
process of translation. The protagonists in *The Twelve
Chairs* are for the most part semi-educated men, but
they all aspire to *kulturnost*, and love to refer to classics
of Russian literature—which they usually misquote.
They also frequently mispronounce foreign words
with comical effect. These no translator could possibly salvage. But the English-speaking reader won't
miss the ridiculous quality of the "updated" version of
The Marriage on a Soviet stage, even if he has never
seen a traditional performance of Gogol's comedy; he
will detect with equal ease the hilarious scheme of
Ostap Bender to "modernize" a famous canvas by
Repin even if he has never seen the original painting.
Fortunately, most of the comic qualities of the novel
are inherent in the actions of the protagonists, and
these are not affected by being translated. They will
only serve to prove once again that, basically, Soviet
Russians are "fed with the same food, hurt with the
same weapons, subject to the same diseases, healed by
the same means, warmed and cooled by the same winter and summer" as all men are.

MAURICE FRIEDBERG

Hunter College 1960

CONTENTS

Part I: THE LION OF STARGOROD

Part II: IN MOSCOW

Contents

Part III: MADAM PETUKHOVA'S TREASURE

Part : I

THE LION
OF STARGOROD

: *1* :

Bezenchuk

and the Nymphs

THERE WERE so many hairdressing establishments and
funeral homes in the regional center of N. that the inhabitants seemed to be born merely in order to have a
shave, get their hair cut, freshen up their heads with
toilet water and then die. In actual fact, people came
into the world, shaved, and died rather rarely in the
regional center of N. Life in N. was extremely quiet.
The spring evenings were delightful, the mud glistened like coal in the light of the moon, and all the
young men of the town were so much in love with
the secretary of the communal-service workers' local
committee that she found difficulty in collecting their
subscriptions.

Matters of life and death did not worry Ippolit
Matveyevich Vorobyaninov, although by the nature
of his work he dealt with them from nine till five
every day, with a half-hour break for lunch.

Each morning, having drunk his ration of hot milk
brought to him by Claudia Ivanovna in a streaky
frosted-glass tumbler, he left the dingy little house
and went outside into the vast street bathed in weird
spring sunlight; it was called Comrade Gubernsky
Street. It was the nicest kind of street you can find in
regional centers. On the left you could see the coffins

of the Nymph funeral home glittering with silver
througn undulating green-glass panes. On the right,
the dusty, plain oak coffins of Bezenchuk, the undertaker, reclined sadly behind small windows from
which the putty was peeling off. Further up, "Master
Baber Pierre and Constantine" promised customers a
"manicure" and "curling performed at home." Still
further on was a hotel with a hairdresser's, and beyond
it a large open space in which a straw-colored calf
stood tenderly licking the rusty sign propped up
against a solitary gateway. The sign read: "Do Us
the Honor" Funeral Home.

Although there were many funeral homes, their
clientele was not wealthy. The "Do Us the Honor"
had gone broke three years before Ippolit Matveyevich settled in the town of N., while Bezenchuk
drank like a fish and had once tried to pawn his best
sample coffin.

People rarely died in the town of N. Ippolit
Matveyevich knew this better than anyone because he
worked in the registry office, where he was in charge
of the registration of deaths and marriages.

The desk at which Ippolit Matveyevich worked
resembled an ancient gravestone. The left-hand corner
had been eaten away by rats. Its wobbly legs quivered
under the weight of bulging tobacco-colored files of
notes, which could provide any required information
on the origins of the town inhabitants and the family
trees that had grown up in the barren regional soil.

On Friday, April 15, 1927, Ippolit Matveyevich
woke up as usual at half past seven and immediately
slipped onto his nose an old-fashioned pince-nez with
a gold nosepiece. He did not wear glasses. At one time,
deciding that it was not hygienic to wear a pince-nez,
he went to the optician and bought himself a pair
of frameless spectacles with gold-plated sidepieces. He
liked the spectacles from the very first, but his wife
(this was shortly before she died) found that they

made him look the very image of Milyukov, and he
gave them to the man who cleaned the yard. Although
he was not shortsighted, the fellow grew accustomed
to the glasses and enjoyed wearing them.

"*Bon jour!*" sang Ippolit Matveyevich to himself as
he lowered his legs from the bed. "*Bon jour*" showed
that he had woken up in a good humor. If he said
"*Guten Morgen*" on awakening, it usually meant that
his liver was playing tricks, that it was no joke being
fifty-two, and that the weather was damp at the time.

Ippolit Matveyevich thrust his legs into prewar
trousers, tied the ribbons around his ankles, and pulled
on short, soft-leather boots with narrow, square toes.
Five minutes later he was neatly arrayed in a yellow
vest decorated with small silver stars and a lustrous
silk jacket that reflected the colors of the rainbow as
it caught the light. Wiping away the drops of water
still clinging to his gray hairs after his ablutions, Ippolit Matveyevich fiercely wiggled his mustache, hesitantly felt his bristly chin, gave his close-cropped silvery hair a brush and, then, smiling politely, went
toward his mother-in-law, Claudia Ivanovna, who had
just come into the room.

"Eppole-et," she thundered, "I had a bad dream
last night."

The word "dream" was pronounced with a French
"r."

Ippolit Matveyevich looked his mother-in-law up
and down. He was six feet two inches tall, and from
that height it was easy for him to regard his mother-
in-law with a certain contempt.

Claudia Ivanovna continued: "I dreamed of the deceased Marie with her hair down and wearing a golden
sash."

The iron lamp with its chain and dusty glass toys
all vibrated at the rumble of Claudia Ivanovna's voice.

"I am very disturbed. I fear something may happen."

These last words were uttered with such force that the square of bristling hair on Ippolit Matveyevich's head moved in different directions. He wrinkled up his face and said slowly:

"Nothing's going to happen, *Maman*. Have you paid for the water?"

It appeared that she had not. Nor had the galoshes been washed. Ippolit Matveyevich disliked his mother-in-law. Claudia Ivanovna was stupid, and her advanced age gave little hope of any improvement. She was stingy in the extreme, and it was only Ippolit Matveyevich's poverty which prevented her giving rein to this passion. Her voice was so strong and fruity that it might well have been envied by Richard the Lion-hearted, at whose shout, as is well known, horses used to kneel. Furthermore, and this was the worst thing of all about her, she had dreams. She was always having dreams. She dreamed of girls in sashes, horses trimmed with the yellow braid worn by dragoons, janitors playing harps, angels in watchmen's fur coats who went for walks at night carrying clappers, and knitting needles which hopped around the room by themselves making a distressing tinkle. An empty-headed woman was Claudia Ivanovna. In addition to everything else, her upper lip was covered by a mustache, each side of which resembled a shaving brush.

Ippolit Matveyevich left the house feeling rather irritated.

Bezenchuk, the undertaker, was standing at the entrance to his tumble-down establishment, leaning against the door with his hands crossed. The regular collapse of his commercial undertakings plus a long period of practice in the consumption of intoxicating drinks had made his eyes bright yellow like a cat's, and they burned with an unfading light.

"Greetings to an honored guest!" he rattled off, seeing Vorobyaninov. "Good morning."

Ippolit Matveyevich politely raised his soiled beaver hat.

"How's your mother-in-law, might I inquire?"

"Mrr-mrr," said Ippolit Matveyevich indistinctly, and, shrugging his shoulders, continued on his way.

"God grant her health," said Bezenchuk bitterly. "Nothin' but losses, durn it." And crossing his hands on his chest, he again leaned against the doorway.

At the entrance to the Nymph funeral home Ippolit Matveyevich was stopped once more.

There were three owners of the Nymph. They all bowed to Ippolit Matveyevich and inquired in chorus about his mother-in-law's health.

"She's well," replied Ippolit Matveyevich. "The things she does! Last night she saw a golden girl with her hair down. It was in a dream."

The three Nymphs exchanged glances and sighed loudly.

These conversations delayed Ippolit Matveyevich on his way, and contrary to his usual practice, he did not arrive at work until the clock on the wall above the slogan "Finish Your Business and Leave" showed five after nine.

Because of his great height, and particularly because of his mustache, Ippolit Matveyevich was known in the office as Maciste,* although the real Maciste had no mustache.

Taking a blue felt cushion out of a drawer in the desk, Ippolit Matveyevich placed it on his chair, aligned his mustache correctly (parallel to the top of the desk) and sat down on the cushion, rising slightly higher than his three colleagues. He was not afraid of getting piles; he was afraid of wearing out his pants, so that was why he used the blue cushion.

* Translator's Note: Maciste was an internationally known Italian actor of the time.

All these operations were watched timidly by two young persons—a boy and a girl. The young man, who wore a cotton padded coat, was completely overcome by the office atmosphere, the chemical smell of the ink, the clock that was ticking loud and fast, and most of all by the sharply worded notice "Finish Your Business and Leave." The young man in the coat had not even begun his business, but he was nonetheless ready to leave. He felt his business was so insignificant that it was shameful to disturb such a distinguished-looking gray-haired citizen as Vorobyaninov. Ippolit Matveyevich also felt the young man's business was a trifling one and could wait, and so he opened folder no. 2 and, with a twitch of the cheek, immersed himself in the papers. The girl, who had on a long jacket edged with shiny black ribbon, whispered something to the young man and, pink with embarrassment, began moving toward Ippolit Matveyevich.

"Comrade," she said, "where do we . . ."

The young man in the coat sighed with pleasure and, unexpectedly for himself, blurted out:

"Get married!"

Ippolit Matveyevich looked thoughtfully at the rail behind which the young couple were standing.

"Birth? Death?"

"Get married?" repeated the young man in the coat and looked round him in confusion.

The girl gave a giggle. Things were going fine. Ippolit Matveyevich set to work with the skill of a magician. In spidery handwriting he recorded the names of the bride and groom in thick registers, sternly questioned the witnesses, who had to be fetched from outside, breathed tenderly and lengthily on the square rubber stamps and then, half rising to his feet, impressed them upon the tattered identification papers. Having received two roubles from the newly-weds "for administration of the sacrament," as he said with a smirk, and given them a receipt, Ippolit Matveyevich drew himself up to his splendid height, automatically pushing out his chest (he had worn a corset at one time). The wide golden rays of the sun fell on his shoulders like epaulets. His appearance was slightly comic, but singularly impressive. The biconcave lenses of his pince-nez flashed white like searchlights. The young couple stood in awe.

"Young people," said Ippolit Matveyevich pompously, "allow me to congratulate you, as they used to say, on your legal marriage. It is very, very nice to see young people like yourselves moving hand in hand toward the realization of eternal ideals. It is very, ve-ery nice!"

Having made this address, Ippolit Matveyevich shook hands with the newly married couple, sat down, and, extremely pleased with himself, continued to read the papers in folder no. 2.

At the next desk the clerks grunted into their inkwells.

The quiet routine of the working day had begun. No one disturbed the deaths-and-marriages desk. Through the window, citizens could be seen making their way home, shivering in the spring chilliness. At exactly midday the cock in the Hammer and Plow co-operative began crowing. Nobody was surprised. Then came the mechanical rattling and squeaking of a car engine. A thick cloud of violet smoke billowed out from Comrade Gubernsky Street, and the clanking grew louder. Through the smoke appeared the outline of the regional-executive-committee car Gos. No. 1 with its minute radiator and bulky body. Floundering in the mud as it went, the car crossed Staropan Square and, swaying from side to side, disappeared in a cloud of poisonous smoke. The clerks remained standing at the window for some time, commenting on the event and attempting to connect it with a possible reduction in staff. A little while later Bezenchuk cautiously went past along the footboards. For days on end he used to wander round the town trying to find out if anyone had died.

The working day was drawing to a close. The bells in the nearby white and yellow belfry began ringing furiously. The windows rattled. The jackdaws rose one by one from the belfry, joined forces over the square, held a brief meeting, and flew off. The evening sky turned ice-gray over the deserted square.

It was time for Ippolit Matveyevich to leave. Everything that was to be born on that day had been born and registered in the thick ledgers. All those wishing to get married had done so and were likewise recorded in the thick registers. And, clearly to the ruin of the undertakers, there had not been a single death. Ippolit Matveyevich packed up his files, put the felt cushion away in the drawer, fluffed up his mustache with a comb, and was just about to leave, having visions of a bowl of steaming soup, when the door burst open and Bezenchuk, the undertaker, appeared on the threshold.

"Greetings to an honored guest," said Ippolit Matveyevich with a smile. "What can I do for you?"

The undertaker's animal-like face glowed in the dusk, but he was unable to utter a word.

"Well?" asked Ippolit Matveyevich more severely.

"Does the Nymph, durn it, really give good service?" said the undertaker vaguely. "Can they really satisfy customers? Why, a coffin needs so much wood alone."

"What?" asked Ippolit Matveyevich.

"It's the Nymph. . . . Three families livin' on one rotten business. And their materials ain't no good, and the finish is worse. What's more, the tassels ain't thick enough, durn it. Mine's an old firm, though. Founded in 1907. My coffins are like pickles, specially selected for the people who know a good coffin."

"What are you talking about? Are you crazy?"

asked Ippolit Matveyevich curtly and moved toward the door. "Your coffins will drive you out of your mind."

Bezenchuk obligingly threw open the door, let Vorobyaninov go out first and then began following him, trembling as though with impatience.

"When the 'Do Us the Honor' was goin', it was all right. There wasn't one firm, not even in Tver, which could touch it in brocade, durn it. But now, I tell you straight, there's nothin' to beat mine. You don't even need to look."

Ippolit Matveyevich turned round angrily, glared at Bezenchuk, and began walking faster. Although he had not had any difficulties at the office that day, he felt rotten.

The three owners of the Nymph were standing by their establishment in the same positions in which Ippolit Matveyevich had left them that morning. They appeared not to have exchanged a single word with one another, yet a striking change in their expressions and a kind of secret satisfaction darkly gleaming in their eyes indicated that they had heard something of importance.

At the sight of his business rivals, Bezenchuk waved his hand in despair and called after Vorobyaninov in a whisper:

"I'll make it thirty-two roubles."

Ippolit Matveyevich frowned and increased his pace.

"You can have credit," added Bezenchuk.

The three owners of the Nymph said nothing. They sped after Vorobyaninov in silence, continually doffing their caps and bowing as they went.

Highly annoyed by the stupid attentions of the undertakers, Ippolit Matveyevich ran up the steps of the porch more quickly than usual, irritably wiped his boots free of mud on one of the steps and, feeling strong pangs of hunger, went into the hallway. He was met by Father Fyodor, priest of the Church of St. Frol and St. Laurence, who had just come out of the inner room and was looking hot and bothered. Holding up his cassock in his right hand, Father Fyodor hurried past toward the door, ignoring Ippolit Matveyevich.

It was then that Ippolit Matveyevich noticed the extra cleanliness and the unsightly disorder of the sparse furniture, and felt a tickling sensation in his nose from the strong smell of medicine. In the outer room Ippolit Matveyevich was met by his neighbor, Kuznetsova, the agronomist. She spoke in a whisper, moving her hand about.

"She's worse. She's just made her confession. Don't make a noise with your boots."

"I'm not," said Ippolit Matveyevich meekly. "What's happened?"

Madam Kuznetsova sucked in her lips and pointed to the door of the inner room:

"Very severe heart attack."

Then, clearly repeating what she had heard, added:

"The possibility of her not recovering should not be discounted. I've been on my feet all day. I came this morning to borrow the meat grinder and saw the door was open. There was no one in the kitchen and no one in this room either. So I thought Claudia Ivanovna had gone to buy flour to make some Easter cake. She'd been going to for some time. You know what the flour is like nowadays. If you don't buy it beforehand . . ."

Madam Kuznetsova would have gone on for a long time describing the flour and the high price of it and how she found Claudia Ivanovna lying by the tiled stove completely unconscious, had not a groan from the next room impinged painfully on Ippolit Matveyevich's ear. He quickly crossed himself with a somewhat feelingless hand and entered his mother-in-law's room.

The Demise
of Madam Petukhova

CLAUDIA IVANOVNA lay on her back with one arm under her head. She was wearing a bright apricot-colored cap of the type that used to be in fashion when ladies wore the "chanticleer" and had just begun to dance the tango.

Claudia Ivanovna's face was solemn, but revealed absolutely nothing. Her eyes were fixed on the ceiling.

"Claudia Ivanovna!" called Ippolit Matveyevich.

His mother-in-law moved her lips rapidly, but instead of the trumpetlike sounds to which his ear was accustomed, Ippolit Matveyevich only heard a groan, soft, high-pitched, and so pitiful that his heart gave a leap. A tear suddenly glistened in one eye and rolled down his cheek like a drop of mercury.

"Claudia Ivanovna," repeated Vorobyaninov, "what's the matter?"

But again he received no answer. The old woman had closed her eyes and slumped to one side.

The agronomist came quietly into the room and led him away like a little boy taken to be washed.

"She's dropped off. The doctor didn't say she was to be disturbed. Listen, dearie, run down to the chemist's. Here's the prescription. Find out how much an ice bag costs."

Ippolit Matveyevich obeyed Madam Kuznetsova, sensing her indisputable superiority in such matters.

It was a long way to the chemist's. Clutching the prescription in his fist like a schoolboy, Ippolit Matveyevich hurried out into the street.

It was almost dark, but against the fading light the frail figure of Bezenchuk could be seen leaning against the wooden gate munching a piece of bread and onion. The three Nymphs were squatting beside him, eating porridge from an iron pot and licking their spoons. At the sight of Vorobyaninov the undertakers stood to attention like soldiers. Bezenchuk shrugged his shoulders petulantly and, pointing to his rivals, said:

"Always in me way, durn 'em."

In the middle of the square, near the bust of the poet Zhukovsky, which was inscribed with the words "Poetry is God in the Sacred Dreams of the Earth," an animated conversation was in progress following the news of Claudia Ivanovna's stroke. The general opinion of the assembled citizens could have been summed up as "We all have to go sometime" and "What the Lord gives, the Lord takes back."

"The hairdresser "Pierre and Constantine"—who readily answered to the name of Andrei Ivanovich, by the way—once again took the opportunity to air his knowledge of medicine, acquired from the Moscow magazine *Ogonyok*.

"Modern science," Andrei Ivanovich was saying, "has achieved the impossible. Take this for example. Let's say a customer gets a pimple on his chin. In the old days that usually resulted in blood poisoning. But they say that nowadays in Moscow—I don't know whether it's true or not—a fresh sterilized shaving brush is used for every customer."

The citizens gave long sighs.

"Aren't you overdoing it a bit, Andrei?"

"How could there be a different brush for every person? That's a good one!"

Prusis, a former member of the proletarian intelligentsia, and now a stall-owner, actually became excited.

"Wait a moment, Andrei Ivanovich. According to the latest census, the population of Moscow is more than two million. That means they'd need more than two million brushes. Seems rather curious."

The conversation was becoming heated, and heaven only knows how it would have ended had not Ippolit Matveyevich appeared at the end of the street.

"He's off to the chemist's again. Things must be bad."

"The old woman will die. Bezenchuk isn't running round the town in a flurry for nothing."

"What does the doctor say?"

"What doctor? Do you think those people in the social-insurance office are really doctors? They're enough to send a healthy man to his grave!"

"Pierre and Constantine," who had been longing for a chance to make a pronouncement on the subject of medicine, looked around cautiously, and said:

"Hemoglobin is what counts nowadays."

Having said that, he fell silent.

The citizens also fell silent, each reflecting in his own way on the mysterious power of hemoglobin.

When the moon rose and cast its minty light on the miniature bust of Zhukovsky, a rude word could clearly be seen chalked on the poet's bronze back.

This inscription had first appeared on June 15, 1897, the same day that the bust had been unveiled. And despite all the efforts of the police, and later the militia, the defamatory word had reappeared each day with unfailing regularity.

The samovars were already singing in the little wooden houses with their outside shutters, and it was time for supper. The citizens stopped wasting their time and went their way. A wind began to blow.

In the meantime Claudia Ivanovna was dying. First she asked for something to drink, then said she had to get up and fetch Ippolit Matveyevich's best boots from the cobbler. One moment she complained of the dust which, as she put it, was enough to make you choke, and the next asked for all the lamps to be lit.

Ippolit Matveyevich paced up and down the room, tired of worrying. His mind was full of unpleasant, practical thoughts. He was thinking how he would have to ask for an advance at the mutual assistance office, fetch the priest, and answer letters of condolence from relatives. To take his mind off these things, Ippolit Matveyevich went out onto the porch. There, in the green light of the moon, stood Bezenchuk, the undertaker.

"So how would you like it, Mr. Vorobyaninov?" asked the undertaker, hugging his cap to his chest.

"Yes, probably," answered Ippolit Matveyevich gloomily.

"Does the Nymph, durn it, really give good service?" said Bezenchuk, becoming agitated.

"Go to the devil! You make me sick!"

"I'm not doin' nothin'. I'm only askin' about the tassels and brocade. How shall I make it? Best quality? Or how?"

"No tassels or brocade. Just an ordinary coffin made of pinewood. Do you understand?"

Bezenchuk put his finger to his lips to show that he understood perfectly, turned round and, managing to balance his cap on his head although he was staggering, went off. It was only then that Ippolit Matveyevich noticed that he was blind drunk.

Ippolit Matveyevich felt singularly upset. He tried to picture himself coming home to an empty, dirty house. He was afraid his mother-in-law's death would deprive him of all those little luxuries and set ways he had acquired with such effort since the revolution—a revolution which had stripped him of much greater luxuries and a grand way of life. "Should I marry?" he wondered. "But whom?" The militia chief's niece, Barbara Stepanovna, Prusis's sister? Or maybe I should hire a housekeeper. But what's the use. She would only drag me around the courts. And it would cost me something, too!"

The future suddenly looked black for Ippolit Matveyevich. Full of indignation and disgust at everything around him, he went back into the house.

Claudia Ivanovna was no longer delirious. Lying high on her pillows, she looked at Ippolit Matveyevich in full command of her faculties, and even sternly, he thought.

"Ippolit Matveyevich," she whispered clearly. "Sit close to me. I want to tell you something."

Ippolit Matveyevich sat down in annoyance, peering into his mother-in-law's thin, bewhiskered face. He made an attempt to smile and say something encouraging, but the smile was hideous and no words of encouragement came to him. An awkward wheezing noise was all he could produce.

"Ippolit," repeated his mother-in-law, "do you remember our drawing-room suite?"

"Which one?" asked Ippolit Matveyevich with that kind of polite attention that is only accorded to the very sick.

"The one . . . upholstered in English chintz."

"You mean the suite in my house?"

"Yes, in Stargorod."

"Yes, I remember it very well . . . a sofa, a dozen chairs and a round table with six legs. It was splendid furniture. Made by Hambs. . . . But why does it come to mind?"

Claudia Ivanovna, however, was unable to answer. Her face had slowly begun to turn the color of copper sulfate. For some reason Ippolit Matveyevich also caught his breath. He clearly remembered the drawing room in his house and its symmetrically arranged walnut furniture with curved legs, the polished parquet floor, the old brown grand piano, and the oval black-framed daguerreotypes of high-ranking relatives on the walls.

Claudia Ivanovna then said in a wooden, apathetic voice:

"I sewed my jewels into the seat of a chair."

Ippolit Matveyevich looked sideways at the old woman.

"What jewels?" he asked mechanically, then, suddenly realizing what she had said, added quickly:

"Weren't they taken when the house was searched?"

"I hid the jewels in a chair," repeated the old woman stubbornly.

Ippolit Matveyevich jumped up and, taking a close look at Claudia Ivanovna's stony face lit by the paraffin lamp, saw she was not raving.

"Your jewels!" he cried, startled at the loudness of his own voice. "In a chair? Who induced you to do that? Why didn't you give them to me?"

"Why should I have given them to you when you squandered away my daughter's estate?" said the old woman quietly and viciously.

Ippolit Matveyevich sat down and immediately stood up again. His heart was noisily sending the blood coursing around his body. He began to hear a ringing in his ears.

"But you took them out again, didn't you? They're here, aren't they?"

The old woman shook her head.

"I didn't have time. You remember how quickly and unexpectedly we had to flee. They were left in the chair . . . the one between the terra-cotta lamp and the fireplace."

"But that was madness! You're just like your daughter," shouted Ippolit Matveyevich loudly.

And no longer concerned for the fact that he was at the bedside of a dying woman, he pushed back his chair with a crash and began prancing about the room.

"I suppose you realize what may have happened to the chairs? Or do you think they're still there in the drawing room in my house, quietly waiting for you to come and get your jewelry?"

The old woman did not answer.

The registry clerk's wrath was so great that the pince-nez fell off his nose and landed on the floor with a tinkle, the gold nosepiece glittering as it passed his knees.

"What? Seventy thousand roubles worth of jewelry hidden in a chair! Heaven knows who may sit on that chair!"

At this point Claudia Ivanovna gave a sob and leaned forward with her whole body toward the edge of the bed. Her hand described a semicircle and reached out to grasp Ippolit Matveyevich, but then fell back onto the violet down quilt.

Squeaking with fright, Ippolit Matveyevich ran to fetch his neighbor.

"I think she's dying," he cried.

The agronomist crossed herself in a businesslike way and, without hiding her curiosity, hurried into Ippolit Matveyevich's house, accompanied by her bearded husband, also an agronomist. In distraction Vorobyaninov wandered into the municipal park.

While the two agronomists and their servants tidied up the deceased woman's room, Ippolit Matveyevich roamed around the park, bumping into benches and mistaking for bushes the young couples numb with early spring love.

The strangest things were going on in Ippolit Matveyevich's head. He could hear the sound of gypsy choirs and orchestras composed of big-breasted women playing the tango over and over again; he imagined the Moscow winter and a long-bodied black trotter that snorted contemptuously at the passers-by. He imagined many different things: a pair of deliciously expensive orange-colored panties, slavish devotion, and a possible trip to Cannes.

Ippolit Matveyevich began walking more slowly and suddenly stumbled over the form of Bezenchuk, the undertaker. The latter was asleep, lying in the middle of the path in his fur coat. The jolt woke him up. He sneezed and stood up briskly.

"Now don't you worry, Mr. Vorobyaninov," he said heatedly, as though continuing the conversation started a while before. "There's lots of work goes into a coffin."

"Claudia Ivanovna's dead," his client informed him.

"Well, God rest her soul," said Bezenchuk. "So the old lady's passed away. Old ladies pass away . . . or they depart this life. It depends who she is. Yours, for instance, was small and plump, so she passed away. But if it's one who's a bit bigger and thinner, then they say she has departed this life. . . ."

"What do you mean 'they say'? Who says?"

"We say. The undertakers. Now you, for instance. You're distinguished-looking and tall, though a bit on the thin side. If you should die, God forbid, they'll say you popped off. But a tradesman, who belonged to the former merchants' guild, would breathe his last. And if it's someone of lower status, say a janitor, or a peasant, we say he has croaked or gone west. But when the high-ups die, say a railroad conductor or someone in the administration, they say he has kicked the bucket. They say: 'You know our boss has kicked the bucket, don't you?' "

Shocked by this curious classification of human morality, Ippolit Matveyevich asked:

"And what will the undertakers say about you when you die?"

"I'm a small fellow. They'll say, 'Bezenchuk's gone,' and nothin' more."

And then he added grimly:

"It's not possible for me to pop off or kick the

bucket; I'm too small. But what about the coffin, Mr. Vorobyaninov? Do you really want one without tassels and brocade?"

But Ippolit Matveyevich, once more immersed in dazzling dreams, walked on without answering. Bezenchuk followed him, working something out on his fingers and muttering to himself as he always did.

The moon had long since vanished and there was a wintry cold. Fragile, waferlike ice covered the puddles. The companions came out on Comrade Gubernsky Street, where the wind was tussling with the hanging shop-signs. A fire engine drawn by skinny horses emerged from the direction of Staropan Square with a noise like the lowering of a blind.

Swinging their canvas legs from the platform, the firemen wagged their helmeted heads and sang in intentionally tuneless voices:

> *"Glory to our fire chief,*
> *Glory to dear Comrade Pumpoff!"*

"They've been having a good time at Nicky's wedding," said Bezenchuk uninterestedly. "He's the fire chief's son." And he scratched himself under his coat. "So you really want it without tassels and brocade?"

By that moment Ippolit Matveyevich had finally made up his mind. "I'll go and find them," he decided, "and then we'll see." And in his jewel-encrusted visions even his deceased mother-in-law seemed nicer than she had actually been. He turned to Bezenchuk and said:

"Go on then, damn you, make it! With brocade! And tassels!"

The Parable
of the Sinner

HAVING HEARD the dying Claudia Ivanovna's confession, Father Fyodor Vostrikov, priest of the Church of St. Frol and St. Laurence, left Vorobyaninov's house in a complete daze and the whole way home kept looking round him distractedly and smiling to himself in confusion. His bewilderment became so great in the end that he was almost knocked down by the district-executive-committee motor car, Gos. No. 1. Struggling out of the cloud of purple smoke issuing from the infernal machine, Father Vostrikov reached the stage of complete distraction, and, despite his venerable rank and middle age, finished the journey at a frivolous half-gallop.

His wife, Catherine, was laying the table for supper. On the days when there was no evening service to conduct, Father Fyodor liked to have his supper early. This time, however, to his wife's surprise, the holy father, having taken off his hat and warm padded cassock, skipped past into the bedroom, locked himself in and began singing the prayer "It Is Meet" in a toneless voice.

His wife sat down on a chair and whispered in alarm:

"He's up to something again."

Father Fyodor's tempestuous soul knew no rest, nor had ever known it. Neither at the time when he was Fedya, a pupil of the Russian Orthodox Church school, nor when he was Fyodor Ivanych, a bewhiskered student at the seminary. Having left the seminary and studied law at the university for three years, Vostrikov became afraid in 1915 of the possibility of mobilization and returned to the church. He was first anointed a deacon, then ordained a priest and appointed to the regional center of N. And the whole time, at every stage of his clerical and secular career, Father Fyodor never lost interest in worldly possessions.

He cherished the dream of possessing his own candle factory. Tormented by the vision of thick ropes of wax being wound onto the factory drums, Father Fyodor devised various schemes that would bring in enough basic capital to buy a little factory in Samara which he had had his eye on for some time.

Ideas occurred to Father Fyodor unexpectedly, and when they did he used to get down to work on the spot. He once started making a marble-like washing soap; he made pounds and pounds, but despite its enormous fat content, the soap would not lather, and it cost twice as much as the Hammer and Plow brand, to boot. For a long time it remained in the liquid state, gradually decomposing on the porch of the house, so that whenever his wife, Catherine, passed it, she burst into tears. The soap was eventually thrown into the cesspool.

Reading in a magazine on animal farming that rabbit meat was as tender as chicken, that rabbits were highly prolific and that a keen farmer could make a mint of money by breeding them, Father Fyodor immediately acquired half a dozen stud rabbits, and two months later, Nerka the dog, terrified by the incredible number of long-eared creatures filling the yard and house, fled to an unknown destination. However, the

wretchedly provincial citizens of the town of N.
proved extraordinarily conservative and, with unusual
unanimity, refused to buy Vostrikov's rabbits. Then
Father Fyodor had a talk with his wife and decided to
enhance his diet with rabbit meat, which was supposed
to be tastier than chicken. The rabbits were roasted
whole, turned into *rissoles* and cutlets, made into soup,
served cold for supper and baked in pies. But to no
avail. Father Fyodor worked it out that even if they
switched exclusively to a diet of rabbit, the family
could not consume more than forty of the creatures a
month, while the monthly increment was ninety,
with the number increasing in a geometrical progression.

The Vostrikovs then decided to sell home-cooked
meals. Father Fyodor spent a whole evening writing
out an advertisement in indelible pencil on neatly cut
sheets of graph paper, announcing the sale of tasty
home-cooked meals prepared in pure butter. The advertisement began "Cheap and Good!" His wife filled
an enamel dish with flour-and-water paste, and late
one evening Father Fyodor went around sticking the
advertisements on all the telegraph poles, and also in
the vicinity of state-owned institutions.

The new idea was a great success. Seven people appeared the first day, among them Bendin, the military-
commissariat clerk, by whose endeavor the town's
oldest monument—an arch of triumph dating from the
time of the Empress Elizabeth—had been pulled down
shortly before, because, as he claimed, it interfered
with the traffic. The dinners were very popular. The
next day there were fourteen customers. There was
hardly enough time to skin the rabbits. For a whole
week things went swimmingly and Father Fyodor even
considered starting up a small fur-trading business,
without a car, when something quite unforeseen took
place.

The Hammer and Plow co-operative, which had

been shut for three weeks for stock-taking, reopened, and some of the counter hands, panting with the effort, rolled a barrel of rotten cabbage into the yard shared with Father Fyodor and dumped the contents into the cesspool. Attracted by the piquant smell, the rabbits hastened to the cesspool, and the next morning an epidemic broke out among the tender rodents. It only raged for three hours, but during that time it finished off two hundred and forty adult rabbits and an uncountable number of offspring.

The shocked Father Fyodor was depressed for two whole months, and it was only now, when returning from Vorobyaninov's house and, to his wife's surprise, locking himself in the bedroom, that he regained his spirits. There was every indication that Father Fyodor had been captivated by some new idea.

Catherine knocked on the bedroom door with a knuckle. There was no reply, but the singing grew louder. A moment later the door opened slightly and through the crack appeared Father Fyodor's face, brightened by a maidenly flush.

"Let me have a pair of scissors quickly, Mother," snapped Father Fyodor.

"But what about your supper?"

"Yes, later on."

Father Fyodor grabbed the scissors, locked the door again, and went over to a mirror hanging on the wall in a black scratched frame.

Beside the mirror was an ancient folk-painting, "The Parable of the Sinner," made from a copperplate and neatly hand-painted. The parable had been a great consolation to Vostrikov after the misfortune with the rabbits. The picture clearly showed the transient nature of all earthly things. The top row was composed of four drawings with meaningful and consolatory captions in Church Slavonic: Shem saith a prayer, Ham soweth wheat, Japheth enjoyeth power, Death overtaketh all. The figure of Death carried a scythe and a

winged hourglass and looked as though it was made of
artificial limbs and orthopedic appliances; it was standing on deserted hilly ground with its legs wide apart,
and its general appearance made it clear that the fiasco
with the rabbits was a mere trifle.

At this moment Father Fyodor preferred "Japheth
enjoyeth power." The drawing showed a fat, opulent
man with a beard sitting on a throne in a small room.

Father Fyodor smiled and, looking closely at himself
in the mirror, began clipping his fine beard. The scissors clicked, the hairs fell to the floor, and five minutes
later Father Fyodor knew he was absolutely no good at
clipping beards. His beard was askew, looked unbe-
coming and even suspicious.

Fiddling about for a while longer, Father Fyodor became highly irritated, called his wife, and, handing her
the scissors, said peevishly:

"You help me, Mother. I just can't manage these rotten hairs."

His wife actually threw up her hands in surprise.

"What have you done to yourself?" she finally managed to say.

"I haven't done anything. I'm trimming my beard.
It seems to have gone askew just here. . . ."

"Heavens!" said his wife, attacking Father Fyodor's
curls. "Surely you're not joining the New Church
movement?"

Father Fyodor was delighted that the conversation
had taken this turn.

"And why shouldn't I join the Renovators, Mother?
They're people, aren't they?"

"Of course they're people," conceded his wife venomously, "but they go to movies and pay alimony."

"Well, then, I'll go to movies as well."

"Go on then!"

"I will!"

"You'll get tired of it. Just look at yourself in the
mirror."

And indeed, a lively black-eyed countenance with a short, odd-looking beard and an absurdly long mustache peered out of the mirror at Father Fyodor.

They trimmed down the mustache to the right proportions.

What happened next amazed Mother still more. Father Fyodor declared that he had to go out for a certain reason that very evening and asked his wife to go round to her brother, the baker, and borrow his fur-collared coat and duck-billed cap for a week.

"I won't go," said his wife and began weeping.

Father Fyodor walked up and down the room for half an hour, frightening his wife by the change in his expression and telling her all sorts of rubbish. Mother could understand only one thing—for no apparent reason Father Fyodor had cut his hair, intended to go off somewhere, and was leaving her for good.

"I'm not leaving you," he kept saying. "I'm not. I'll be back in a week. A man can have a job to do, after all. Can he or can't he?"

"No, he can't," said his wife.

Father Fyodor even had to strike the table with his fist, although he was normally a mild person in his treatment of his near ones. He did so cautiously, since he had never done it before, and, greatly alarmed, his wife threw a kerchief around her head and ran to fetch the civilian clothing from her brother.

Left alone, Father Fyodor thought for a moment, muttered, "It's not easy for the women, either," and pulled out a small tin trunk from under the bed. This type of trunk is mostly found among Red Army soldiers. It is usually lined with striped paper on top of which is a picture of Budyonny or the lid of a "Beach" cigarette box depicting three lovelies on the pebbly beach at Batumi. The Vostrikovs' trunk was also lined with shots, but, to Father Fyodor's annoyance, they were not of Budyonny or Batumi beauties. His wife had covered the inside of the trunk with photographs cut out of the magazine *Chronicle of the 1914 War*. They included "The Capture of Peremyshl," "The Distribution of Comforts to Enlisted Men in the Trenches," and all sorts of other things.

Removing the books that were lying at the top (a set of the *Russian Pilgrim* for 1913; a fat tome, *The History of the Schism,* and a brochure entitled *A Russian in Italy*, the cover of which showed a smoking Vesuvius), Father Fyodor reached down into the very bottom of the trunk and drew out an old shabby hat belonging to his wife. Wincing at the smell of mothballs which suddenly assailed him from the trunk, Father Fyodor tore apart the lace and trimmings and took from the hat a heavy sausage-shaped object covered with linen. The sausage-shaped object contained twenty ten-rouble gold coins, all that was left of Father Fyodor's business ventures.

With a habitual movement of the hand, he lifted his cassock and stuffed the sausage into the pocket of his striped trousers. He then went over to the chest of drawers and took twenty roubles in three- and five-rouble notes from a candy box. There were twenty roubles left in the box.

"That will do for the housekeeping," he decided.

] CHAPTER [

: *4* :

The Muse of Travel

AN HOUR BEFORE the evening-mail train was due in, Father Fyodor, dressed in a short coat which came just below the knee, and carrying a wicker basket, stood in line in front of the booking office and kept looking apprehensively at the station entrance. He was afraid that in spite of his insistence, his wife might come to see him off, and then Prusis, the stall-owner, who was sitting in the buffet and treating the income-tax collector to a glass of beer, would immediately recognize him. Father Fyodor stared with shame and surprise at his striped pants, now exposed to the view of the entire laity.

Boarding a train in which none of the seats was reserved proceeded in its usually scandalous way. Bowed by the weight of enormous sacks, passengers ran from the front of the train to the back and then to the front again. Father Fyodor followed them in a daze. Like everyone else, he spoke to the conductors in an ingratiating tone, like everyone else he was afraid he had been given the "wrong" ticket, and it was only when he was finally allowed into a coach that his customary calm returned and he even became happy.

The locomotive hooted at the top of its voice and the train moved off, carrying Father Fyodor into the unknown distance on business that was mysterious, yet promised great things.

An interesting thing, the right of way. The man in the street who finds himself on it feels a certain urgency in himself and soon turns into a passenger, a consignee, or simply a trouble-maker without a ticket, who makes life difficult for the teams of conductors and platform ticket-inspectors.

The moment a passenger approaches the right of way, which he amateurishly calls a railroad station, his life is completely changed. He is immediately surrounded by predatory porters in white aprons and with nickel badges on their chests, and his luggage is obsequiously picked up. From that moment, the citizen no longer is his own master.

He is a passenger and begins to perform all the duties of one. These duties are many, though they are not unpleasant.

Passengers eat a lot. Ordinary mortals do not eat during the night, but passengers do. They eat fried chicken, which is expensive, hard-boiled eggs, which are bad for the stomach, and olives. Whenever the train passes over a switch, the numerous teapots in the rack clatter together, and legless chickens (the legs have been torn out by the roots by passengers) jump up and down in their newspaper wrapping.

The passengers, however, are oblivious to all this. They tell each other jokes. Every three minutes the whole compartment rocks with laughter; then there is a silence and a soft-spoken voice tells the following story:

"An old Jew lay dying. Around him were his wife and children. 'Is Monya here?' asks the old Jew with difficulty. 'Yes, she's here.' 'Has Auntie Brana come?' 'Yes.' 'And where's Grandma? I don't see her.' 'She's over here.' 'And Isaac?' 'He's here, too.' 'What about the children?' 'They're all here.' 'Then who's left in the store?' "

This very moment the teapots begin rattling and the
chickens fly up and down in the rack, but the passengers do not notice. Each one has a favorite story ready,
eagerly awaiting its turn. A new raconteur, nudging
his neighbors and calling out in a pleading tone, "Have
you heard this one?" finally gains attention and begins:

"A Jew comes home and gets into bed beside his
wife. Suddenly he hears a scratching noise under the
bed. The Jew reaches with his hand underneath the
bed and asks: 'Is that you, Fido?' And Fido licks his
hand and says: 'Yes, it's me.'"

The passengers collapse with laughter; the dark
night cloaks the countryside. Restless sparks fly from
the funnel, and the slim signals in their luminous green
spectacles fastidiously flash past, staring above the
train.

An interesting thing, the right of way! Long, heavy
trains race to all parts of the country. The way is open
at every point. The green light can be seen everywhere; the track is clear. The polar express goes up to
Murmansk. The K-1 shoots out of Kursk Station
bound for Tiflis. The far-eastern courier rounds the
Baikal and approaches the Pacific at full speed.

The Muse of Travel is calling. She has already
plucked Father Fyodor from his quiet regional cloister
and cast him into some unknown province. Even Ippolit Matveyevich Vorobyaninov, former marshal of
the nobility and now a clerk in a registry office, is
stirred to the depths of his heart and is highly excited
by the prospect of great things.

People speed all over the country. Some of them are
looking for scintillating brides thousands of miles away,
while others, in pursuit of treasure, leave their jobs in
the post office and rush like schoolboys to Aldan.
Others simply sit at home tenderly stroking an im-
minent hernia and reading the works of Count Salias,
bought for five kopeks instead of a rouble.

.   .   .

The day after the funeral, kindly arranged by Bezen-chuk, the undertaker, Ippolit Matveyevich went to work and, as part of the duties with which he was charged, duly registered in his own hand the demise of Claudia Ivanovna Petukhova, aged fifty-nine, house-wife, nonparty member, resident of the regional center of N., by origin a member of the upper class of the province of Stargorod. After this, Ippolit Matveyevich granted himself a two-week vacation due to him, took forty-one roubles pay, said goodbye to his colleagues, and went home. On the way he stopped at the chem-ist's.

The chemist, Leopold Grigorevich, who was called Lipa by his friends and family, stood behind the red-lacquered counter, surrounded by frosted-glass bottles of poison, nervously trying to sell the fire chief's sister-in-law "Ango cream for sunburn and freckles; gives the skin an exceptional whiteness." The fire chief's sister-in-law, however, was asking for "Rachelle pow-der, goldish in color; gives the skin a tan not normally acquirable." The chemist had only the Ango cream in stock, and the battle between these two very different cosmetics raged for half an hour. Lipa won in the end and sold the fire chief's sister-in-law some lipstick and a bugovar, which is a device similar in principle to the samovar, except that it looks like a watering can and catches bugs.

"What can I get you?"

"Something for the hair."

"To make it grow, to remove it, or to dye it?"

"Not to make it grow," said Ippolit Matveyevich. "To dye it."

"We have a wonderful hair dye called Titanic. We got it from the customs people; it was confiscated. It's a jet black. A bottle containing a six months' supply costs three roubles, twelve kopeks. I can recommend it to you as a good friend."

Ippolit Matveyevich turned the bottle in his hands, looked at the label with a sigh, and put down his money on the counter.

He went home and, with a feeling of revulsion, began pouring Titanic onto his head and mustache. A stench filled the house.

By the time dinner was over, the stench had cleared, the mustache had dried and become matted and was very difficult to comb. The jet-black color turned out to have a greenish hue, but there was no time for a second try.

Taking from his mother-in-law's jewel box a list of the gems, found the night before, Ippolit Matveyevich counted up his cash in hand, locked the house, put the key in his back pocket and took the no. 7 express to Stargorod.

The Smooth Operator

AT HALF PAST ELEVEN a young man aged about twenty-eight entered Stargorod from the direction of the village of Chmarovka to the northeast. A waif ran along behind him.

"Mister!" cried the boy gaily, "gimme ten kopeks!"

The young man took a warm apple out of his pocket and handed it to the waif, but the child still kept running behind. Then the young man stopped and, looking ironically at the boy, said quietly:

"Perhaps you'd also like the key of the apartment where the money is?"

The presumptuous waif then realized the complete futility of his pretensions and dropped behind.

The young man had not told the truth. He had no money, no apartment where it might have been found and no key with which to open it. He did not even have a coat. The young man entered the town in a green suit tailored to fit at the waist and an old woolen scarf wound several times around his powerful neck. On his feet were patent-leather boots with orange-colored suede uppers. He had no socks on. The young man carried an astrolabe.

Approaching the market, he broke into a song: "O, Bayadere, tum-ti-ti, tum-ti-ti."

In the market he found plenty going on. He squeezed into the line of vendors selling their wares spread out on the ground before them, stood the astrolabe in front of him and began shouting:

"Who wants an astrolabe? Here's an astrolabe going cheap. Special reduction for delegations and women's work divisions!"

At first the unexpected supply met with little demand; the delegations of housewives were more interested in obtaining commodities in short supply and were milling around the cloth and drapery stalls. An agent from the Stargorod criminal-investigation department passed the astrolabe vendor twice, but since the instrument in no way resembled the typewriter stolen the day before from the Central Union of Dairy Co-operatives, the agent stopped glaring at the young man and passed on.

By lunchtime the astrolabe had been sold to a repairman for three roubles.

"It measures by itself," he said, handing over the astrolabe to its purchaser, "provided you have something to measure."

Having rid himself of the calculating instrument, the happy young man had lunch in the Tasty Corner snack bar, and then went to have a look at the town. He passed along Soviet Street, came out into Red Army Street (previously Greater Pushkin Street), crossed Co-operative Street and found himself again on Soviet Street. But it was not the same Soviet Street from which he had come. There were two Soviet Streets in the town. Greatly surprised by this fact, the young man carried on and found himself in Lena Massacre Street (formerly Denisov Street). He stopped outside no. 28, a pleasant two-storied private house, which bore a sign saying:

USSR   RSFSR
SECOND SOCIAL SECURITY OFFICE
OF THE
STARGOROD PROVINCE INSURANCE ADMINISTRATION

and requested a light from the janitor, who was sitting by the entrance on a stone bench.

"Tell me, dad," said the young man, taking a puff, "are there any marriageable young girls in this town?"

The old janitor did not show the least surprise.

"For some a mare'd be a bride," he answered, readily striking up a conversation.

"I have no more questions," said the young man quickly.

And he immediately asked another question: "A house like this and no girls in it?"

"It's a long while since there've been any young girls here," replied the old man. "This is a state institution —a home for old-age women pensioners."

"I see. For ones born before historical materialism?"

"That's it. They were born when they were born."

"And what was here in the house before the days of historical materialism?"

"When was that?"

"In the old days. Under the former regime."

"Oh, in the old days my master used to live here."

"A member of the *bourgeoisie?*"

"*Bourgeoisie* yourself! I told you. He was a marshal of the nobility."

"You mean he was working-class?"

"Working-class yourself! He was a marshal of the nobility."

The conversation with the intelligent janitor so poorly versed in the class structure of society might have gone on for heaven knows how long had not the young man got down to business.

"Listen, Granddad," he said, "what about a drink?"

"All right, buy me one!"

They were gone an hour. When they returned, the janitor was the young man's best friend.

"Right, then, I'll stay the night with you," said the newly acquired friend.

"Since you're a good man, you can stay here for the rest of your life if you like."

Having achieved his aim, the young man promptly went down into the janitor's room, took off his orange-colored boots, and, stretching out on a bench, began thinking out a plan of action for the following day.

The young man's name was Ostap Bender. Of his background he would usually give only one detail. "My dad," he used to say, "was a Turkish citizen." During his life this son of a Turkish citizen had had many occupations. His lively nature prevented him from devoting himself to any one thing for long and kept him roving through the country, finally bringing him to Stargorod without any socks and without a key, apartment, or money.

Lying in the janitor's room, which was so warm that it stank, Ostap Bender sorted out in his mind two possibilities for a career.

He could become a polygamist and calmly move on from town to town, taking with him a suitcase containing his latest wife's valuables, or he could go to the Stargorod Commission for the Improvement of Children's Living Conditions the next day and suggest they undertake the popularization of a brilliantly devised, though as yet unpainted, picture entitled "The Bolsheviks Answer Chamberlain" based on Repin's famous canvas, "The Zaporozhe Cossacks Answer the Sultan." If it worked, this variation could bring in four hundred or so roubles.

The two possibilities had been thought up by Ostap during his last stay in Moscow. The polygamy idea was conceived after reading a law-court report in the evening paper, which clearly stated that the convicted man was given only a two-year sentence, while the second idea came to Bender as he was looking round the Association of Revolutionary Artists' exhibition, having got in with a free pass.

Both possibilities had their drawbacks, however. To begin a career as a polygamist without a heavenly gray polka-dot suit was unthinkable. Moreover, at least ten roubles would be needed for purposes of representation and seduction. He could get married, of course, in his green field-suit, since his virility and good looks were absolutely irresistible to the provincial belles looking for husbands, but that would have been, as Ostap used to say, "poor workmanship." The question of the painting was not all smooth sailing, either. There might be difficulties of a purely technical nature. It might be awkward, for instance, to show Comrade Kalinin in a fur cap and white cape, while Comrade Chicherin was stripped to the waist. They could be depicted in ordinary dress, of course, but that would not be quite the same thing.

"It wouldn't have the right effect!" said Ostap aloud.

At this point he noticed that the janitor had been prattling away for some time, apparently reminiscing about the previous owner of the house.

"The police chief used to salute him. . . . I'd go and wish him a happy new year, let's say, and he'd give me three roubles. At Easter, let's say, he'd give me another three roubles . . . Then on his birthday, let's say. In a year I'd get as much as fifteen roubles from wishin' him. He even promised to give me a medal. 'I want my janitor to have a medal,' he used to say. That's what he would say: 'Tikhon, consider that you already have the medal.' "

"And did he give you one?"

"Wait a moment. . . . 'I don't want a janitor without a medal,' he used to say. He went to St. Petersburg to get me a medal. Well, the first time it didn't work out. The officials didn't want to give me one. 'The

Tsar,' he used to say, 'has gone abroad. It isn't possible just now.' So the master told me to wait. 'Just wait a bit, Tikhon,' he used to say, 'you'll get your medal.' "

"And what happened to this master of yours? Did they bump him off?"

"No one bumped him off. He went away. What was the good of him stayin' here with the soldiers? . . . Do they give medals to janitors nowadays?"

"Sure. I can arrange one for you."

The janitor looked at Bender with veneration.

"I can't be without one. It's that kind of work."

"Where did your master go?"

"Heaven knows. People say he went to Paris."

"Ah, white acacia—the *émigré's* flower! So he's an *émigré*?"

"*Émigré* yourself. . . . He went to Paris, so people say. And the house was taken over for old women. You greet them every day, and they don't even give you a ten-kopek bit! Yes, he was some master!"

At that moment the rusty bell above the door began to ring. The janitor ambled over to the door, opened it, and stood back in complete amazement.

On the top step stood Ippolit Matveyevich Vorobyaninov with a black mustache and black hair. His eyes behind his pince-nez had a pre-revolutionary twinkle.

"Master!" bellowed Tikhon with delight. "Back from Paris!"

Ippolit Matveyevich became embarrassed by the presence of the stranger whose bare purple feet he had just spotted protruding from behind the table, and was about to leave again when Ostap Bender briskly jumped up and made a low bow.

"This isn't Paris, but you're welcome to our abode."

Ippolit Matveyevich felt himself forced to say something.

"Hello, Tikhon. I certainly haven't come from Paris. Where did you get that strange idea from?"

But Ostap Bender, whose long and noble nose had caught the scent of roast meat, did not give the janitor time to utter a word.

"Splendid," he said, squinting. "You haven't come from Paris. You've no doubt come from Kologriv to visit your deceased grandmother."

As he spoke, he tenderly embraced the janitor and pushed him outside the door before the old man had time to realize what was happening. When he finally gathered his wits, all he knew was that his master had come back from Paris, that he himself had been pushed out of his own room, and that he was clutching a rouble note in his left hand.

Carefully locking the door, Bender turned to Vorobyaninov, who was still standing in the middle of the room, and said:

"Take it easy, everything's all right! My name's Bender. You may have heard of me!"

"No, I haven't," said Ippolit Matveyevich nervously.

"No, how could the name of Ostap Bender be known in Paris? Is it warm there just now? It's a nice city. I have a married cousin there. She recently sent me a silk handkerchief by registered mail."

"What rubbish is this?" exclaimed Ippolit Matveyevich. "What handkerchief? I haven't come from Paris at all. I've come from . . ."

"Marvelous! You've come from Morshansk!"

Ippolit Matveyevich had never had dealings with so spirited a young man as Ostap Bender and began to feel peculiar.

"Well, I'm going now," he said.

"Where are you going? You don't need to hurry anywhere; the secret police will come for you anyway."

Ippolit Matveyevich was speechless. He undid his coat with its threadbare velvet collar and sat down on the bench, glaring at Bender.

"I don't know what you mean," he said in a low voice.

"That's no harm; you soon will. Just one moment."

Ostap put on his orange-colored boots and walked up and down the room.

"Which frontier did you cross? Was it the Polish, Finnish, or Rumanian frontier? An expensive pleasure, I imagine. A friend of mine recently crossed the frontier. He lives in Slavuta, on our side, and his wife's parents live on the other. He had a row with his wife over a family matter; she comes from a temperamental family. She spat in his face and ran away to her parents across the frontier. The fellow sat around for a few days but found things weren't going well. There was no dinner and the room was dirty, so he decided to make it up with her. He waited till night and then crossed over to his mother-in-law. But the frontier guards nabbed him, trumped up a charge, and gave him six months. Later on he was expelled from the trade union. The wife, they say, has now gone back, the fool, and her husband is in the workhouse. She is able to take him things. . . . Did you come that way, too?"

"Honestly," protested Ippolit Matveyevich, suddenly feeling himself in the power of the talkative young man who had come between him and the jewels. "Honestly, I'm a citizen of the RSFSR. I can show you my identification papers if you want."

"With printing being as well developed as it is in the West, the forgery of Soviet identification papers is nothing. A friend of mine even went as far as forging American dollars. And you know how difficult it is to forge dollars. The paper has those different-colored little lines on it. It requires great technique. He managed to get rid of them on the Moscow black market. It turned out later that his grandfather, a notorious currency-dealer, had bought them all in Kiev and gone absolutely broke. The dollars were counterfeit, after all. So your papers may not help you very much either.'

Despite his annoyance at having to sit in a smelly janitor's room and listen to an insolent young man burbling about the shady dealings of his friends, instead of actively searching for the jewels, Ippolit Matveyevich could not bring himself to leave. He felt great trepidation at the thought that the young stranger might spread it round the town that the ex-marshal had come back. That would be the end of everything, and he might be put in jail as well.

"Don't tell anyone you saw me," said Ippolit Matveyevich. "They might really think I'm an *émigré*."

"That's more like it! First we have an *émigré* who has returned to his home town, and then we find he is afraid the secret police will catch him."

"But I've told you a hundred times, I'm not an *émigré!*"

"Then who are you? Why are you here?"

"I've come from N. on certain business."

"What business?"

"Personal business."

"And then you say you're not an *émigré*? A friend of mine . . ."

At this point, Ippolit Matveyevich, driven to despair by the stories of Bender's friends, and seeing that he was not getting anywhere, gave in.

"All right," he said. "I'll tell you everything."

"Anyway, it might be difficult without an accomplice," he thought to himself, "and this fellow seems to be a really shady character. He might be useful."

] CHAPTER [

: *6* :

The Diamond Haze

IPPOLIT MATVEYEVICH took off his stained beaver hat, combed his mustache, which gave off a shower of sparks at the touch of the comb, and, having cleared his throat in determination, told Ostap Bender, the first rogue who had come his way, what his dying mother-in-law had told him about her jewels.

During the account, Ostap jumped up several times and, turning to the iron stove, said delightedly:

"Things are moving, gentlemen of the jury. Things are moving."

An hour later they were both sitting at the rickety table, their heads close together, reading the long list of jewelry which had at one time adorned the fingers, neck, ears, bosom, and hair of his mother-in-law.

Ippolit Matveyevich adjusted the pince-nez, which kept falling off his nose, and said emphatically:

"Three strings of pearls . . . Yes, I remember them. Two with forty pearls and the long one had a hundred and ten. A diamond pendant . . . Claudia Ivanovna used to say it was worth four thousand roubles; an antique."

Next came the rings: not thick, silly, and cheap engagement rings, but fine, lightweight rings set with

pure, polished diamonds; heavy, dazzling earrings that
bathe a small female ear in multicolored light; bracelets
shaped like serpents, with emerald scales; a clasp bought
with the profit from a fourteen-hundred-acre harvest;
a pearl necklace that could only be worn by a famous
prima donna; to crown everything was a diadem worth
forty thousand roubles.

Ippolit Matveyevich looked round him. A grass-
green emerald light blazed up and shimmered in the
dark corners of the janitor's dirty room. A diamond
haze hung near the ceiling. Pearls rolled across the table
and bounced along the floor. The room swayed in the
mirage of gems.

The sound of Ostap's voice brought the excited Ippolit Matveyevich back to earth.

"Not a bad choice. The stones have been tastefully
selected, I see. How much did all this jazz cost?"

"Seventy to seventy-five thousand."

"Hm . . . Then it's worth a hundred and fifty thousand now."

"Really as much as that?" asked Ippolit Matveyevich
jubilantly.

"Not less than that. However, if I were you, dear
friend from Paris, I wouldn't give a damn about it."

"What do you mean, not give a damn?"

"Just that. Like they used to before the advent of
historical materialism."

"Why?"

"I'll tell you. How many chairs were there?"

"A dozen. It was a drawing-room suite."

"Your drawing-room suite was probably used for
firewood long ago."

Ippolit Matveyevich was so alarmed that he actually
stood up.

"Take it easy. I'll take charge. The hearing is continued. Incidentally, you and I will have to conclude a
little deal."

Breathing heavily, Ippolit Matveyevich nodded his
assent. Ostap Bender then began stating his conditions.

"In the event of acquisition of the treasure, as a direct partner in the concession and as technical adviser,
I receive sixty per cent. You needn't pay my social
security; I don't care about that."

Ippolit Matveyevich turned gray.

"That's daylight robbery!"

"And how much did you intend offering me?"

"Well . . . er . . . five per cent, or maybe even ten
per cent. You realize, don't you, that's fifteen thousand
roubles!"

"And that's all?"

"Yes. . . ."

"Maybe you'd like me to work for nothing and also
give you the key of the apartment where the money
is?"

"In that case, I'm sorry," said Vorobyaninov through
his nose. "I have every reason to believe I can manage
the business by myself."

"Aha! In that case, I'm sorry," retorted the splendid
Ostap. "I have just as much reason to believe, as Andy
Tucker used to say, that I can also manage your busi-
ness by myself."

"You villain!" cried Ippolit Matveyevich, beginning
to shake.

Ostap remained unmoved.

"Listen, gentleman from Paris, do you know your
jewels are practically in my pocket? And I'm only interested in you as long as I wish to ensure your old
age."

Ippolit Matveyevich realized at this point that iron
hands had gripped his throat.

"Twenty per cent," he said morosely.

"And my grub?" asked Ostap with a sneer.

"Twenty-five."

"And the key of the apartment?"

"But that's thirty-seven and a half thousand!"

"Why be so precise? Well, all right, I'll settle for fifty per cent. We'll go halves."

The haggling continued, and Ostap made a further concession. Out of respect for Vorobyaninov, he was prepared to work for forty per cent.

"That's sixty thousand!" cried Vorobyaninov.

"You're a rather nasty man," retorted Bender. "You're too fond of money."

"And I suppose you aren't?" squeaked Ippolit Matveyevich in a flutelike voice.

"No, I'm not."

"Then why do you want sixty thousand?"

"On principle!"

Ippolit Matveyevich took a deep breath.

"Well, are things moving?" pressed Ostap.

Vorobyaninov breathed heavily and said humbly: "Yes, things are moving."

"It's a bargain, District Chief of the Comanchi!"

As soon as Ippolit Matveyevich, hurt by the nickname, "Chief of the Comanchi," had demanded an apology, and Ostap, in a formal apology, had called him "Field Marshal," they set about working out their disposition.

At midnight Tikhon, the janitor, hanging on to all the garden fences on the way and clinging to the lamp posts, tottered home to his cellar. To his misfortune, there was a full moon.

"Ah! The intellectual proletarian! Officer of the Broom!" exclaimed Ostap, catching sight of the doubled-up janitor.

The janitor began making low-pitched, passionate noises of the kind that are sometimes heard when a lavatory suddenly gurgles heatedly and fussily in the stillness of the night.

"That's nice," said Ostap to Vorobyaninov. "Your janitor is rather a vulgar fellow. Is it possible to get as drunk as that on a rouble?"

"Yes, it is," said the janitor unexpectedly.

"Listen, Tikhon," began Ippolit Matveyevich. "Have you any idea what happened to my furniture, old man?"

Ostap carefully supported Tikhon so that the words could flow freely from his mouth. Ippolit Matveyevich waited tensely. But the janitor's mouth, in which every other tooth was missing, only produced a deafening yell:

"Haa-aapy daa-aays . . ."

The room was filled with an almighty din. The janitor industriously sang the whole song through. He moved about the room bellowing, one moment sliding senseless under a chair, the next moment hitting his head against the brass weights of the clock, and then going down on one knee. He was terribly happy.

Ippolit Matveyevich was at a loss to know what to do.

"Cross-examination of the witnesses will have to be adjourned until tomorrow morning," said Ostap. "Let's go to bed."

They carried the janitor, who was as heavy as a chest of drawers, to the bench.

Vorobyaninov and Ostap decided to sleep together in the janitor's bed. Under his jacket, Ostap had on a red-and-black checked cowboy shirt; under the shirt, he was not wearing anything. Under Ippolit Matveyevich's yellow vest, already familiar to readers, however, he was wearing another, light-blue worsted vest.

"There's a vest worth buying," said Ostap enviously. "Just my size. Sell it to me!"

Ippolit Matveyevich felt it would be awkward to refuse to sell the vest to his new friend and direct partner in the concession.

Frowning, he agreed to sell it at its original price—eight roubles.

"You'll have the money when we sell the treasure,"

said Bender, taking the vest, still warm from Voroby-aninov's body.

"No, I can't do it like that," said Ippolit Matveye-vich, flushing. "Please give it back."

Ostap's delicate nature was revulsed.

"There's stinginess for you," he cried. "We under-take business worth a hundred and fifty thousand and you squabble over eight roubles! You want to learn to live it up!"

Ippolit Matveyevich reddened still more, and taking a notebook from his pocket, he wrote in neat hand-writing:

25/IV/27
Issued to Comrade Bender
Rs. 8

Ostap took a look at the notebook.

"Oho! If you're going to open an account for me, then at least do it properly. Enter the debit and credit. Under 'debit' don't forget to write down the sixty thousand roubles which you owe me, and under 'credit' put down the vest. The balance is in my favor—59,992 roubles. I can live a bit longer."

Thereupon Ostap fell into a silent, childlike sleep. Ippolit Matveyevich took off his wooden wristlets and his baronial boots, left on his darned Jaeger underwear and crawled under the blanket, sniffling as he went. He felt very awkward. On the outside of the bed there was not enough blanket, and it was cold. On the inside, he was warmed by the smooth operator's body, vibrant with ideas.

All three had dreams.

Vorobyaninov had bad dreams about microbes, the criminal-investigation department, velvet shirts, and Be-zenchuk, the undertaker, in a tuxedo, but unshaven.

Ostap dreamed of: Fujiyama; the head of the Dairy Produce Co-operative; and Tarras Bulba selling picture post cards of the Dnieper.

And the janitor dreamed that a horse escaped from the stable. He looked for it all night in the dream and woke up in the morning worn-out and gloomy, not having found it. For some time he looked in surprise at the people sleeping in his bed.

Not understanding anything, he took his broom and went out into the street to carry out his immediate duties, which were to sweep up the horse droppings and shout at the old-women pensioners.

Traces of the Titanic

IPPOLIT MATVEYEVICH woke up as usual at half past seven, mumbled *"Guten Morgen,"* and went over to the washbasin. He washed himself with avidity, cleared his throat, noisily rinsed his face, and shook his head to get rid of the water which had run into his ears. He dried himself with satisfaction, but on taking the towel away from his face, Ippolit Matveyevich noticed that it was stained with the same black color that he had used to dye his horizontal mustache two days before. Ippolit Matveyevich's heart sank. He rushed to get his pocket mirror. The mirror reflected a large nose and the left-hand side of a mustache as green as the grass in spring. He hurriedly shifted the mirror to the right. The right-hand mustachio was the same revolting color. Bending his head slightly, as though trying to butt the mirror, the unhappy man perceived that the jet black still reigned supreme in the center of his square of hair, but that the edges were bordered with the same green color.

Ippolit Matveyevich's whole being emitted a groan so loud that Ostap Bender opened his eyes.

"You're out of your mind!" exclaimed Bender, and immediately closed his sleepy lids.

"Comrade Bender," whispered the victim of the Titanic imploringly.

Ostap woke up after a great deal of shaking and persuasion. He looked closely at Ippolit Matveyevich and burst into a howl of laughter. Turning away from the founder of the concession, the chief director of operations and technical adviser rocked with laughter, seized hold of the top of the bed, cried "Stop, you're killing me!" and again was convulsed with mirth.

"That's not nice of you, Comrade Bender," said Ippolit Matveyevich and twitched his green mustache.

This gave new strength to the almost exhausted Ostap, and his hearty laughter continued for ten minutes. Regaining his breath, he suddenly became very serious.

"Why are you glaring at me like a soldier at a louse? Take a look at yourself."

"But the chemist told me it would be a jet-black color and wouldn't wash off with either hot water or cold water, soap or paraffin. It was contraband."

"Contraband? All contraband is made in Little Arnaut Street in Odessa. Show me the bottle. . . . Look at this! Did you read this?"

"Yes."

"What about this bit in small print? It clearly states that after washing with hot or cold water, soap or paraffin, the hair should not be rubbed with a towel, but dried in the sun or in front of a primus stove. Why didn't you do so? What can you do now with that greenery?"

Ippolit Matveyevich was very depressed. Tikhon came in, and seeing his master with a green mustache, crossed himself and asked for money to have a drink.

"Give this hero of labor a rouble," suggested Ostap, "only kindly don't charge it to me. It's a personal matter between you and your former colleague. Wait a minute, Dad, don't go away! There's a little matter to discuss."

Ostap had a talk with the janitor about the furniture, and five minutes later the concessionaires knew the whole story. The entire furniture had been taken away to the housing division in 1919, with the exception of one drawing-room chair that had first been in Tikhon's charge, but was later taken from him by the assistant warden of the second social-security office.

"Is it here in the house then?"

"That's right."

"Tell me, old fellow," said Ippolit Matveyevich, his heart beating fast, "when you had the chair, did you . . . ever repair it?"

"It didn't need repairin'. Workmanship was good in those days. The chair could last another thirty years."

"Right, off you go, old fellow. Here's another rouble and don't tell anyone I'm here."

"I'll be a tomb, Citizen Vorobyaninov."

Sending the janitor on his way and with a cry of "Things are moving," Ostap Bender again turned to Ippolit Matveyevich's mustache.

"It will have to be dyed again. Give me some money and I'll go to the chemist's. Your Titanic is no damn good, except for dogs. In the old days they really had good dyes. A racing expert once told me an interesting story. Are you interested in horse-racing? No? A pity; it's exciting. Well, anyway . . . there was once a well-known trickster called Count Drutsky. He lost five hundred thousand roubles on races. King of the losers! So when he had nothing left except debts and was thinking about suicide, a shady character gave him a wonderful piece of advice for fifty roubles. The count went away and came back a year later with a three-year-old Orloff trotter. From that moment on the count not only made up all his losses, but won three hundred thousand on top. Broker—that was the name of the horse—had an excellent pedigree and always came in first. He actually beat McMahon in the Derby by a whole length. Terrific! . . . But then Kurochkin

—heard of him?—noticed that all the horses of the Orloff breed were losing their coats, while Broker, the
darling, stayed the same color. There was an unheard-
of scandal. The count got three years. It turned out
that Broker wasn't an Orloff at all, but a crossbreed
that had been dyed. Crossbreeds are much more spirited than Orloffs and aren't allowed within yards of
them! Which? There's a dye for you! Not quite like
your mustache!"

"But what about the pedigree? You said it was a
good one."

"Just like the label on your bottle of Titanic—counterfeit! Give me the money for the dye."

Ostap came back with a new mixture.

"It's called 'Naiad.' It may be better than the Titanic.
Take your coat off!"

The ceremony of re-dying began. But the "Amazing
chestnut color making the hair soft and fluffy" when
mixed with the green of the Titanic unexpectedly
turned Ippolit Matveyevich's head and mustache all
colors of the rainbow.

Vorobyaninov, who had not eaten since morning,
furiously cursed all the perfumeries, both those state-
owned and the illegal ones on Little Arnaut Street in
Odessa.

"I don't suppose even Aristide Briand had a mustache like that," observed Ostap cheerfully. "However,
I don't recommend living in Soviet Russia with ultra-
violet hair like yours. It will have to be shaved off."

"I can't do that," said Ippolit Matveyevich in a
deeply grieved voice. "That's impossible."

"Why? Has it some association or other?"

"I can't do that," repeated Vorobyaninov, lowering
his head.

"Then you can stay in the janitor's room for the rest
of your life, and I'll go for the chairs. The first one is
upstairs, by the way."

"All right, shave it then!"

Bender found a pair of scissors and in a flash snipped off the mustache, which fell silently to the floor. When the hair had been cropped, the technical adviser took a yellowed Gillette razor from his pocket and a spare blade from his billfold, and began shaving Ippolit Matveyevich, who was almost in tears by this time.

"I'm using my last blade on you, so don't forget to credit me with two roubles for the shave and haircut."

"Why so expensive?" Ippolit managed to ask, although he was convulsed with grief. "It should only coast forty kopeks."

"For reasons of security, Comrade Field Marshal!" promptly answered Ostap.

The sufferings of a man whose head is being shaved with a safety razor are incredible. This became clear to Ippolit Matveyevich from the very beginning of the operation.

But all things come to an end.

"There! The hearing continues! Those suffering from nerves shouldn't look."

Ippolit Matveyevich shook himself free of the nauseating tufts that until so recently had been distinguished gray hair, washed himself and, feeling a strong tingling sensation all over his head, looked at himself in the mirror for the hundredth time that day. He was unexpectedly pleased by what he saw. Looking at him was the careworn, but rather youthful, face of an unemployed actor.

"Right, forward march, the bugle is sounding!" cried Ostap. "I'll make tracks for the housing division, while you go to the old women."

"I can't," said Ippolit Matveyevich. "It's too painful for me to enter my own house."

"I see. A touching story. The exiled baron! All right, you go to the housing division, and I'll get busy here. Our meeting place is the janitor's room. Platoon: 'shun!'"

: 8 :

The Bashful Chiseler

THE ASSISTANT WARDEN of the Second Office of the Stargorod Social Security Administration was a shy little thief. His whole being protested against stealing, yet it was impossible for him not to steal. He stole and was ashamed of himself. He stole constantly and was constantly ashamed of himself, which was why his smoothly shaven cheeks always burned with a blush of confusion, shame, bashfulness, and embarrassment. The assistant warden's name was Alexander Yakovlevich, and his wife's name was Alexandra Yakovlevna. He used to call her Sashchen, and she used to call him Alchen. The world has never seen such a bashful chiseler as Alexander Yakovlevich.

He was not only the assistant warden, but also the chief warden. The previous one had been dismissed for rudeness to the inmates, and had been appointed conductor of a symphony orchestra. Alchen was completely different from his ill-bred boss. Under the system of fuller workdays, he took upon himself the running of the home, treating the pensioners with marked courtesy, and introducing important reforms and innovations.

Ostap Bender pulled the heavy oak door of the Vorobyaninov home and found himself in the hall. There was a smell of burnt porridge. From the upstairs rooms came the confused sound of voices, like a distant "hooray" from a line of troops. There was no one about and no one appeared. An oak staircase with two flights of once lacquered stairs led upward. Only the rings were now left; there was no sign of the stair rods that had once held the carpet in place.

"The Comanchi chief lived in vulgar luxury," thought Ostap as he went upstairs.

In the first room, which was spacious and light, fifteen or so old women in dresses made of the cheapest mouse-gray woolen cloth were sitting in a circle.

Stretching forward their necks and keeping their eyes on a healthy-looking man in the middle, the old women were singing:

> *"We hear the sound of distant jingling,*
> *The troika's on its round;*
> *Far into the distance stretches*
> *The sparkling snowy ground."*

The choirmaster, wearing a shirt and trousers of the same mouse-gray material, was beating time with both hands and, turning from side to side, kept shouting:

"Descants, softer! Kokushkina, not so loud!"

He caught sight of Ostap, but unable to restrain the movement of his hands, he merely glared at the newcomer and continued conducting. The choir increased its volume with an effort, as though singing through a pillow.

> *"Ta-ta-ta, ta-ta-ta, ta-ta-ta,*
> *Te-ro-rom, tu-ru-rum, tu-ru-rum . . ."*

"Can you tell me where I can find the assistant warden?" asked Ostap, breaking into the first pause.

"What do you want, Comrade?"

Ostap shook the conductor's hand and inquired amiably: "National folksongs? Very interesting! I'm the fire inspector."

The assistant warden looked ashamed.

"Yes, yes," he said, with embarrassment. "Very opportune. I was actually going to write you a report."

"There's nothing to worry about," said Ostap magnanimously. "I'll write the report myself. Let's take a look at the premises."

Alchen dismissed the choir with a wave of his hand, and the old women made off with little steps of delight.

"Come this way," invited the assistant warden.

Before going any further, Ostap scrutinized the furniture in the first room. It consisted of a table, two garden benches with iron legs (one of them had the name "Nicky" carved on the back), and a light-brown harmonium.

"Do they use primus stoves or anything of that kind in this room?"

"No, no. This is where our recreational activities are held. We have a choir, a drama circle, painting, drawing, and music."

When he reached the word "music," Alexander Yakovlevich blushed. First his chin turned red, then his forehead and cheeks. Alchen felt very ashamed. He had sold all the instruments belonging to the wind section a long time before. The feeble lungs of the old women had never produced anything more than a puppylike squeak from them, anyway. It was ridiculous to see such a mass of metal in so helpless a condition. Alchen had not been able to resist selling the wind section, and now he felt very guilty.

A slogan written in large letters on a piece of the same mouse-gray woolen cloth spanned the wall between the windows. It said:

A BRASS BAND IS THE PATH
TO COLLECTIVE CREATIVITY

"Very good," said Ostap. "A recreation room does not present any fire hazard. Let's go on."

Passing through the front rooms of Vorobyaninov's house, Ostap could see no sign of a walnut chair with curved legs and English chintz upholstery. The ironed-smooth walls were plastered with directives issued to the Second Office. Ostap read them and, from time to time, asked enthusiastically:

"Are the chimneys swept regularly? Are the stoves working properly?"

And receiving exhaustive answers, moved on.

The fire inspector made a diligent search for at least one corner of the house which might constitute a fire hazard, but in that respect everything seemed to be in order. His other hunt, however, was less successful. Ostap went into the dormitories. As he appeared, the old women stood up and bowed low. The rooms contained beds covered with blankets, as hairy as a dog's coat, with the word "Feet" woven at one end. Below the beds were trunks, which at the initiative of Alexander Yakovlevich, who liked to do things in a military fashion, projected exactly one third of their length.

Everything in the Second Office was marked by its extreme modesty; the furniture that consisted solely of garden benches taken from Alexander Boulevard (now named in honor of the Proletarian Voluntary Saturdays), the paraffin lamps bought at the local market, and the very blankets with that frightening word, "Feet." One aspect of the house, however, had been made to last and was developed on a grand scale—to wit, the door springs.

Door springs were Alexander Yakovlevich's passion. Sparing no effort, he fitted all the doors in the house with springs of different types and systems. There were very simple ones in the form of an iron rod; compressed-air ones with cylindrical brass pistons; there were ones with pulleys that raised and lowered heavy

bags of shot. There were springs which were so complex in design that the local mechanic could only shake
his head in wonder. And all the cylinders, springs, and
counterweights were very powerful, slamming doors
shut with the swiftness of a mousetrap. Whenever the
mechanisms operated, the whole house shook. With
pitiful squeals, the old women tried to escape the onslaught of the doors, but not always with success. The
doors gave the fugitives a thump in the back, and at
the same time, a counterweight shot past their ears
with a dull rasping sound.

As Bender and the assistant warden walked around
the house, the doors fired a noisy salute.

But the feudal magnificence had nothing to hide: the
chair was not there. As the search progressed, the fire
inspector found himself in the kitchen. Porridge was
cooking in a large copper pot and gave off the smell
that the smooth operator had noticed in the hall. Ostap
wrinkled his nose and said:

"What is it cooking in? Lubricating oil?"

"It's pure butter, I swear it is," said Alchen, blushing
to the roots of his hair. "We buy it from the farm." He
felt very ashamed.

"Anyway, it's not a fire risk," observed Ostap.

The chair was not in the kitchen, either. There was
only a stool, occupied by the cook wearing a cap and
apron of mouse-gray woolen material.

"Why is everybody's clothing gray? That cloth isn't
even fit to wipe the windows with!"

The shy Alchen was even more embarrassed.

"We don't receive enough funds." He was disgusted
with himself.

Ostap looked at him disbelievingly and said: "That
is no concern of the fire brigade which I am at present
representing."

Alchen was alarmed.

"We've taken all the necessary fire precautions," he

declared. "We even have a fire extinguisher. An Eclair."

The fire inspector reluctantly proceeded in the direction of the fire extinguisher, peeping into the lumber rooms as he went. The red-iron nose of the extinguisher caused the inspector particular annoyance, despite the fact that it was the only object in the house which had any connection with fire precautions.

"Where did you get it? At the market?"

And without waiting for an answer from the thunderstruck Alexander Yakovlevich, he removed the Eclair from the rusty nail on which it was hanging, broke the capsule without warning, and quickly pointed the nose in the air. But instead of the expected stream of foam, all that came out was a high-pitched hissing which sounded like the ancient hymn tune "How Glorious Is Our Lord on Zion."

"You obviously did get it at the market," said Ostap, his earlier opinion confirmed. And he put back the fire extinguisher, which was still hissing, in its place.

They moved on, accompanied by the hissing.

"Where can it be?" wondered Ostap. "I don't like the look of things." And he made up his mind not to leave the place until he had found out the truth.

While the fire inspector and the assistant warden were crawling about the attics, considering fire precautions in detail and examining the chimneys, the Second Office of the Stargorod Social Security Administration carried on its daily routine.

Dinner was ready. The smell of burnt porridge had appreciably increased, and it overpowered all the sourish smells inhabiting the house. There was a rustling in the corridors. Holding iron bowls full of porridge in front of them with both hands, the old women cautiously emerged from the kitchen and sat down at a large table, trying not to look at the refectory slogans, composed by Alexander Yakovlevich and painted by his wife. The slogans read:

FOOD IS THE SOURCE OF HEALTH
ONE EGG CONTAINS AS MUCH FAT
AS A HALF POUND OF MEAT
BY CAREFULLY MASTICATING YOUR FOOD
YOU HELP SOCIETY
MEAT IS BAD FOR YOU

These sacred words aroused in the old ladies memories of teeth that had disappeared before the revolution, eggs that had been lost at approximately the same
time, meat that was inferior to eggs in fat, and perhaps
even the society that they were deprived of the opportunity of helping by carefully masticating.

Seated at table in addition to the old women were
Isidor, Afanasy, Cyril, and Oleg, and also Pasha Emilyevich. Neither in age nor sex did these young men fit
into the pattern of social security, but they were the
younger brothers of Alchen, and Pasha Emilyevich
was Alexandra Yakovlevna's cousin, once removed.
The young men, the oldest of whom was the thirty-
two-year-old Pasha Emilyevich, did not consider their
life in the pensioners' home in any way abnormal.
They lived on the same basis as the old women; they
too had government-property beds and blankets with
the word "Feet"; they were clothed in the same mouse-
gray material as the old women, but on account of their
youth and strength they ate better than the latter.
They stole everything in the house that Alchen did
not manage to steal himself. Pasha could put away four
pounds of fish at one go, and he once did so, leaving
the house dinnerless.

Hardly had the old women had time to taste their
porridge when the younger brothers and Pasha Emilyevich rose from the table, having gobbled down their
share, and went belching into the kitchen to look for
something more digestible.

The meal continued. The old women began jabber-
ing:

"Now they'll stuff themselves full and start bawling songs."

"Pasha Emilyevich sold the chair from the recreation room this morning. A second-hand dealer took it away by the back door."

"Just you see. He'll come home drunk tonight."

At this moment the pensioners' conversation was interrupted by a trumpeting noise that even drowned the hissing of the fire extinguisher, and a husky voice began:

". . . vention . . ."

The old women hunched their shoulders and, ignoring the loud-speaker in the corner on the floor, continued eating in the hope that fate would spare them, but the loud-speaker cheerfully went on:

"Yevdokkkkkkrrrakkkkh viduso . . . valuable invention. Railroadman of the Murmansk Railroad, Comrade Sokutsky, S Samara, O Oriel, K Kaliningrad, U Urals, Ts Tsaritsina, K Kalin-grad, Y York. Sokuts-ky."

The trumpet wheezed and renewed the broadcast in a thick voice.

". . . vented a system of light signals for snow plows. The invention has been approved by Dorizul. . . ."

The old women floated away to their rooms like gray ducklings. The loud-speaker, jigging up and down by its own power, blared away into the empty room:

"And we will now play some Novgorod folk music."

Far, far away, in the center of the earth, someone strummed a balalaika and a blackearth Battistini broke into song:

> "*On the wall the bugs were sitting,*
> *Blinking at the sky;*
> *Then they saw the tax inspector*
> *And crawled away to die.*"

In the center of the earth the verses brought forth a storm of activity. A horrible gurgling was heard from the loud-speaker. It was something between thunderous applause and the eruption of an underground volcano.

Meanwhile the disheartened fire inspector had descended an attic ladder backwards and was now in the kitchen again, where he saw five citizens digging into a barrel of sauerkraut and bolting it down. They ate in silence. Pasha Emilyevich alone waggled his head in the style of an epicurean and, wiping some strings of cabbage from his mustache, observed:

"It's a sin to eat cabbage like this without vodka."

"Is this a new intake of women?" asked Ostap.

"They're orphans," replied Alchen, shouldering the inspector out of the kitchen and surreptitiously shaking his fist at the orphans.

"Children of the Volga Region?"

Alchen was confused.

"A trying heritage from the Tsarist regime?"

Alchen spread his arms as much as to say: "There's nothing you can do with a heritage like that."

"Coeducation by the composite method?"

Without further hesitation the bashful Alchen invited the fire inspector to take potluck and lunch with him.

Potluck that day happened to be a bottle of Zubrovka vodka, home-pickled mushrooms, minced herring, Ukrainian beet soup containing first-grade meat, chicken and rice, and stewed apples.

"Sashchen," said Alexander Yakovlevich, "I want you to meet a comrade from the province fire-precaution administration."

Ostap made his hostess a theatrical bow and paid her such an interminable and ambiguous compliment that he could hardly get to the end of it. Sashchen, a buxom woman, whose good looks were somewhat marred by sideburns like those which Tsar Nicholas used to have, laughed softly and took a drink with the two men.

"Here's to your communal services," exclaimed Ostap.

The lunch went off gaily, and it was not until they reached the stewed fruit that Ostap remembered the point of his visit.

"Why is it," he asked, "that the furnishings are so skimpy in your establishment?"

"What do you mean?" said Alchen. "What about the harmonium?"

"Yes, I know, *vox humana*. But you have absolutely nothing at all of any taste to sit on. Only garden benches."

"There's a chair in the recreation room," said Alchen in an offended tone. "An English chair. They say it was left over from the original furniture."

"By the way, I didn't see your recreation room. How is it from the point of view of fire hazard? It won't let you down, I hope. I had better see it."

"Certainly."

Ostap thanked his hostess for the lunch and left.

No primus was used in the recreation room; there was no portable stove of any kind; the chimneys were in a good state of repair and were cleaned regularly, but the chair, to the incredulity of Alchen, was missing. They ran to look for it. They looked under the beds and under the trunks; for some reason or other they moved back the harmonium; they questioned the old women, who kept looking at Pasha Emilyevich timidly, but the chair was just not there. Pasha Emilyevich himself showed great enthusiasm in the search. When all had calmed down, Pasha still kept wandering from room to room, looking under decanters, shifting iron teaspoons, and muttering:

"Where can it be? I saw it myself this morning. It's ridiculous!"

"It's depressing, girls," said Ostap in an icy voice.

"It's absolutely ridiculous!" repeated Pasha Emilyevich impudently.

At this point, however, the Eclair fire extinguisher, which had been hissing the whole time, took a high F, which only the People's Artist, Nezhdanova, can do, stopped for a second and then emitted its first stream of foam, which soaked the ceiling and knocked the cook's cap off. The first stream of foam was followed by another, mouse gray in color, which bowled over young Isidor Yakovlevich. After that the extinguisher began working smoothly. Pasha Emilyevich, Alchen and all the surviving younger brothers raced to the spot.

"Well done," said Ostap. "An idiotic invention!"

As soon as the old women were left alone with Ostap and without the boss, they at once began complaining:

"He's brought his family into the home. They eat up everything."

"The piglets get milk and we get porridge."

"He's taken everything out of the house."

"Take it easy, girls," said Ostap, retreating. "You need someone from the labor-inspection department. The senate hasn't empowered me. . . ."

The old women were not listening.

"And that Pasha Melentyevich. He went and sold a chair today. I saw him myself."

"Who did he sell it to?" asked Ostap quickly.

"He sold it . . . that's all. He was going to steal my blanket. . . ."

A fierce struggle was going on in the corridor. But mind finally triumphed over matter and the extinguisher, trampled under Pasha Emilyevich's feet of iron, gave a last dribble and was silent forever.

The old women were sent to clean the floor. The fire inspector bowed his head and, waddling slightly, went up to Pasha Emilyevich.

"A friend of mine," began Ostap importantly, "also used to sell government property. He now lives a holy life in the workhouse."

"I find your groundless accusations strange," said Pasha, who smelled strongly of foam.

"Who did you sell the chair to?" asked Ostap in a ringing whisper.

Pasha Emilyevich, who had supernatural understanding, realized at this point that he was about to be beaten, if not kicked.

"To a second-hand dealer."

"What's his address?"

"I'd never seen him before."

"Never?"

"No, honestly."

"I ought to bust you in the mouth," said Ostap dreamily, "only Zarathustra wouldn't allow it. Get to hell out of here!"

Pasha Emilyevich smiled fawningly and began walking away.

"Come back, you abortion," cried Ostap haughtily. "What was the dealer like?"

Pasha Emilyevich described him in detail, while Ostap listened carefully. The interview was concluded by Ostap with the words: "This clearly has nothing to do with fire precautions."

In the corridor the bashful Alchen went up to Ostap and gave him a gold piece.

"That comes under Article 114 of the Criminal Code," said Ostap. "Bribing officials in the course of their duty."

Nevertheless he took the money and, without taking leave of Alexander Yakovlevich, went toward the door. The door, which was fitted with a powerful contraption, opened with an effort and gave Ostap a one-and-a-half-ton shove in the backside.

"Good shot!" said Ostap, rubbing the affected part. "The hearing is continued."

] CHAPTER [

: *9* :

Where Are Your Curls?

WHILE OSTAP was inspecting the Second Social Security Office, Ippolit Matveyevich had left the janitor's room and was wandering along the streets of his home town, feeling the chill on his shaven head.

Along the roadway trickled clear spring water. There was a constant splashing and plopping as diamond drops dripped from the roof tops. Sparrows hunted for manure, and the sun rested on the roofs. Golden carthorses drummed their hoofs against the bare roadway and, turning their ears downward, listened with pleasure to their own sound. On the damp telegraph poles the wet advertisements, "I teach the guitar by the number system" and "Social-science lessons for those preparing for the People's Conservatory," were all wrinkled up, and the letters had run. A platoon of Red Army soldiers in winter helmets crossed a puddle that began at the Stargorod co-operative shop and stretched as far as the province planning administration, the pediment of which was crowned with plaster tigers, figures of victory, and cobras.

Ippolit Matveyevich walked along, looking with interest at the people passing him in both directions. As one who had spent the whole of his life and also the

revolution in Russia, he was able to see how the way of
life was changing and acquiring a new countenance.
He had become used to this fact, but he seemed to be
used to only one point on the globe—the regional center of N. Now he was back in his home town, he realized he understood nothing. He felt just as awkward
and strange as though he really were an *émigré* just
back from Paris. In the old days, whenever he rode
through the town in his carriage, he used invariably to
meet friends or people he knew by sight. But now he
had gone four blocks along Lena Massacre Street and
there was no friend to be seen. They had vanished, or
they might have changed so much that they were no
longer recognizable, or perhaps they had become unrecognizable because they wore different clothes and
different hats. Perhaps they had changed their walk.
In any case, they were no longer there.

Ippolit walked along, pale, cold, and lost. He completely forgot that he was supposed to be looking for
the housing division. He crossed from sidewalk to sidewalk and turned into side streets, where the uninhib-
ited carthorses were quite intentionally drumming
their hoofs. There was more of winter in the side
streets, and rotting ice was still to be seen in places.
The whole town was a different color; the blue houses
had become green and the yellow ones gray. The fire
indicators had disappeared from the fire tower, the fire-
man no longer walked up and down it, and the streets
were much noisier than Ippolit Matveyevich could remember.

On Greater Pushkin Street, Ippolit Matveyevich was
amazed by the tracks and overhead cables of the street
railway, which he had never seen in Stargorod before.
He had not read the papers and did not know that the
two streetcar routes to the station and the market were
due to be opened on May Day. At one moment Ippolit
Matveyevich felt he had never left Stargorod, and the

next moment it was like a place completely unfamiliar to him.

Engrossed in these thoughts, he reached Marx and Engels Street. Here he re-experienced a childhood feeling that at any moment a friend would appear from round the corner of the two-storied house with the long balcony. He even stopped walking in anticipation. But the friend did not appear. The first person to come round the corner was a glazier with a box of Bohemian glass and a dollop of copper-colored putty. Then came a swell in a suede cap with a yellow leather peak. He was pursued by some children and elementary-school boys carrying books tied with straps.

Suddenly Ippolit Matveyevich felt a hotness in his palms and a sinking feeling in his stomach. A stranger with a kindly face was coming straight toward him, carrying a chair by the middle, as one would a violoncello. Suddenly developing hiccups, Ippolit Matveyevich looked closely at the chair and immediately recognized it.

Yes! It was a Hambs chair upholstered in flowered English chintz somewhat darkened by the storms of the revolution; it was a walnut chair with curved legs. Ippolit Matveyevich felt as though a gun had gone off in his ear.

"Knives and scissors sharpened! Razors set!" cried a baritone voice nearby.

And immediately came the shrill echo:

"Soldering and repairing!"

"Moscow *News*, magazine *Giggler, Red Meadow*."

Somewhere up above, a glass pane was removed with a crash. The truck from the grain-mill-and-elevator-construction administration passed by, shaking the town. A militiaman blew his whistle. Everything brimmed over with life. There was no time to be lost.

With a leopardlike spring, Ippolit Matveyevich leaped toward the repulsive stranger and silently tugged at the chair. The stranger tugged the other way. Still holding onto one leg with his left hand, Ippolit Matveyevich then began forcibly detaching the stranger's fat fingers from the chair.

"Thief!" whispered the stranger, gripping the chair more firmly.

"Just a moment, just a moment!" mumbled Ippolit Matveyevich, continuing to unstick the stranger's fingers.

A crowd began to gather. Three or four people were already standing nearby, watching the struggle with lively interest.

They both glanced around in alarm and, without looking at one another or letting go of the chair, rapidly moved on as though nothing were the matter.

"What's happening?" wondered Ippolit Matveyevich in dismay.

What the stranger was thinking was impossible to say, but he was walking in a most determined way.

They kept going more and more quickly until they saw a clearing scattered with bits of brick and other building materials at the end of a blind alley and turned into it simultaneously. Ippolit Matveyevich's strength now increased fourfold.

"Give it to me!" he shouted, doing away with all ceremony.

"Help!" exclaimed the stranger, almost inaudibly.

Since both of them had their hands occupied with the chair, they began kicking one another. The stranger's boots had metal studs, and at first Ippolit Matveyevich came off badly. He soon adjusted himself, however, and, skipping to the left and right as though doing a *crakovyak*, managed to dodge his opponent's blows, trying at the same time to catch him in the stomach. He was not successful, since the chair was in the way, but he did manage to land him a kick on the kneecap, after which the enemy could only lash out with one leg.

"Oh, Lord!" whispered the stranger.

It was then that Ippolit Matveyevich saw that the stranger who had carried off his chair in the most outrageous manner was none other than Father Fyodor, priest of the Church of St. Frol and St. Laurence.

"Father!" he exclaimed, removing his hands from the chair in astonishment.

Father Vostrikov turned purple and finally loosed his grip. The chair, no longer supported by either of them, fell to the brick-strewn ground.

"Where's your mustache, my dear Ippolit Matveyevich?" asked the cleric as caustically as possible.

"And what about your curls? You used to have curls, I believe!"

Ippolit Matveyevich's words conveyed utter contempt. He threw Father Fyodor a look of singular disgust and, tucking the chair under his arm, turned to go. But Father Fyodor had now recovered from his embarrassment and was not going to yield Vorobyaninov such an easy victory. With a cry of "No, I'm sorry," he grasped hold of the chair again. Their initial position was restored. The two opponents stood clutching the chair and, moving from side to side, sized one another up like cats or boxers.

The tense pause lasted a whole minute.

"So you're after my property, Holy Father?" said Ippolit Matveyevich through clenched teeth and kicked the holy father in the hip.

Father Fyodor feinted and then viciously kicked the marshal in the groin, making him double up.

"It's not your property."

"Whose then?"

"Not yours!"

"Whose then?"

"Not yours!"

"Whose then? Whose?"

Spitting at each other in this way, they kept kicking furiously.

"Whose property is it then?" screeched the marshal, sinking his foot in the holy father's stomach.

"It's nationalized property," said the holy father firmly, overcoming his pain.

"Nationalized?"

"Yes, nationalized."

They were jerking out the words so quickly that they ran together.

"Who nationalized it?"

"The Soviet Government. The Soviet Government."

"Which government?"

"The working people's government."

"Aha!" said Ippolit Matveyevich icily. "The government of workers and peasants?"

"Yes!"

"Hmm . . . then maybe you're a member of the Communist Party, Holy Father?"

"Maybe I am!"

Ippolit Matveyevich could no longer restrain himself and with a shriek of "Maybe you are" spat juicily in Father Fyodor's kindly face. Father Fyodor immediately spat in Ippolit Matveyevich's face and also found his mark. They had nothing with which to wipe away the spittle since they were still holding the chair. Ippolit Matveyevich made a noise like a door opening and thrust the chair at his enemy with all his might. The enemy fell over, dragging the panting Vorobyaninov with him. The struggle continued in the stalls.

Suddenly there was a crack and both front legs broke off simultaneously. Forgetting about one another, the opponents began tearing the walnut treasure-chest to pieces. The flowered English chintz split with the heart-rending scream of a sea gull. The back was torn off with a mighty tug. The treasure hunters ripped off the sacking together with the brass tacks and, grazing their hands on the springs, buried their fingers in the woolen stuffing. The disturbed springs hummed. Five minutes later the chair had been picked clean. Bits and pieces were all that was left. Springs rolled in all directions, and the wind blew the rotten wool all over the clearing. The curved legs lay in a hole. There were no jewels.

"Well, did you find anything?" asked Ippolit Matveyevich, panting.

Father Fyodor, all covered with tufts of wool, puffed and said nothing.

"You crook!" shouted Ippolit Matveyevich, "I'll break your neck, Father Fyodor!"

"I'd like to see you!" retorted the priest.

"Where are you going all covered in fluff?"

"Mind your own business!"

"Shame on you, Father! You're nothing but a thief!"

"I've stolen nothing from you."

"How did you find out about this? You used the sacrament of confession for your own ends. Very nice! Very fine!"

With an indignant "Fooh!" Ippolit Matveyevich left the clearing and, brushing his sleeve as he went, made for home. At the corner of Lena Massacre and Yerogeyev streets he caught sight of his partner. The technical adviser and director general of the concession was having the suede uppers of his boots cleaned with canary polish; he was standing half turned with one foot slightly raised. Ippolit Matveyevich hurried up to him. The director was gaily crooning the shimmy:

> *"The camels used to do it,*
> *The barracudas used to dance it,*
> *Now the whole world's doing the shimmy."*

"Well, how was the housing division?" he asked in a businesslike way, and immediately added:

"Wait a moment. Don't tell me now; you're too excited. Cool down a little."

Giving the shoeshiner seven kopeks, Ostap took

Vorobyaninov by the arm and led him down the street. He listened very carefully to everything the agitated Ippolit Matveyevich told him.

"Aha! A small black beard? Right! A coat with a sheepskin collar? I see. That's the chair from the pensioners' home. It was bought today for three roubles."

"But wait a moment. . . ."

And Ippolit Matveyevich told the chief concessionaire all about Father Fyodor's low tricks.

Ostap's face clouded.

"Too bad," he said. "Just like a detective story. We have a mysterious rival. We must steal a march on him. We can always break his head later."

While the friends were having a snack in the Stenka Razin beer hall and Ostap was asking questions about the past and present state of the housing division, the day came to an end.

The golden carthorses became brown again. The diamond drops grew cold in mid-air and plopped onto the ground. In the beer halls and the Phoenix restaurant the price of beer went up. Evening had come; the street lights on Greater Pushkin Street lit up and a detachment of Pioneers went by, stamping their feet on the way home from their first spring outing.

The tigers, figures of victory, and cobras on top of the province-planning administration shone mysteriously in the light of the advancing moon.

As he made his way home with Ostap, who was now suddenly silent, Ippolit Matveyevich gazed at the tigers and cobras. In his time, the building had housed the Provincial Government and the citizens had been proud of their cobras, considering them one of the sights of Stargorod.

"I'll find them," thought Ippolit Matveyevich, looking at one of the plaster figures of victory.

The tigers swished their tails lovingly, the cobras contracted with delight, and Ippolit Matveyevich's heart was filled with determination.

: *10* :

The Mechanic, the Parrot and the Fortuneteller

No. 7 PERELESHINSKY STREET was not one of Stargorod's best buildings. Its two stories were constructed in the style of the Second Empire and were embellished with timeworn lion heads, singularly reminiscent of the once well-known writer Artsybashev. There were exactly seven of these Artsybashevian physiognomies, one for each of the windows facing onto the street. The faces had been placed at the keystone of each window.

There were two other embellishments on the building, though these were of a purely commercial nature. On one side hung the radiant sign:

ODESSA ROLL BAKERY
MOSCOW
BUN ARTEL

The sign depicted a young man wearing a tie and ankle-length French trousers. In one dislocated hand he held a fabulous cornucopia from which poured an avalanche of ocher-colored buns; whenever necessary, these were passed off as Moscow rolls. The young man had a sexy smile on his face. On the other side, the Fastpack packing office announced itself to prospective clients by a black board with round gold lettering.

Despite the appreciable difference in the signs and also the capital possessed by the two dissimilar enterprises, they both engaged in the same business, namely, speculation in all types of fabrics: coarse wool, fine wool, cotton, and, whenever silk of good color and design came their way, silk as well.

Passing through the tunnel-like gateway and turning right into the yard with its cement well, you could see two doorways without porches, giving straight onto the angular stones of the yard. A dulled brass plate with a name engraved in script was fixed to the right-hand door:

> V. M. POLESOV

The left-hand door was fitted with a piece of whitish tin:

> FASHIONS AND MILLINERY

This was also only for show.

Inside the fashions-and-millinery workroom there was no esparterie, no trimmings, no headless dummies with soldierly bearing, nor any large heads for elegant ladies' hats. Instead, the three-room apartment was occupied by an immaculately white parrot in red shorts. The parrot was riddled with fleas, but could not complain since it was unable to talk. For days on end it used to crack sunflower seeds and spit the husks through the bars of its tall, circular cage onto the carpet. It only needed a concertina and new squeaky galoshes to resemble a peasant on a spree. Dark-brown patterned curtains flapped at the window. Dark-brown hues predominated in the apartment. Above the piano was a reproduction of Boecklin's "Isle of the Dead" in a fancy frame of dark-green oak, covered with glass. One corner of the glass had been broken off some time before, and the flies had added so many finishing touches to the picture at this bared section that it merged completely with the frame. What was going on in that section of the "Isle of the Dead" was quite impossible to say.

The owner herself was sitting in the bedroom and laying out cards, resting her arms on an octagonal table covered by a dirty Richelieu tablecloth. In front of her sat the widow, Gritsatsuyeva, in a fluffy shawl.

"I should warn you, young lady, that I don't take less than fifty kopeks for a session," said the fortune-teller.

The widow, whose anxiousness to find a new husband knew no bounds, agreed to pay the price.

"But tell me the future as well, please," she said plaintively.

"You will be represented by the Queen of Clubs."

"I was always the Queen of Hearts," objected the widow.

The fortuneteller consented apathetically and began combining the cards. A rough estimation of the widow's lot was ready in a few minutes. Both major and minor difficulties awaited the widow, but near to her heart was the King of Clubs who had befriended the Queen of Diamonds.

A fair copy of the prediction was made from the widow's hand. The lines of her hand were clean, powerful, and faultless. Her life line stretched so far that it ended up at her pulse and, if it told the truth, the widow ought to live till doomsday. The head line and line of brilliancy gave reason to believe that she would give up her grocery business and present mankind with master works in the realm of art, science, and social studies. Her Mounts of Venus resembled Manchurian volcanoes and revealed marvelous reserves of love and affection.

The fortuneteller explained all this to the widow, using the words and phrases current among graphologists, palmists, and horse traders.

"Thank you, madam," said the widow. "Now I know who the King of Clubs is. And I know who the Queen of Diamonds is, too. But what about the King? Does that mean marriage?"

"It does, young lady."

The widow went home in a dream, while the fortuneteller threw the cards into a drawer, yawned, displaying the mouth of a fifty-year-old woman, and went into the kitchen. There she busied herself with the meal that was warming on a Graetz stove; wiping her hands on her apron like a cook, she took a chipped-enamel pail and went into the yard to fetch water.

She walked across the yard, dragging her flat feet. Her drooping breasts wobbled lazily inside her dyed blouse. Her head was crowned with graying hair. She was an old woman, she was dirty, she regarded everyone with suspicion, and she had a sweet tooth. If Ippolit Matveyevich had seen her now, he would never have recognized Elena Bour, his former mistress, about whom the clerk of the court had once said in verse that "her lips were inviting and she was so spritely!" At the well, Madam Bour was greeted by her neighbor, Victor Mikhailovich Polesov, the mechanic-intellectual, who was collecting water in an empty gasoline can. Polesov had the face of an operatic Mephistopheles who is carefully rubbed with burnt cork just before he has to go on.

As soon as they had exchanged greetings, the neighbors got down to a discussion of the affair concerning the whole of Stargorod.

"What times we live in!" said Polesov ironically.

"Yesterday I went all over the town but couldn't find a three-eighths-inch die anywhere. There wasn't any. And to think—they're going to open a street railway!"

Elena Stanislavovna, who had as much idea about three-eighths-inch dies as a student of the Leonardo da Vinci ballet school who thinks that cream comes from cream tarts, expressed her sympathy.

"The shops we have now! Nothing but lines and no shops. And the names of the shops are so dreadful. Stargiko!"

"But I'll tell you something else, Elena Stanislavovna. They have four General Electric Company motors left. And they just about work, although the chassis are junk. The windows haven't any shock absorbers. I've seen them myself. The whole lot rattles. Horrible! And the other engines are from Kharkov. Made entirely by the State Non-Ferrous Metallurgy Industry."

The mechanic stopped talking in irritation. His black face glistened in the sun. The whites of his eyes were yellowish. Among the artisans owning cars in Stargorod, of whom there were many, Victor Polesov was the most gauche, and most frequently made an ass of himself. The reason for this was his overebullient nature. He was an ebullient idler. He was forever effervescing. In his own workshop in the second yard of no. 7 Pereleshinsky Street, he was never to be found. The extinguished portable furnaces stood deserted in the middle of his stone shed, the corners of which were cluttered up with punctured tires, torn Triangle tire covers, rusty locks (so enormous you could have locked cities with them), fuel cans with the names "Indian" and "Wanderer," a sprung baby carriage, a useless dynamo, rotted rawhide belts, oil-stained rope, worn emery paper, an Austrian bayonet, and a great deal of other broken, bent, and dented junk. Clients could never find Victor Mikhailovich. He was always out somewhere giving orders. He had no time for work. It was impossible for him to stand by and watch a horse and cart drive into his or anyone else's yard. He immediately went out and, clasping his hands behind his back, watched the carter's actions with contempt. Finally he could bear it no longer.

"Where do you think you're going?" he used to shout in a horrified voice. "Move over!"

The startled carter would move the cart over.

"Where do you think you're moving to, wretch?" Victor Polesov cried, rushing up to the horse. "In the old days you would have got a slap for that, then you would have moved over."

Having given orders in this way for half an hour or so, Polesov would be just about to return to his workshop, where a broken bicycle pump awaited repair, when the peaceful life of the town would be disturbed by some other contretemps. Either two carts entangled their axles in the street and Victor Mikhailovich would show them the best and quickest way to separate them, or workmen would be replacing a telegraph pole and Polesov would check that it was perpendicular with his own plumb line brought specially from the workshop; or, finally, a fire engine would go past and Polesov, excited by the noise of the siren and burned up with curiosity, would chase after it.

But from time to time Polesov was seized by a mood of practical activity. For several days he used to shut himself up in his workshop and work in silence. Children ran freely about the yard and shouted what they liked, carters described any circles in the yard, carts completely stopped entangling their axles and fire engines and hearses sped to the fire unaccompanied—Victor Mikhailovich was working. One day after a bout of this kind, he emerged from the workshop with a motorcycle, pulling it like a ram by the horns; the motorcycle was made up of parts of cars, fire extinguishers, bicycles and typewriters. It had a one-and-a-half horsepower Wanderer engine and Davidson wheels, while the other essential parts had lost the name of the original maker. A piece of cardboard with the words "Trial Run" hung on a cord from the saddle. A crowd gathered. Without looking at anyone, Victor Mikhailovich gave the pedal a twist with his hand. There was no spark for at least ten minutes, but then came a metallic splutter and the contraption shuddered and enveloped itself in a cloud of filthy smoke. Polesov jumped into the saddle, and the motorcycle, accelerating madly, carried him through the tunnel into the middle of the roadway and stopped dead. Polesov was about to get off and investigate the mysterious vehicle when it suddenly reversed and, whisking its creator through the same tunnel, stopped at its original point of departure in the yard, grunted peevishly, and blew up. Victor Mikhailovich escaped by a miracle and during the next bout of activity used the bits of the motorcycle to make a stationary engine, very similar to a real one—except that it did not work.

The crowning glory of the mechanic-intellectual's academic activity was the epic of the gates of no. 5, the next-door building. The housing co-operative that owned the building signed a contract with Victor Polesov under which he undertook to repair the iron gates and paint them any color he liked. For its part, the housing co-operative agreed to pay Victor Mikhailovich Polesov the sum of twenty-one roubles, seventy-five kopeks, subject to approval by the special committee. The official stamps were charged to the contractor.

Victor Mikhailovich carried off the gates like Samson. He set to work in his shop with enthusiasm. It took several days to unrivet the gates. They were taken to pieces. Iron curlicues lay in the baby carriage; iron bars and spikes were piled under the workbench. It took another few days to inspect the damage. Then a great disaster occurred in the town. A water main burst on Drovyanaya Street, and Polesov spent the rest of the week at the scene of the misfortune, smiling ironically, shouting at the workmen, and looking into the hole in the ground every few minutes.

As soon as his organizational ardor had somewhat abated, Polesov returned to his gates, but it was too late. The children from the yard were already playing with the iron curlicues and spikes of the gates of no. 5. Seeing the wrathful mechanic, the children dropped their playthings and fled. Half the curlicues were missing and were never found. After that Polesov lost interest in the gates.

But then terrible things began to happen in no. 5, which was now wide open. The wet linen was stolen from the attics, and one evening someone even carried off a samovar that was singing in the yard. Polesov himself took part in the pursuit, but the thief ran at quite a pace, even though he was holding the steaming samovar in front of him, and, looking over his shoulder, covered Victor Mikhailovich, who was keeping in front of everyone, with foul abuse. The one who suffered most, however, was the yard keeper from no. 5. He lost his nightly wage since there were now no gates, there was nothing to open, and residents returning from a spree had no one to give a tip to. At first the yard keeper kept coming to ask if the gates would soon be finished; then he tried praying, and finally made vague threats. The housing co-operative sent Polesov written reminders, and there was talk of taking the matter to court. The situation had grown more and more tense.

Standing by the well, the fortuneteller and the mechanic-enthusiast continued their conversation.

"Given the absence of seasoned sleepers," cried Victor Mikhailovich for the whole yard to hear, "it won't be a street railway, but plain misery!"

"When will all this end!" said Elena Stanislavovna. "We live like savages!"

"There's no end to it. . . . Yes. Do you know who I saw today? Vorobyaninov."

In her amazement, Elena Stanislavovna leaned against the wall, continuing to hold the full pail of water in mid-air.

"I had gone to the communal-services building to extend my contract for the hire of the workshop and was going down the corridor when suddenly two people came toward me. One of them seemed familiar; he looked like Vorobyaninov. Then they asked me what the building had been in the old days. I told them it used to be a girls' secondary school and later the housing division. I asked them why they wanted to know, but they just said 'Thanks' and went off. Then I saw clearly that it really was Vorobyaninov, only without his mustache. The other one with him was a fine-looking fellow. Obviously a former officer. And then I thought . . ."

At that moment Victor Mikhailovich noticed something unpleasant. Breaking off what he was saying, he grabbed his can and promptly hid behind the trash bin. Into the yard sauntered the yard keeper from no. 5. He stopped by the well and began looking round at the outhouses. Not seeing Polesov anywhere, he asked sadly:

"Isn't Vick, the mechanic, here yet?"

"I really don't know," said the fortuneteller. "I don't know at all."

And with unusual nervousness she hurried off to her apartment, spilling water from the pail.

The yard keeper stroked the cement block at the top of the well and went over to the workshop. Two paces beyond the sign:

```
┌─────────────────────────────────────────┐
│                                           │
│    ENTRANCE TO METAL WORKSHOP             │
│                                           │
└─────────────────────────────────────────┘
```

was the sign:

```
┌──────────────────────────────────┐
│                                    │
│        METAL WORKSHOP              │
│   AND PRIMUS STOVE REPAIRS         │
│                                    │
└──────────────────────────────────┘
```

under which there hung a heavy padlock. The yard keeper kicked the padlock and said with loathing:

"Ugh, filth!"

He stood by the workshop for another two or three minutes working up the most venomous feelings, then wrenched off the sign with a crash, took it to the well in the middle of the yard, and, standing on it with both feet, began making an unholy row.

"You thieves in no. 7!" howled the yard keeper. "Riffraff of all kinds! Seven-sired viper! With secondary education! I don't give a damn for his secondary education! Damn mess!"

During this, the seven-sired viper with secondary education was sitting behind the trash bin and feeling depressed.

Window frames flew open with a bang, and amused tenants poked their heads out.

People strolled into the yard from outside, in curiosity. At the sight of an audience, the yard keeper became even more heated.

"Fitter-mechanic!" he cried. "Damn aristocrat!"

The yard keeper's parliamentary expressions were richly interspersed with swear words, to which he gave preference. The members of the fair sex crowding around the windows were very annoyed at the yard keeper, but stayed where they were.

"I'll push his face in!" he raged. "Education!"

While the scene was at its height, a militiaman appeared and quietly began hauling the fellow off to the precinct. He was assisted by some young toughs from Fastpack.

The yard keeper put his arms around the militiaman's neck and burst into tears.

The danger was past.

A weary Victor Mikhailovich then jumped out from behind the trash bin. There was a stir among the audience.

"Bum!" cried Polesov in the wake of the procession, "I'll show you! You louse!"

The yard keeper was weeping bitterly and could not hear. He was carried to the precinct, and the sign "Metal Workshop and Primus Stove Repair" was also taken along as factual evidence.

Victor Mikhailovich bristled with fury for some time.

"Sons of bitches!" he said, turning to the spectators. "Conceited bums!"

"That's enough, Victor Mikhailovich," called Elena Stanislavovna from the window. "Come in here a moment."

She placed a dish of stewed fruit in front of Polesov and, pacing up and down the room, began asking him questions.

"But I tell you it was him; without his mustache, but definitely him," said Polesov, shouting as usual. "I know him well. It was the spitting image of Vorobyaninov."

"Not so loud, for heaven's sake! Why do you think he's here?"

An ironic smile appeared on Polesov's face.

"Well, what do you think?"

He chuckled with even greater irony.

"At any rate, not to sign a treaty with the Bolsheviks."

"Do you think he's in danger?"

The reserves of irony amassed by Polesov over the ten years since the revolution were inexhaustible. A

series of smiles of varying force and skepticism lit
up his face.

"Who isn't in danger in Soviet Russia, expecially a
man in Vorobyaninov's position. Mustaches, Elena
Stanislavovna, are not shaved off for nothing."

"Has he been sent from abroad?" asked Elena Stanislavovna, almost choking.

"Definitely," replied the brilliant mechanic.

"What is his purpose here?"

"Don't be childish!"

"I must see him all the same."

"Do you know what you're risking?"

"I don't care. After ten years of separation I cannot
do otherwise than see Ippolit Matveyevich."

And it actually seemed to her that fate had parted
them while they were still in love with one another.

"I beg you to find him. Find out where he is. You
go everywhere; it won't be difficult for you. Tell him
I want to see him. Do you hear?"

The parrot in the red shorts, which had been dozing
on its perch, was startled by the noisy conversation;
it turned upside down and froze in that position.

"Elena Stanislavovna," said the mechanic, half rising
and pressing his hands to his chest, "I will contact
him."

"Would you like some more stewed fruit?" asked
the fortuneteller, deeply touched.

Victor Mikhailovich consumed the stewed fruit
irritably, gave Elena Stanislavovna a lecture on the
faulty construction of the parrot's cage, and then left
with instructions to keep everything strictly secret.

: *11* :

The "Mirror of Life" Index

THE NEXT DAY the partners saw that it was no longer convenient to live in the janitor's room. Tikhon kept muttering away to himself and had become completely stupid, having seen his master first with a black mustache, then with a green one, and finally with no mustache at all. There was nothing to sleep on. The room stank of rotting manure, brought in on Tikhon's new felt boots. His old ones stood in the corner and did not help to purify the air, either.

"I declare the reunion over," said Ostap. "We must move to a hotel."

Ippolit Matveyevich trembled. "I can't."

"Why not?"

"I shall have to register."

"Aren't your papers in order?"

"My papers are in order, but my name is well known in the town. Rumors will spread."

The concessionaires reflected for a while in silence.

"How do you like the name Michelson?" suddenly asked the splendid Ostap.

"Which Michelson? The senator?"

"No. The member of the Soviet trade-workers' union."

"I don't get you."

"That's because you lack technical experience. Don't be naïve!"

Bender took a union card out of his green jacket and handed it to Ippolit Matveyevich.

"Konrad Karlovich Michelson, aged forty-eight, nonparty member, bachelor; union member since 1921 and a person of excellent character; a good friend of mine and seems to be a friend of children. . . . But you needn't be friendly to children. The militia doesn't require that of you."

Ippolit Matveyevich turned red. "But is it right?"

"Compared with our concession, this misdeed, though it does come under the penal code, is as innocent as the children's game of 'Rats.' "

Vorobyaninov nevertheless balked at the idea.

"You're an idealist, Konrad Karlovich. You're lucky, otherwise you might have to become a Papa Christosopulo or Zlovunov."

There followed immediate consent, and without saying goodbye to Tikhon, the concessionaires went out into the street.

They stopped at the Sorbonne furnished rooms. Ostap threw the whole of the small hotel staff into confusion. First he looked at the seven-rouble rooms, but disliked the furnishings. The cleanliness of the five-rouble rooms pleased him more, but the carpets were shabby and there was an objectionable smell. In the three-rouble rooms everything was satisfactory except for the pictures.

"I can't live in the same room as landscapes," said Ostap.

They had to take a room for one rouble, eighty. It had no landscapes, no carpets, and the furniture was very conservative—two beds and a night table.

"Stone Age style," observed Ostap with approval. "I hope there aren't any prehistoric monsters in the mattresses."

"Depends on the season," replied the cunning cleaner. "If there's a provincial convention of some kind, then of course there aren't any, because we have many visitors and we clean the place thoroughly before they arrive. But at other times you may find some. They come across from the Livadia rooms next door."

That day the concessionaires visited the Stargorod communal services, where they obtained the information they required. It turned out that the housing division had been disbanded in 1921 and that its voluminous records had been merged with those of the communal services.

The smooth operator got down to business. By evening the partners had found out the address of the head of the records department, Bartholomew Korobeinikov, a former clerk in the Tsarist town administration and now an office-employment official.

Ostap attired himself in his worsted vest, dusted his jacket against the back of a chair, demanded a rouble, twenty kopeks from Ippolit Matveyevich, and set off to visit the record keeper. Ippolit Matveyevich remained at the Sorbonne hotel and paced up and down the narrow gap between the two beds in agitation. The fate of the whole enterprise was in the balance that cold, green evening. If they could get hold of copies of the orders for the distribution of the furniture requisitioned from Vorobyaninov's house, half the battle had been won. There would still be tremendous difficulties facing them, but at least they would be on the right track.

"If only we can get the orders," whispered Ippolit Matveyevich to himself, lying on the bed, "if only we can get them."

The springs of the battered mattress nipped him like fleas, but he did not feel them. He still only had a vague idea of what would follow once the orders had been obtained, but was sure everything would go swimmingly.

Engrossed in his rosy dream, Ippolit Matveyevich tossed about on the bed. The springs bleated underneath him.

Ostap had to cross the entire town. Korobeinikov lived in Gusishe, on the outskirts.

It was an area populated largely by railroad workers. From time to time a snuffling locomotive would back its way along the walled-off embankment, above the houses. For a second the roof tops were lit by the blaze from the firebox. Now and then empty freighters went by, and from time to time detonators could be heard exploding. Amid the huts and temporary wooden barracks stretched the long brick walls of still damp apartment houses.

Ostap passed an island of lights—the railroad workers' club—checked the address from a piece of paper, and halted in front of the record keeper's house. He rang a bell marked "Please Ring" in embossed letters.

After prolonged questioning as to "Who do you want?" and "What is it about?" the door was opened, and he found himself in a dark, cupboard-cluttered hallway. Someone breathed on him in the darkness, but did not speak.

"Is Citizen Korobeinikov here?" asked Ostap.

The person who had been breathing took Ostap by the arm and led him into a dining room lit by a hanging kerosene lamp. Ostap saw in front of him a prissy little old man with an unusually flexible spine. There was no doubt that this was Citizen Korobeinikov himself. Without waiting for an invitation, Ostap moved up a chair and sat down.

The old man looked fearlessly at the high-handed stranger and remained silent. Ostap amiably began the conversation.

"I've come on business. You work at the communal-services records office, don't you?"

The old man's back started moving and arched affirmatively.

"And you worked before that in the housing division?"

"I have worked everywhere," he answered gaily.

"Even in the Tsarist town administration?"

Here Ostap smiled graciously. The old man's back contorted for some time and finally ended up in a position implying that his employment in the Tsarist town administration was something long passed and that it was not possible to remember everything for sure.

"And may I ask what I can do for you?" said the host, regarding his visitor with interest.

"You may," answered the visitor. "I am Vorobyaninov's son."

"Whose? The marshal's?"

"Yes."

"Is he still alive?"

"He's dead, Citizen Korobeinikov. He's gone to his rest."

"Yes," said the old man without any particular grief, "a sad event. But I didn't think he had any children."

"He didn't," said Ostap amiably in confirmation.

"What do you mean?"

"I'm from a morganatic marriage."

"Not by any chance Elena Stanislavovna's son?"

"Right!"

"How is she?"

"Mom's been in her grave some time."

"I see. I see. How sad."

And the old man gazed at Ostap with tears of sympathy in his eyes, although that very day he had seen Elena Stanislavovna at the meat stalls in the market.

"We all pass away," he said, "but please tell me on what business you're here, my dear . . . I don't know your name."

"Voldemar," promptly replied Ostap.

"Vladimir Ippolitovich, very good."

The old man sat down at the table covered with patterned oilcloth and peered into Ostap's eyes.

In carefully chosen words, Ostap expressed his grief at the loss of his parents. He much regretted that he had invaded the privacy of the respected record keeper so late at night and disturbed him by the visit, but hoped that the respected record keeper would forgive him when he knew what had brought him.

"I would like to have some of my dad's furniture," concluded Ostap with inexpressible filial love, "as a keepsake. Can you tell me who was given the furniture from Dad's house?"

"That's difficult," said the old man after a moment's thought. "Only a well-to-do person could manage that. What's your profession, may I ask?"

"I have my own refrigeration plant in Samara, run on artel lines."

The old man looked dubiously at young Vorobyaninov's green suit, but made no comment.

"A smart young man," he thought.

"A typical old bastard," decided Ostap, who had by then completed his observation of Korobeinikov.

"So there you are," said Ostap.

"So there you are," said the record keeper. "It's difficult, but possible."

"And it involves expense," suggested the refrigeration-plant owner helpfully.

"A small sum . . ."

" 'Is nearer one's heart,' as Maupassant used to say. The information will be paid for."

"All right then, seventy roubles."

"Why so much? Are oats so expensive nowadays?"

The old man quivered slightly, wriggling his spine.

"Joke if you will. . . ."

"I accept, Dad. Cash on delivery. When shall I come?"

"Have you the money on you?"

Ostap eagerly slapped his pocket.

"Then now, if you like," said Korobeinikov triumphantly.

He lit a candle and led Ostap into the next room. Besides a bed, obviously slept in by the owner of the house himself, the room contained a desk piled with account books and a wide office cupboard with open shelves. The printed letters A, B, C down to the rearguard letter Z were glued to the edges of the shelves. Bundles of orders bound with new string lay on the shelves.

"Oho!" exclaimed the delighted Ostap. "A full set of records at home."

"A complete set," said the record keeper modestly. "Just in case, you know. The communal services don't need them and they might be useful to me in my old age. We're living on top of a volcano, you know. Anything can happen. Then people will rush off to find their furniture, and where will it be? It will be here. This is where it will be. In the cupboard. And who will have preserved it? Who will have looked after it? Korobeinikov! So the gentlemen will say thank you to the old man and help him in his old age. And I don't need very much; ten roubles an order will do me. Otherwise, they might as well look for the wind in the field. They won't find the furniture without me."

Ostap looked at the old man in rapture.

"A marvelous office," he said. "Complete mechanization. You're an absolute hero of labor!"

The flattered record keeper began explaining the details of his pastime. He opened the thick registers.

"It's all here," he said, "the whole of Stargorod. All the furniture. Who it was taken from and who it was given to. And here's the alphabetical index—the mirror of life! Whose furniture do you want to know about? Angelov, first-guild merchant? Certainly. Look under A. A, Ak, Am, An, Angelov. The number? Here it is—82742. Now give me the stock book. Page 142. Where's

Angelov? Here he is. Taken from Angelov on December 18, 1918: Baecker grand piano, one, no. 97012; piano stools, one, soft; bureaus, two; wardrobes, four (two mahogany); bookcases, one . . . and so on. And who was it all given to? Let's look at the distribution register. The same number. Issued to. The bookcase to the town military committee, three wardrobes to the Lark boarding school, another wardrobe for the personal use of the secretary of the Stargorod Province Food Office. And where did the piano go? The piano went to the social-security administration, and it's there to this day."

"I don't think I saw a piano there," thought Ostap, remembering Alchen's shy little face.

"Or, for instance, Murin, head of the town council. So we look under M. It's all here. The whole town. Pianos, settees, pier glasses, chairs, divans, poofs, chandeliers . . . even dinner services."

"Well," said Ostap, "they ought to erect a monument to you. But let's get to the point. The letter V, for example."

"The letter V it is," responded Korobeinikov willingly. "In one moment. Vm, Vn, Vorotsky, no. 48238, Vorobyaninov, Ippolit Matveyevich, your father, God rest his soul, was a man with a big heart . . . A Baecker piano, no. 54809. Chinese vases, marked, four, from the Sèvres factory in France; Aubusson carpets, eight, different sizes; a tapestry, 'The Shepherd Boy'; a tapestry, 'The Shepherd Girl'; Tekke carpets, two; Khorassan carpets, one; stuffed bears with dish, one; a bedroom suite to seat twelve; a dining-room suite to seat sixteen; a drawing-room suite to seat twelve, walnut, made by Hambs."

"And who was given it?" asked Ostap impatiently.

"We're just coming to that. The stuffed bear with dish went to the second militia precinct. The 'Shepherd Boy' tapestry went to the art treasure collection; the 'Shepherd Girl' tapestry to the water-transport

club; the Aubusson, Tekke, and Khorassan carpets to
the ministry of foreign trade. The bedroom suite went
to the hunters' trade union; the dining-room suite to
the Stargorod branch of the chief tea administration.
The walnut suite was divided up. The round table and
one chair went to the second social-security office, a
curved-back settee was given to the housing division
(it's still in the hall, and the bastards have spilled grease
all over the covering); one chair went to Comrade
Gritsatsuyev as an invalid of the imperialist war, at his
own request, granted by Comrade Burkin, head of the
housing division. Ten chairs went to Moscow to the
furniture museum, in accordance with a circular sent
round by the ministry of education . . . Chinese vases,
marked . . ."

"Well done!" said Ostap jubilantly. "That's more
like it! Now it would be nice to see the actual orders."

"In a moment. We'll come to the orders in a moment. Letter V, no. 48328."

The old man went up to the cupboard and, standing
on tiptoe, took down the appropriate bundle.

"Here you are. All your father's furniture. Do you
want all the orders?"

"What would I do with all of them? Just something
to remind me of my childhood. The drawing-room
suite . . . I remember how I used to play on the Khorassan carpet in the drawing room, looking at the 'Shepherd Boy' tapestry. . . . I had a fine time, a wonderful
childhood. So let's stick to the drawing-room suite,
Dad."

Lovingly the old man began to open up the bundle
of green counterfoils and searched for the orders in
question. He took out five of them. One was for ten
chairs, two for one chair each, one for the round table,
and one for the tapestry.

"Just see. They're all in order. You know where each
item is. All the counterfoils have the addresses on them
and also the receiver's own signature. So no one can

back out if anything happens. Perhaps you'd like Madam Popova's furniture? It's very good and also made by Hambs."

But Ostap was motivated solely by love for his parents; he grabbed the orders, stuffed them in the depths of his pocket and declined the furniture belonging to General Popov's wife.

"May I make out a receipt?" inquired the record keeper, adroitly arching himself.

"You may," said Ostap amiably. "Make it out, Champion of an Idea!"

"I will then."

"Do that!"

They went back into the first room. Korobeinikov made out a receipt in neat handwriting and handed it smilingly to his visitor. The chief concessionaire took the piece of paper with two fingers of his right hand in a singularly courteous manner and put it in the same pocket as the precious orders.

"Well, so long for now," he said, squinting. "I think I've given you a lot of trouble. I won't burden you any more with my presence. Good-by, King of the Office!"

The dumfounded record keeper limply took the offered hand.

"Goodbye!" repeated Ostap.

He moved toward the door.

Korobeinikov was at a loss to understand. He even looked on the table to see if the visitor had left any money there. Then he asked very quietly:

"What about the money?"

"What money?" said Ostap, opening the door. "Did I hear you say something about money?"

"Of course! For the furniture; for the orders!"

"Honestly, chum," crooned Ostap, "I swear by my late father, I'd be glad to, but I haven't any; I forgot to draw from my checking account."

The old man began to tremble and put out a puny hand to restrain his nocturnal visitor.

"Don't be a fool," said Ostap menacingly. "I'm telling you in plain Russian—tomorrow means tomorrow. So long! Write to me!"

The door slammed. Korobeinikov opened it and ran into the street, but Ostap had gone. He was soon on his way past the bridge. A locomotive passing overhead illuminated him with its lights and covered him with smoke.

"Things are moving," cried Ostap to the engineer, "things are moving, gentlemen of the jury!"

The engineer could not hear; he waved his hand, and the wheels of the locomotive began pulling the steel elbows of the cranks with still greater force. The locomotive raced away.

Korobeinikov stood for a few moments in the icy wind and then went back into his hovel, cursing like a trooper. He stopped in the middle of the room and kicked the table with rage. The clog-shaped ash tray with the word "Triangle" on it jumped up and down, and the glass clinked against the decanter.

Never before had Bartholomew Korobeinikov been so wretchedly deceived. He could deceive anyone he liked, but this time he had been fooled with such brilliant simplicity that all he could do was stand for some time, lashing out at the thick legs of the table.

In Gusishe, Korobeinikov was known as Bartholomeich. People only turned to him in cases of extreme need. He acted as a pawnbroker and charged cannibalistic rates of interest. He had been doing this for several years and had never once been caught. But now he had been cheated at his own game, a business from which he expected great profits and a secure old age.

"A fine thing!" he cried, remembering the lost orders. "From now on money in advance. How could I have bungled it like that? I gave him the walnut suite

with my own hands. The 'Shepherd Boy' alone is price-
less. Done by hand. . . ."

An uncertain hand had been ringing the bell marked
"Please Ring" for some time and Korobeinikov hardly
had time to remember that the outside door was still
open, when there was a heavy thud, and the voice of a
man entangled in a maze of cupboards called out:

"How do I get in?"

Korobeinikov went into the hallway, took hold of
somebody's coat (it felt like coarse cloth), and pulled
Father Fyodor into the dining room.

"I humbly apologize," said Father Fyodor.

After ten minutes of innuendoes and sly remarks on
both sides, it came to light that Citizen Korobeinikov
definitely did have some information regarding Vorobyaninov's furniture and that Father Fyodor was not
averse to paying for it. Furthermore, to the record
keeper's great amusement, the visitor turned out to be
the late marshal's own brother, and he passionately desired to keep something in memory of him, for example, a walnut drawing-room suite. The suite had
very happy boyhood associations for Vorobyaninov's
brother.

Korobeinikov asked a hundred roubles. The visitor
rated his brother's memory considerably lower than
that, say thirty roubles. They agreed on fifty.

"I'd like the money first," said the record keeper.
"It's a rule of mine."

"Does it matter if I give it to you in ten-rouble gold
pieces?" asked Father Fyodor, hurriedly, tearing open
the lining of his coat.

"I'll take them at the official rate of exchange. Today's rate is nine and a half."

Vostrikov took five yellow coins from the sausage,
added two and a half in silver, and pushed the pile over
to the record keeper. The latter counted the coins
twice, scooped them up into one hand and, requesting
his visitor to wait, went to fetch the orders. Bartholo-

meich did not need to reflect for long; he opened the "mirror of life" index at the letter P, quickly found the right number and took down a bundle of orders for Popova, the general's wife. Disemboweling the bundle, he selected the order for twelve walnut chairs from the Hambs factory, issued to Comrade Bruns, resident of 34 Vineyard Street. Marveling at his own artfulness and dexterity, he chuckled to himself and took the order to the purchaser.

"Are they all in one place?" asked the purchaser.

"All there together. It's a splendid suite. You'll lick your lips. Anyway, I don't need to tell you, you know yourself!"

Father Fyodor rapturously gave the record keeper a prolonged handshake and, colliding innumerable times with the cupboards in the hall, fled into the darkness of the night.

For quite a while longer Bartholomeich chuckled to himself at the customer he had cheated. He spread the gold coins out in a row on the table and sat there for a long time, gazing dreamily at the bright yellow discs.

"What is it about Vorobyaninov's furniture that attracts them?" he wondered. "They're out of their minds."

He undressed, said his prayers without much attention, lay down on the narrow cot, and fell into a troubled sleep.

: *12* :

A Passionate Woman
Is a Poet's Dream

DURING THE NIGHT the cold was completely consumed. It became so warm that the feet of early passers-by began to ache. The sparrows chirped various nonsense. Even the hen that emerged from the kitchen into the hotel yard felt a surge of strength and tried to take off. The sky was covered with small dumplinglike clouds and the trash bin reeked of violets and *soupe paysanne*. The wind lazed under the eaves. Tomcats lounged on the roof tops and, half closing their eyes, condescendingly watched the yard, across which the room cleaner, Alexander, was hurrying with a bundle of dirty washing.

Things began stirring in the corridors of the Sorbonne. Delegates were arriving from other regions for the opening of the street railway. A whole crowd of them got down from a wagon bearing the name of the Sorbonne hotel.

The sun was warming to its fullest extent. Up flew the corrugated iron shutters of the shops, and workers in Soviet institutions on their way to work in padded coats breathed heavily and unbuttoned themselves, feeling the heaviness of spring.

On Co-operative Street an overloaded truck belong-

ing to the grain-mill-and-elevator-construction administration broke a spring, and Victor Polesov arrived at
the scene to give advice.

From the room furnished with down-to-earth luxury (two beds and a night table) came a horselike
snorting and neighing. Ippolit Matveyevich was happily washing himself and blowing his nose. The smooth
operator lay in bed inspecting the damage to his boots.

"By the way," he said, "kindly settle your debt."

Ippolit Matveyevich surfaced from under his towel
and looked at his partner with bulging, pince-nezless
eyes.

"Why are you staring at me like a soldier at a louse?
What are you surprised about? The debt? Yes! You
owe me some money. I forgot to tell you yesterday
that I had to pay, with your authority, seventy roubles
for the orders. Herewith the receipt. Sling over thirty-
five roubles. Concessionaires, I hope, share the expenses on an equal footing?"

Ippolit Matveyevich put on his pince-nez, read the
receipt and, sighing, passed over the money. But even
that could not dampen his spirits. The riches were in
their hands. The thirty-rouble speck of dust vanished
in the glitter of a diamond mountain.

Smiling radiantly, Ippolit Matveyevich went out into
the corridor and began strolling up and down. His
plans for a new life to be built on a foundation of precious stones brought him great comfort. "And the holy
father," he gloated, "has been taken for a ride. He'll see
as much of the chairs as his beard."

Reaching the end of the corridor, Vorobyaninov
turned round. The cracked white door of room no. 13
opened wide, and out toward him came Father Fyodor
in a blue tunic encircled by a shabby black cord with a
fluffy tassel. His kindly face was beaming with happiness. He had also come into the corridor for a walk.
The rivals approached one another several times, looking at each other triumphantly as they passed. At the

two ends of the corridor they both turned simultaneously and approached again. . . . Ippolit Matveyevich's heart was bursting with joy. Father Fyodor was
experiencing a similar feeling. They were both sorry
for the defeated enemy. By the time they reached the
fifth lap, Ippolit Matveyevich could restrain himself no
longer.

"Good morning, Father," he said with inexpressible
sweetness.

Father Fyodor mustered all the sarcasm with which
God had endowed him and replied with:

"Good morning, Ippolit Matveyevich."

The enemies parted. When their paths next crossed,
Vorobyaninov said casually:

"I hope I didn't hurt you at our last meeting."

"Not at all, it was very pleasant meeting you," replied the other jubilantly.

They moved apart again. Father Fyodor's physiog-
nomy began to disgust Ippolit Matveyevich.

"I don't suppose you're saying Mass any more?" he
remarked at the next encounter.

"There's nowhere to say it. The parishioners have
run off to various places in search of treasure."

"Their own treasure, mark you. Their own!"

"I don't know whose it is, but just that they're looking for it."

Ippolit Matveyevich wanted to say something nasty
and even opened his mouth to do so, but was unable to
think of anything and angrily returned to his room. At
that moment, the son of a Turkish citizen, Ostap
Bender, emerged from the room in a light-blue vest,
and, treading on his own laces, went toward Vostrikov.
The roses on Father Fyodor's cheeks whithered and
turned to ash.

"Do you buy rags and bones?" he asked menacingly.
"Chairs, entrails, cans of boot polish?"

"What do you want?" whispered Father Fyodor.

"I want to sell you an old pair of pants."

The priest stiffened and moved away.

"Why are you silent like an archbishop at a party?"

Father Fyodor slowly walked toward his room.

"We buy old stuff and steal new stuff!" called Ostap after him.

Vostrikov lowered his head and stopped by the door. Ostap continued taunting him.

"What about the britches, my dear cleric? Will you take them? There's also the sleeves of a vest, the middle of a doughnut, and the ears of a dead donkey. The whole lot is going retail—it's cheaper. And they're not hidden in chairs, so you won't need to look for them."

The door shut behind the cleric.

Ostap sauntered back satisfied, his laces flopping against the carpet.

As soon as his massive figure was sufficiently far away, Father Fyodor quickly poked his head round the door and, with long pent-up indignation, squeaked:

"Fool yourself!"

"What's that?" cried Ostap, promptly turning back, but the door was already shut and the only sound was the click of the lock.

Ostap bent down to the keyhole, cupped his hand to his mouth, and said clearly:

"How much is opium for the people?"

There was silence behind the door.

"Dad, you're a nasty man," said Ostap loudly.

That very moment the point of a pencil shot out of the keyhole and wiggled in the air in an attempt to sting Father Fyodor's enemy. The concessionaire jumped back in time and grasped the pencil. Separated by the door, the adversaries began a tug of war with the pencil. Youth was victorious, and the pencil, clinging like a splinter, slowly crept out of the keyhole. Ostap returned with the trophy to his room, where the partners were still more elated.

"And the enemy's in flight, flight, flight," crooned Ostap.

He carved a rude word with a pocket knife on the edge of the pencil, ran into the corridor, pushed the pencil through the priest's keyhole, and hurried back.

The friends got out the green counterfoils and began a careful examination of them.

"This one's for the 'Shepherd Girl' tapestry," said Ippolit Matveyevich dreamily. "I bought it from a St. Petersburg antique dealer."

"To hell with the 'Shepherd Girl,' " said Ostap, tearing the order to ribbons.

"A round table . . . probably from the suite . . ."

"Give me the table. To hell with the table!"

Two orders were left: one for ten chairs transferred to the furniture museum in Moscow, and the other for the chair given to Comrade Gritsatsuyev in Plekhanov Street, Stargorod.

"Have your money ready," said Ostap. "We may have to go to Moscow."

"But there's a chair here!"

"One chance in ten. Pure mathematics. Anyway, Citizen Gritsatsuyev may have lit the stove with it."

"Don't joke like that!"

"Don't worry, *lieber Vater* Konrad Karlovich Michelson, we'll find them. It's a sacred cause!"

"We'll be wearing cambric footcloths and eating Margo cream."

"I have a hunch the jewels are in that very chair."

"Oh, you have a hunch, do you. What other hunches do you have? None? All right. Let's work the Marxist way. We'll leave the sky to the birds and deal with the chairs ourselves. I can't wait to meet the imperialist war invalid, Citizen Gritsatsuyev, at 15 Plekhanov Street. Don't lag behind, Konrad Karlovich. We'll plan as we go."

As they passed Father Fyodor's door, the vengeful son of a Turkish citizen gave it a kick. There was a low snarling from the harassed rival inside.

"Don't let him follow us!" said Ippolit Matveyevich in alarm.

"After today's meeting of the ministers aboard the yacht no *rapprochement* is possible. He's afraid of me."

The friends did not return till evening. Ippolit Matveyevich looked worried. Ostap was beaming. He was wearing new raspberry-colored shoes with round rubber heel taps, green-and-black checked socks, a cream cap, and a silk-mixture scarf of a brightly colored Rumanian shade.

"It's there all right," said Vorobyaninov, reflecting on his visit to the widow Gritsatsuyeva, "but how are we going to get hold of it? By buying it?"

"Certainly not!" said Ostap. "Besides being a totally unproductive expense, that would start rumors. Why one chair, and why that chair in particular?"

"What shall we do?"

Ostap lovingly inspected the heels of his new shoes.

"*Chic moderne*," he said. "What shall we do? Don't worry, Judge, I'll take on the operation myself. No chair can withstand these shoes."

Ippolit Matveyevich brightened up.

"You know, while you were talking to Mrs. Gritsatsuyeva about the flood, I sat down on our chair and I honestly felt something hard underneath me. They're there, I'll swear to it. They're there, I know it."

"Don't get excited, Citizen Michelson."

"We must steal it during the night; honestly, we must steal it!"

"For a marshal of the nobility your methods are too crude. Anyway, do you know the technique? Maybe you have a traveling kit with a set of skeleton keys. Get rid of the idea. It's a typical scummy trick to rob a poor widow."

Ippolit Matveyevich pulled himself together.

"It's just that we must act quickly," he said imploringly.

"Only cats are born quickly," said Ostap instructively. "I'll marry her."

"Who?"

"Madam Gritsatsuyeva."

"Why?"

"So that we can rummage inside the chair quietly and without any fuss."

"But you'll tie yourself down for life!"

"The things we do for the concession!"

"For life!" said Ippolit Matveyevich in a whisper.

He threw up his hands in amazement. His pastorlike face was bristly and his bluish teeth showed they had not been cleaned since the day he left the town of N.

"It's a great sacrifice," whispered Ippolit Matveyevich.

"Life!" said Ostap. "Sacrifice! What do you know about life and sacrifices? Do you think that just because you were evicted from your own house you've tasted life? And just because they requisitioned one of your imitation Chinese vases it's a sacrifice? Life, gentlemen of the jury, is a complex affair, but, gentlemen of the jury, a complex affair which can be managed as simply as opening a box. All you have to do is to know how to open it. Those who don't—have had it."

Ostap polished his crimson shoes with the sleeve of his jacket, played a flourish with his lips and went off.

Toward morning he rolled into the room, took off his shoes, put them on the bedside table and, stroking the shiny leather, murmured tenderly:

"My little friends."

"Where were you?" asked Ippolit Matveyevich, half asleep.

"At the widow's," replied Ostap in a dull voice.

Ippolit Matveyevich raised himself on one elbow.

"And are you going to marry her?"

Ostap's eyes sparkled.

"I'll have to make an honest woman of her now."

Ippolit Matveyevich gave a croak of embarrassment.

"A passionate woman," said Ostap, "is a poet's dream. Provincial straightforwardness. Such tropical women have long vanished from the center of the country, but they can still be found in outlying spots."

"When's the wedding?"

"The day after tomorrow. Tomorrow's impossible. It's May Day, and everything's shut."

"But what about our own business? You're getting married . . . but we may have to go to Moscow."

"What are you worried about? The hearing is continued."

"And the wife?"

"Wife? The little diamond widow? She's our last concern. A sudden summons to the capital. A short report to be given to the junior council of ministers. A farewell scene and a roast chicken for the journey. We'll travel in comfort. Go to sleep. Tomorrow we have a holiday."

: *13* :

Breathe Deeper: You're Excited!

ON THE MORNING of May Day, Victor Polesov, consumed by his usual thirst for activity, hurried out into
the street and headed for the center. At first he was unable to find any suitable outlet for his talents, since
there were still few people about and the reviewing
stands, guarded by mounted militiamen, were empty.
By nine o'clock, however, bands had begun purring,
wheezing, and whistling in various parts of the town.
Housewives came running out of their gates.

A column of musicians'-union officials in soft collars
somehow strayed into the middle of the railroad workers' contingent, getting in their way and upsetting everyone.

A truck disguised as a green plyboard locomotive
with the serial letter "S" kept running into the musicians from behind, eliciting shouts from the bowels of
the locomotive in the direction of the toilers of the
oboe and flute:

"Where's your supervisor? You're not supposed to
be on Red Army Street! Can't you see you're causing a
road block?"

At this point, to the misfortune of the musicians,
Victor Polesov intervened.

"That's right! You're supposed to turn into the blind alley here. They can't even organize a parade! Scandalous!"

The children were riding in trucks belonging to the Stargorod communal services and the grain-mill-and-elevator-construction administration. The youngest ones stood at the sides of the truck and the bigger ones in the middle. The junior army waved paper flags and thoroughly enjoyed themselves. It was crowded, noisy, and hot. Every minute there were bottlenecks, and every other minute they were cleared. To pass the time during the bottlenecks the crowd tossed old men and activists in the air. The old men wailed in squeaky voices, while the activists sailed up and down with serious faces in silence. One merry column of people mistook Polesov for a supervisor as he was trying to squeeze through them and began tossing him. Polesov thrashed about like Punchinello.

Then came an effigy of the British minister, Chamberlain, being beaten on the top hat with a cardboard hammer by a worker possessing a model anatomical physique. This was followed by a truck carrying three members of the Communist youth league in tails and white gloves. They kept looking at the crowd with embarrassment.

"Basil!" shouted someone from the sidewalk, "you bourgeois! Give back those suspenders!"

Girls were singing. Alchen was marching along with a group of social-security workers with a large red bow on his chest. As he went he crooned in a nasal voice:

> *From the forests of Siberia*
> *To the British Sea,*
> *There's no one superior*
> *To the Red Army. . . .*

At a given command, gymnasts disjointedly shouted out something unintelligible.

Everything walked, rode, and marched to the new

streetcar depot from where at exactly one o'clock the first electric streetcar in Stargorod was due to move off.

No one knew exactly when the construction of the street railway had been begun. Sometime back in 1920, when voluntary Saturday work was introduced, railroad workers and ropemakers had marched to Gusishe to the accompaniment of music and spent the whole day digging holes. They dug a great number of large, deep holes. A comrade in an engineer's cap had run about among the diggers, followed by a foreman carrying colored poles. Work had continued at the same spot the next Saturday. Two holes dug in the wrong place had to be filled in again. The comrade descended on the foreman and demanded an explanation. Then fresh holes had been dug that were even bigger and deeper. Next, the bricks were delivered and the real builders arrived. They set about laying the foundations, but then everything quieted down. The comrade in the engineer's cap still appeared now and then at the deserted building site and wandered round and round the brick-lined pit, muttering:

"Cost accounting!"

He tapped the foundations with a stick and then hurried home, covering his frozen ears with his hands.

The engineer's name was Treukhov.

The idea of the streetcar depot, the construction of which ceased abruptly at the foundation stage, was conceived by Treukhov in 1912, but the Tsarist town council had rejected the project. Two years later Treukhov stormed the town council again, but the war prevented any headway. Then the revolution interfered, and now the new economic plan, cost accounting, and capital recovery interfered. The foundations were overgrown with flowers in the summer, and in the winter children turned them into a snow-slide.

Treukhov dreamed of great things. He was sick and tired of working in the town-improvement department of the Stargorod communal services, tired of mending the curbs, and tired of estimating the cost of billboards. But the great things did not pan out. The streetcar project, resubmitted for consideration, became bogged down at the higher instances of the provincial administration; it was approved by one and rejected by another, passed on to the capital, regardless of approval or rejection, became covered in dust, and no money was forthcoming.

"It's barbarous!" Treukhov shouted at his wife. "No money, indeed! But they have money to pay for cab drivers and for carting merchandise to the station! The Stargorod cab drivers would rob their own grandmothers! It's a pillagers' monopoly, of course. Just try carrying your own stuff to the station! A street railway would pay for itself in six years."

His withered mustache drooped angrily, and his snub-nosed face worked convulsively. He took some blueprints out of the desk and showed them to his wife for the thousandth time. They were plans for a terminus, depot, and twelve streetcar routes.

"To hell with twelve routes! They can wait. But three! Three! Stargorod will choke without them!"

Treukhov snorted and went into the kitchen to chop wood. He did all the household chores himself. He designed and built a cradle for the baby and also constructed a washing machine. For a while he washed the clothes in it himself, explaining to his wife how to work the machine. At least a fifth of Treukhov's salary went on subscriptions to foreign technical literature. To make ends meet he gave up smoking.

He took his project to Gavrilin, the new chief of the Stargorod communal services who had been transferred from Samarkand. The new chief, deeply tanned by the Turkistan sun, listened to Treukhov for some time, though without particular attention, and finally said:

"In Samarkand, you know, we don't need a street

railway. Everyone rides donkeys. A donkey cost three roubles—dirt cheap—and it can carry about three hundred pounds. Just a little donkey; it's amazing!"

"But that's Asia," said Treukhov angrily. "A donkey costs three roubles. but you need thirty roubles a year to feed it."

"And how many times do you think you can travel on your street railway for thirty roubles? Three hundred. And that's not even every day for a year."

"Then you'd better send for some of your donkeys," shouted Treukhov and rushed out of the office, slamming the door.

Whenever he met Treukhov from that time on, the new chief would ask derisively:

"Well, then, shall we send for donkeys or build a street railway?"

Gavrilin's face was like a smoothly peeled radish. His eyes were filled with cunning.

About two months later Gavrilin sent for the engineer and said to him earnestly:

"I have a little plan. One thing is clear, though; there's no money, and a street railway is not a donkey to be bought for three roubles. We'll have to get some funds. What practical solution is there? A shareholding company? What else? A loan repayable with interest! How long will it take for the street railway to pay for itself?"

"Six years from the opening of the first three routes."

"Well, let's say ten years then. Now, the shareholding company. Who will buy the shares? The food co-operatives and the central union of dairy co-operatives. Do the ropemakers need a street railway? Yes, they do. We will be despatching freight cars to the railroad station. So that's the ropemakers. The ministry of transport may contribute something, and also the province-executive committee. That's definite. And once we've got things going, the State Bank and the Commercial Bank will give us loans. So that's my little plan. It is going to be discussed at the executive-committee meeting on Friday, and if they agree, the rest is up to you."

Treukhov stayed up till the early hours, excitedly washing clothes and explaining to his wife the advantages of streetcars over horse-drawn transportation.

The decision taken on the Friday was favorable. But that was when the trouble started. It proved very difficult to form the shareholding company. The ministry of transport kept changing its mind about becoming a shareholder. The food co-operatives tried their best to avoid taking fifteen per cent of the shares and only wanted to take ten per cent. The shares were finally distributed, though not without a few skirmishes. Gavrilin was sent for by the province control commission and reprimanded for using his position to exert pressure. But everything came out all right, and then it was only a question of beginning.

"Well, Comrade Treukhov," said Gavrilin, "get cracking! Do you think you'll manage? Well and good. It's not like buying a donkey."

Treukhov immersed himself in his work. The great things which he had dreamed of for years had finally arrived. Estimates were made, a construction program drawn up, and the materials ordered. The difficulties arose where they were least expected. It was found that there were no professional cement experts in Stargorod, so they had to be assigned from Leningrad. Gavrilin tried to force the pace, but the plants could not deliver the machinery for eighteen months, whereas it was actually needed within a year at the latest. A threat to order the machinery from abroad, however, brought about the required effect. Then there were minor difficulties. First it was impossible to find shaped iron of the right size, then unseasoned sleepers were received instead of seasoned ones. The

right ones were finally delivered, but Treukhov, who
had gone personally to the seasoning plant, rejected
sixty per cent of the sleepers. There were defects in
the cast-iron parts, and the timber was damp. Gavrilin
made frequent visits to the building sites in his ancient,
wheezing Fiat and had rows with Treukhov.

While the terminus and depot were being erected,
the citizens of Stargorod merely made jokes.

In the Stargorod *Truth* the streetcar story was reported by "the Prince of Denmark," writer of humorous pieces, known to the whole town under the
pen name of "Flywheel." Not less than three times a
week, in a long account, Flywheel expressed his irritation at the slowness of the construction. The newspaper's third column—which used to abound with
such skeptical headlines as "No sign of a club,"
"Around the weak points," "Inspections are needed,
but what is the point of the shine and long tails?"
"Good and . . . bad," "What we like and what we
don't," "Deal with the saboteurs of education," and
"It's time to put an end to red tape"—began to present
readers with such sunny and encouraging headlines at
the top of Flywheel's reports as "How we are living
and how we are building," "Giant will soon start
work," "Modest builder," and so on in that vein.

Treukhov used to open the newspaper with a shudder and, feeling disgust for the brotherhood of writers,
read such cheerful lines about himself as:

. . . I'm climbing over
the rafters with the wind
whistling in my ears.

Above me is the in-
visible builder of our
powerful street railway,
that thin, pug-nosed man
in a shabby cap with
crossed hammers.

It brings to mind
Pushkin's poem: "There
he stood, full of great
thoughts, on the bank.
. . ."

I approach him. Not
a breath of air. The raf-
ters do not stir.

I ask him: How is the

work progressing? En-
gineer Treukhov's ugly
face brightens up. . . .
 He shakes my hand
and says:
 "Seventy per cent of
the target has been
reached."

[The article ended
like this:]

He shakes my hand
in farewell. The rafters
creak behind me.
 Builders scurry to and
fro.
 Who could forget the
feverish activity of the
building site or of the
homely face of our
builder?

FLYWHEEL

The only thing that saved Treukhov was that he had
no time to read the papers and sometimes managed to
miss Comrade Flywheel's jottings.

On one occasion Treukhov could not restrain himself, and he wrote a carefully worded and malicious
reply.

 "Of course [he
wrote], you can call a
bolt a transmission, but
people who do so know
nothing about building.
And I would like to
point out to Comrade
Flywheel that the only
time rafters creak is

when the building is
about to fall down. To
speak of rafters in this
way is much the same
as claiming that a vio-
loncello can give birth
to children.

 "Yours, [etc.]"

After that the indefatigable prince stopped visiting
the building site, but his reports continued to grace the
third column, standing out sharply against a background of such prosaic headlines as "15,000 roubles
growing rusty," "Housing Hitches," "Materials are
weeping," and "Curiosities and tears."

The construction was nearing its end. Rails were
welded by the thermite method, and they stretched
without gaps from the station to the slaughterhouse,
and from the market to the cemetery.

In the beginning it was intended to time the opening of the street railway for the ninth anniversary of the October revolution, but the car-building plant was unable to supply the cars by the promised date and made some excuse about "fittings." The opening had to be postponed until May Day. By this date everything was definitely ready.

Wandering about, the concessionaires reached Gusishe at the same time as the processions. The whole of Stargorod was there. The new depot was decorated with garlands of evergreen; the flags flapped, and the wind rippled the banners. A mounted militiaman galloped after the ice-cream seller who had somehow got into the circular space cordoned off by railway workers. A rickety platform, as yet empty, with a public-address system, rose between the two gates of the depot. Delegates began mounting the platform. A combined band of communal-service workers and rope-makers was trying out its lungs. The drum lay on the ground.

A Moscow correspondent in a shaggy cap wandered around inside the depot, which contained ten light-green streetcars numbered 701 to 710. He was looking for the chief engineer in order to ask him a few questions on the subject of street railways. Although the correspondent had already prepared in his mind the report on the opening of the street railway with a summary of the speeches, he nevertheless conscientiously continued his search, his only complaint being the absence of a bar.

The crowds sang, yelled, and chewed sunflower seeds while waiting for the railway to be opened.

The presidium of the province executive committee mounted the platform. The Prince of Denmark stammered out a few phrases to his fellow writer. The newsreel cameramen from Moscow were expected any moment.

"Comrades," said Gavrilin, "I declare the official

meeting on the occasion of the opening of the Stargorod street railway open."

The brass trumpets sprang into action, sighed, and
played the International right through three times.

"Comrade Gavrilin will now give a report," cried
Comrade Gavrilin.

The Prince of Denmark (Flywheel) and the guest
from Moscow both wrote in their notebooks, without
collusion:

"The ceremony opened with a report by Comrade
Gavrilin, Chairman of the Stargorod Communal Services. The crowd listened attentively."

The two correspondents were people of completely
different types. The Muscovite was young and single,
while Flywheel was burdened with a large family and
had passed his forties some time ago. One had lived in
Moscow all his life, while the other had never been
there. The Muscovite liked beer, while Flywheel never
let anything but vodka pass his lips. Despite this difference in character, age, habits, and upbringing, however, the impressions of both the journalists were cast
in the same hackneyed, second-hand, dust-covered
phrases. Their pencils began scratching and another
observation was recorded in the notebooks: "On this
day of festivity it is as though the streets of Stargorod
have grown wider. . . ."

Gavrilin began his speech in a good and simple
fashion. "Building a street railway is not like buying a
donkey."

A loud guffaw was suddenly heard from Ostap
Bender in the crowd; he had appreciated the remark.
Heartened by the response, Gavrilin, without knowing
why himself, suddenly switched to the international
situation. Several times he attempted to bring his speech
back on the rails, but, to his horror, found that he was
unable to. The international words just flowed out by
themselves, against the speaker's will. After Chamberlain, to whom Gavrilin devoted half an hour, the inter-

national arena was taken by the American Senator
Borah; the crowd wilted. The correspondents both
wrote: "The speaker described the international situation in vivid language. . . ." Gavrilin, now worked up,
made some nasty comments about the Rumanian nobility and then turned to Mussolini. It was only toward
the end of his speech that he was able to suppress his
second international nature and say in a good, businesslike way:

"And so, Comrades, I think that the streetcar which
is about to leave the depot . . . is leaving on whose account? Yours, of course, Comrades—and that of all
workers who have really worked, not from fear, Comrades, but from conscience. It is also due, Comrades,
to that honest Soviet specialist, chief engineer Treukhov. We must thank him as well."

A search for Treukhov was made, but he was not to
be found. The representative of the dairy co-operatives,
who had been itching to speak, squeezed through to
the front of the platform, waved his hand, and began
speaking loudly of the international situation. At the
end of the speech, both correspondents promptly jotted down as they listened to the feeble applause: "Loud
applause turning into an ovation." They both wondered whether "turning into an ovation" wasn't too
strong. The Muscovite made up his mind to cross it
out. Flywheel sighed and left it.

The sun rapidly rolled down an inclined plane. Slogans resounded from the platform, and the band played
a flourish. The sky became a vivid dark blue and the
meeting went on and on. Both the speakers and the
listeners had felt for some time that something was
wrong, that the meeting had gone on much too long
and that the street railway should be started up as soon
as possible. But they had all become so used to talking
that they could not stop.

Treukhov was finally found. He was covered with

dirt and took a long time to wash his face and hands before going onto the platform.

"Comrade Treukhov, chief engineer, will now say a
few words," announced Gavrilin jubilantly. "Well, say
something, I said all the wrong things," he added in a
whisper.

Treukhov wanted to say a number of things. About
voluntary Saturday work, the difficulties of his work,
and about everything that had been done and remained
to do. And there was a lot to be done: the town ought
to do away with the horrible market; there were covered glass buildings to be constructed; a permanent
bridge could be built instead of the present temporary
one, which was swept away each year by the ice drifts,
and finally there was the plan for a very large meat-
refrigeration plant.

Treukhov opened his mouth and, stuttering, began. "Comrades! The international position of our
State . . ."

And then he went on to burble such boring truisms
that the crowd, now listening to its sixth international
speech, lost interest.

It was only when he had finished that Treukhov realized he had not said a word about the street railway.
"It's a shame," he said to himself, "we have absolutely
no idea how to speak."

He remembered hearing a speech by a French Communist at a meeting in Moscow. The Frenchman was
talking about the bourgeois press. "Those acrobats of
the pen, those virtuosos of farce, those jackals of the
rotary press," he had exclaimed. The first part of his
speech had been delivered in the key of A, the second
in C, and the final part, the pathétique, had been in the
key of E. His gestures were moderate and elegant.

"But we only make a mess of things," decided
Treukhov. "It would be better if we didn't talk at all."

It was completely dark when the chairman of the

province executive committee snipped the red tape sealing off the depot. Workers and representatives of public organizations noisily began taking their seats in the streetcars. There was a tinkling of bells and the first streetcar, driven by Treukhov himself, sailed out of the depot to the accompaniment of deafening shouts from the crowd and groans from the band. The illuminated cars seemed even more dazzling than in the daytime. They made their way through Gusishe in a line; passing under the railroad bridge, they climbed easily into the town and turned into Greater Pushkin Street. The band was in the second streetcar; poking their trumpets out of the windows they played the Budyonny march.

Gavrilin, in a conductor's coat and with a bag across his shoulders, smiled tenderly as he jumped from one car to another, ringing the bell at the wrong time and handing out invitations to:

	GALA EVENING *at the* COMMUNAL SERVICES WORKERS' CLUB
on May 1 at 9 P.M.	*Program:* 1. Report by Comrade Mosin. 2. Award of certificates by the Communal Services Workers' Union. 3. Informal half: Grand Concert, family supper and bar.

On the platform of the last car stood Victor Polesov, who had somehow or other been included among the guests of honor. He sniffed the motor. To his extreme surprise, it looked perfectly all right and seemed to be working normally. The glass in the windows was not rattling, and, looking at the panes closely, he saw that they were padded with rubber. He had already made

several comments to the driver and was now considered by the public to be an expert on streetcar
matters in the West.

"The pneumatic brake isn't working too well,"
said Polesov, looking triumphantly at the passengers.
"It's not sucking!"

"Nobody asked you," replied the driver. "It will no
doubt suck all right."

Having made a festive round of the town, the cars
returned to the depot, where a crowd was waiting for
them. Treukhov was tossed in the air beneath the full
glare of electric lights. They also tried tossing Gavrilin,
but since he weighed almost 216 pounds and did not
soar very high, he was quickly set down again. Comrade Mosin and various technicians were also tossed.
Victor Polesov was then tossed for the second time
that day. This time he did not kick with his legs, but
soared up and down, gazing sternly and seriously at
the starry sky. As he soared up for the last time, Polesov noticed that the person holding him by the foot
and laughing nastily was none other than the former
marshal of the nobility, Ippolit Matveyevich Vorobyaninov. Polesov politely freed himself and went a
short distance away, still keeping the marshal in sight.
Observing that Ippolit Matveyevich and the young
stranger with him, clearly an ex-officer, were leaving,
he cautiously started to follow them.

As soon as everything was over, and Comrade
Gavrilin was sitting in his lilac Fiat waiting for Treukhov to issue final instructions so that they could then
drive together to the club, a Ford station wagon containing the newsreel cameramen drove up to the depot
gates.

A man wearing twelve-sided horn-rimmed spectacles and a sleeveless leather coat was the first to
spring nimbly out of the vehicle. A long pointed
beard grew straight out of his Adam's apple. A second
man carried the camera and kept tripping over a long

scarf of the type that Ostap Bender usually called "chic moderne." Next came assistants, lights, and girls.

The whole group tore into the depot with loud shouts.

"Attention!" cried the bearded owner of the leather coat. "Nick, set the lights up!"

Treukhov turned crimson and went over to the late arrivals.

"Are you the newsreel reporters?" he asked. "Why didn't you come during the day?"

"When is the railway going to be opened?"

"It has already been opened."

"Yes, yes, we are a little late. We came across some good nature shots. There was loads of work. A sunset! But, anyway, we'll manage. Nick, lights! Close-up of a turning wheel. Close-up of the feet of the moving crowd. Lyuda, Milochka, start walking! Nick, action! Off you go! Keep walking, keep walking! That's it, thank you! Now we'll take the builder. Comrade Treukhov? Would you mind, Comrade Treukhov? No, not like that. Three quarters. Like this, it's more original! Against a streetcar . . . Nick! Action! Say something!"

"I . . . I . . . honestly, I feel so awkward!"

"Splendid! Good! Say something else! Now you're talking to the first passenger. Lyuda, come into the picture! That's it. Breathe deeper, you're excited! . . . Nick! A close-up of their legs! Action! That's it. Thanks very much. Cut!"

Gavrilin clambered out of the throbbing Fiat and went to fetch his missing friend. The producer with the hairy Adam's apple came to life.

"Nick! Over here! A marvelous character type. A worker! A streetcar passenger. Breathe deeper, you're excited! You've never been in a streetcar before. Breathe!"

Gavrilin wheezed malevolently.

"Marvelous! Milochka, come here! Greetings from

the young Communists! Breathe deeper, you're excited! That's it! Swell! Nick, cut!"

"Aren't you going to film the street railway?" asked Treukhov shyly.

"You see," lowed the leather producer, "the lighting conditions make it difficult. We'll have to fill in the shots in Moscow. 'Bye-'bye!"

The newsreel reporters disappeared quicker than lightning.

"Well, let's go and relax, pal," said Gavrilin. "What's this? You smoking!"

"I've begun smoking," confessed Treukhov. "I couldn't stop myself."

At the family gathering, the hungry Treukhov smoked one cigarette after another, drank three glasses of vodka, and became hopelessly drunk. He kissed everyone and they kissed him. He tried to say something nice to his wife, but only burst into laughter. Then he shook Gavrilin's hand for a long time and said:

"You're a strange one! You should learn to build railroad bridges. It's a wonderful science, and the chief thing is that it's so simple. A bridge across the Hudson . . ."

Half an hour later he was completely gone and made a Philipic against the bourgeois press.

"Those acrobats of the press, those hyenas of the pen! Those virtuosos of the rotary printing machine!" he cried.

His wife took him home in a horse-cab.

"I want to go by streetcar," he said to his wife. "Can't you understand? If there's a street railway, we should use it. Why? First, because it's an advantage!"

Polesov followed the concessionaires, spent some time mustering his courage, and finally, waiting until there was no one about, went up to Vorobyaninov.

"Good evening, Mr. Ippolit Matveyevich!" he said respectfully.

Vorobyaninov turned pale. "I don't think I know you," he mumbled.

Ostap stuck out his right shoulder and went up to the mechanic-intellectual. "Come on now, what is it that you want to tell my friend?"

"Don't be alarmed," whispered Polesov, "Elena Stanislavovna sent me."

"What! Is she here?"

"Yes, and she wants to see you."

"Why?" asked Ostap. "And who are you?"

"I . . . Don't you think anything of the sort, Ippolit Matveyevich. You don't know me, but I remember you very well."

"I'd like to visit Elena Stanislavovna," said Vorobyaninov indecisively.

"She's very anxious to see you."

"Yes, but how did she find out?"

"I saw you in the corridor of the communal services building and thought to myself for a long time: 'I know that face.' Then I remembered. Don't worry about anything, Ippolit Matveyevich. It will all be absolutely secret."

"Do you know the woman?" asked Ostap in a businesslike way.

"Mm . . . yes. An old friend."

"Then we might go and have supper with your old friend. I'm famished and all the shops are shut."

"We probably can."

"Let's go, then. Lead the way, mysterious stranger."

And Victor Mikhailovich, continually looking behind him, led the partners through the back yards to the fortuneteller's house on Pereleshinsky Street.

: *14* :

The "Alliance of the Sword and Plowshare"

WHEN A WOMAN grows old, many unpleasant things may happen to her: her teeth may fall out, her hair may thin out and turn gray, she may become short-winded, she may unexpectedly develop fat or grow extremely thin, but her voice never changes. It remains just as it was when she was a schoolgirl, a bride, or some young rake's mistress.

That was why Vorobyaninov trembled when Polesov knocked at the door and Elena Stanislavovna answered: "Who's that?" His mistress's voice was the same as it had been in 1899 just before the opening of the Paris Fair. But as soon as he entered the room, squinting on account of the light, he saw that there was not a trace of her former beauty left.

"How you've changed," he said involuntarily.

The old woman threw herself onto his neck. "Thank you," she said, "I know what you risk by coming here to see me. You're the same chivalrous knight. I'm not going to ask you why you're here from Paris. I'm not curious, you see."

"But I haven't come from Paris at all," said Ippolit Matveyevich in confusion.

"My colleague and I have come from Berlin," Ostap

corrected her, nudging Ippolit Matveyevich, "but it's not advisable to talk about it too loudly."

"Oh, how pleased I am to see you," shrilled the fortuneteller. "Come in here, into this room. And I'm sorry, Victor Mikhailovich, but couldn't you come back in half an hour?"

"Oh!" Ostap remarked. "The first meeting. Difficult moments! Allow me to withdraw as well. May I come with you, dear Victor Mikhailovich?"

The mechanic trembled with joy. They both went off to Polesov's apartment, where Ostap, sitting on a piece of one of the gates of no. 5 Pereleshinsky Street, outlined his phantasmagoric ideas for the salvation of the motherland to the dumbstruck artisan.

An hour later they returned to find the old couple lost in reminiscence.

"And do you remember, Elena Stanislavovna?" Ippolit Matveyevich was saying.

"And do you remember, Ippolit Matveyevich?" Elena Stanislavovna was saying.

"The psychological moment for supper seems to have arrived," thought Ostap, and, interrupting Ippolit Matveyevich, who was recalling the elections to the Tsarist town council, said: "They have a very strange custom in Berlin. They eat so late that you can't tell whether it's an early supper or a late lunch."

Elena Stanislavovna gave a start, took her rabbit's eyes off Vorobyaninov, and dragged herself into the kitchen.

"And now we must act, act, and act," said Ostap, lowering his voice to a conspiratorial whisper. He took Polesov by the arm. "The old woman is reliable, isn't she, and won't give us away?"

Polesov joined his hands as though praying.

"What's your political credo?"

"Always!" replied Polesov delightedly.

"You support Kirillov, I hope?"

"Yes, indeed." Polesov stood at attention.

"Russia will not forget you," Ostap rapped out.

Holding a cookie in his hand, Ippolit Matveyevich listened in dismay to Ostap, but there was no holding the smooth operator. He was carried away. He felt inspired and ecstatically pleased at this above-average blackmail. He paced up and down like a leopard.

This was the state in which Elena Stanislavovna found him as she carted in the samovar from the kitchen. Ostap gallantly ran over to her, took the samovar without stopping, and placed it on the table. The samovar gave a peep and Ostap decided to act.

"Madam," he said, "we are happy to see in you . . ."

He did not know whom he was happy to see in Elena Stanislavovna. He had to start again. Of all the flowery expressions of the Tsarist regime, only one kept coming to mind—"has graciously commanded." This was out of place, so he began in a businesslike way.

"Strict secrecy. A state secret." He pointed to Vorobyaninov. "Who do you think this powerful old man is? Don't say you don't know. He's the master mind, the father of Russian democracy and a person close to the emperor."

Ippolit Matveyevich drew himself up to his splendid height and goggled in confusion. He had no idea what was happening, but, knowing from experience that Ostap Bender never did anything without good reason, kept silent. Polesov was thrilled. He stood with his chin tucked in like someone about to begin a parade.

Elena Stanislavovna sat down on a chair and looked at Ostap in fright.

"Are there many of us in the town?" he asked outright. "What's the general feeling?"

"Given the absence . . ." said Polesov and began a muddled account of his troubles. These included that conceited bum, the yard keeper from no. 5, the three-eighths-inch dies, the street railway, and so on.

"Good!" snapped Ostap. "Elena Stanislavovna! With your assistance we want to contact the best people in the town who have been forced underground by a cruel fate. Who can we ask to come here?"

"Who can we ask! Maxim Petrovich and his wife."

"No women," Ostap corrected her. "You will be the only pleasant exception. Who else?"

From the discussion, in which Polesov also took an active part, it came to light that they could ask Maxim Petrovich Charushnikov, a former Tsarist town councilor, who had now in some miraculous way been raised to the rank of a Soviet official; Dyadyev, owner of Fastpack; Kislarsky, chairman of the Odessa roll bakery of the Moscow Bun artel; and two young men who were nameless but fully reliable.

"In that case, please ask them to come here at once for a small conference. In the greatest secrecy."

Polesov began speaking. "I'll fetch Maxim Petrovich, Nikesha, and Vladya, and you, Elena Stanislavovna, be so good as to run down to Fastpack for Kislarsky."

Polesov sped off. The fortuneteller looked reverently at Ippolit Matveyevich and also went off.

"What does this mean?" asked Ippolit Matveyevich.

"It means," retorted Ostap, "that you're behind the times."

"Why?"

"Because! Excuse a vulgar question, but how much money do you have?"

"What money?"

"All kinds—including silver and copper."

"Thirty-five roubles."

"And I suppose you intended to recover the entire outlay on the enterprise with that much money?"

Ippolit Matveyevich was silent.

"Here's the point, dear boss. I reckon you understand me. You will have to be the master mind and person close to the emperor for an hour or so."

"Why?"

"Because we need capital. Tomorrow's my wedding. I'm not a beggar. I want to have a good time on that memorable day."

"What do I have to do?" groaned Ippolit Matveyevich.

"You have to keep quiet. Puff out your cheeks now and then to look important."

"But that's . . . fraudulence!"

"Who are you to talk, Count Tolstoy or Darwin? That comes well from a man who was only yesterday preparing to break into Gritsatsuyeva's apartment at night and steal her furniture. Don't think too much. Just keep quiet and don't forget to puff out your cheeks."

"Why involve ourselves in such a dangerous business. We might be betrayed."

"Don't worry about that. I don't bet on poor odds. We'll work it so that none of them understands anything. Let's have some tea."

While the concessionaires were eating and drinking, and the parrot was cracking sunflower seeds, the guests began arriving at the apartment.

Nikesha and Vladya came with Victor Mikhailovich. He was hesitant to introduce the young men to the master mind. They sat down in a corner and watched the father of Russian democracy eating cold veal. Nikesha and Vladya were complete and utter gawks. Both were in their late twenties and were apparently very pleased at being invited to the meeting.

Charushnikov, the former Tsarist town councilor, was a fat, elderly man. He gave Ippolit Matveyevich a prolonged handshake and peered into his face.

Under the supervision of Ostap, the old-timers began exchanging reminiscences.

As soon as the conversation was moving smoothly, Ostap turned to Charushnikov. "Which regiment were you in?"

Charushnikov took a deep breath. "I . . . I . . . wasn't, so to speak, in any, since I was entrusted with the confidence of society and was elected to office."

"Are you a member of the upper class?"

"Yes, I was."

"I hope you still are. Stand firm! We shall need your help. Has Polesov told you? We will be helped from abroad. It's only a question of public opinion. The organization is strictly secret. Be careful!"

Ostap chased Polesov away from Nikesha and Vladya and asked them with genuine severity: "Which regiment were you in? You will have to serve your fatherland. Are you members of the upper class? Very good. The West will help us. Stand firm! Contributions—I mean the organization—will be strictly secret. Be careful!"

Ostap was carried away. Things seemed to be going well. Ostap led the owner of Fastpack into a corner as soon as Elena Stanislavovna had introduced him, advised him to stand firm, inquired which regiment he had served in, and promised him assistance from abroad and complete secrecy of the organization. The first reaction of the owner of Fastpack was a desire to get away from the conspiratorial apartment as soon as possible. He felt that his firm was too solvent to engage in such a risky business. But taking a look at Ostap's athletic figure, he hesitated and began thinking: "Supposing . . . Anyway, it all depends on what kind of sauce this thing will be served with."

The tea-party conversation livened up. The initiated religiously kept the secret and chatted about the town.

The last to arrive was citizen Kislarsky, who, being neither a member of the upper class nor a former guardsman, immediately sized up the situation after a brief talk with Ostap.

"Stand firm! said Ostap instructively.

Kislarsky promised he would.

"As a representative of private enterprise, you cannot ignore the cries of the people."

Kislarsky saddened sympathetically.

"Do you know who that is sitting there?" asked Ostap, pointing to Ippolit Matveyevich.

"Of course," said Kislarsky. "It's Mr. Vorobyaninov."

"That," said Ostap, "is the master mind, the father of Russian democracy and a person close to the emperor."

"Two years solitary confinement at best," thought Kislarsky, beginning to tremble. "Why did I have to come here?"

"The secret 'Alliance of the Sword and Plowshare,'" whispered Ostap ominously.

"Ten years" flashed through Kislarsky's mind.

"You can leave, by the way, but I warn you, we have a long reach."

"I'll show you, you son of a bitch," thought Ostap. "You'll not get away from here for less than a hundred roubles."

Kislarsky became like marble. That day he had had such a good, quiet dinner of chicken gizzards and soup with nuts, and knew nothing of the terrible "Alliance of the Sword and Plowshare." He stayed. The words "long reach" made an unfavorable impression on him.

"Citizens," said Ostap, opening the meeting, "life dictates its own laws, its own cruel laws. I am not going to talk about the aim of our gathering—you all know it. Our aim is sacred. From everywhere we hear cries. From every corner of our huge country people are calling for help. We must extend a helping hand and we will do so. Some of you have work and eat bread and butter; others earn on the side and eat caviar sandwiches. All of you sleep in your own beds and cover yourselves with warm blankets. It is only the young children, the waifs and strays, who are not looked after. These flowers of the street, or, as the white-collar proletarians call them, 'flowers in asphalt,' deserve a better lot. We must help them, gentlemen of the jury, and, gentlemen of the jury, we will do so."

The smooth operator's speech caused different reactions among the audience.

Polesov could not understand his young friend, the guards officer. "What children?" he wondered. "Why children?"

Ippolit Matveyevich did not even try to understand. He was completely fed up with the whole business and sat there in silence, puffing out his cheeks.

Elena Stanislavovna became melancholy.

Nikesha and Vladya gazed in devotion at Ostap's sky-blue vest.

The owner of Fastpack was extremely pleased. "Nicely put," he decided. "With that sauce I might even give some money. If it's successful, I get the credit. If it's not, I don't know anything about it. I just helped the children and that's all."

Charushnikov exchanged a significant look with Dyadyev and, giving the speaker his due for conspiratorial ability, continued rolling pellets of bread across the table.

Kislarsky was in seventh heaven. "What a brain," he thought. He felt he had never loved waifs and strays as much as that evening.

"Comrades," Ostap continued, "immediate help is required. We must tear these children from the clutches of the street, and we will do so. We will help these children. Let us remember that these children are the flowers of life. I now invite you to make your contributions and help the children—the children alone and no one else. Do you understand me?"

Ostap took a receipt book from his side pocket.

"Please make your contributions. Ippolit Matveyevich will vouch for my authority."

Ippolit Matveyevich puffed out his cheeks and bowed his head. At this, even the dopey Nikesha and Vladya, and the fidgety mechanic, too, realized the point of Ostap's allusions.

"In order of seniority, gentlemen," said Ostap. "We'll begin with dear Maxim Petrovich."

Maxim Petrovich fidgeted and forced himself to give thirty roubles. "In better times I'd give more," he declared.

"Better times will soon be coming," said Ostap.

"Anyway, that had nothing to do with the children who I am at present representing."

Nikesha and Vladya gave eight roubles.

"That's not much, young men."

The young men reddened.

Polesov ran home and brought back fifty.

"Well done, hussar," said Ostap. "For a car-owning hussar working by himself that's enough for the first time. What say the merchants?"

Dyadyev and Kislarsky haggled for some time and complained about taxes.

Ostap was unmoved. "I consider such talk out of place in the presence of Ippolit Matveyevich."

Ippolit Matveyevich bowed his head. The merchants contributed two hundred roubles each for the benefit of the children.

"Four hundred and eighty-eight roubles in all," announced Ostap. "Hm . . . twelve roubles short of a round figure."

Elena Stanislavovna, who had been trying to stand firm for some time, went into the bedroom and brought back the necessary twelve roubles in a bag.

The remaining part of the meeting was more subdued and less festive in nature. Ostap began to get frisky. Elena Stanislavovna drooped completely. The guests gradually dispersed, respectfully taking leave of the organizers.

"You will be given special notice of the date of our

next meeting," said Ostap as they left. "It's strictly secret. The cause must be kept secret. It's also in your own interests, by the way."

At these words, Kislarsky felt the urge to give another fifty roubles and not to come to any more meetings. He only just restrained himself.

"Right," said Ostap, "let's get moving. Ippolit Matveyevich, you, I hope, will take advantage of Elena Stanislavovna's hospitality and spend the night here. It will be a good thing for the conspiracy if we separate for a time, anyway, as a blind. I'm off."

Ippolit Matveyevich was winking broadly, but Ostap pretended he had not noticed and went out into the street.

Having gone a block, he remembered the five hundred honestly earned roubles in his pocket.

"Cabby!" he cried. "Take me to the Phoenix."

The cabby leisurely drove Ostap to a closed restaurant.

"What's this! Shut?"

"On account of May Day."

"Damn them! All the money in the world and nowhere to have a good time. All right, then, take me to Plekhanov Street. Do you know it?"

"What was the street called before?" asked the cabby.

"I don't know."

"How can I get there? I don't know it, either."

Ostap nevertheless ordered him to drive on and find it.

For an hour and a half they cruised around the dark and empty town, asking watchmen and militiamen the way. One militiaman racked his brains and at length informed them that Plekhanov Street was none other than the former Governor Street.

"Governor Street! I've been taking people to Governor Street for twenty-five years."

"Then drive there!"

They arrived at Governor Street, but it turned out to be Karl Marx and not Plekhanov Street.

The frustrated Ostap renewed his search for the lost street, but was not able to find it.

The dawn cast a pale light on the face of the moneyed martyr who had been prevented from disporting himself.

"Take me to the Sorbonne hotel!" he shouted. "A fine driver you are! You don't even know Plekhanov!"

The widow Gritsatsuyeva's palace glittered. At the head of the banquet table sat the King of Clubs—the son of a Turkish citizen. He was elegant and drunk. The guests were talking loudly.

The young bride was no longer young. She was at least thirty-five. Nature had endowed her generously. She had everything: breasts like watermelons, a bulging nose, brightly colored cheeks, and a powerful neck. She adored her new husband and was afraid of him. She did not therefore call him by his first name, or by his patronymic, which she had not managed to find out, anyway, but by his surname—Comrade Bender.

Ippolit Matveyevich was sitting on his cherished chair. All through the wedding feast he bounced up and down, trying to feel something hard. From time to time he did. Whenever this happened, the people present pleased him, and he began shouting "Kiss the bride" furiously.

Ostap kept making speeches and proposing toasts. They drank to public education and the irrigation of Uzbekistan. Later on the guests began to depart. Ippolit Matveyevich lingered in the hall and whispered to Bender:

"Don't waste time, they're there."

"You're a moneygrubber," replied the drunken Ostap. "Wait for me at the hotel. Don't go anywhere.

I may come at any moment. Settle the hotel bill and have everything ready. Adieu, Field Marshal! Wish me good night!"

Ippolit Matveyevich did so and went back to the Sorbonne to worry.

Ostap turned up at five in the morning carrying the chair. Ippolit Matveyevich was speechless. Ostap put down the chair in the middle of the room and sat on it.

"How did you manage it?" Vorobyaninov finally got out.

"Very simple. Family style. The widow was asleep and dreaming. It was a pity to wake her. 'Don't wake her at dawn!' Too bad! I had to leave a note. 'Going to Novokhopersk to make a report. Won't be back to dinner. Your own Bunny.' And I took the chair from the dining room. There aren't any streetcars running at this time of the morning, so I rested on the chair on the way."

Ippolit Matveyevich flung himself toward the chair with a burbling sound.

"Go easy," said Ostap, "we must avoid making a noise." He took a pair of pliers out of his pocket, and work soon began to hum. "Did you lock the door?" he asked.

Pushing aside the impatient Vorobyaninov, he neatly laid open the chair, trying not to damage the flowered chintz.

"This kind of cloth isn't to be had any more; it should be preserved. There's a dearth of goods and nothing can be done about it."

Ippolit Matveyevich was driven to a state of extreme irritation.

"There," said Ostap quietly. He raised the covering and groped among the springs with both his hands. The network of veins stood out on his forehead.

"Well?" Ippolit Matveyevich kept repeating in various keys. "Well? Well?"

"Well and well," said Ostap irritably. "One chance in eleven . . ." He thoroughly examined the inside of the chair and concluded: "And this chance isn't ours."

He stood up straight and dusted his knees. Ippolit Matveyevich flung himself on the chair.

The jewels were not there. Vorobyaninov's hands dropped, but Ostap was in good spirits as before.

"Our chances have now increased."

He began walking up and down the room.

"It doesn't matter. The chair cost the widow twice as much as it did us."

He took a gold brooch set with colored stones, a hollow bracelet of imitation gold, half a dozen gold teaspoons, and a tea strainer out of his side pocket.

In his grief Ippolit Matveyevich did not even realize that he had become an accomplice in common or garden theft.

"A shabby trick," said Ostap, but you must agree I couldn't leave my beloved without something to remember her by. However, we haven't any time to lose. This is only the beginning. The end will be in Moscow. And a furniture museum is not like a widow —it'll be a bit more difficult.

The partners stuffed the pieces of the chair under the bed and, having counted their money (together with the contributions for the children's benefit, they had five hundred and thirty-five roubles), drove to the station to catch the Moscow train.

They had to drive right across the town.

On Co-operative Street they caught sight of Polesov running along the sidewalk like a startled antelope. He was being pursued by the yard keeper from no. 5 Pereleshinsky Street. Turning the corner, the concessionaires just had time to see the yard keeper catch up with Polesov and begin bashing him. Polesov was shouting "Help!" and "Bum!"

Until the train departed they sat in the men's room to avoid meeting the beloved.

The train whisked the friends toward the noisy capital. They pressed against the window.

The cars were speeding over Gusishe.

Suddenly Ostap let out a roar and seized Vorobyaninov by the biceps. "Look, look!" he cried. "Quick! It's Alchen, that son of a bitch!"

Ippolit Matveyevich looked downward. At the bottom of the embankment a tough-looking young man with a mustache was pulling a wheelbarrow loaded with a light-brown harmonium and five window frames. A shamefaced citizen in a mouse-gray shirt was pushing the barrow.

The sun pushed its way through the dark clouds. The crosses on the churches glittered.

"Pashka! Going to market?"

Pasha Emilyevich raised his head but only saw the buffers of the last coach; he began working even harder with his legs.

"Did you see that?" asked Ostap delightedly. "Terrific! That's the way to work!"

Ostap slapped the mournful Vorobyaninov on the back.

"Don't worry, Dad! Never say die! The hearing is continued. Tomorrow evening we'll be in Moscow."

Part : II

IN MOSCOW

A Sea of Chairs

STATISTICS know everything.

It has been calculated with precision how much plowland there is in the USSR, with subdivisions into black earth, loam, and loess. All citizens of both sexes have been recorded in those neat, thick registers—so familiar to Ippolit Matveyevich Vorobyaninov—the registry office ledgers. It is known how much of a certain food is consumed yearly by the average citizen in the Republic. It is known how much vodka is imbibed as an average by this average citizen, with a rough indication of the tidbits consumed with it. It is known how many hunters, ballerinas, revolving lathes, dogs of all breeds, bicycles, monuments, girls, lighthouses, and sowing machines there are in the country.

How much life, full of fervor, emotion, and thought, there is in those statistical tables!

Who is this rosy-cheeked individual sitting at a table with a napkin tucked into his collar and putting away the steaming victuals with such relish? He is surrounded with herds of miniature bulls. Fattened pigs have congregated in one corner of the statistical table. Countless numbers of sturgeon, burbot, and chekhon fish splash about in a special statistical pool. There are hens sitting on the individual's head, hands, and shoulders. Tame geese, ducks, and turkeys fly through cirrus clouds. Two rabbits are hiding under the table. Pyramids and Towers of Babel made of bread rise above the horizon. A small fortress of jam is washed by a river of milk. A pickle the size of the leaning tower of Pisa appears on the horizon. Platoons of wines, spirits, and liqueurs march behind ramparts of salt and pepper. Tottering along in the rear in a miserable bunch come the soft drinks: the non-combatant soda waters, lemonades, and wire-encased syphons.

Who is this rosy-cheeked individual—a gourmand and a toss-pot—with a sweet tooth? Gargantua, King of the Dipsodes? Silaf Voss? The legendary soldier, Jacob Redshirt? Lucullus?

It is not Lucullus. It is Ivan Ivanovich Sidorov or Sidor Sidorovich Ivanov—an average citizen who consumes all the victuals described in the statistical table as an average throughout his life. He is a normal consumer of calories and vitamins, a quiet forty-year-old bachelor, who works in a habadashery and knitwear store.

You can never hide from statistics. They have exact information not only on the number of dentists, sausage shops, syringes, janitors, film directors, prostitutes, thatched roofs, widows, cabdrivers, and bells; they even know how many statisticians there are in the country.

But there is one thing that they do not know.

They do not know how many chairs there are in the USSR.

There are many chairs.

The census calculated the population of the Union Republics at a hundred and forty-three million people. If we leave aside ninety million peasants who prefer benches, boards, and earthen seats, and in the east of the country, shabby carpets and rugs, we still have fifty million people for whom chairs are objects of prime necessity in their everyday lives. If we take into account possible errors in calculation and the habit of certain citizens in the Soviet Union of sitting on the fence, and then halve the figure just in case, we find that there cannot be less than twenty-six and a half million chairs in the country. To make the figure truer we will take off another six and a half million. The twenty million left is the minimum possible number.

Amid this sea of chairs made of walnut, oak, ash, rosewood, mahogany, and Karelian birch, amid chairs made of fir and pinewood, the heros of this novel are to find one Hambs walnut chair with curved legs, containing Madam Petukhova's treasure inside its chintz-upholstered belly.

The concessionaires lay on the upper berths still asleep as the train cautiously crossed the Oka river and, increasing its speed, began nearing Moscow.

] CHAPTER [

: *16* :

The Brother Berthold Schwartz Hostel

LEANING against one another, Ippolit Matveyevich and Ostap stood at the open window of the unupholstered railroad car and gazed at the cows slowly descending the embankment, the pine needles, and the plank platforms of the country stations.

The traveler's stories had all been told. Tuesday's copy of the Stargorod *Truth* had been read right through, including the advertisements, and was now covered in grease spots. The chickens, eggs, and olives had all been consumed.

All that remained was the most wearisome lap of the journey—the last hour before Moscow.

Merry little country houses came bounding up to the embankment from areas of sparse woodland and clumps of trees. Some of them were wooden palaces with verandas of shining glass and newly painted iron roofs. Some were simple wooden cabins with tiny square windows, real traps for their inmates.

While the passengers scanned the horizon with the air of experts and told each other about the history of Moscow, muddling up what they vaguely remembered about the battle of Kalka, Ippolit Matveyevich was trying to picture the furniture museum. He imagined a tremendously long corridor lined with chairs. He saw himself walking rapidly along between them.

"We still don't know what the museum will be like . . . how things will turn out," he was saying nervously.

"It's time you had some shock treatment, Marshal. Stop having premature hysterics! If you can't help suffering, at least suffer in silence."

The train bounced over the switches and the signals opened their mouths as they watched it. The railroad tracks multiplied constantly and proclaimed the approach of a huge junction. Grass disappeared from the sides and was replaced by cinder; freight trains whistled and signalmen hooted. The din suddenly increased as the train dived in between two lines of empty freight trucks and, clicking like a turnstile, began counting them off.

The tracks kept dividing.

The train leapt out of the corridor of trucks and the sun came out. Down below, by the very ground, switch signals like hatchets moved rapidly backward and forward. There came a shriek from a turntable where depot workers were herding a locomotive into its stall.

The train's joints creaked as the brakes were suddenly applied. Everything squealed and set Ippolit Matveyevich's teeth on edge. The train came to a halt by an asphalt platform.

It was Moscow. It was Ryazan station, the freshest and newest of all the Moscow terminals.

None of the eight other Moscow stations had such vast, high-ceilinged halls as the Ryazan. The entire Yaroslavl station with all its pseudo-Russian heraldic ornamentation could easily have fitted into the large buffet-restaurant of the Ryazan.

The concessionaires pushed their way through to the exit and found themselves on Kalanchev Square. On their right towered the heraldic birds of Yaroslavl station. Directly in front of them was October station, painted in two colors dully reflecting the light. The clock showed five after ten. The clock on top of the Yaroslavl said exactly ten o'clock. Looking up at the Ryazan-station clock, with its zodiac dial, the travelers noted that it was five to ten.

"Very convenient for dates," said Ostap. "You always have ten minutes grace."

The coachman made a kissing sound with his lips and they passed under the bridge. The majestic panorama of the capital unfolded before them.

"Where are we going, by the way?" Ippolit Matveyevich asked.

"To visit nice people," Ostap replied. "There are masses of them in Moscow and they're all my friends."

"And we're staying with them?"

"It's a hostel. If we can't stay with one, we can always go to another."

On Hunter's Row there was confusion. Unlicensed hawkers were running about in disorder like geese, with their trays on their heads. A militiaman trotted along lazily after them. Some waifs were sitting beside an asphalt vat, breathing in the pleasant smell of boiling tar.

They came out on Arbat Square, passed along Prechistenka Boulevard, and, turning right, stopped in a small street called Sivtsev Vrazhek.

"What building is that?" Ippolit Matveyevich asked.

Ostap looked at the pink house with a projecting attic and answered: "The Brother Berthold Schwartz hostel for chemistry students."

"Was he really a monk?"

"No, no, I'm joking. It's the Semashko hostel."

As befits the normal run of student hostels in Moscow, this building had long been lived in by people whose connection with chemistry was somewhat remote. The students had gone their ways; some of them had completed their studies and gone off to take up jobs, and some had been expelled for failing their exams. It was the latter group which, growing from year to year, had formed something between a housing co-operative and a feudal settlement in the little pink house. In vain had ranks of freshmen sought to invade the hostel; the ex-chemists were highly resourceful and repulsed all assaults. The house was finally given up as a bad job and disappeared from the housing programs of the Moscow realty administration. It was as though it had never existed. It did exist, however, and there were people living in it.

The concessionaires went upstairs to the second floor and turned into a corridor that was in complete darkness.

"Light and airy!" said Ostap.

Suddenly someone wheezed in the darkness, just by Ippolit Matveyevich's elbow.

"Don't be alarmed," Ostap observed. "That wasn't in the corridor, but behind the wall. Plyboard, as you know from physics, is an excellent conductor of sound. Careful! Hold on to me! There should be a safe here somewhere."

The cry uttered at that moment by Ippolit Matveyevich as he hit his chest against a sharp steel corner showed that there definitely was a safe there somewhere.

"Did you hurt yourself?" Ostap inquired. "That's nothing. That's physical pain. I'd hate to think how much moral suffering has gone on here. There used to be a skeleton here belonging to a student called Ivanopulo. He bought it at the market, but was afraid to keep it in his room. So visitors first bumped into the safe and then the skeleton fell on top of them. Pregnant women were always very annoyed."

The partners wound their way up a spiral staircase to the large attic, which was divided by plyboard partitions into long slices five feet wide. The rooms were like pencil boxes, the only difference being that

besides pens and pencils they contained people and
primus stoves as well.

"Are you there, Nicky?" Ostap asked quietly, stopping at a central door.

The response was an immediate stirring and chattering in all five pencil boxes.

"Yes," came the answer from behind the door.

"That fool's visitors have arrived too early again!"
whispered a woman's voice in the last box on the left.

"Let a fellow sleep, can't you!" growled box no. 2.

There was a delighted hissing from the third box.

"It's the militia to see Nicky about that window he
smashed yesterday."

No one spoke in the fifth pencil box; instead came
the hum of a primus and the sound of kissing.

Ostap pushed open the door with his foot. The
whole of the plyboard erection gave a shake and the
concessionaires entered Nicky's cell.

The scene that met Ostap's eye was horrible, despite
its outward innocence. The only furniture in the room
was a red-striped mattress resting on four bricks. But
it was not that which disturbed Ostap, who had long
been aware of the state of Nicky's furniture; nor was
he surprised to see Nicky himself, sitting on the
legged mattress. It was the heavenly creature sitting
beside him who made Ostap's face cloud over immediately. Such girls never make good business associates.
Their eyes are too blue and the lines of their necks
too clean for that sort of thing. They make mistresses
or, what is worse, wives—beloved wives. And, indeed,
Nicky addressed this creature as Liza and made funny
faces at her.

Ippolit Matveyevich took off his beaver cap, and
Ostap led Nicky out into the corridor, where they
conversed at length in whispers.

"A splendid morning, madam," said Ippolit Matveyevich.

The blue-eyed madam laughed and, without any

apparent bearing on Ippolit Matveyevich's remark, began telling him what fools the people in the next box were.

"They light the primus on purpose so that they won't be heard kissing. But think how silly that is. We can all hear. The point is they don't hear anything themselves because of the primus. Look, I'll show you."

And Nicky's wife, who had mastered all the secrets of the primus stove, said loudly: "The Zveryevs are fools!"

From behind the wall came the infernal hissing of the primus stove and the sound of kisses.

"You see! They can't hear anything. The Zveryevs are fools, asses, and cranks! You see!"

"Yes," said Ippolit Matveyevich.

"We don't have a primus, though. Why? Because we eat at the vegetarian canteen, although I'm against a vegetarian diet. But when Nicky and I were married, he was longing for us to eat together in the vegetarian canteen, so that's why we go there. I'm actually very fond of meat, but all you get there is rissoles made of noodles. Only please don't say anything to Nicky."

At this point Nicky and Ostap returned.

"Well, then, since we definitely can't stay with you, we'll go and see Pantelei."

"That's right, fellows," cried Nicky, "go and see Ivanopulo. He's a good sport."

"Come and visit us," said Nicky's wife. "My husband and I will always be glad to see you."

"There they go inviting people again!" said an indignant voice in the last pencil box. "As though they didn't have enough visitors!"

"Mind your own business, you fools, asses, and cranks!" said Nicky's wife without raising her voice.

"Do you hear that, Ivan Andreyevich?" said an agitated voice in the last box. "They insult your wife and you say nothing."

Invisible commentators from the other boxes added their voices to the fray and the verbal cross-fire increased. The partners went downstairs to Ivanopulo.

The student was not at home. Ippolit Matveyevich lit a match and saw that a note was pinned to the door. It read: "Will not be back before nine. Pantelei."

"That's no harm," said Ostap, "I know where the key is." He groped underneath the safe, produced a key, and unlocked the door.

Ivanopulo's room was exactly the same size as Nicky's, but, being a corner room, had one wall made of brick; the student was very proud of it. Ippolit Matveyevich noted with dismay that he did not even have a mattress.

"This will do nicely," said Ostap. "Quite a decent size for Moscow. If we all three lie on the floor, there will even be some room to spare. I wonder what that son of a bitch, Pantelei, did with the mattress."

The window looked out onto a narrow street. A militiaman was walking up and down outside the little house opposite, built in the style of a Gothic tower, which housed the embassy of a minor power. Behind the iron gates some people could be seen playing tennis. The white ball flew backward and forward accompanied by short exclamations.

"Out!" said Ostap. "And the standard of play is not good. However, let's have a rest."

The concessionaires spread newspapers on the floor and Ippolit Matveyevich brought out the cushion which he carried with him.

Ostap dropped down onto the papers and dozed off. Ippolit Matveyevich was already asleep.

: 17 :

Have Respect for Mattresses, Citizens!

"LIZA, let's go and have dinner!"

"I don't feel like it. I had dinner yesterday."

"I don't get you."

"I'm not going to eat phony rabbit."

"Oh, don't be silly!"

"I can't exist on vegetarian sausages."

"Today you can have apple pie."

"I just don't feel like it."

"Not so loud. Everything can be heard."

The young couple changed voices to a stage whisper.

Two minutes later Nicky realized for the first time in three months of married life that his beloved liked sausages of carrot, potato, and pea less than he did.

"So you prefer dog meat to a vegetarian diet," cried Nicky, disregarding the eavesdropping neighbors in his burst of anger.

"Not so loud, I say!" shouted Liza. "And then you're nasty to me! Yes, I do like meat. At times. What's so bad about that?"

Nicky said nothing in his amazement. This was an unexpected turn of events. Meat would make an enormous, unfillable hole in his budget. The young husband strolled up and down beside the mattress on which the red-faced Liza was sitting curled up into a ball, and made some desperate calculations.

The job of tracing blueprints at the Technopower design office brought Nicky Kalachov no more than forty roubles, even in the best months. He did not pay any rent for the apartment. There was no housing authority in that jungle settlement and rent was an abstract concept. Ten roubles went on Liza's cutting and sewing lessons. Dinner for the two of them (one first course of monastery beet soup and a second course of phony rabbit or genuine noodles) consumed in two honestly halved portions in the "Thou Shalt Not Steal" vegetarian canteen took thirteen roubles each month from the married couple's budget. The rest of their money dwindled away heavens knows where. This disturbed Nicky most of all. "Where does the money go?" he used to wonder, drawing a thin line with a special pen on sky-blue tracing paper. A change to meat-eating under these circumstances would mean ruin. That was why Nicky had spoken so heatedly.

"Just think of eating the bodies of dead animals. Cannibalism in the guise of culture. All diseases stem from meat."

"Of course they do," said Liza with modest irony: "angina, for instance."

"Yes, they do—including angina. Don't you believe me? The organism is weakened by the continual consumption of meat and is unable to resist infection."

"How stupid!"

"It's not stupid. It's the stupid person who tries to stuff his stomach full without bothering about the quantity of vitamins."

Nicky suddenly became quiet. An emormous pork chop had loomed up before his inner eye, driving the insipid, uninteresting baked noodles, porridge, and potato nonsense further and further into the background. It seemed to have just come out of the pan. It was sizzling, bubbling, and giving off spicy fumes. The bone stuck out like the barrel of a dueling pistol.

"Try to understand," said Nicky, "a pork chop takes away a week of a man's life."

"Let it," said Liza. "Phony rabbit takes away six months. Yesterday when we were eating that carrot entree I felt I was going to die. Only I didn't want to tell you."

"Why didn't you want to tell me?"

"I hadn't the strength. I was afraid of crying."

"And aren't you afraid now?"

"Now I don't care." Liza began sobbing.

"Leo Tolstoy," said Nicky in a quavering voice, "didn't eat meat either."

"No," retorted Liza, hiccuping through her tears, "the count ate asparagus."

"Asparagus isn't meat."

"But when he was writing *War and Peace* he did eat meat. He did! He did! And when he was writing *Anna Karenina* he stuffed himself and stuffed himself."

"Do shut up!"

"Stuffed himself! Stuffed himself!"

"And I suppose while he was writing *The Kreutzer Sonata* he also stuffed himself?" asked Nicky venomously.

"*The Kreutzer Sonata* is short. Just imagine him trying to write *War and Peace* on vegetarian sausages!"

"Anyway, why do you keep nagging me about your Tolstoy?"

"Me nag *you* about Tolstoy! I like that. Me nag you!"

There was loud merriment in the pencil boxes. Liza hurriedly pulled a blue knitted hat onto her head.

"Where are you going?"

"Leave me alone. I have something to do."

And she fled.

"Where can she have gone?" Nicky wondered. He listened hard.

"Women like you have a lot of freedom under the Soviet regime," said a voice in the last pencil box on the left.

"She's gone to drown herself," decided the third pencil box.

The fifth pencil box lit the primus and got down to the routine kissing.

Liza ran from street to street in agitation.

It was that Sunday hour when lucky people carry mattresses along the Arbat from the market.

Newly married couples and Soviet farmers are the principal purchasers of spring mattresses. They carry them upright, clasping them with both arms. Indeed, how can they help clasping those blue, shiny-flowered foundations of their happiness!

Citizens! Have respect for a blue-flowered spring mattress. It's a family hearth. The be all and the end all of furnishings and the essence of domestic comfort; a base for love-making; the father of the primus. How sweet it is to sleep to the democratic hum of its springs. What marvelous dreams a man may have when he falls asleep on its blue hessian. How great is the respect enjoyed by a mattress owner.

A man without a mattress is pitiful. He does not exist. He does not pay taxes; he has no wife; friends will not lend him money "until Wednesday"; cab drivers shout rude words after him and girls laugh at him. They do not like idealists.

People without mattresses largely write such verse as:

> *It's nice to rest in a rocking chair*
> *To the quiet tick of a Bouret clock,*

When snowflakes swirlingly fill the air
And the daws pass, like dreams, in a flock.

They compose the verse at high desks in the post office, delaying the efficient mattress owners who come to send telegrams.

A mattress changes a man's life. There is a certain attractive, unfathomed force hidden in its covering and springs. People and things come together to the alluring ring of its springs. It summons the income-tax collector and girls. They both want to be friends with the mattress owner. The tax collector does so for fiscal reasons and for the benefit of the state, and the girls do so unselfishly, obeying the laws of nature.

Youth begins to bloom. Having collected his tax like a bumblebee gathering spring honey, the tax collector flies away with a joyful hum to his district hive. And the fast-retiring girls are replaced by a wife and a Jewel No. 1 primus.

A mattress is insatiable. It demands sacrifices. At night it makes the sound of a bouncing ball. It needs a bookcase. It needs a table with thick stupid legs. Creaking its springs, it demands drapes, a door curtain, and pots and pans for the kitchen. It shoves people and says to them:

"Go on! Buy a washboard and rolling pin!"

"I'm ashamed of you, man. You haven't yet got a carpet."

"Work! I'll soon give you children. You need money for diapers and a baby carriage."

A mattress remembers and does everything in its own way.

Not even a poet can escape the common lot. Here he comes, carrying one from the market, hugging it to his soft belly with horror.

"I'll break down your resistance, poet," says the mattress. "You no longer need to run to the post office to write poetry. And, anyway, is it worth writing?

Work and the balance will always be in your favor.
Think about your wife and children!

"I haven't a wife," cries the poet, staggering back
from his sprung teacher.

"You will have! But I don't guarantee she will be
the loveliest girl on earth. I don't even know whether
she will be kind. Be prepared for anything. You will
have children."

"I don't like children."

"You will."

"You frighten me, Citizen Mattress."

"Shut up, you fool. You don't know everything.
You'll also obtain credit from the Moscow wood-
working factory."

"I'll kill you, mattress!"

"Puppy! If you dare to, the neighbors will denounce
you to the housing authority."

So every Sunday lucky people cruise around Moscow to the joyful sound of mattresses.

But that is not the only thing, of course, which
makes a Moscow Sunday. Sunday is museum day.

There is a special group of people in Moscow who
know nothing about art, are not interested in archi-
tecture, and do not like historical monuments. These
people visit museums solely because they are housed
in splendid buildings. These people stroll through the
dazzling rooms, look enviously at the frescoes, touch
the things they are requested not to touch, and mut-
ter continually:

"My, how they used to live!"

They are not concerned with the fact that the
murals were painted by the Frenchman Puvis de Cha-
vannes. They are only concerned with how much it
cost the former owner of the house. They go up
staircases with marble statues on the landings and try
to imagine how many footmen used to stand there,
what wages were paid to them, and how much they
received in tips. There is china on the mantelpiece,

but they disregard it and decide that a fireplace is not such a good thing, as it uses up a lot of wood. In the oak-paneled dining room they do not examine the wonderful carving. They are troubled by one thought: what did the former merchant-owner used to eat there and how much would that be at the present cost of living.

People like this can be found in any museum. While the conducted tours are cheerfully moving from one work of art to another, this kind of person stands in the middle of the room and, looking in front of him, sadly moans:

"My, how they used to live!"

Liza ran along the street, stifling her tears. Her thoughts spurred her on. She was thinking about her poor and unhappy life.

"If we just had a table and two more chairs, it would be fine. And we'll have a primus in the long run. We must get organized."

She slowed down, suddenly remembering her quarrel with Nicky. Furthermore, she felt hungry. Hatred for her husband suddenly welled up in her.

"It's simply disgraceful," she said aloud.

She felt even more hungry.

"Very well, then, I know what I'll do."

And Liza blushingly bought a slice of bread and sausage from a vendor. Hungry as she was, it was awkward eating in the street. She was, after all, a mattress owner and understood the subtleties of life. Looking around, she turned into the entrance to a large two-storied house. Inside she attacked the slice of bread and sausage with great avidity. The sausage was delicious. A large group of tourists entered the doorway. They looked at Liza by the wall as they passed.

"Let them look!" decided the infuriated Liza.

: *18* :

The Furniture Museum

LIZA wiped her mouth with a handkerchief and brushed the crumbs off her blouse. She felt happier. She was standing in front of a notice that read:

MUSEUM OF FURNITURE MAKING

To return home would be awkward. She had no one she could go and see. There were twenty kopeks in her pocket. So Liza decided to begin her life of independence with a visit to the museum. Checking her cash in hand, she went into the lobby.

Inside she immediately bumped into a man with a shabby beard who was staring at a malachite column with a grieved expression and muttering through his mustache:

"People sure lived well!"

Liza looked respectfully at the column and went upstairs.

For ten minutes or so she sauntered through small square rooms with ceilings so low that people entering them looked like giants.

The rooms were furnished in the style of the period

of the Emperor Paul with mahogany and Karelian
birch furniture that was austere, magnificent, and mili-
tant. Two square dressers, the doors of which were
crisscrossed with spears, stood opposite a writing desk.
The desk was vast. Sitting at it would have been like
sitting at the Theater Square with the Bolshoi theater
with its colonnade and four bronze horses drawing
Apollo to the first night of "The Red Poppy" as an
inkwell. At least, that is how it seemed to Liza, who
was being reared on carrots like a rabbit. There were
high-backed chairs in the corners of the room with
tops twisted to resemble the horns of a ram. The sun-
shine lay on their peach-colored covers.

The chairs looked very inviting, but it was forbidden to sit on them.

Liza made a mental comparison between the price-
less Empire chair and her red-striped mattress. The
result was not too bad. She read the plate on the wall
which gave a scientific and ideological justification
of the period, and, regretting that she and Nicky did
not have a room in this palatial building, went out,
unexpectedly finding herself in a corridor.

Along the left-hand side, at floor level, was a line of
semicircular windows. Through them Liza could see
below her a huge columned hall with two rows of
large windows. The hall was also full of furniture, and
visitors strolled about inspecting it. Liza stood still.
Never before had she seen a room under her feet.

Marveling and thrilling at the sight, she stood for
some time gazing downward. Suddenly she noticed
the friends she had made that day, Bender and his
traveling companion, the distinguished-looking old
man with the shaven head; they were moving from
the chairs toward the desks.

"Good," said Liza. "Now I won't be so bored."

She brightened up considerably, ran downstairs, and
immediately lost her way. She came to a red drawing
room in which there were about forty pieces of furni-

ture. It was walnut furniture with curved legs. There
was no exit from the drawing room, so she had to run
back through a circular room with windows at the top,
apparently furnished with nothing but flowered cushions.

She hurried past Renaissance brocade chairs, Dutch
dressers, a large Gothic bed with a canopy resting on
four twisted columns. In a bed like that a person would
have looked no larger than a nut.

At length Liza heard the drone of a batch of tourists
as they listened inattentively to the guide unmasking
the imperialistic designs of Catherine II in connection
with the deceased empress's love of Louis Quinze
furniture.

This was in fact the large columned hall with the
two rows of large windows. Liza made toward the far
end, where her acquaintance, Comrade Bender, was
talking heatedly to his shaven-headed companion.

As she approached, she could hear a sonorous voice
saying:

"The furniture is chic moderne, but not apparently
what we want."

"No, but there are other rooms as well. We must
examine everything systematically."

"Hello!" said Liza.

They both turned around and immediately frowned.

"Hello, Comrade Bender. I'm glad I've found you.
It's boring by myself. Let's look at everything together."

The concessionaires exchanged glances. Ippolit Matveyevich assumed a dignified air, although the idea
that Liza might delay their important search for the
chair with the jewels was not a pleasant one.

"We are typical provincials," said Bender impatiently. "But how did you get here, Miss Moscow?"

"Quite by accident. I had a row with Nicky."

"Really?" Ippolit Matveyevich observed.

"Well, let's leave this room," Ostap said.

"But I haven't looked at it yet. It's so nice."

"That's done it!" Ostap whispered to Vorobyaninov. And, turning to Liza, he added: "There's absolutely nothing to see here. The style is decadent. The Kerensky period."

"I'm told there's some Hambs furniture somewhere here," Ippolit Matveyevich declared. "Maybe we should see that."

Liza agreed and, taking Vorobyaninov's arm (she thought him a remarkably nice representative of science), went toward the exit. Despite the seriousness of the situation at this decisive moment in the treasure hunt, Bender laughed good-humoredly as he walked behind the couple. He was amused at the chief of the Comanchi in the role of a cavalier.

Liza was a great hindrance to the concessionaires. Whereas they could determine at a glance whether or not the room contained the furniture they were after, and if not, automatically make for the next, Liza browsed at length in each section. She read all the printed tags, made cutting remarks about the other visitors, and dallied at each exhibit. Completely without realizing it, she was mentally adapting all the furniture she saw to her own room and requirements. She did not like the Gothic bed at all. It was too big. Even if Nicky in some miraculous way acquired a room six yards square, the medieval couch still would not fit into it. Liza walked round and round the bed, measuring its true area in paces. She was very happy. She did not notice the sour faces of her companions, whose chivalrous natures prevented them from heading for the Hambs room at full pelt.

"Let's be patient," Ostap whispered. "The furniture won't run away. And don't squeeze the girl, Marshal, I'm jealous!"

Vorobyaninov laughed smugly.

The rooms went on and on. There was no end to them. The furniture of the period of the Emperor

Alexander was displayed in batches. Its relatively small size delighted Liza.

"Look, look!" she cried, seizing Ippolit Matveyevich by the sleeve. "You see that bureau? That would suit our room wonderfully, wouldn't it?"

"Charming furniture," said Ostap testily. "But decadent."

"I've been in here already," said Liza as she entered the red drawing room. "I don't think it's worth stopping here."

To her astonishment, the indifferent companions were standing stock-still by the door like sentries.

"Why have you stopped? Let's go on. I'm tired."

"Wait," said Ippolit Matveyevich, freeing his arm. "One moment."

The large room was crammed with furniture. Hambs chairs were arranged along the wall and around a table. The couch in the corner was also encircled by chairs. Their curved legs and comfortable backs were excitingly familiar to Ippolit Matveyevich. Ostap looked at him questioningly. Vorobyaninov was flushed.

"You're tired, young lady," he said to Liza. "Sit down here a moment to rest while he and I walk around a bit. This seems to be an interesting room."

They sat Liza down. Then the concessionaires went over to the window.

"Are they the ones?" Ostap asked.

"It looks like it. I must have a closer look."

"Are they all here?"

"I'll just count them. Wait a moment." Vorobyaninov began shifting his eyes from one chair to another. "Just a second," he said at length, "twenty chairs! That can't be right. There are only supposed to be twelve."

"Take a good look. They may not be the right ones."

They began walking among the chairs.

"Well?" Ostap asked impatiently.

"The back doesn't seem to be the same as in mine."

"So they aren't the ones?"

"No, they're not."

"What a waste of time it was taking up with you!"

Ippolit Matveyevich was completely crushed.

"All right," said Ostap, "the hearing is continued. A chair isn't a needle in a haystack. We'll find it. Give me the orders. We will have to establish unpleasant contact with the museum curators. Sit down beside the girl and wait. I'll be back soon."

"Why are you so depressed?" asked Liza. "Are you tired?"

Ippolit Matveyevich tried not to answer.

"Does your head ache?"

"Yes, slightly. I have worries, you know. The lack of a woman's affection has an effect on one's tenor of life."

Liza was at first surprised, and then, looking at her bald-headed companion, felt truly sorry for him. Vorobyaninov's eyes were full of suffering. His pince-nez could not hide the sharply outlined bags underneath them. The rapid change from the quiet life of a clerk in a district registry office to the uncomfortable, irksome existence of a diamond hunter and adventurer had left its mark. Ippolit Matveyevich had become extremely thin and his liver had started paining him. Under the strict supervision of Bender he was losing his own personality and rapidly being absorbed by the powerful intellect of the son of a Turkish citizen. Now that he was left alone for a minute with the charming Liza, he felt an urge to tell her about his trials and tribulations, but did not dare to do so.

"Yes," he said, gazing tenderly at his companion, "that's how it is. How are you, Elizabeth . . ."

"Petrovna. And what's your name?"

They exchanged names and patronymics.

"A tale of true love," thought Ippolit Matveyevich,

peering into Liza's simple face. So passionately and so irresistibly did the old marshal want a woman's affection that he immediately seized Liza's tiny hand in his own wrinkled hands and began talking enthusiastically of Paris. He wanted to be rich, extravagant, and irresistible. He wanted to captivate a beauty from the all-women orchestra and drink champagne with her in a private dining room to the sound of music. What was the use of talking to a girl who knew absolutely nothing about women's orchestras or wine, and who by nature would not appreciate the delight of that kind of life? But he so much wanted to be attractive! Ippolit Matveyevich enchanted Liza with his account of Paris.

"Are you a scientist?" asked Liza.

"Yes, to a certain extent," replied Ippolit Matveyevich, feeling that since first meeting Bender he had regained some of the nerve which he had lost in recent years.

"And how old are you, if it's not an indiscreet question?"

"That has nothing to do with the science which I am at present representing."

Liza was squashed by the prompt and apt reply. "But, anyway—thirty, forty, fifty?"

"Almost. Thirty-seven."

"Oh! You look much younger."

Ippolit Matveyevich felt happy. "When will you give me the pleasure of seeing you again?" he asked through his nose.

Liza was very ashamed. She wriggled about on her seat and felt miserable. "Where has Comrade Bender got to?" she asked in a thin voice.

"So when, then?" asked Vorobyaninov impatiently. "When and where shall we meet?"

"Well, I don't know. Whenever you like."

"Is today all right?"

"Today?"

"Please!"

"Well, all right. Today, if you like. Come and see us."

"No, let's meet outside. The weather's so wonderful at present. Do you know the poem 'It's mischievous May, it's magical May, who is waving his fan of freshness'?"

"Is that by Zharov?"

"Mmm . . . I think so. Today, then? And where?"

"How strange you are. Anywhere you like. By the safe, if you want. Do you know it? As soon as it's dark."

Hardly had Ippolit Matveyevich time to kiss Liza's hand, which he did solemnly and in three installments, when Ostap returned. He was very businesslike.

"Excuse me, mademoiselle," he said quickly, "but my friend and I cannot see you home. A small but important matter has arisen. We have to go somewhere urgently."

Ippolit Matveyevich caught his breath. "Goodbye, Elizabeth Petrovna," he said hastily. "I'm very, very sorry, but we're in a terrible hurry."

The partners ran off, leaving the astonished Liza in the room so abundantly furnished with Hambs chairs.

"If it weren't for me," said Ostap as they went downstairs, "not a damn thing would get done. Take your hat off to me! Go on! Don't be afraid! Your head won't fall off! Listen! The museum has no use for your furniture. The right place for it is not a museum, but the barracks of a punishment battalion. Are you satisfied with the situation?"

"What nerve!" exclaimed Vorobyaninov, who had begun to free himself from the other's powerful intellect.

"Silence!" said Ostap coldly. "You don't know what's happening. If we don't get hold of your furni-

ture, everything's lost. We'll never see it. I have just
had a depressing conversation with the curator of this
historical refuse dump."

"Well, and what did he say?" cried Ippolit Matveyevich. "This curator of yours?"

"He said all he needed to. Don't worry. 'Tell me,'
I said to him, 'how do you explain the fact that the
furniture requisitioned in Stargorod and sent to your
museum isn't here?' I asked him politely, of course, as
a comrade. 'Which furniture?' he asks. 'Such cases do
not occur in my museum.' I immediately shoved the
orders under his nose. He began rummaging in the
files. He searched for about half an hour and finally
came back. Well, guess what happened to the furniture!"

"Not lost?" squeaked Vorobyaninov.

"No, just imagine! Just imagine, it remained safe
and sound through all the confusion. As I told you, it
has no museum value. It was dumped in a storehouse
and only yesterday, mind you, only yesterday, after
seven years [it had been in the storehouse *seven
years*], it was sent to be auctioned. The auction is
being held by the chief scientific administration. And
provided no one bought it either yesterday or this
morning, it's ours."

"Quick!" Ippolit Matveyevich shouted.

"Cab!" Ostap yelled.

They got in without even arguing about the price.

"Pray for me, pray! Don't be afraid, Hofmarshal!
Wine, women, and cards will be provided. Then we'll
settle for the light-blue vest as well."

As friskily as foals, the concessionaires tripped into
the Petrovka arcade where the auction rooms were
located.

In the first auction room they caught sight of what
they had long been chasing. All ten chairs were lined
along the wall. The upholstery had not even become
darker, nor had it faded or been in any way spoiled.

The chairs were as fresh and clean as when they had first been removed from the supervision of the zealous Claudia Ivanovna.

"Are those the ones?" asked Ostap.

"My God, my God," Vorobyaninov kept repeating. "They're the ones. The very ones. There's no doubt this time."

"Let's make certain, just in case," said Ostap, trying to remain calm.

They went up to an auctioneer.

"These chairs are from the furniture museum, aren't they?"

"These? Yes, they are."

"And they're for sale?"

"Yes."

"At what price?"

"No price yet. They're up for auction."

"Aha! Today?"

"No. The auction has finished for today. Tomorrow at five."

"And they're not for sale at the moment?"

"No. Tomorrow at five."

They could not leave the chairs at once, just like that.

"Do you mind if we have a look at them?" Ippolit Matveyevich stammered.

The concessionaires examined the chairs at great length, sat on them, and, for the sake of appearances, looked at the other lots. Vorobyaninov was breathing hard and kept nudging Ostap.

"Take your hat off to me, Marshal!"

Ippolit Matveyevich was not only prepared to take his hat off to Ostap; he was even ready to kiss the soles of his crimson boots.

"Tomorrow, tomorrow, tomorrow," he kept saying.

He felt an urge to sing.

Voting the European Way

WHILE THE FRIENDS were leading a cultured and edify-
ing way of life, visiting museums and making passes
at girls, the double-widow Gritsatsuyeva, a fat and
feeble woman, was consulting and conspiring with her
neighbors in Plekhanov Street, Stargorod.

They examined the note left by Bender in groups,
and even held it up to the light. But it had no water-
mark, and even if it had, the mysterious squiggles of
the splendid Ostap would not have been any clearer.

Three days passed. The horizon remained clear.
Neither Bender, the tea strainer, the imitation-gold
bracelet, nor the chair returned. These animate and
inanimate objects had all disappeared in the most puz-
zling way.

The widow then decided to take drastic measures.
She went to the office of the Stargorod *Truth*, where
they briskly concocted for her the following notice:

> MISSING FROM HOME. I implore any-
> one knowing the whereabouts of Com.
> Bender to inform me. Aged 25-30,
> brown hair, last seen dressed in a green
> suit, yellow boots, and a blue vest.

Information on the above person will
be suitably rewarded. Gritsatsuyeva,
15 Plekhanov St.

"Is he your son?" they asked sympathetically in the
office.

"Husband!" replied the martyr, covering her face
with a handkerchief.

"Your husband!"

"Why? He's legal."

"Nothing. You really ought to go to the militia."

The widow was alarmed. She was terrified of the
militia. She left, accompanied by curious glances.

Three times did the columns of the Stargorod *Truth*
send out their summons, but the great land was silent.
No one came forward who knew the whereabouts of a
brown-haired man in yellow boots. No one came forward to collect the suitable reward. The neighbors
continued to gossip.

People became used to the Stargorod street railway
and rode it without trepidation. The conductors
shouted "Full up" in fresh voices and everything proceeded as though the railway had been going since the
time of St. Vladimir the Red Sun. Disabled persons
of all categories, women and children and Victor Polesov sat at the front of the streetcar. To the cry of
"Fares please," Polesov used to answer "Season" and
remain next to the driver. He did not have a season
ticket, nor could he have had one.

The sojourn of Vorobyaninov and the smooth operator left a deep imprint on the town.

The conspirators carefully kept the secret entrusted
to them. Even Polesov kept it, despite the fact that he
was dying to blurt out the exciting secret to the first
person he met. But then, remembering Ostap's powerful shoulders, he stood firm. He only poured out his
heart in conversations with the fortuneteller.

"What do you think, Elena Stanislavovna?" he would ask. "How do you explain the absence of our leaders?"

Elena Stanislavovna was also very intrigued, but she had no information.

"Don't you think, Elena Stanislavovna," continued the indefatigable mechanic, "that they're on a special mission at present?"

The fortuneteller was convinced that this was the case. Their opinion was apparently shared by the parrot in the red shorts as well. It looked at Polesov with a round, knowing eye as if to say: "Give me some seeds and I'll tell you all about it. You'll be governor, Victor. All the mechanics will be in your charge. And the yard keeper from no. 15 will remain as before—a conceited bum."

"Don't you think we ought to carry on without them, Elena Stanislavovna? Whatever happens, we can't sit around doing nothing."

The fortuneteller agreed and remarked: "He's a hero, our Ippolit Matveyevich."

"He *is* a hero, Elena Stanislavovna, that's clear. But what about the officer with him? A go-getting fellow. Say what you like, Elena Stanislavovna, but things can't go on like this. They definitely can't."

And Polesov began to act. He made regular visits to all the members of the secret society "Sword and Plowshare," pestering Kislarsky, the canny owner of the Odessa roll bakery of the "Moscow Bun" artel, in particular. At the sight of Polesov, Kislarsky's face darkened. And his talk of the need to act drove the timid bun-maker to distraction.

Toward the week end they all met at Elena Stanislavovna's in the room with the parrot. Polesov was bursting with energy.

"Stop blathering, Victor," said the clear-thinking Dyadyev. "What have you been careering round the town for days on end for?"

"We must act!" cried Polesov.

"Act yes, but certainly not shout. This is how I see the situation, gentlemen. Once Ippolit Matveyevich has spoken, his words are sacred. And we must assume we haven't long to wait. How it will all take place, we don't need to know; there are military people to take care of that. We are the civilian contingent—representatives of the town intelligentsia and merchants. What's important for us? To be ready. Do we have anything? Do we have a center? No. Who will be governor of the town? There's no one. But that's the main thing, gentlemen. I don't think the British will stand on ceremony with the Bolsheviks. That's our first sign. It will all change very rapidly, gentlemen, I assure you."

"Well, we don't doubt that in the least," said Charushnikov, puffing out his cheeks.

"And a very good thing you don't. What do you think, Mr. Kislarsky? And you, young men?"

Nikesha and Vladya both looked absolutely certain of a rapid change, while Kislarsky happily nodded assent, having gathered from what the head of the Fastpack firm had said that he would not be required to participate directly in any armed clashes.

"What are we to do?" asked Polesov impatiently.

"Wait," said Dyadyev. "Follow the example of Mr. Vorobyaninov's companion. How smart! How shrewd! Did you notice how quickly he got around to assistance to the waifs and strays? That's how we should all act. We're only helping the children. So, gentlemen, let's nominate our candidates."

"We propose Ippolit Matveyevich Vorobyaninov as Marshal of the Nobility," exclaimed the young Nikesha and Vladya.

Charushnikov coughed condescendingly. "What do you mean! Nothing less than a minister for him. Higher, if you like. Make him a dictator."

"Come, come, gentlemen," said Dyadyev, "a marshal is the last thing to think about. We need a governor. I think . . ."

"You, Mr. Dyadyev," cried Polesov ecstatically. "Who else is there to take the reins in our province."

"I am most flattered by your confidence . . ." Dyadyev began, but at this point Charushnikov, who had suddenly turned pink, began to speak.

"The question, gentlemen," he said in a strained voice, "ought to have been aired."

He tried not to look at Dyadyev.

The owner of Fastpack also looked at his boots, which had wood shavings sticking to them.

"I don't object," he said. "Let's put it to the vote. Secret ballot or a show of hands?"

"We don't need to do it the Soviet way," said Charushnikov in a hurt voice. "Let's vote in an honest European way, by secret ballot."

They voted on pieces of paper. Dyadyev received four votes and Charushnikov two. Someone had abstained. It was clear from Kislarsky's face that it was he. He did not wish to spoil his relations with the future governor, whoever he might be.

When Polesov excitedly announced the results of the honest European ballot, there was silence in the room. They tried not to look at Charushnikov. The unsuccessful candidate for governor sat in humiliation.

Elena Stanislavovna felt very sorry for him, as she had voted in his favor. Charushnikov obtained his second vote by voting for himself; he was, after all, well versed in electoral procedure.

"Anyway, I propose Monsieur Charushnikov as mayor," said the kindly Elena Stanislavovna immediately.

"Why 'anyway'?" asked the magnanimous governor. "Not anyway, but him and no one else. Mr. Charushnikov's public activity is well known to us all."

"Hear, hear!" they all cried.

"Then can we consider the election accepted?"

The humiliated Charushnikov livened up and even tried to protest. "No, no, gentlemen, I request a vote. It's even more necessary to vote for a mayor than for a governor. If you wish to show me your confidence, gentlemen, I ask you to hold a ballot."

Pieces of paper poured into the empty sugar bowl.

"Six votes in favor and one abstention."

"Congratulations, Mr. Mayor," said Kislarsky, whose face gave away that he had abstained this time, too. "Congratulations!"

Charushnikov swelled with pride.

"And now it only remains to take some refreshment, your excellency," he said to Dyadyev. "Polesov, nip down to the October. Do you have any money?"

Polesov made a mysterious gesture with his hand and ran off. The elections were temporarily adjourned and resumed after supper.

As ward of the educational region they appointed Raspopov, former director of a private school, and now a second-hand book dealer. He was greatly praised. It was only Vladya who protested suddenly, after his third glass of vodka.

"We mustn't elect him. He gave me bad marks in logic at the graduation exams."

They all went for Vladya.

"At such a decisive hour, you must not think of your own good. Think of the fatherland."

They brainwashed Vladya so quickly that he even voted in favor of his tormentor. Raspopov was elected by seven votes with one abstention.

Kislarsky was offered the post of chairman of the stock-exchange committee. He did not object, but abstained during the voting just in case.

Drawing from among friends and relatives, they elected a chief of police, a head of the assay office, and a customs and excise inspector; they filled the vacan-

cies of regional public prosecutor, judge, clerk of the
court, and other court officials; they appointed chair-
men of the Zemstvo and merchants' council, the
children's welfare committee, and, finally, the shop-
owners' council. Elena Stanislavovna was elected ward
of the "Drop of Milk" and "White Flower" societies.
On account of their youth, Nikesha and Vladya were
appointed special-duty clerks attached to the governor.

"Wait a minute," exclaimed Charushnikov suddenly.
"The governor has two clerks and what about me?"

"A mayor is not entitled to special-duty clerks."

"Then give me a secretary."

Dyadyev consented. Elena Stanislavovna also had
something to say.

"Would it be possible," she said, faltering, "I know
a young man, a nice and well-brought-up boy. Madam
Cherkesova's son. He's a very, very nice and clever
kid. He hasn't a job at present and has to keep going
to the employment office. He's even a trade-union
member. They promised to find work for him in the
union. Couldn't you take him? His mother would be
very grateful."

"It might be possible," said Charushnikov graciously. "What do you think, gentlemen? All right. I
think that could be arranged."

"Right, then—that seems to be about all," Dyadyev
observed.

"What about me?" a high-pitched, nervous voice
suddenly said.

They all turned around. A very upset Victor Polesov was standing in the corner next to the parrot.
Tears were bubbling on his black eyelids. The guests
all felt very ashamed, remembering that they had been
drinking Polesov's vodka and that he was basically
one of the organizers of the Stargorod branch of the
"Sword and Plowshare."

Elena Stanislavovna seized her head and gave a horrified screech.

"Victor Mikhailovich!" they all gasped. "Pal! Shame on you! What are you doing in the corner? Come out at once."

Polesov came near. He was suffering. He had not expected such callousness from his comrades in the "Sword and Plowshare."

Elena Stanislavovna was unable to restrain herself. "Gentlemen," she said, "this is awful. How could you forget Victor Mikhailovich, so dear to us all?" She got up and kissed the mechanic-aristocrat on his sooty forehead. "Surely Victor Mikhailovich is worthy of being a ward or a police chief."

"Well, Victor Mikhailovich," asked the governor, "do you want to be a ward?"

"Well of course, he would make a splendid, humane ward," put in the mayor, swallowing a mushroom and frowning.

"But what about Raspopov? You've already nominated Raspopov."

"Yes, indeed, what shall we do with Raspopov?"

"Make him a fire chief, eh?"

"A fire chief!" exclaimed Polesov, suddenly becoming excited.

A picture of fire engines, the glare of lights, the sound of the siren and the drumming of hoofs suddenly flashed through his mind. Axes glimmered, torches wavered, the ground heaved, and black dragons carried him to a fire at the town theater.

"A fire chief! I want to be a fire chief!"

"Well, that's fine. Congratulations! You're now the fire chief."

"Let's drink to the prosperity of the fire brigade," said the chairman of the stock-exchange committee sarcastically.

They all went for him.

"You were always Left Wing! We know you!"

"What do you mean, gentlemen, Left Wing?"

"We know, we know!"

"Left Wing!"

"All Jews are Left Wing!"

"Honestly, gentlemen, I don't understand such jokes."

"You're Left Wing, don't try to hide it!"

"He dreams about Milyukov at night."

"Cadet! You're a Cadet."

"The Cadets sold Finland," cried Charushnikov suddenly.

"And took money from the Japanese. They split the Armenians."

Kislarsky could not endure the stream of groundless accusations. Pale, his eyes blazing, the chairman of the stock-exchange committee grasped hold of his chair and said in a ringing voice:

"I was always a supporter of the Tsar's October manifesto and still am."

They began to sort out who belonged to which party.

"Democracy above all, gentlemen," said Charushnikov. "Our town government must be democratic."

"But without Cadets! They did us dirty in 1917."

"I hope," said the governor acidly, "that there aren't any so-called Social Democrats among us."

There was nobody present more Left Wing than the Octobrists, represented at the meeting by Kislarsky. Charushnikov declared himself to be the "center." The extreme Right Wing was the fire chief. He was so Right Wing that he did not know which party he belonged to.

They talked about war.

"Quite soon," said Dyadyev.

"There'll be a war."

"I advise stocking up with a few things before it's too late."

"Do you think so?" asked Kislarsky in alarm.

"Well, what do you think? Do you suppose you can get anything in wartime? Flour will disappear from the market right away. Silver coins will vanish completely. There'll be all sorts of paper currency, and stamps will have the same value as notes, and all that sort of thing."

"War, that's for sure."

"You may think differently, but I'm spending all my spare cash on buying up essential commodities," said Dyadyev.

"And what about your textile business?"

"Textiles can look out for themselves, but the flour and sugar are important."

"That's what I advise you. I urge you, even."

Polesov laughed derisively. "How can the Bolsheviks fight? What with? What will they fight with? Old-fashioned rifles. And the Air Force? A prominent communist told me that they only have . . . well, how many planes do you think they have?"

"About two hundred."

"Two hundred? Not two hundred, but thirty-two. And France had eighty thousand fighters."

It was past midnight when they all went home.

"Yes, indeed. They've got the Bolsheviks worried."

The governor took the mayor home. They both walked with an exaggeratedly even pace.

"Governor!" Charushnikov was saying. "How can you be a governor when you aren't even a general!"

"I shall be a civilian governor. Why, are you jealous? I'll jail you whenever I want. You'll have your fill of jail from me."

"You can't jail me. I've been elected and entrusted with authority."

"They prefer elected people in jail."

"Kindly don't try to be funny," shouted Charushnikov for all the street to hear.

"What are you shouting for, you fool?" said the

governor. "Do you want to spend the night in the militia station?"

"I can't spend the night in the militia station," retorted the mayor. "I'm a government employee."

A star twinkled. The night was enchanting. The argument between the governor and the mayor continued down Second Soviet Street.

From Seville to Granada

WAIT A MINUTE NOW, where is Father Fyodor? Where is the shorn priest from the Church of St. Frol and St. Laurence? Was he not about to go to see citizen Bruns at 34 Vineyard Street? Where is that treasure seeker in angel's clothing and sworn enemy of Ippolit Vorobyaninov, at present cooling his heels in the dark corridor by the safe.

Gone is Father Fyodor. He has been spirited away. They say he was seen at Popasnaya station on the Donets railroad, hurrying along the platform with a teapot full of hot water.

Greedy is Father Fyodor. He wants to be rich. He is chasing around Russia in search of the furniture belonging to Popova, the general's wife, which actually does not contain a darn thing.

He is on his way through Russia. And all he does is write letters to his wife:

Letter from Father Fyodor
written from Kharkov Station to his wife
in the district center of N.

My Darling Catherine Alexandrovna,

I owe you an apology. I have left you alone, poor thing, at a time like this.

I must tell you everything. You will understand and, I hope, agree.

It was not, of course, to join the new church movement that I went. I had no intention of doing so, God forbid!

Now read this carefully. We shall soon begin to live differently. You remember I told you about the candle factory. It will be ours, and perhaps one or two other things as well. And you won't have to cook your own meals or have boarders any more. We'll go to Samara and hire servants.

I'm on to something, but you must keep it absolutely secret: don't even tell Marya Ivanovna. I'm looking for treasure. Do you remember the deceased Claudia Ivanovna, Vorobyaninov's mother-in-law? Just before her death, Claudia Ivanovna disclosed to me that her jewels were hidden in one of the drawing-room chairs (there were twelve of them) at her house in Stargorod.

Don't think, Katey, that I'm just a common thief. She bequeathed them to me and instructed me not to let Ippolit Matveyevich, her lifelong tormentor, get them.

That's why I left so suddenly, you poor thing.

Don't condemn me.

I went to Stargorod, and what do you think—that old woman-chaser turned up as well. He had found out. He must have tortured the old woman before she died. Horrible man! And there was some criminal traveling with him: he had hired himself a thug. They fell upon me and tried to get rid of me. But I'm not one to be trifled with: I didn't give in.

At first I went off on a false track. I only found one chair in Vorobyaninov's house (it's now a home for pensioners); I was carrying the chair to my room in the Sorbonne Hotel when suddenly a man came around the corner roaring like a lion and rushed at me, seizing the chair. We almost had a fight. He wanted to shame me. Then I looked closely and who was it but Vorobyaninov. Just imagine, he had shaved off his mustache and shaved his head, the crook. Shameful at his age.

We broke open the chair, but there was nothing there. It was not until later that I realized I was on the wrong track. But at that moment I was very distressed.

I felt outraged and I told that old libertine the truth to his face.

What a disgrace, I said, at your age. What mad things are going on in Russia nowadays when a marshal of the nobility pounces on a minister of the church like a lion and rebukes him for not being in the Communist Party. You're a low fellow, I said, you tormented Claudia Ivanovna and you want someone else's property—which is now state-owned and no longer his.

He was ashamed and went away—to the brothel, I imagine.

So I went back to my room in the Sorbonne and started to make plans. I thought of something that bald-headed fool would never have dreamed of. I decided to find the person who had distributed the requisitioned furniture. So you see, Katey, I did well to study law at college: it has served me well. I found the person in question the next day. Bartholomeich, a very decent old man. He lives quietly with his grandmother and works hard to earn his living. He gave me all the documents. It's true I had to reward him for the service. I'm now out of money (I'll come to that). It turned out that all twelve chairs from Vorobyaninov's house went to engineer Bruns at 34 Vineyard Street. Note that all the chairs went to one person, which I had not expected (I was afraid the chairs might have gone to different places). I was very pleased at this. Then I met that wretch Vorobyaninov in the Sorbonne again. I gave him a good talking to and didn't spare his friend, the thug, either. I was very afraid they might find out my secret, so I hid in the hotel until they left.

Bruns turned out to have moved from Stargorod to Kharkov in 1923 to take up an appointment. I learned from the janitor that he had taken all his furniture and was looking after it very carefully. He's said to be a shrewd person.

I'm now sitting in the station at Kharkov and writing for this reason: first, I love you very much and keep thinking of you, and, second, Bruns is no longer here. But don't despair. Bruns is now working in Rostov at the New-Ros-Cement plant. I have just enough money for the fare. I'm leaving in an hour's time on a mixed passenger-freight train. Please stop by your brother-in-law's, my sweet, and get fifty roubles from him (he owes it to me and promised to pay) and send it to: Fyodor Ivanovich Vostrikov, Central Post Office, Rostov, to await collection. Send a money order by mail to economize. It will cost thirty kopeks.

What's the news in the town?

Has Kondratyevna been to see you? Tell Father Cyril that I'll be back soon and that I've gone to see my dying aunt in Voronezh. Be economical. Is Evstigneyev still having meals? Give him my regards. Say I've gone to my aunt.

How's the weather? It's already summer here in Kharkov. A noisy city, the center of the Ukrainian Republic. After the provinces it's like being abroad.

Please do the following:

1) send my summer cassock to the cleaner (it's better to spend Rs. 3 on cleaning than waste money on buying a new one); 2) look after yourself; and 3)

when you write to Gulka, mention casually that I've
gone to Voronezh to see my aunt.
Give everyone my regards. Say I'll be back soon.
With tender kisses and blessings,
Your husband,
Fedya.

N.B. Where can Vorobyaninov be roving about at the
moment?

Love dries a man up. The bull lows with desire. The
rooster cannot keep still. The marshal of the nobility
loses his appetite.
Leaving Ostap and the student Ivanopulo in a bar,
Ippolit Matveyevich made his way to the little pink
house and took up his stand by the safe. He could hear
the sounds of trains leaving for Castille and the splash
of departing steamers.

> *As in far off Alpujarras*
> *The golden mountains fade*

His heart was fluttering like a pendulum. There was
a ticking in his ears.

> *And guitars strum out their summons*
> *Come forth, my pretty maid.*

Uneasiness spread along the corridor. Nothing could
thaw the cold of the safe.

> *From Seville to Granada*
> *Through the stillness of the night*

Phonographs droned in the pencil boxes. Primuses
hummed like bees.

> *Comes the sound of serenading*
> *Comes the ring of swords in fight.*

In short, Ippolit Matveyevich was head over heels in love with Liza Kalachov.

Many people passed Ippolit Matveyevich in the corridor, but they all smelled of either tobacco, vodka, disinfectant, or stale soup. In the obscurity of the corridor it was possible to distinguish people only by their smell or the heaviness of their tread. Liza had not come by. Ippolit Matveyevich was sure of that. She did not smoke, drink vodka, or wear boots with iron taps. She could not have smelled of iodine or cod's head. She could only exude the tender fragrance of rice pudding or tastily prepared hay, on which Mrs. Nordman-Severov fed the famous painter Repin for such a long time.

And then he heard light, uncertain footsteps. Someone was coming down the corridor, bumping into its elastic walls and murmuring sweetly.

"Is that you, Elizabeth Petrovna?" asked Ippolit Matveyevich.

"Can you tell me where the Pfefferkorns live?" a deep voice replied. "I can't see a damn thing in the dark!"

Ippolit Matveyevich said nothing in his alarm. The Pfefferkorn seeker waited for an answer but, not getting one, moved on, puzzled.

It was nine o'clock before Liza came. They went out into the street under a caramel green evening sky.

"Where shall we go?" asked Liza.

Ippolit Matveyevich looked at her pale, shining face and, instead of saying "I am here, Inezilla, beneath thy window," began to talk long-windedly and tediously about the fact that he had not been in Moscow for a long time and that Paris was infinitely better than the Russian capital, which was always a large, badly planned village, whichever way you turned it.

"This isn't the Moscow I remember, Elizabeth Petrovna. Now there's a stinginess everywhere. In my

day we spent money like water. 'We only live once.'
There's a song called that."

They walked the length of Prechistenka Boulevard
and came out onto the embankment by the Church of
Christ the Savior.

A line of black-brown fox tails stretched along the
far side of Moskvoretsk Bridge. The power stations
were smoking like a squadron of ships. Streetcars rattled across the bridge and boats moved up and down
the river. An accordion was sadly telling its tale.

Taking hold of Ippolit Matveyevich's hand, Liza
told him about her troubles: the quarrel with her husband, the difficulty of living with eavesdropping
neighbors, the ex-chemists, and the monotony of a
vegetarian diet.

Ippolit Matveyevich listened and began thinking.
Devils were aroused in him. He visualized a wonderful
supper. He decided he must in some way or other
make an overwhelming impression on the girl.

"Let's go to the theater," he suggested.

"The movies are better," said Liza, "they're
cheaper."

"Why think of the money? A night like this and
you worry about the cost!"

The devils in him threw prudence to the wind, set
the couple in a cab, without haggling about the fare,
and took them to the Ars movie theater. Ippolit Matveyevich was splendid. He bought the most expensive seats. They did not wait for the show to finish,
however. Liza was used to cheaper seats nearer the
screen and could not see so well from the thirty-
fourth row.

In his pocket Ippolit Matveyevich had half the sum
obtained by the concessionaires from the Stargorod
conspirators. It was a lot of money for Vorobyaninov,
so unaccustomed to luxury. Excited by the possibility
of an easy conquest, he was ready to dazzle Liza with

the scale of his entertaining. He considered himself admirably equipped for this, and proudly remembered how easily he had once won the heart of Elena Bour. It was part of his nature to spend money extravagantly and showily. He had been famous in Stargorod for his good manners and ability to converse with any woman. He thought it would be amusing to use his prerevolutionary polish on conquering a little Soviet girl, who had never seen anything or known anything.

With little persuasion Ippolit Matveyevich took Liza to the Prague, the showpiece of the Moscow union of consumer societies, the best place in Moscow, as Bender used to say.

The Prague awed Liza by the copious mirrors, lights, and flower pots. This was excusable; she had never before been in a restaurant of this kind. But the mirrored room unexpectedly awed Ippolit Matveyevich, too. He was out of touch and had forgotten about the world of restaurants. Now he felt ashamed of his baronial boots with square toes, prerevolutionary trousers, and yellow, star-spangled vest.

They were both embarrassed and stopped suddenly at the sight of the rather mixed public.

"Let's go over there in the corner," suggested Vorobyaninov, although there were tables free just by the stage, where the orchestra was scraping away at the stock potpourri from the "Bayadere."

Liza quickly agreed, feeling that all eyes were upon her. The social lion and lady-killer, Vorobyaninov, followed her awkwardly. The social lion's shabby pants drooped baggily from his thin behind. The lady-killer hunched his shoulders and began polishing his pince-nez in an attempt to cover up his embarrassment.

No one took their order. Ippolit Matveyevich had not expected this. Instead of gallantly conversing with his lady, he remained silent, sighed, tapped the table timidly with an ash tray, and coughed incessantly. Liza looked around her with curiosity; the silence became unnatural. But Ippolit Matveyevich could not think of anything to say. He had forgotten what he usually said in such cases.

"We'd like to order," he called to waiters as they flew past.

"Just coming, sir," cried the waiters without stopping.

A menu was eventually brought, and Ippolit Matveyevich buried himself in it with relief.

"But veal cutlets are two twenty-five, a filet is two twenty-five, and vodka is five roubles," he mumbled.

"For five roubles you get a large decanter, sir," said the waiter, looking around impatiently.

"What's the matter with me?" Ippolit Matveyevich asked himself in horror. "I'm making myself ridiculous."

"Here you are," he said to Liza with belated courtesy, "you choose something. What would you like?"

Liza felt ashamed. She saw how haughtily the waiter was looking at her escort, and realized he was doing something wrong.

"I'm not at all hungry," she said in a shaky voice. "Or wait, have you anything vegetarian?"

"We don't serve vegetarian dishes. Maybe a ham omelet?"

"All right, then," said Ippolit Matveyevich, having made up his mind, "bring us some sausages. You'll eat sausages, won't you, Elizabeth Petrovna?"

"Yes, certainly."

"Sausages, then. These at a rouble twenty-five each. And a bottle of vodka."

"It's in a decanter."

"Then a large one."

The public-catering employee gave the defenseless Liza a knowing look.

"What will you have with the vodka? Fresh caviar? Smoked salmon?"

The registry-office employee continued to rage in Ippolit Matveyevich. "Nothing," he said rudely. "How much are the salted gherkins? All right, let me have two."

The waiter hurried away and silence reigned once more at the table. Liza was the first to speak.

"I've never been here before. It's very nice."

"Ye-es," said Vorobyaninov slowly, working out the cost of what they had ordered. "Never mind," he thought, "I'll drink some vodka and loosen up a bit. I feel so awkward at the moment."

But when he had drunk the vodka and accompanied it with a gherkin, he did not loosen up, but rather became more gloomy. Liza did not drink anything. The tension continued. Then someone else approached the table and, looking tenderly at Liza, tried to sell them flowers.

Ippolit Matveyevich pretended not to notice the be-whiskered flower seller, but he kept hovering near the table. It was quite impossible to say nice things with him there.

They were saved for a while by the cabaret. A well-fed man in a morning coat and patent-leather shoes came onto the stage.

"Well, here we are again," he said breezily, addressing the public. "Next on our program we have the well-known Russian folk singer Barbara Godlevskaya."

Ippolit Matveyevich drank his vodka and said nothing. Since Liza did not drink and kept wanting to go home, he had to hurry to finish the whole decanter.

By the time the singer had been replaced by an entertainer in a ribbed velvet shirt, who came onto the stage and began to sing:

> *Roaming,*
> *You're always roaming*
> *As though with all the life outside*
> *Your appendix will be satisfied,*
> > *Roaming,*
> > *Ta-ra-ra-ra . . .*

Ippolit Matveyevich was already well in his cups and, together with all the other customers in the restaurant, whom half an hour earlier he had considered rude and niggardly Soviet thugs, was clapping in time to the music and joining in the chorus:

> > *Roaming,*
> > *Ta-ra-ra-ra . . .*

He kept jumping up and going to the men's room without excusing himself. The nearby tables had already begun calling him uncle, and invited him over for a glass of beer. But he did not go. He suddenly became proud and suspicious. Liza stood up determinedly.

"I'm going. You stay. I can go home by myself."

"Certainly not! As a member of the upper class I cannot allow that."

"*Garson!* The check! Bums!"

Ippolit Matveyevich stared at the check for some time, swaying in his chair.

"Nine roubles, twenty kopeks," he muttered. "Perhaps you'd also like the key of the apartment where the money is."

He ended up by being led cautiously downstairs by the arm. Liza could not escape, since the social lion had the cloakroom ticket.

In the first side street Ippolit Matveyevich leaned against Liza and began to paw her. Liza fought him off.

"Stop it!" she cried. "Stop it! Stop it!"

"Let's go to a hotel," Vorobyaninov urged.

Liza freed herself with difficulty and, without taking aim, punched the lady-killer on the nose. The pince-nez with the gold nosepiece fell to the ground and, getting in the way of one of the square-toed baronial boots, broke with a crunch.

> *The evening breeze*
> *Sighs through the trees*

Choking back her tears, Liza ran home down Silver Lane.

> *Loud and fast*
> *Flows the*
> *Gualdalquivir.*

The blinded Ippolit Matveyevich trotted off in the opposite direction, shouting "Stop! Thief!"

Then he cried for a long time and, still weeping, bought a full basket of bagels from an old woman. Reaching the Smolensk market, now empty and dark, he walked up and down for some time, throwing the bagels all over the place like a sower sowing seed. As he went, he shouted in a tuneless voice:

> *Roaming,*
> *You're always roaming,*
> *Ta-ra-ra-ra . . .*

Later on he befriended a cabdriver, poured out his heart to him, and told him in a muddled way about the jewels.

"A gay old gentleman," exclaimed the cabdriver.

Ippolit Matveyevich was really in a gay mood. The gaiety was clearly of a rather reprehensible nature, be-cause he woke up at about eleven the next day in the local precinct. Of the two hundred roubles with which he had shamefully begun his night of enjoy-ment and pleasure, only twelve remained.

He felt like death. His spine ached, his liver hurt, and his head felt as if he was wearing a lead pot on it.

But the most awful thing was that he could not remember how and where he could have spent so much
money. On the way home he had to stop at the optician's to have new lenses fitted in his pince-nez.

Ostap looked in surprise at the bedraggled figure of
Ippolit Matveyevich for some time but said nothing.
He was cold and ready for battle.

] CHAPTER [
: *21* :

Punishment

THE AUCTION was due to begin at five o'clock. Citizens were allowed in to inspect the lots at four. The friends arrived at three o'clock and spent a whole hour looking at a machine-building exhibition next door.

"It looks as though by tomorrow," said Ostap, "given good will on both sides, we ought to be able to buy that little locomotive. A pity there's no price tag on it. It's nice to own your own locomotive."

Ippolit Matveyevich was in a highly nervous state. The chairs alone could console him.

He did not leave them until the moment the auctioneer, in checked trousers and a beard reaching to his Russian covert-coat tunic, mounted the stand.

The concessionaires took their places in the fourth row on the right. Ippolit Matveyevich began to get very excited. He thought the chairs would be sold at once, but they were actually the third item on the list, and first came the usual auction junk: odd pieces of dinner services embellished with coats of arms; a sauce dish; a silver glass holder; a Petunin landscape; a bead handbag; a brand-new primus burner; a small bust of Napoleon; linen brassiers; a tapestry "Hunter shooting wild duck," and other trash.

They had to be patient and wait. It was hard to wait when the chairs were all there; the goal was within reach.

"What a rumpus there'd be," thought Ostap, "if they knew what little goodies were being sold here today in the form of those chairs."

"A figure depicting Justice!" announced the auctioneer. "Made of bronze. In perfect condition. Five roubles. Who'll bid more? Six and a half on the right. Seven at the end. Eight roubles in front in the first row. Going for eight roubles. Going. Gone to the first row in front."

A girl with a receipt book immediately hurried over to the citizen in the first row.

The auctioneer's hammer rose and fell. He sold an ash tray, some crystal glass, and a porcelain powder bowl.

Time dragged painfully.

"A bronze bust of Alexander the Third. Would make a good paperweight. No use for anything else. Going at the marked price one bust of Alexander the Third."

There was laughter among the audience.

"Buy it, Marshal," said Ostap sarcastically. "You like that sort of thing."

Ippolit Matveyevich made no reply; he could not take his eyes off the chairs.

"No offers? The bust of Alexander the Third is removed from sale. A figure depicting Justice. Apparently the twin of the one just sold. Basil, hold up the Justice. Five roubles. Who'll give me more?"

There was a snuffling sound from the first row. The citizen evidently wanted a complete set of Justices.

"Five roubles for the bronze Justice."

"Six!" sang out the citizen.

"Six roubles in front. Seven. Nine roubles on the right at the end."

"Nine and a half," said the lover of Justice quietly, raising his hand.

"Nine and a half in front. Going for nine and a half. Going. Gone!"

The hammer came down and the girl hastened over to the citizen in the first row.

He paid up and wandered off into the next room to receive his bronze.

"Ten chairs from a palace," said the auctioneer suddenly.

"Why from a palace?" gasped Ippolit Matveyevich quietly.

Ostap became angry. "To hell with you! Listen and stop fooling!"

"Ten chairs from a palace. Walnut. Period of Alexander the Second. In perfect condition. Made by the cabinet maker Hambs. Basil, hold one of the chairs under the light."

Basil seized the chair so roughly that Ippolit Matveyevich half stood up.

"Sit down, you damned idiot," hissed Ostap. "Sit down, I tell you. You make me sick!"

Ippolit Matveyevich's jaw had dropped. Ostap was pointing like a setter. His eyes shone.

"Ten walnut chairs. Eighty roubles."

There was a stir in the room. Something of use in the house was being sold.

One after another the hands flew up. Ostap remained calm.

"Why don't you bid?" snapped Vorobyaninov.

"Get out!" retorted Ostap, clenching his teeth.

"A hundred and twenty roubles at the back. A hundred and twenty-five in the next seat. A hundred and forty."

Ostap calmly turned his back on the stand and surveyed his competitors.

The auction was at its height. Every seat was taken.

The lady sitting directly behind Ostap was tempted by the chairs and, after a few words with her husband ("Beautiful chairs! Heavenly workmanship, Sanya. And from a palace!"), put up her hand.

"A hundred and forty-five, fifth row on the right. Going!"

The stir died down. Too expensive.

"A hundred and forty-five, going for the second time."

Ostap was apathetically examining the stucco cornice. Ippolit Matveyevich was sitting with his head down, trembling.

"One hundred and forty-five. Gone!"

But before the shiny black hammer could strike the plyboard stand, Ostap had turned around, thrown up his hand, and said quite quietly: "Two hundred."

All the heads turned toward the concessionaires. Peaked caps, cloth caps, and yachting caps and hats were set in action. The auctioneer raised his bored face and looked at Ostap.

"Two hundred," he said. "Two hundred in the fourth row on the right. Any more bids? Two hundred roubles for a palace suite of walnut furniture consisting of ten pieces. Going at two hundred roubles to the fourth row on the right. Going!"

The hand with the hammer was poised above the stand.

"Mama!" said Ippolit Matveyevich loudly.

Ostap, pink and calm, smiled. The hammer came down making a heavenly sound.

"Gone," said the auctioneer. "Young lady, fourth row on the right."

"Well, chairman, was that effective?" asked Ostap. "What would you do without a technical adviser, I'd like to know?"

Ippolit Matveyevich grunted happily. The young lady trotted over to them.

"Was it you who bought the chairs?"

"Yes, us!" Ippolit Matveyevich burst out. "Us! Us! When can we have them?"

"Whenever you please. Now if you like."

The tune "Roaming, you're always roaming" went madly round and round in Ippolit Matveyevich's head. "The chairs are ours! Ours! Ours!" His whole body was shouting it. "Ours!" cried his liver. "Ours!" endorsed his appendix.

He was so overjoyed that he suddenly felt twitches in the most unexpected places. Everything vibrated, rocked, and crackled under the pressure of unheard-of bliss. He saw the train approaching the St. Gotthard. On the open platform of the last car stood Ippolit Matveyevich in white trousers, smoking a cigar. Edelweiss fell gently onto his head, which was again covered with shining, aluminum-gray hair. He was on his way to the garden of Eden.

"Why two hundred and thirty and not two hundred?" said a voice next to him.

It was Ostap speaking; he was fiddling with the receipt.

"Fifteen per cent commission is included," answered the girl.

"Well, I suppose that's all right. Here you are."

Ostap took out his billfold, counted out two hundred roubles, and turned to the director in chief of the enterprise.

"Let me have thirty roubles, pal, and make it snappy. Can't you see the young lady's waiting?"

Ippolit Matveyevich made no attempt at all to get the money.

"Well? Why are you staring at me like a soldier at a louse? Are you crazy with joy or something?"

"I don't have the money," stammered Ippolit Matveyevich at length.

"Who doesn't?" asked Ostap very quietly.

"I don't."

"And the two hundred roubles?"

"I . . . I . . . lost it."

Ostap looked at Vorobyaninov and quickly realized the meaning of the flabbiness of the face, the green pallor of the cheeks, and the bags under the swollen eyes.

"Give me the money," he whispered with loathing, "you old bastard!"

"Well, are you going to pay?" asked the girl.

"One moment," said Ostap with a charming smile, "there's been a slight hitch."

There was still a faint hope that they might persuade her to wait for the money.

Here Ippolit Matveyevich, who had now recovered his senses, broke into the conversation.

"Just a moment," he spluttered. "Why is there commission? We don't know anything about that. You should have warned us. I refuse to pay the thirty roubles."

"Very well," said the girl curtly, "I'll see to that."

Taking the receipt, she hurried back to the auctioneer and had a few words with him.

The auctioneer immediately stood up. His beard glistened in the strong light of the electric lamps.

"In accordance with auctioneering regulations," he stated, "persons refusing to pay the full sum of money for items purchased must leave the hall. The sale of the chairs is revoked."

The dazed friends sat motionless.

The effect was terrific. There was rude guffawing from the onlookers. Ostap remained seated, however. He had not suffered such a blow for a long time.

"You're asked to leave."

The auctioneer's singsong voice was firm.

The laughter in the room grew louder.

So they left. Few people have ever left an auction room with more bitterness.

Vorobyaninov went first. With his bony shoulders

hunched up, and in his shrunken jacket and silly baronial boots, he walked like a crane; he felt the warm
and friendly glance of the smooth operator behind.

The concessionaires stopped in the room next to
the auction hall. They could now only watch the proceedings through a glass door. The path back was
barred. Ostap maintained a friendly silence.

"An outrageous system," murmured Ippolit Matveyevich timidly. "Downright disgraceful! We should
complain to the militia."

Ostap said nothing.

"No, but really, it's a hell of a thing." Ippolit Matveyevich continued ranting. "Making the working
people pay through the nose. Honestly! Two hundred
and thirty roubles for ten old chairs. It's mad!"

"Yes," said Ostap woodenly.

"Isn't it?" said Vorobyaninov again. "It's mad!"

"Yes."

Ostap went up close to Vorobyaninov and, having
looked around, hit the marshal a quick, hard, and unobserved blow in the side. "That's for the militia.
That's for the high price of chairs for working people
of all countries. That's for going after girls at night.
That's for being a dirty old man."

Ippolit Matveyevich took his punishment without a
sound.

From the side it looked as though a respectful son
was conversing with his father, except that the father
was shaking his head too vigorously.

"Now get out of here!"

Ostap turned his back on the director of the enterprise and began watching the auction hall. A moment
later he looked around.

Ippolit Matveyevich was still standing there, with
his hands by his sides.

"Oh! You're still here, life and soul of the party! Go
on, get out!"

"Comrade Bender," Vorobyaninov implored, "Comrade Bender!"

"Go on, go! And don't come back to Ivanopulo's. I'll throw you out."

Ostap did not turn around again. Something was going on in the hall which interested him so much that he opened the glass door slightly and began listening.

"That's done it," he muttered.

"What has?" asked Vorobyaninov obsequiously.

"They're selling the chairs separately, that's what. Maybe you'd like to buy one? Go ahead, I'm not stopping you. I doubt, though, whether they'll let you in. And you haven't much money, I gather."

In the meantime, in the auction hall, the auctioneer, feeling that he would be unable to make any member of the public cough up two hundred roubles all at once (too large a sum for the small fry left), decided to obtain his price in bits and pieces. The chairs came up for auction again, but this time in lots.

"Four chairs from a palace. Made of walnut. Upholstered. Made by Hambs. Thirty roubles. Who'll give me more?"

Ostap had soon regained his former power of decision and sang-froid.

"You stay here, you ladies' favorite, and don't go away. I'll be back in five minutes. You stay here and see who buys the chairs. Don't miss a single one."

Ostap had thought of a plan—the only one possible under the difficult circumstances facing them.

He hurried out into the Petrovka, made for the nearest asphalt vat, and had a businesslike conversation with some waifs.

Five minutes later he was back as promised with the waifs waiting ready at the entrance to the auction rooms.

"They're being sold," whispered Ippolit Matveyevich. "Four and then two have already gone."

"See what you've done!" said Ostap. "Be glad. We had them in our hands . . . in our hands, don't you realize!"

From the hall came a squeaky voice of the kind endowed only to auctioneers, croupiers, and glaziers.

". . . and a half on my left. Three. One more chair from the palace. Walnut. In perfect condition. And a half on the right. Going for three and a half in front."

Three chairs were sold separately. The auctioneer announced the sale of the last chair. Ostap choked with fury. He let fly at Vorobyaninov again. His abusive remarks were full of bitterness. Who knows how far Ostap might not have gone in this satirical exercise had he not been interrupted by the approach of a man in a brown Lodz suit. He waved his plump hands, bowed, and jumped up and down and backward and forward as though playing tennis.

"Tell me, is there really an auction here?" he asked Ostap hurriedly. "Yes? An auction. And are they really selling things here? Wonderful."

The stranger jumped backward, his face wreathed with smiles.

"So they're really selling things here? And one can buy cheaply? First rate. Very, very much so. Ah!"

Swinging his hips, the stranger rushed into the hall past the bewildered concessionaires and bought the last chair so quickly that Vorobyaninov could only croak. With the receipt in his hand the stranger ran up to the collection counter.

"Tell me, do I get the chair now? Wonderful! Ah! Ah!"

Bleating endlessly and moving about the whole time, the stranger loaded the chair onto a cab and drove off. A waif ran behind, hot on his trail.

The new chair owners gradually dispersed by cab and on foot. Ostap's junior agents hared after them. Ostap himself left and Vorobyaninov timidly followed him. The day had been like a nightmare. Everything had happened so quickly and not at all as anticipated.

On Sivtsev Vrazhek, pianos, mandolins, and accordions were celebrating the spring. Windows were wide open. Flower pots lined the windowsills. Displaying his hairy chest, a fat man stood by a window in his suspenders and sang. A cat slowly made its way along a wall. Kerosene lamps blazed above the food stalls.

Nicky was strolling about outside the little pink house. Seeing Ostap, who was walking in front, he greeted him politely and then went up to Vorobyaninov. Ippolit Matveyevich greeted him cordially. Nicky, however, was not going to waste time.

"Good evening," he said and, unable to control himself, boxed Ippolit Matveyevich's ears. As he did so he uttered a phrase, which in the opinion of Ostap, who was witnessing the scene, was a rather vulgar one.

"That's what everyone will get," said Nicky in a childish voice, "who tries . . ."

Who tries exactly what, Nicky did not specify. He stood on tiptoe and, closing his eyes, slapped Vorobyaninov's face.

Ippolit Matveyevich raised his elbow slightly but did not dare utter a sound.

"That's right," said Ostap, "and now on the neck. Twice. That's it. Can't be helped. Sometimes the eggs have to teach a lesson to the chicken that gets out of hand. Once more, that's it. Don't be shy. Don't hit him any more on the head, it's his weakest point."

If the Stargorod conspirators had seen the master mind and father of Russian democracy at that crucial moment, it can be taken for certain that the secret alliance of the "Sword and Plowshare" would have ended its existence.

"That's enough, I think," said Nicky, hiding his hand in his pocket.

"Just once more," implored Ostap.

"To hell with him. He'll know next time."

Nicky went away. Ostap went upstairs to Ivanopu-

lo's and looked down. Ippolit Matveyevich stood sideways to the house, leaning against the iron railing of
the embassy.

"Citizen Michelson," he called. "Konrad Karlovich.
Come inside. I permit you."

Ippolit Matveyevich entered the room in slightly
better spirits. "Unheard-of impudence," he exclaimed
angrily. "I could hardly control myself."

"Dear, dear," sympathized Ostap. "What has the
modern youth come to? Terrible young people! Chase
after other people's wives. Spend other people's
money. Complete decadence. But tell me, does it really
hurt when they hit you on the head?"

"I'll challenge him to a duel!"

"Fine! I can recommend a good friend of mine. He
knows the dueling code by heart and has two brooms
quite suitable for a struggle to the death. You can have
Ivanopulo and his neighbor on the right as seconds.
He's an ex-honorary citizen of the city of Kologriv
and still even brags about the title. Or you can have a
duel with meat grinders—it's more elegant. Each
wound is definitely fatal. The wounded adversary is
automatically turned into a meat ball. How do you
like the idea, Marshal?"

At that moment there was a whistle from the street
and Ostap went down to receive the reports from his
young agents.

The waifs had coped splendidly with their mission.
Four chairs had gone to the Columbus theater. The
waif explained in detail how the chairs were transported in a wheelbarrow, unloaded, and carted into
the building through the stage door. Ostap already
knew the location of the theater.

Another young pathfinder said that two chairs had
been taken away in a cab. The boy did not seem to be
very bright. He knew the street where the chair had
been taken and even remembered the number of the

apartment was 17, but could not remember the number of the house.

"I ran too quick," said the waif. "It went out of my head."

"You won't get any money," declared the boss.

"But, mister! I'll show you the place."

"All right, stay here. We'll go there together."

The citizen with the bleat turned out to live on Sadovaya Spasskaya. Ostap jotted down the exact address in a notebook.

The eighth chair had been taken to the House of the Peoples. The boy who had followed this chair proved to have initiative. Overcoming barriers in the form of the commandant's office and numerous messengers, he had found his way into the building and discovered the chair had been bought by the editor of the *Lathe* newspaper.

Two boys had not yet come back. They arrived almost simultaneously, panting and tired.

"Barrack Street in the Clear Lakes district."

"Number?"

"Nine. And the apartment is nine. There were Tatars living in the yard next door. I carried the chair the last part of the way. We went on foot."

The final messenger brought sad tidings. At first everything had been all right, but then everything had gone all wrong. The purchaser had taken his chair into the freight yard of October Station and it had not been possible to slip in after him, as there were armed soldiers of the special military region of the ministry of transport standing at the gates.

"He left by train, most likely," said the waif, concluding his report.

This greatly disconcerted Ostap. Rewarding the waifs royally, one rouble each (except for the herald from Varsonofefsky Street, who had forgotten the number and was told to come back the next day), the

technical adviser went back inside and, ignoring the
many questions put to him by the disgraced chairman
of the board, began to scheme.

"Nothing's lost yet. We have the addresses and
there are many old and reliable tricks for getting the
chairs: simple friendship; a love affair; friendship with
housebreaking; barter; and money. The last is the
most reliable. But there isn't much money."

Ostap glanced ironically at Ippolit Matveyevich.
The smooth operator had regained his usual clarity
of thought and mental balance. It would, of course, be
possible to get the money. Their reserve included the
picture "Chamberlain Answers the Bolsheviks," the
tea strainer, and full opportunity for continuing a career of polygamy.

The only trouble was the tenth chair. There was a
trail to follow, but only a diffuse and vague one.

"Well, anyway," Ostap decided aloud, "we can easily bet on those odds. I'll stake nine to one. The hearing is continued. Do you hear? You, member of the
jury?"

Ellochka the Cannibal

WILLIAM SHAKESPEARE's vocabulary has been estimated by the experts at twelve thousand words. The vocabulary of a Negro from the Mumbo Jumbo tribe amounts to three hundred words.

Ellochka Shukin managed easily and fluently on thirty.

Here are the words, phrases, and interjections which she fastidiously picked from the great, rich, and expressive Russian language:

1. Don't be rude.

2. Ho-ho (expresses irony, surprise, delight, loathing, joy, contempt, and satisfaction, according to the circumstances).

3. Great!

4. Dismal (applied to everything—for example: "dismal Pete has arrived," "dismal weather," or a "dismal cat").

5. Gloom.

6. Ghastly (for example: when meeting a close female acquaintance, "a ghastly meeting").

7. Kid (applied to all male acquaintances, regardless of age or social position).

8. Don't tell me how to live!

9. Like a child ("I beat him like a child" when playing cards, or "I brought him down like a child," evidently when talking to a lease holder).

10. Ter-r-rific!

11. Fat and good-looking (used to describe both
animate and inanimate objects).

12. Let's go by horse-cab (said to her husband).

13. Let's go by taxi (said to male acquaintances).

14. You're all white at the back! (joke).

15. Just imagine!

16. Ula (added to a name to denote affection—for
example: Mishula, Zinula).

17. Oho! (irony, surprise, delight, loathing, joy,
contempt, and satisfaction).

The extraordinarily small number of words remaining were used as connecting links between Ellochka
and department-store assistants.

If you looked at the photographs of Ellochka Shukin which her husband, engineer Ernest Pavlovich
Shukin, had hanging over his bed (one profile and the
other full face), you would easily see her pleasantly
high and curved forehead, big liquid eyes, the cutest
little nose in the whole of the province of Moscow, and
a chin with a small beauty spot.

Men found Ellochka's height flattering. She was
petite, and even the puniest little men looked hefty
he-men beside her.

She had no particular distinguishing features; she
did not need them. She was pretty.

The two hundred roubles which her husband earned
each month at the Electroluster factory was an insult to Ellochka. It was of no help at all in the tremendous battle which she had been waging for the past
four years since the time when she acquired the social
status of housewife and Shukin's wife. The battle was
waged at full pressure. It absorbed all her resources.
Ernest Pavlovich took home work to do in the eve-

ning, refused to have servants, lit the primus himself, put out the trash, and even cooked meat balls.

But it was all useless. A dangerous enemy was ruining the household more and more every year. Four years earlier Ellochka had noticed that she had a rival across the ocean. The misfortune had come upon Ellochka one happy evening while she was trying on a very pretty crepe de chine blouse. It made her look almost a goddess.

"Ho-ho!" she exclaimed, summing up by that cannibal cry the amazingly complex emotions which had overcome her.

More simply, the emotions could have been expressed by the following: men will become excited when they see me like this. They will tremble. They will follow me to the edge of the world, hiccuping with love. But I shall be cold. Are you really worthy of me? I am still the prettiest girl of all. No one in the world has such an elegant blouse as this.

But there were only thirty words, so Ellochka selected the most expressive one—"Ho-ho!"

It was at this hour of greatness that Fimka Sóbak came to see her. She brought with her the icy breath of January and a French fashion magazine. Ellochka got no further than the first page. A glossy photograph showed the daughter of the American billionaire, Vanderbilt, in an evening dress. It showed furs and plumes, silks and pearls, an unusually simple cut and a stunning hairdo. That settled everything.

"Oho!" said Ellochka to herself.

That meant "she or me."

The next morning found Ellochka at the hairdresser's, where she relinquished her beautiful black plait and had her hair dyed red. Then she was able to climb another step up the ladder leading her to the glittering paradise frequented by billionaires' daughters, who were not fit to hold a candle to housewife Shukin. A dog skin made to look like muskrat was bought with a loan and added the finishing touch to the evening dress.

Mister Shukin, who had long cherished the dream of buying a new drawing board, became rather depressed.

The dog-trimmed dress was the first well-aimed blow at Miss Vanderbilt. The snooty American girl was then dealt three more in succession. Ellochka bought a chinchilla tippet (Russian rabbit caught in Tula Province) from Fimka Sóbak, a private furrier, acquired a hat made of dove-gray Argentine felt, and converted her husband's new jacket into a stylish tunic. The billionaire's daughter was shaken, but the affectionate Daddy Vanderbilt had evidently come to the rescue.

The latest number of the magazine contained a portrait of the cursed rival in four different styles: 1) in black-brown fox; 2) with a diamond star on her forehead; 3) in a flying suit (high boots, a very thin green coat and gauntlets, the tops of which were encrusted with medium-size emeralds), and 4) in a ball dress (cascades of jewelry and a little silk).

Ellochka mustered her forces. Daddy Shukin obtained a loan from the mutual-assistance fund, but they would only give him thirty roubles. The desperate new effort radically undermined the household economy. The battle had to be waged on all fronts. Not long before some snapshots of the Miss in her new castle in Florida had been received. Ellochka, too, had to acquire new furniture. She bought two upholstered chairs at an auction. (Successful buy! Wouldn't have missed it for the world.) Without asking her husband, Ellochka took the money from the dinner funds. There were ten days and four roubles left to the fifteenth.

Ellochka transported the chairs down Varsonofefsky Street in style. Her husband was not at home, but soon arrived carrying a brief case.

"The dismal husband has arrived," said Ellochka distinctly.

All her words were pronounced distinctly and popped out as smartly as peas from a pod.

"Hello, Ellochka, what's all this? Where did the chairs come from?"

"Ho-ho!"

"No, really?"

"Ter-r-rific!"

"Yes, they're nice chairs.

"Great!"

"A present from someone?"

"Oho!"

"What? Do you mean you bought them? Where did the money come from? The housekeeping money? But I've told you a thousand times . . ."

"Ernestula, don't be rude!"

"How could you do a thing like that? We won't have anything to eat!"

"Just imagine!"

"But it's outrageous! You're living beyond your means."

"You're kidding."

"No, no. You're living beyond your means."

"Don't tell me how to live!"

"No, let's have a serious talk. I get two hundred roubles . . ."

"Gloom!"

"I don't take bribes, don't steal money, and don't know how to counterfeit it. . . ."

"Ghastly!"

Ernest Pavlovich dried up.

"The point is this," he said after a while; "we can't go on this way."

"Ho-ho!" said Ellochka, sitting down on the new chair.

"We will have to get a divorce."

"Just imagine!"

"We're not compatible. I . . ."

"You're a fat and good-looking kid."

"How many times have I told you not to call me a kid."

"You're kidding!"

"And where did you get that idiotic jargon from?

"Don't tell me how to live!"

"Oh, hell!" cried the engineer.

"Don't be rude, Ernestula!"

"Let's get divorced peaceably."

"Oho!"

"You won't prove anything to me. This argument . . ."

"I'll beat you like a child."

"No, this is absolutely intolerable. Your arguments cannot prevent me from taking the step forced upon me. I'm going to get the moving man."

"You're kidding!"

"We'll divide up the furniture equally."

"Ghastly!"

"You'll get a hundred roubles a month. Even a hundred and twenty. The room will be yours. Live how you like, I can't go on this way."

"Great!" said Ellochka with contempt.

"I'll move in with Ivan Alexeyevich."

"Oho!"

"He's gone to the country and left me his apartment for the summer. I have the key. . . . Only there's no furniture."

"Ter-r-rific!"

Five minutes later Ernest Pavlovich came back with the janitor.

"I'll leave the wardrobe. You need it more. But I'll have the desk, if you don't mind. And take this chair, janitor. I'll take one of the chairs. I think I have the right to, don't I?"

Ernest Pavlovich gathered his things into a large bundle, wrapped his boots up in paper, and turned toward the door.

"You're all white at the back," said Ellochka in a phonographic voice.

"Goodbye, Ella."

He hoped that this time at least his wife would refrain from her usual metallic vocables. Ellochka also felt the seriousness of the occasion. She strained herself, searching for suitable words for the parting. They soon came to mind.

"Going by taxi? Ter-r-rific!"

The engineer hurtled downstairs like an avalanche.

Ellochka spent the evening with Fimka Sóbak. They discussed a singularly important event which threatened to upset world economy.

"It seems they will be worn long and wide," said Fimka, sinking her head into her shoulders like a hen. "Gloom!"

Ellochka looked admiringly at Fimka Sóbak. Mlle Sobak was reputed to be a cultured girl and her vocabulary contained about a hundred and eighty words. One of the words was one that Ellochka would not even have dreamed of. It was the meaningful word "homosexuality."

Fimka Sóbak was undoubtedly a cultured girl.

The animated conversation lasted well into the night.

At ten the next morning the smooth operator arrived at Varsonofefsky Street. In front of him ran the waif from the day before. He pointed out the house.

"You're not telling stories?"

"Of course not, mister. In there, through the front door."

Bender gave the boy an honestly earned rouble.

"That's not enough," said the boy, like a cabdriver.

"The ears of a dead donkey. Get them from Pushkin. On your way, defective one!"

Ostap knocked at the door without the least idea of what excuse he would use for his visit. In conversations with young ladies he preferred inspiration.

"Oho?" asked a voice behind the door.

"On business," replied Ostap.

The door opened and Ostap went into a room which could only have been furnished by someone with the imagination of a woodpecker. The walls were covered with picture postcards of film stars, dolls, and Tambov tapestries. Against this dazzling background it was difficult to make out the little occupant of the room. She was wearing a gown made from one of Ernest Pavlovich's shirts, trimmed with some mysterious fur.

Ostap knew at once how he should behave in such high society. He closed his eyes and took a step backward. "A beautiful fur!" he exclaimed.

"You're kidding," said Ellochka tenderly. "It's Mexican jerboa."

"It can't be. You were deceived. You were given a much better fur. It's Shanghai leopard. Yes, leopard. I recognize it by the shade. You see how it reflects the sun. Just like emerald!"

Ellochka had dyed the Mexican jerboa with green water color herself and so the morning visitor's praise was particularly pleasing.

Without giving her time to recover, the smooth operator poured out everything he had ever heard about furs. After that they discussed silk, and Ostap promised to make his charming hostess a present of several thousand silkworms which he claimed had been brought for him by the chairman of the Central Executive Committee of Uzbekistan.

"You're the right kind of kid," observed Ellochka as a result of the first few minutes of friendship.

"You're surprised, of course, by this early visit by a stranger."

"Ho-ho!"

"But I've come on a delicate matter."

"You're kidding."

"You were at the auction yesterday and made a remarkable impression on me."

"Don't be rude!"

"Heavens! To be rude to such a charming woman would be inhuman."

"Ghastly!"

The conversation continued along these lines, now and then producing splendid results.

But all the time Ostap's compliments became briefer and more watery. He had noticed that the second chair was not there. It was up to him to find a clue. By interspersing his questions with flowery Eastern flattery he found out all about the events of the day before in Ellochka's life.

"Something new," he thought, "the chairs are crawling around like roaches."

"Sell me the chair, dear lady," said Ostap unexpectedly. "I like it very much. Only with your woman's intuition could you have chosen such an artistic object. Sell it to me, young lady, and I'll give you seven roubles."

"Don't be rude, kid," said Ellochka slyly.

"Ho-ho!" said Ostap, trying to make her understand.

"I must approach her differently," he decided. "Let's suggest an exchange."

"You know that in Europe now and in the best homes in Philadelphia they've reintroduced the ancient custom of pouring tea through a strainer? It's remarkably effective and elegant."

Ellochka pricked up her ears.

"A diplomat I know has just arrived back from Vienna and brought me one as a present. It's an amusing thing."

"It must be great," said Ellochka with interest.

"Oho! Ho-ho! Let's make an exchange. You give me the chair and I'll give you the tea strainer. Do you want to?"

The sun rolled about in the strainer like an egg. Spots of light danced on the ceiling. A dark corner of the room was suddenly lit up. The strainer made the same overwhelming impression on Ellochka as an old tin can makes on a Mumbo Jumbo cannibal. In such circumstances the cannibal shouts at the top of his voice. Ellochka, however, merely uttered a quiet "Ho-ho."

Without giving her time to recover, Ostap put the strainer down on the table, took the chair, and having found out the address of the charming lady's husband, courteously bowed his way out.

Absalom Vladimirovich Iznurenkov

THERE FOLLOWED a busy time for the concessionaires. Ostap contended that the chairs should be struck while the iron was hot. Ippolit Matveyevich was granted an amnesty, although Ostap, from time to time, would ask him such questions as:

"Why the hell did I ever take up with you? What do I need you for, anyway? You ought to go home to your registry office where the corpses and newborn babies are waiting for you. Don't make the infants suffer. Go back there!"

But in his heart the smooth operator had become very much attached to the wild marshal. "Life wouldn't be such fun without him," he thought. And he would glance now and then at Ippolit Matveyevich, whose head was just beginning to sprout a new crop of silvery hair.

Ippolit Matveyevich's initiative was allotted a fair share of the work schedule. As soon as the placid Ivanopulo had gone out, Bender would try to drum into his partner's head the surest way to get the treasure.

"Act boldly. Don't ask too many questions. Be more cynical—people like it. Don't do anything through a third party. People are smart. No one's going to hand you the jewels on a plate. But don't do anything criminal. We've got to keep on the right side of the law."

The search progressed, however, without any great
success. The criminal code plus a large number of
bourgeois prejudices retained by the citizens of the
capital made things difficult. People just could not
tolerate nocturnal visits through their windows, for
instance. The work could only be done legally.

The same day that Ostap visited Ellochka Shukin
a new piece of furniture appeared in Ivanopulo's room.
It was the chair bartered for the tea strainer, the third
trophy of the expedition. The partners had long since
passed the stage where the hunt for the jewels aroused
strong feelings in them, where they clawed open the
chairs and gnawed the springs.

"Even if there's nothing in them," Ostap said, "you
must realize we've earned at least ten thousand roubles.
Every chair opened increases our chances. What does
it matter if there's nothing in the little lady's chair?
We don't have to break it to pieces. Let Ivanopulo furnish his room with it. It will be pleasanter for us too."

That day the concessionaires trooped out of the
little pink house and went off in different directions.
Ippolit Matveyevich was entrusted with the stranger
with the bleat from Sadovaya Spasskaya Street; he was
given twenty-five roubles to cover expenses, ordered
to keep out of bars and not to come back without the
chair. For himself the smooth operator chose Ellochka's
husband.

Ippolit Matveyevich crossed the city in a no. 6 bus.
As he bounced up and down on the leather seat, almost
hitting his head against the roof, he wondered how he
would find out the bleating stranger's name, what excuse to make for visiting him, what his first words
should be and how to get to the point.

Alighting at the Red Gates, he found the right house
from the address Ostap had written down, and began
walking up and down outside. He could not bring

himself to go inside. It was an old, dirty Moscow hotel, which had been converted into a housing co-operative, and was resided in, to judge by the shabby frontage, by tenants who persistently avoided their payments.

For a long time Ippolit Matveyevich remained by the entrance, continually approaching and reading the handwritten notice threatening neglectful tenants until he knew it by heart; then, finally, still unable to think of anything, he went up the stairs to the second floor. There were several doors along the corridor. Slowly, as though going up to the blackboard in school to prove a theorem he had not properly learned, Ippolit Matveyevich approached room 41. A visiting card was pinned upside-down to the door by one thumbtack.

```
ʌOʞИƎᴚՈNZI

qɔıʌoɹıɯıpɐ⅂Λ ɯolɐsq∀
```

In a complete daze, Ippolit Matveyevich forgot to knock. He opened the door, took three zombie-like steps forward and found himself in the middle of the room.

"Excuse me," he said in a strangled voice, "can I see Comrade Iznurenkov?"

Absalom Vladimirovich did not reply. Vorobyaninov raised his head and saw there was no one in the room.

It was not possible to guess the proclivities of the occupant from the outward appearance of the room. The only thing that was clear was that he was a bachelor and had no domestic help. On the window-sill lay a piece of paper containing bits of sausage skin. The low divan by the wall was piled with newspapers. There were a few dusty books on the small bookshelf. Photographs of tomcats, little cats, and female cats looked down from the walls. In the middle of the room, next to a pair of dirty shoes which had toppled over sideways, was a walnut chair. Crimson wax seals dangled from all the pieces of furniture, including the chair from the Stargorod mansion. Ippolit Matveyevich paid no attention to this. He immediately forgot about the criminal code and Ostap's admonition, and ran toward the chair.

At this moment the papers on the divan began to stir. Ippolit Matveyevich started back in fright. The papers moved a little way and fell onto the floor; from beneath them emerged a small, placid tomcat. It looked uninterestedly at Ippolit Matveyevich and began to wash itself, catching at its ear, face, and whiskers with its paw.

"Bah!" said Ippolit Matveyevich and dragged the chair toward the door. The door opened for him and there on the threshold stood the occupant of the room, the stranger with the bleat. He was wearing a coat under which could be seen a pair of lilac shorts. He was carrying his pants in his hand.

It could be said that there is no one like Absalom Vladimirovich Iznurenkov in the whole Republic. The Republic valued his services. He was of great use to it. But, for all that, he remained unknown, though he was just as skilled in his art as Chaliapin was in singing, Gorky in writing, Capablanca in chess, Melnikov in ice-skating, and that very large-nosed and brown Assyrian occupying the best place on the corner of Tverskaya and Kamerger streets was in cleaning black boots with brown polish.

Chaliapin sang. Gorky wrote great novels. Capablanca prepared for his match against Alekhine. Melnikov broke records. The Assyrian made citizens' shoes shine like mirrors. Absalom Iznurenkov made jokes.

He never made them without reason, just for the effect. He made them to order for humorous journals. On his shoulders he bore the responsibility for highly important campaigns, and supplied most of the Moscow satirical journals with subjects for cartoons and humorous anecdotes.

Great men make jokes twice in their lifetime. The jokes increase their fame and go down in history. Iznurenkov produced no less than sixty first-rate jokes a month, which everyone retold with a smile, but he nonetheless remained in obscurity. Whenever one of Iznurenkov's witticisms was used as a caption for a cartoon, the glory went to the artist. The artist's name was placed above the cartoon. Iznurenkov's name did not appear.

"It's terrible," he used to cry. "It's impossible for me to sign my name. What am I supposed to sign? Two lines?"

And he continued his virulent campaign against the enemies of society—dishonest members of co-operatives, embezzlers, Chamberlain, and bureaucrats. He aimed his sting at bootlickers, apartment-block superintendents, owners of private property, hooligans, citizens reluctant to lower their prices, and industrial executives who tried to avoid economy drives.

As soon as the journals came out, the jokes were repeated in the circus arena, reprinted in the evening press without reference to the source, and offered to audiences from the variety stage by "entertainers writing their own words and music."

Iznurenkov managed to be funny about fields of activity in which you would not have thought it was possible to say anything funny. From the arid desert of excessive increases in the cost of production Iznurenkov managed to extract a hundred or so masterpieces of wit. Heine would have given up in despair had he been asked to say something funny and at the same time socially useful about the unfair tariff rates on slow-delivery freight consignments; Mark Twain would have fled from the subject, but Iznurenkov remained at his post. He chased from one editorial office to another, bumping into ash-tray stands and bleating. In ten minutes the subject had been worked out, the cartoon devised, and the caption added.

When he saw a man in his room just about to remove the chair with the seal, Absalom Iznurenkov waved his pants, which had just been pressed at the tailor's, gave a jump, and screeched: "That's ridiculous! I protest! You have no right. There's a law, after all. It's not intended for fools, but you may have heard the furniture can stay another two weeks! I shall complain to the Public Prosecutor. After all, I'm going to pay!"

Ippolit Matveyevich stood motionless, while Iznurenkov threw off his coat and, without moving away from the door, pulled on the pants over his fat, Chichikovian legs. Iznurenkov was portly, but his face was thin.

Vorobyaninov had no doubt in his mind that he was about to be seized and hauled off to the police. He was therefore very surprised when the occupant of the room, having adjusted his dress, suddenly became calmer.

"You must understand," he said in a tone of conciliation, "I cannot agree to it."

Had he been in Iznurenkov's shoes, Ippolit Matveyevich would certainly not have agreed to his chairs being stolen in broad daylight either. But he did not know what to say, so he kept silent.

"It's not my fault. It's the fault of the musicians' organization. Yes, I admit I didn't pay for the hired piano for eight months. But at least I didn't sell it, although there was plenty of opportunity. I was honest, but they behaved like crooks. They took away the piano, and then went to court about it and had an inventory of my furniture made. There's nothing to put on the inventory. All this furniture constitutes work tools. The chair is a work tool as well."

Ippolit Matveyevich was beginning to see the light.

"Put that chair down!" screeched Iznurenkov suddenly. "Do you hear, you bureaucrat?"

Ippolit Matveyevich obediently put down the chair and mumbled: "I'm sorry, there's been a misunderstanding. It often happens in this kind of work!"

At this Iznurenkov brightened up terrifically. He began running about the room singing: "And in the morning she smiled again before her window." He did not know what to do with his hands. They flew all over the place. He started tying his tie, then left off without finishing. He took up a newspaper, then threw it on the floor without reading anything.

"So you aren't going to take away the furniture today? . . . Good . . . Ah! Ah!"

Taking advantage of this favorable turn of events, Ippolit Matveyevich moved toward the door.

"Wait!" called Iznurenkov suddenly. "Have you ever seen such a cat? Tell me, isn't it really extraordinarily fluffy?"

Ippolit Matveyevich found the cat in his trembling hands.

"First rate," babbled Absalom Vladimirovich, not knowing what to do with his excess of energy. "Ah! Ah!"

He rushed to the window, clapped his hands, and began making slight but frequent bows to two girls who were watching him from a window of the house opposite. He stamped his feet and gave sighs of longing.

"Girls from the suburbs! The finest fruit! . . . First rate! . . . Ah! . . . 'And in the morning she smiled again before her window.' "

"I'm leaving now, Citizen," said Ippolit Matveyevich stupidly.

"Wait, wait!" Iznurenkov suddenly became excited. "Just one moment! Ah! Ah! The cat . . . Isn't it extraordinarily fluffy? Wait . . . I'll be with you in a moment."

He dug into all his pockets with embarrassment, ran
to the side, came back, looked out of the window, ran
aside, and again returned.

"Forgive me, my dear fellow," he said to Vorobyaninov, who had stood with folded arms like a soldier
during all these operations.

With these words he handed the marshal a half-
rouble piece.

"No, no, please don't refuse. All labor must be rewarded."

"Much obliged," said Ippolit Matveyevich, surprised
at his own resourcefulness.

"Thank you, dear fellow. Thank you, dear friend."

As he went down the corridor, Ippolit Matveyevich
could hear bleating, screeching, and shouts of delight
coming from Iznurenkov's room.

Outside in the street, Vorobyaninov remembered
Ostap, and trembled with fear.

Ernest Pavlovich Shukin was wandering about the
empty apartment obligingly loaned to him by a friend
for the summer, trying to decide whether or not to
have a bath.

The three-room apartment was at the very top of a
nine-story building. The only thing in it besides a desk
and Vorobyaninov's chair was a pier glass. It reflected
the sun and hurt his eyes. The engineer lay down on
the desk and immediately jumped up again. It was red-
hot.

"I'll go and have a wash," he decided.

He undressed, felt cooler, inspected himself in the
mirror, and went into the bathroom. A coolness enveloped him. He climbed into the bath, doused himself with water from a blue enamel mug, and soaped
himself generously. Covered in lather, he looked like
a Christmas-tree decoration.

"Feels good," said Ernest Pavlovich.

Everything was fine. It was cool. His wife was not there. He had complete freedom ahead of him. The engineer knelt down and turned on the faucet in order to wash off the soap. The faucet gave a gasp and began making slow, undecipherable noises. No water came out. Ernest Pavlovich inserted a slippery little finger into the faucet. Out poured a thin stream of water and then nothing more. Ernest Pavlovich frowned, stepped out of the bath, lifting each leg in turn, and went into the kitchen. Nothing was forthcoming from the faucet there, either.

Ernest Pavlovich shuffled through the rooms and stopped in front of the mirror. The soap was stinging his eyes, his back itched, and suds were dripping onto the floor. Listening to make certain there was still no water running in the bath, he decided to call the janitor.

"He can at least bring up some water," decided the engineer, wiping his eyes and slowly getting furious, "or else I'm in a mess."

He looked out of the window. Down below, at the bottom of the well of the building, there were some children playing.

"Janitor!" shouted Ernest Pavlovich. "Janitor!"

No one answered.

Then Ernest Pavlovich remembered that the janitor lived at the front of the building under the stairway. He stepped out onto the cold tiled floor and, keeping the door open with one arm, leaned over the banister. There was only one apartment on that landing, so Ernest Pavlovich was not afraid of being seen in his strange suit of soapsuds.

"Janitor!" he shouted downstairs.

The word rang out and reverberated noisily down the stairs.

"Hoo-hoo!" it echoed.

"Janitor! Janitor!"

"Hum-hum! Hum-hum!"

It was at this point that the engineer, impatiently shifting from one bare foot to the other, suddenly slipped and, to regain his balance, let go of the door.

The brass bolt of the Yale lock clicked into place and the door shut fast. The wall shook. Not appreciating the irrevocable nature of what had happened, Ernest Pavlovich pulled at the door handle. The door did not budge.

In dismay the engineer pulled the handle again several times and listened, his heart beating fast. There was a churchlike evening stillness. A little light still filtered through the multicolored glass of the high window.

"A fine thing to happen," thought Shukin.

"You son of a bitch" he said to the door.

Downstairs, voices broke through the silence like exploding squibs. Then came the muffled bark of a dog in one of the rooms.

Someone was pushing a baby carriage upstairs.

Ernest Pavlovich walked timidly up and down the landing.

"Enough to drive you crazy!"

It all seemed too outrageous to have actually happened. He went up to the door and listened again. Suddenly he heard a different sort of noise. At first he thought it was someone walking about in the apartment.

"Somebody may have got in through the back door," he thought, although he knew that the back door was locked and that no one could have got in.

The monotonous sound continued. The engineer held his breath and suddenly realized that the sound was that of running water. It was evidently pouring from all the faucets in the apartment. Ernest Pavlovich almost began howling.

The situation was awful. A full-grown man with a mustache and higher education was standing on a ninth-floor landing in the center of Moscow, naked except for a covering of bursting soapsuds. There was nowhere he could go. He would rather have gone to jail than show himself in that state. There was only one thing to do—hide. The bubbles were bursting and making his back itch. The lather on his face had already dried; it made him look as though he had the mange and puckered his skin like a hone.

Half an hour passed. The engineer kept rubbing himself against the whitewashed walls and groaning, and made several unsuccessful attempts to break in the door. He became dirty and horrible.

Shukin decided to go downstairs to the janitor at any price.

"There's no other way out. None. The only thing to do is hide in the janitor's room."

Breathing heavily and covering himself with his hand as men do when they enter the water, Ernest Pavlovich began creeping downstairs along the banister. He reached the landing between the eighth and ninth floors.

His body reflected multicolored rhombuses and squares of light from the window. He looked like Harlequin secretly listening to a conversation between Columbine and Pierrot. He had just turned to go down the next flight when the lock of an apartment door below snapped open and a girl came out carrying a ballet dancer's attaché case. Ernest Pavlovich was back on his landing before the girl had gone one step. He was practically deafened by the terrible beating of his heart.

It was half an hour before the engineer had recovered sufficiently to make another sortie. This time he was fully determined to rush down at full speed, ignoring everything, and reach the promised janitor's room.

He started off. Silently taking four stairs at a time, the engineer raced downstairs. On the landing of the sixth floor he stopped for a moment. This was his undoing. Someone was coming up.

"Insufferable brat!" said a woman's voice, amplified many times by the stairway. "How many times do I have to tell him!"

Obeying instinct rather than reason, like a cat pursued by dogs, Ernest Pavlovich tore up to the ninth floor again.

Back on his own landing, all covered with wet footmarks, he silently burst into tears, tearing his hair and swaying convulsively. The hot tears ran through the coating of soap and formed two wavy furrows.

"Oh, my God!" moaned the engineer. "Oh, Lord. Oh, Lord!"

There was no sign of life. Then he heard the noise of a truck going up the street. So there was life somewhere!

Several times more he tried to bring himself to go downstairs, but his nerve gave way each time. He might as well have been in a burial vault.

"Someone's left a trail behind him, the pig!" he heard an old woman's voice say from the landing below.

The engineer ran to the wall and butted it several times with his head. The most sensible thing to do, of course, would have been to keep shouting until someone came, and then put himself at their mercy. But Ernest Pavlovich had completely lost his ability to reason; breathing heavily he wandered round and round the landing.

There was no way out.

: 24 :

The Automobile Club

IN THE EDITORIAL OFFICES of the large daily newspaper
Lathe, located on the second floor of the House of the
Peoples, reserve material was hurriedly being got ready
for the typesetters.

News items and articles were selected from the
reserve (material which had been set up but not included in the previous number) and the number of
lines occupied were counted up; then began the daily
haggling for space.

The newspaper was able to print forty-four hundred
lines in all on its four pages. This had to include everything: cables, articles, social events, letters from correspondents, advertisements, one satirical sketch in verse
and two in prose, cartoons, photographs, and the
special sections, such as theater, sports, chess, the
editorial, second editorial, reports from Soviet Party
and trade-union organizations, serialized novels, features on life in the capital, subsidiary items under the
title of "Snippets," popular-science articles, radio programs, and other odds and ends. In all, about ten thousand lines of material from all sections was set up, so
that the distribution of space was usually accompanied
by dramatic scenes.

The first person to run to the editor was the chess editor, Maestro Sudeikin. He posed a polite though bitter question. "What? No chess today?"

"No room," replied the editor. "There's a long special feature. Three hundred lines."

"But today's Saturday. Readers are expecting the Sunday section. I have the answers to problems, I have a splendid study by Neunyvako, and I also have—"

"All right, how much do you want?"

"Not less than a hundred and fifty."

"All right, if it's answers to problems, we'll give you sixty lines."

The maestro tried for another thirty so that at least the Neunyvako could go in (the wonderful Tartokover vs. Bogolyubov game had been lying about for a month), but was rebuffed.

Persidsky, the reporter, arrived. "Do you want some impressions of the Plenum?" he asked softly.

"Of course," cried the editor. "It was held the day before yesterday, after all!"

"I have the Plenum," said Persidsky even more softly, "and two sketches, but they won't give me any room."

"Why won't they? Who did you talk to? Have they gone crazy?"

The editor hurried off to have an argument. He was followed by Persidsky, intriguing as he went; behind them both ran a member of the advertisement section.

"We have Sekarov fluid," he cried gloomily.

The office manager trailed along after them, dragging a chair he had bought at an auction for the editor.

"The fluid can go in on Thursday. Today we're printing our supplements!"

"You won't make much from the free advertisements, while the fluid has been paid for."

"Very well, we'll clear up the matter in the night editor's office. Give the advertisement to Pasha. He's just going there."

The editor sat down to read the editorial. He was immediately interrupted from that entertaining occupation. The next to arrive was the artist.

"Aha!" said the editor, "very good! I have a subject for a cartoon in view of the latest cable from Germany."

"What about this?" said the artist. " 'The Steel Helmet and the General Situation in Germany'?"

"All right, you work something out and then show it to me."

The artist went back to his department. He took a square of drawing paper and sketched an emaciated dog in pencil. On the dog's head he drew a German helmet with a spike. Then he turned to the wording. On the animal's body he printed the word "Germany"; then he printed "Danzig Corridor" on its curly tail, "Dreams of Revenge" on its jaw, "Dawes Plan" on its collar, and "Stresemann" on its protruding tongue. In front of the dog the artist drew a picture of Poincaré holding a piece of meat in his hand. He thought of something to write on the piece of meat, but the meat was too small and the word would not fit in. Anyone less quick-witted than a cartoonist would have lost his head, but, without a second thought, the artist drew a shape like a label of the kind that is tied to the neck of a bottle near the piece of meat and wrote "French Guarantees of Security" in minute letters inside it. So that Poincaré should not be confused with any other French statesman, he wrote the word "Poincaré" on the stomach. The drawing was ready.

The desks of the art department were covered with foreign magazines, large-size pairs of scissors, and bottles of India ink and whiting. Bits of photographs—a shoulder, a pair of legs, and a section of countryside—lay about on the floor.

There were five artists who scraped the photographs with Gillette razor blades to brighten them up; they also improved the contrast by touching them up with India ink and whiting, and wrote their names and the size (3 ¾ squares, 2 columns, and so on) on the reverse side, since these directions are required in zincography.

There was a foreign delegation sitting in the chief editor's office. The office interpreter looked into the speaker's face and, turning to the chief editor, said: "Comrade Arnaud would like to know . . ."

They were discussing the running of a Soviet newspaper. While the interpreter was explaining to the chief editor what Comrade Arnaud wanted to know, Arnaud, in velvet plus fours, and all the other foreigners looked curiously at a red pen with a No. 86 nib which was leaning against the wall in the corner. The nib almost touched the ceiling and the holder was as wide as an average man's body at the thickest part. It was quite possible to write with it; the nib was a real one although it was actually bigger than a large pike.

"Hohoho!" laughed the foreigners. "Colossal!"

The pen had been presented to the editorial office by a correspondent's congress.

Sitting on Vorobyaninov's chair, the chief editor smiled and, nodding first toward the pen and then at his guests, happily explained things to them.

The clamor in the offices continued. Persidsky brought in an article by Semashko and the editor promptly deleted the chess section from the third page. Maestro Sudeikin no longer battled for Neunyvako's wonderful study; he was only concerned about saving the solutions. After a struggle more tense than his match with Lasker at the San Sebastian tournament, he won a place at the expense of "Life and the Law."

Semashko was sent to the compositors. The editor

buried himself once more in the editorial. He had decided to read it at all costs, just for the sporting
interest.

He had just reached the bit that said ". . . but the
contents of the pact are such that, if the League of
Nations registers it, we will have to admit that . . ."
when "Life and the Law," a hairy man, came up to
him. The editor continued reading, avoiding the eyes
of "Life and the Law," and making unnecessary notes
on the editorial.

"Life and the Law" went around to the other side
of him and said in a hurt voice: "I don't understand."

"Uhunh," said the editor, trying to play for time.
"What's the matter?"

"The matter is that on Wednesday there was no
'Life and the Law,' on Friday there was no 'Life and
the Law,' on Thursday you carried only a case of
alimony which you had in reserve, and on Saturday
you're leaving out a trial which has been written up
for some time in all other papers. It's only us who—"

"Which other papers?" cried the editor. "I haven't
seen it."

"It will appear again tomorrow and we'll be too
late."

"But when you were asked to report the Chubarov
case, what did you write? It was impossible to get a
line out of you. I know. You were reporting the case
for the evening paper."

"How do you know?"

"I know. I was told."

"In that case I know who told you. It was Persidsky.
The same Persidsky who blatantly uses the editorial-
office services to send material to Leningrad."

"Pasha," said the editor quietly, "fetch Persidsky."

"Life and the Law" sat indifferently on the window
ledge. In the garden behind him birds and young
skittle players could be seen busily moving about.
They litigated for some time. The editor ended the

hearing with a smart move: he threw out the chess and replaced it with "Life and the Law." Persidsky was given a warning.

It was five o'clock, the busiest time for the office.

Smoke curled above the overheated typewriters. The reporters dictated in voices harshened by their haste. The senior typist shouted at the rascals who slipped in their material unobserved and out of turn.

Down the corridor came the office poet. He was courting a typist, whose modest hips unleashed his poetic emotions. He used to lead her to the end of the corridor by the window and murmur words of love to her, to which she usually replied: "I'm working overtime today and I'm very busy."

That meant she loved another.

The poet generally got in the way and asked all his friends the same favor with monotonous regularity. "Let me have ten kopeks for the streetcar."

He sauntered into the local correspondents' room in search of the sum. Wandering about between the desks at which the readers were working, and fingering the piles of despatches, he renewed his efforts. The readers, the most hardboiled people in the office (they were made that way by the need to read through a hundred letters a day, scrawled by hands which were more used to axes, paintbrushes, and wheelbarrows than a pen), were silent.

The poet visited the despatch office and finally migrated to the clerical section. But besides not getting the ten kopeks, he was buttonholed by Avdotyev, a member of the Young Communist League, who proposed that the poet should join the Automobile Club. The poet's enamored soul was enveloped in a cloud of gasoline fumes. He took two paces to the side, changed into third gear, and disappeared from sight.

Avdotyev was not a bit discouraged. He believed in the triumph of the automobile idea. In the editor's room he carried on the struggle, on the sly, which also prevented the editor from finishing the editorial.

"Listen, Alexander Josifovich, wait a moment, it's a serious matter," said Avdotyev, sitting down on the editor's desk. "We've formed an automobile club. Would the editorial office give us a loan of five hundred roubles for eight months?"

"You need have no doubt."

"Why? Do you think it's a dead duck?"

"I don't think, I know. How many members are there?"

"A large number already."

For the moment the club only consisted of the organizer, but Avdotyev did not enlarge on this.

"For five hundred roubles we can buy a car at the 'graveyard.' Yegorov has already picked one out there. He says the repairs won't come to more than five hundred. That's a thousand altogether. So I thought of recruiting twenty people, each of whom will give fifty. Anyway, it'll be fun. We'll learn to drive. Yegorov will be the instructor and in three months' time, by August, we'll all be able to drive. We'll have a car and each one in turn can go where he likes."

"What about the five hundred for the purchase?"

"The mutual-assistance fund will provide that on interest. We'll pay it off. So I'll put you down, shall I?"

But the editor was rather bald, hard-worked, and enslaved by his family and apartment, liked to have a rest after dinner on the settee, and read *Pravda* before going to sleep. He thought for a moment and then declined.

Avdotyev approached each desk in turn and repeated his fiery speech. His words had a dubious effect on the old men, which meant for him anyone above the age of twenty. They snapped at him, excusing themselves by saying they were already friends of children and regularly paid twenty kopeks a year for the benefit of the poor mites. They would like to join, but . . .

"But what?" cried Avdotyev. "Supposing we had a car today? Yes, supposing we put down a blue six-cylinder Packard in front of you for fifteen kopeks a year, with gas and oil paid for by the government?"

"Go away," said the old men. "It's the last call, you're preventing us from working."

The automobile idea was fading and beginning to give off fumes when a champion of the new enterprise was finally found. Persidsky jumped back from the telephone with a crash and, having listened to Avdotyev, said: "You're tackling it the wrong way. Give me the sheet. Let's begin at the beginning."

Accompanied by Avdotyev, Persidsky began a new round.

"You, you old mattress," he said to a blue-eyed boy, "you don't even have to give any money. You have bonds from '27, don't you? For how much? For five hundred? All the better. You hand over the bonds to the club. The capital comes from the bonds. By August we will have cashed all the bonds and bought the car."

"What happens if my bond wins a prize?" asked the boy defiantly.

"How much do you expect to win?"

"Fifty thousand."

"We'll buy cars with the money. And the same thing if I win. And the same if Avdotyev wins. In other words, no matter whose bonds win, the money will be spent on cars. Do you understand now? You crank! You'll drive along the Georgian Military Highway in your own car. Mountains, you idiot! And 'Life and the Law,' social events, accidents, and the young lady—you know, the one who does the films—will all go rolling along behind you in their own cars as well. Well? Well? You'll be courting!"

In the depths of his heart no bond holder believes in the possibility of a win. At the same time he is

jealous of his neighbors' and friends' bonds. He is dead
scared that they will win and that he, the eternal
loser, will be left out in the cold. Hence the hope of
a win on the part of an office colleague drew the bond
holders into the new club. The only disturbing thought
was that none of their bonds would win. That seemed
rather unlikely, though, and, furthermore, the Automobile Club had nothing to lose, since one car from
the graveyard was guaranteed from the capital earned
from the bonds.

In five minutes twenty people had been recruited.
As soon as it was all over, the editor arrived, having
heard about the club's alluring prospects.

"Well, fellows," he said, "why shouldn't I put my
name down on the list?"

"Why not, old man," replied Avdotyev, "only not
on our list. We have a full complement and no new
members are being admitted for the next five years.
You'd do better to enroll yourself as a friend of children. It's cheap and sure. Twenty kopeks a year and
no need to drive anywhere."

The editor looked sheepish, remembered that he was
indeed on the old side, sighed, and went back to finish
reading the entertaining editorial.

He was stopped in the corridor by a good-looking
man with a Circassian face.

"Say, Comrade, where's the editorial office of the
Lathe?"

It was the smooth operator.

] CHAPTER [

: 25 :

Conversation
with a Naked Engineer

OSTAP'S APPEARANCE in the editorial offices was preceded by a number of events of some importance.

Not finding Ernest Pavlovich at home (the apartment was locked and the owner probably at work), the smooth operator decided to visit him later on, and in the meantime he wandered about the town. Tortured by a thirst for action, he crossed streets, stopped in squares, made eyes at militiamen, helped ladies into buses, and generally gave the impression by his manner that the whole of Moscow with its monuments, streetcars, vegetable vendors, churches, stations, and hoardings had gathered at his home for a party. He walked among the guests, spoke courteously to them, and found something nice to say to each one. So many guests at one party somewhat tired the smooth operator. Furthermore, it was after six o'clock and time to visit engineer Shukin.

But fate had decided that before seeing Ernest Pavlovich, Ostap had to be delayed a couple of hours in order to sign a statement for the militia.

On Sverdlov Square the smooth operator was knocked down by a horse. A timid white animal descended on him out of the blue and gave him a shove with its bony chest. Bender fell down, breaking out in a sweat. It was very hot. The white horse loudly apologized and Ostap briskly jumped up. His powerful frame was undamaged. This was all the more reason for a scene.

The hospitable and friendly host of Moscow was unrecognizable. He waddled up to the embarrassed old man driving the cab and punched him in his padded back. The old man took his punishment patiently. A militiaman came running up.

"I insist you report the matter," cried Ostap with emotion.

His voice had a metallic ring of a man whose most sacred feelings had been hurt. And, standing by the wall of the Maly Theater, on the very spot where there would later be a statue to the Russian dramatist Ostrovsky, Ostap signed a statement and granted a brief interview to Persidsky, who had come hurrying over. Persidsky did not shirk his arduous duties. He carefully noted down the victim's name and sped on his way.

Ostap majestically set off again. Still feeling the effects of the clash with the white horse, and experiencing a belated regret for not having been able to give the cabdriver a belt on the neck as well, Ostap reached Shukin's house and went up to the seventh floor, taking two stairs at a time. A heavy drop of liquid struck him on the head. He looked up and a thin trickle of dirty water caught him right in the eye.

"Someone needs his nose punched for tricks like that," decided Ostap.

He hurried upward. A naked man covered with white fungus was sitting by the door of Shukin's apartment with his back to the stairs. He was sitting on the tiled floor, holding his head in his hands and rocking from side to side.

The naked man was surrounded by water coming from under the apartment door.

"Oh-oh-oh," groaned the naked man. "Oh-oh-oh."

"Is it you pouring the water about?" asked Ostap irritably. "What a place to take a bath. You must be crazy!"

The naked man looked at Ostap and burst into tears.

"Listen, Citizen, instead of crying, you ought to go to the bathroom. Look at yourself. Just like a picador."

"The key," moaned the engineer.

"What key?" asked Ostap.

"Of the ap-ap-apartment."

"Where the money is?"

The naked man was hiccuping at an incredible rate.

Nothing could confuse Ostap. He began to see the light. And, finally, when he realized what had happened, he almost fell over the banister with laughter.

"So you can't get into the apartment. But it's so simple."

Trying not to dirty himself against the naked engineer, Ostap went up to the door, slid a long yellow fingernail into the Yale lock, and carefully began moving it up and down, and left and right.

The door opened noiselessly and the naked man rushed into the flooded apartment with a howl of delight.

The faucets were gushing. In the dining room the water had formed a whirlpool. In the bedroom it had made a calm lake, on which a pair of slippers were floating about as serenely as swans. Some cigarette ends had collected together in a corner like a shoal of sleepy fish.

Vorobyaninov's chair was standing in the dining room, where the flood of water was greatest. Small white waves lapped against all four legs. The chair was rocking slightly and appeared to be about to float away from its pursuer. Ostap sat down on it and drew up his feet. Ernest Pavlovich, now himself again, turned off all the faucets with a cry of "Pardon me!! Pardon me!" rinsed himself, and appeared before Bender stripped to the waist in a pair of wet pants rolled up to the knee.

"You absolutely saved my life," he exclaimed with feeling. "I apologize for not shaking your hand, but I'm all wet. You know, I almost went crazy."

"You seemed to be getting on that way."

"I found myself in a horrible situation."

And Ernest Pavlovich gave the smooth operator full details of the misfortune which had befallen him, first laughing nervously, and then becoming more sober as he relived the awful experience.

"Had you not come, I would have died," he said in conclusion.

"Yes," said Ostap, "something similar once happened to me, too. Even a bit worse."

The engineer was now so interested in anything concerned with such situations that he put down the pail in which he was collecting water, and began listening attentively.

"It was just like what happened to you," began Bender, "only it was winter, and not in Moscow, but Mirgorod during one of those merry little periods of occupation between Makhno and Tyuntyunik in '19. I was living with a family. Terrible Ukrainians! Typical property owners. A one-story house and loads of different junk. You should note that with regard to sewage and other facilities, they have only cesspools in Mirgorod. Well, one night I nipped out in my underclothes right into the snow. I wasn't afraid of catching cold—it was only going to take a moment. I nipped out and automatically closed the door behind me. It was about twenty degrees below. I knocked, but got no answer. You can't stand in one spot or you freeze. I knocked, ran about, knocked, and ran around, but there was no answer. And the thing is that not one of those devils was asleep. It was a terrible night; the dogs were howling and there was a sound of shots somewhere nearby. And there's me running about the snowdrifts in my summer shorts. I kept knocking for almost an hour. I was nearly done. And why didn't they open the door—what do you think? They were busy hiding their property and sewing up their money in cushions. They thought it was a police raid. I nearly slaughtered them afterward."

This was all very close to the engineer's heart.

"Yes," said Ostap, "so you are engineer Shukin."

"Yes, but please don't tell anyone about this. It would be awkward."

"Oh, sure! *Entre nous* and *tête à tête*, as the French say. But I came to see you for a reason, Comrade Shukin."

"I'll be extremely pleased to help you."

"*Grand merci*. It's a piddling matter. Your wife asked me to stop by and collect this chair. She said she needed it to make a pair. And she intends sending you an armchair."

"Certainly," exclaimed Ernest Pavlovich. "Only too happy. But why should you bother yourself? I can take it for you. I can do it today."

"No, no. It's no bother at all for me. I live nearby."

The engineer fussed about and saw the smooth operator as far as the door, beyond which he was afraid to go, despite the fact that the key had been carefully placed in the pocket of his wet pants.

Former student Ivanopulo was presented with another chair. The upholstery was admittedly somewhat the worse for wear, but it was nevertheless a splendid chair and exactly like the first one.

Ostap was not worried by the failure of the chair, the fourth in line. He was familiar with all the tricks of fate.

It was the chair that had vanished into the freight yard of October Station which cut like a huge dark mass through the well-knit pattern of his deductions. His thoughts about that chair were depressing and raised grave doubts.

The smooth operator was in the position of a roulette player who only bet on numbers; one of that breed of people who want to win thirty-six times their stake all at once. The situation was even worse than that. The concessionaires were playing a kind of roulette in which zero could come up eleven out of twelve times. And, what was more, the twelfth number was out of sight, and heaven knows where, and possibly contained a marvelous win.

The chain of distressing thoughts was interrupted by the advent of the director in chief. His appearance alone aroused forebodings in Ostap.

"Oho!" said the technical adviser. "I see you're making progress. Only don't joke with me. Why have you left the chair outside? To have a laugh at my expense?"

"Comrade Bender," muttered the marshal.

"Why are you trying to unnerve me? Bring it here at once. Don't you see that the new chair that I am sitting on has made your acquisition many times more valuable?"

Ostap leaned his head to one side and squinted.

"Don't torment the child," he said at length in his deep voice. "Where's the chair? Why haven't you brought it?"

Ippolit Matveyevich's muddled report was interrupted by shouts from the floor, sarcastic applause, and cunning questions. Vorobyaninov concluded his report to the unanimous laughter of the listeners.

"What about my instructions?" said Ostap menacingly. "How many times have I told you it's a sin to steal. Even back in Stargorod you wanted to rob my wife, Madame Gritsatsuyeva; even then I realized you had the character of a petty criminal. The most this propensity will ever get you is six months inside. For a master mind, and father of Russian democracy, your scale of operations isn't very grand. And here are the results. The chair has slipped through your fingers. Not only that, you've spoiled an easy job. Just try making another visit there. That Absalom will tear your head off. It's lucky for you that you were helped by that ridiculous fluke, or else you'd have been behind bars, misguidedly waiting for me to bring you things. I shan't bring you anything, so keep that in mind. What's Hecuba to me? After all, you're not my mother, sister, or lover."

Ippolit Matveyevich stood looking at the ground in acknowledgment of his worthlessness.

"The point is this, chum. I see the complete uselessness of our working together. At any rate, working with as uncultured a partner as you for forty per cent is absurd. *Volens, nevolens,* I must state new conditions."

Ippolit Matveyevich began breathing. Up to that moment he had been trying not to breathe.

"Yes, my ancient friend, you are suffering from organizational impotence and greensickness. Accordingly, your share is decreased. Honestly, do you want twenty per cent?"

Ippolit Matveyevich shook his head firmly.

"Why not? Too little for you?"

"T-too little."

"But after all, that's thirty thousand roubles. How much do you want?"

"I'll accept forty."

"Daylight robbery!" cried Ostap, imitating the marshal's intonation during their historic haggling in the janitor's room. "Is thirty thousand too little for you? You want the key of the apartment as well?"

"It's you who wants the key of the apartment," babbled Ippolit Matveyevich.

"Take twenty before it's too late, or I might change my mind. Take advantage of my good mood."

Vorobyaninov had long since lost the air of smugness with which he had begun the search for the jewels.

The ice that had started moving in the janitor's room, the ice that had crackled, cracked, and smashed against the granite embankment, had broken up and melted. It was no longer there. Instead there was a wide stretch of rushing water which bore Ippolit Matveyevich along with it, buffeting him from side to side, first knocking him against a beam, then tossing him against the chairs, then carrying him away from them. He felt inexpressible fear. Everything frightened him. Along the river floated refuse, patches of oil, broken hen coops, dead fish, and a ghastly-looking cap. Perhaps it belonged to Father Fyodor, a duck-bill cap blown off by the wind in Rostov. Who knows? The end of the path was not in sight. The former marshal of the nobility was not being washed ashore nor had he the strength or wish to swim against the stream.

He was carried out into the open sea of adventure.

Two Visits

LIKE AN unswaddled babe who clenches and un-
clenches its waxen fists without stopping, moves its
legs, waggles its cap-covered head, the size of a large
Antonov apple, and blows bubbles through its mouth,
Absalom Vladimirovich Iznurenkov was eternally in a
state of unrest. He moved his plump legs, waggled his
shaven chin, produced sighing noises, and made gestures with his hairy arms as though doing gym-
nastics on the end of strings.

He led a very busy life, appeared everywhere, and
made suggestions while tearing down the street like a
frightened chicken; he talked to himself very rapidly
as though working out the premium on a stone, iron-
roofed building. The whole secret of his life and
activity was that he was organically incapable of
concerning himself with any one matter, subject, or
thought for longer than a minute.

If his joke was not successful and did not cause
instant mirth, Iznurenkov, unlike others, did not attempt to persuade the chief editor that the joke was
good and required reflection for complete appreciation; he immediately suggested another one.

"What's bad is bad," he used to say, "and finish it off."

When in shops, Iznurenkov caused a commotion by appearing and disappearing so rapidly in front of the salespeople, and buying boxes of chocolates so expansively, that the cashier expected to receive at least thirty roubles. But Iznurenkov, dancing up and down by the cash desk and pulling at his tie as though it choked him, would throw down a crumpled three-rouble note onto the glass plate and make off, bleating gratefully.

If this man had been able to stay still for even as little as two hours, the most unexpected things might have happened.

He might have sat down at a desk and written a marvelous novel, or perhaps an application to the mutual-assistance fund for a permanent loan, or a new clause in the law on the exploitation of housing space, or a book entitled *How to Dress Well and Behave in Society*.

But he was unable to do so. His madly working legs carried him off, the pencil flew out of his gesticulating hands, and his thoughts jumped from one thing to another.

Iznurenkov ran about the room, and the seals on the furniture shook like the earrings on a gypsy dancer. A giggling girl from the suburbs sat on the chair.

"Ah! Ah!" cried Absalom Vladimirovich, "divine! Ah! Ah! First rate! You are Queen Margot."

The queen from the suburbs laughed respectfully, though she understood nothing.

"Have some chocolate, do! Ah! Ah! Charming."

He kept kissing her hands, admiring her modest attire, pushing the cat into her lap, and asking, fawningly: "He's just like a parrot, isn't he? A lion. A real lion. Tell me, isn't he extraordinarily fluffy? And his tail. It really is a huge tail, isn't it?"

The cat then went flying into the corner, and, pressing his hands to his milk-white chest, Absalom Vladimirovich began bowing to someone outside the window. Suddenly a valve popped open in his madcap mind and he began to be witty about his visitor's physical and spiritual attributes.

"Is that brooch really made of glass? Ah! Ah! What brilliance. Honestly, you dazzle me. And tell me, is Paris really a big city? Is there really an Eiffel Tower there? Ah! What hands! What a nose!"

He did not kiss the girl. It was enough for him to pay her compliments. And he talked without end. The flow of compliments was interrupted by the unexpected appearance of Ostap.

The smooth operator fiddled with a piece of paper and asked sternly: "Does Iznurenkov live here? Is that you?"

Absalom Vladimirovich peered uneasily into the stranger's stony face. He tried to read in his eyes exactly what demands were forthcoming; whether it was a fine for breaking a streetcar window during a conversation, a summons for not paying his rent, or a contribution to a magazine for the blind.

"Come on, Comrade," said Ostap harshly, "that's not the way to do things—kicking out a sheriff."

"What sheriff?" Iznurenkov was horrified.

"You know very well. I'm now going to remove the furniture. Kindly remove yourself from that chair, Citizeness," said Ostap sternly.

The young citizeness, who a moment before had been listening to verse by the most lyrical poets, rose from her seat.

"No, don't move," cried Iznurenkov, sheltering the chair with his body. "They have no right."

"You'd better not talk about rights, Citizen. You should be more conscientious. Let go of the furniture! The law must be obeyed."

With these words, Ostap seized the chair and shook it in the air.

"I'm removing the furniture," said Ostap resolutely.

"No, you're not."

"What do you mean, I'm not, when I am?" Ostap chuckled, carrying the chair into the corridor.

Absalom kissed his lady's hand and, inclining his head, ran after the severe judge. The latter was already on the way downstairs.

"And I say you have no right. By law the furniture can stay another two weeks, and it's only three days so far. I may pay!"

Iznurenkov buzzed around Ostap like a bee, and in this manner they reached the street. Absalom Vladimirovich chased the chair right up to the end of the street. There he caught sight of some sparrows hopping about by a pile of manure. He looked at them with twinkling eyes, began muttering to himself, clapped his hands, and, bubbling with laughter, said:

"First rate! Ah! Ah! What a subject!"

Engrossed in working out the subject, he gaily turned around and rushed home, bouncing as he went. He only remembered about the chair when he arrived back and found the girl from the suburbs standing in the middle of the room.

Ostap took the chair away by cab.

"Take note," he said to Ippolit Matveyevich, "the chair was obtained with my bare hands. For nothing. Do you understand?"

When they had opened the chair, Ippolit Matveyevich's spirits were low.

"The chances are continually improving," said Ostap, "but we haven't a kopek."

"Why?"

"Maybe there aren't any jewels at all."

Ippolit Matveyevich waved his hands so violently that his jacket rode up.

"In that case everything's fine. Let's hope that Ivanopulo's estate need only be increased by one more chair."

"There was something in the paper about you today, Comrade Bender," said Ippolit Matveyevich obsequiously.

Ostap frowned. He did not like the idea of his name being front-page news. "What are you blathering about? Which newspaper?"

Ippolit Matveyevich triumphantly opened the *Lathe*. "Here it is. In the section 'What Happened Today.'"

Ostap became a little calmer; he was only worried about denouncements in the sections "Our Caustic Comments" and "Take the Malefactors to Court."

Sure enough, there in nonpareil type in the section "What Happened Today" was the item:

KNOCKED DOWN BY
A HORSE

CITIZEN O. BENDER WAS KNOCKED DOWN YESTERDAY ON SVERDLOV SQUARE BY HORSE-CAB NO. 8974. THE VICTIM WAS UNHURT EXCEPT FOR SLIGHT SHOCK.

"It was the cabdriver who suffered slight shock, not me," grumbled O. Bender. "The idiots! They write and write and don't know what they're writing about. Aha! So that's the *Lathe*. Very, very pleasant. Do you realize, Vorobyaninov, that this report might have been written by someone sitting on our chair? A fine thing that is!"

The smooth operator lapsed into thought. He had found an excuse to visit the newspaper office.

Having found out from the editor that all the rooms on both sides of the corridor were occupied by the editorial offices, Ostap assumed a naïve air and made a round of the premises. He had to find out which room contained the chair.

He strode into the union committee room, where a meeting of the young motorists was in progress, but saw at once there was no chair there and moved on to the next room. In the clerical office he pretended to be waiting for a resolution; in the reporters' room he asked where it was they were selling the wastepaper as advertised; in the editor's office he asked about subscriptions, and in the humorous sketch section he wanted to know where they accepted notices concerning lost documents.

By this method he eventually arrived at the chief editor's office, where the chief editor was sitting on the concessionaires' chair bawling into a telephone.

Ostap needed time to scrutinize the terrain.

"Comrade Editor, you have published a downright slanderous statement about me."

"What slanderous statement?"

Taking his time, Ostap unfolded a copy of the *Lathe*. Glancing around at the door, he saw it had a Yale lock. By removing a small piece of glass in the door it would be possible to slip a hand through and unlock it from the inside.

The chief editor read the item which Ostap pointed out to him.

"Where do you see a slanderous statement there?"

"Of course, this bit:

> 'The victim was unhurt except
> for slight shock.' "

"I don't understand."

Ostap looked tenderly at the chief editor and the chair.

"Am I likely to be shocked by some cabdriver? You have disgraced me in the eyes of the world. You must publish an apology."

"Listen, Citizen," said the chief editor, "no one has disgraced you. And we don't publish apologies for such minor points."

"Well, I shall not let the matter rest, at any rate," said Ostap as he left the room.

He had seen all he wanted.

The Marvelous Workhouse Basket

THE STARGOROD BRANCH of the ephemeral "Sword and Plowshare" and the young toughs from Fastpack formed a line outside the "Grainproducts" meal shop.

Passers-by kept stopping.

"What's the line for?" asked the citizens.

In a tiresome line outside a shop there is always one person whose readiness to chatter increases with his distance from the shop doorway. And farthest of all stood Polesov.

"Things have reached a pretty pitch," said the fire chief. "We'll soon be eating oilcake. Even 1919 was better than this. There's only enough flour in the town for four days."

The citizens twirled their mustaches disbelievingly and argued with Polesov, quoting the Stargorod *Truth*.

Having proved to Polesov as easily as pie that there was as much flour available as they needed and that there was no need to panic, the citizens ran home, collected all their ready cash, and joined the flour line.

When they had bought up all the flour in the store, the toughs from Fastpack switched to groceries and formed a tea and sugar line.

In three days Stargorod was in the grip of a food

and commodity crisis. Representatives from the co-
operatives and state-owned trading organizations proposed that until the arrival of food supplies, already on
their way, the sale of edibles should be restricted to a
pound of sugar and five pounds of flour a head.

The next day an antidote to this was found.

At the head of the sugar line stood Alchen. Behind
him was his wife, Sashchen, Pasha Emilyevich, four
Yakovleviches and all fifteen old-women pensioners in
their woolen dresses. As soon as he had bled the store
of twenty-two pounds of sugar, Alchen led his line
across to the other co-operatives, cursing Pasha Emilyevich as he went for gobbling up his ration of one
pound of granulated sugar. Pasha poured the sugar
into his palm and transferred it to his enormous mouth.
Alchen fussed about all day. To avoid such unforeseen losses, he took Pasha from the line and put him
onto carrying the goods purchased to the local market.
There Alchen slyly sold the booty of sugar, tea, and
marquisette to the privately owned stalls.

Polesov stood in line chiefly for reasons of principle. He had no money, so he could not buy anything,
anyway. He wandered from line to line, listening to
the conversations, made nasty remarks, raised his eye-
brows significantly, and complained about conditions.
The result of his insinuations was that rumors began
to go around that some sort of underground organization had arrived from Mech and the Urals with a supply of swords and plowshares.

Governor Dyadyev made ten thousand roubles in
one day. What the chairman of the stock-exchange
committee made, even his wife did not know.

The idea that he belonged to a secret society gave
Kislarsky no rest. The rumors in the town were the last
straw. After a sleepless night, the chairman of the
stock-exchange committee made up his mind that the
only thing that could shorten his term of imprison-
ment was to make a clean breast of it.

"Listen, Henrietta," he said to his wife, "it's time to transfer the textiles to your brother-in-law."

"Why, will they really come for you?" asked Henrietta Kislarsky.

"They might. Since there isn't any freedom of trade in the country, I'll have to go to jail some time or other."

"Shall I prepare your underwear? What misery for me to have to keep taking you things. But why don't you become a Soviet employee? After all, my brother-in-law is a trade-union member and he doesn't do too badly."

Henrietta did not know that fate had promoted her husband to the rank of chairman of the stock-exchange committee. She was therefore calm.

"I may not come back tonight," said Kislarsky, "in which case bring me some things tomorrow to the jail. But please don't bring any cream cookies. What kind of fun is it eating cold tarts?"

"Perhaps you ought to take the primus?"

"Do you think I would be allowed a primus in my cell? Give me my basket."

Kislarsky had a special workhouse basket. Made to order, it was fully adapted for all purposes. When opened out, it acted as a bed, and when half open, it could be used as a table. Moreover, it could be substituted for a cupboard; it had shelves, hooks, and drawers. His wife put some cold supper and fresh underwear into the all-purpose basket.

"You don't need to see me off," said her experienced husband. "If Rubens comes for the money, tell him there isn't any. Goodbye! Rubens can wait."

And Kislarsky walked sedately out into the street, carrying the workhouse basket by the handle.

"Where are you going, Citizen Kislarsky?" Polesov hailed him.

He was standing by a telegraph pole and shouting encouragement to a post-office worker who was clambering up toward the insulators, gripping the pole with iron claws.

"I'm going to confess," answered Kislarsky.

"What about?"

"The 'Sword and Plowshare.' "

Victor Mikhailovich was speechless. Kislarsky sauntered toward the province public prosecutor's office, sticking out his little egg-shaped belly, which was encircled by a wide belt with an outside pocket.

Victor Mikhailovich flapped his wings and flew off to see Dyadyev.

"Kislarsky's a provocateur," cried Polesov. "He's just gone to squeal on us. He's even still in sight."

"What? And with his basket?" said the horrified governor of Stargorod.

"Yes."

Dyadyev kissed his wife, shouted to her that if Rubens came he was not to get any money, and raced out into the street. Victor Mikhailovich turned a circle, clucked like a hen that has just laid an egg, and rushed to find Nikesha and Vladya.

In the meantime, Kislarsky sauntered slowly along in the direction of the prosecutor's office. On the way he met Rubens and had a long talk with him.

"And what about the money?" asked Rubens.

"My wife will give it to you."

"And why are you carrying that basket?" Rubens inquired suspiciously.

"I'm going to the steam baths."

"Well, have a good steam!"

Kislarsky then called in at the state-owned candy store, formerly the Bonbons de Varsovie, drank a cup of coffee, and ate a piece of layer cake. It was time to repent. The chairman of the stock-exchange committee went into the reception room of the prosecutor's office. It was empty. Kislarsky went up to a door marked "Province Public Prosecutor" and knocked politely.

"Come in," said a familiar voice.

Kislarsky went inside and halted in amazement. His egg-shaped belly immediately collapsed and wrinkled like a date. What he saw was totally unexpected.

The desk behind which the prosecutor was sitting was surrounded by members of the powerful "Sword and Plowshare" organization. Judging from their gestures and plaintive voices, they had confessed to everything.

"Here he is," said Dyadyev, "the ringleader and Octobrist."

"First of all," said Kislarsky, putting down the basket on the floor and approaching the desk, "I am not an Octobrist; next, I have always been sympathetic toward the Soviet regime, and third, the ringleader is not me, but Comrade Charushnikov, whose address is—"

"Red Army Street!" shouted Dyadyev.

"Number three!" chorused Nikesha and Vladya.

"Inside the yard on the right!" added Polesov. "I can show you."

Twenty minutes later they brought in Charushnikov, who promptly denied ever having seen any of the persons present in the room before in his life, and then, without pausing, went on to denounce Elena Stanislavovna.

It was only when he was in his cell, wearing clean underwear and stretched out on his workhouse basket, that the chairman of the stock-exchange committee felt happy and at ease.

During the crisis Madam Gritsatsuyeva-Bender managed to stock up with enough provisions and commodities for her shop to last at least four months. Regaining her calm, she began pining once more for her young husband, who was languishing at meetings of the Junior Council of Ministers. A visit to the fortuneteller brought no reassurance.

Alarmed by the disappearance of the Stargorod Areopagus, Elena Stanislavovna dealt the cards with outrageous negligence. The cards first predicted the end of the world, then a meeting with her husband in a government institution in the presence of an enemy—the King of Spades.

What is more, the actual fortunetelling ended up rather oddly, too. Police agents arrived (Kings of Spades) and took away the prophetess to a government institution (the public prosecutor's office).

Left alone with the parrot, the widow was about to leave in confusion when the parrot struck the bars of its cage with its beak and spoke for the first time in its life.

"The times we live in!" it said sardonically, covering its head with one wing and pulling a feather from underneath.

Madam Gritsatsuyeva-Bender made for the door in fright.

A stream of heated, muddled words followed her. The ancient bird was so upset by the visit of the police and the removal of its owner that it began shrieking out all the words it knew. A prominent place in its repertoire was occupied by Victor Polesov.

"Given the absence . . ." said the parrot testily.

And, turning upside-down on its perch, it winked at the widow, who had stopped motionless by the door, as much as to say: "Well, how do you like it, widow?"

"Mother!" gasped Gritsatsuyeva.

"Which regiment were you in?" asked the parrot in Bender's voice. "Cr-r-r-rash! Europe will help us."

As soon as the widow had fled, the parrot straightened its shirt front and uttered the words which people had been trying unsuccessfully for years to make it say.

"Pretty Polly!"

The widow fled howling down the street. At her house an agile old man was waiting for her. It was Bartholomeich.

"It's about the advertisement," said Bartholomeich. "I've been here for two hours."

The heavy hoof of presentiment struck the widow a blow in the heart.

"Oh," she intoned, "it's been a grueling experience."

"Citizen Bender left you, didn't he? It was you who put the advertisement in, wasn't it?"

The widow sank onto the sacks of flour.

"How weak your constitution is," said Bartholomeich sweetly. "I'd first like to find out about the reward. . . ."

"Oh, take everything. I need nothing any more . . ." burbled the sensitive widow.

"Right, then. I know the whereabouts of your sonny boy, O. Bender. How much is the reward?"

"Take everything," repeated the widow.

"Twenty roubles," said Bartholomeich dryly.

The widow rose from the sacks. She was covered with flour. Her flour-dusted eyelashes flapped frenziedly. "How much?" she asked.

"Fifteen roubles." Bartholomeich lowered his price. He sensed it would be difficult making the wretched woman even cough up three roubles.

Trampling the sacks underfoot, the widow advanced on the old man, called upon the heavenly powers to bear witness, and with their assistance drove a hard bargain.

"Well, all right, make it five roubles. Only I want the money in advance, please: it's a rule of mine."

Bartholomeich took two newspaper clippings from his notebook and, without letting go of them, began reading.

"Take a look at these in order. You wrote 'Missing

from home . . . I implore, etc.' That's right, isn't it? That's the Stargorod *Truth*. And this is what they wrote about your little boy in the Moscow newspapers. Here . . . 'Knocked down by a horse.' No, don't smile, madam, just listen . . . 'Knocked down by a horse.' But alive. Alive, I tell you. Would I ask for money for a corpse? So that's it . . . 'Knocked down by a horse. Citizen O. Bender was knocked down yesterday on Sverdlov Square by horse-cab number 8974. The victim was unhurt except for slight shock.' So I'll give you these documents and you give me the money in advance. It's a rule of mine."

Sobbing, the widow handed over the money. Her husband, her dear husband in yellow boots lay on distant Moscow soil and a cab-horse, breathing flames, was kicking his blue worsted chest.

Bartholomeich's sensitive nature was satisfied with the decent reward. He went away, having explained to the widow that further clues to her husband's whereabouts could definitely be found at the offices of the *Lathe*, where naturally everything was known.

Letter from Father Fyodor written in Rostov at the Milky Way hot-water stall to his wife in the regional center of N.

My darling Kate,

A fresh disaster has befallen me, but I'll come to that. I received the money in good time, for which sincere thanks. On arrival in Rostov I went at once to the address. New-Ros-Cement is an enormous establishment; no one there had ever heard of Engineer Bruns. I was about to despair completely when they gave me an idea. Try the personnel office, they said. I did. Yes, they told me, we did have someone of that name; he was doing responsible work, but left us last year to go to Baku to work for As-Oil as an accident-prevention specialist.

Well, my dear, my journey will not be as brief as I expected. You write that the money is running out. It can't be helped, Catherine. It won't be long now. Have patience, pray to God, and sell my diagonal-cloth student's uniform. And there'll soon be other expenses to be borne of another nature. Be ready for everything.

The cost of living in Rostov is awful. I paid Rs. 2.25 for a hotel room. I haven't enough to get to Baku. I'll cable you from there if I'm successful.

The weather here is very hot. I carry my coat around with me. I'm afraid to leave anything in my room—they'd steal it before you had time to turn around. The people here are sharp.

I don't like Rostov. It is considerably inferior to Kharkov in population and geographical position. But don't worry, Mother, God willing, we'll take a trip to Moscow together. Then you'll see it's a completely West European city. And then we will go to live in Samara near our factory.

Has Vorobyaninov come back? Where can he be? Is Estigneyev still having meals? How's my cassock since it was cleaned? Make all our friends believe I'm at my aunt's deathbed. Write the same thing to Gulenka.

Yes! I forgot to tell you about a terrible thing that happened to me today.

I was gazing at the quiet Don, standing by the bridge and thinking about our future possessions. Suddenly a wind came up and blew my cap into the river. It was your brother's, the baker's. I was the only one to see it. I had to make a new outlay and buy an English cap for Rs. 2.50. Don't tell your brother anything about what happened. Tell him I'm in Voronezh.

I'm having trouble with my underwear. I wash it

in the evening and if it hasn't dried by the morning, I put it on damp. It's even pleasant in the present heat.

With love and kisses,
Your husband eternally,
Fedya.

The Hen and
the Pacific Rooster

PERSIDSKY THE REPORTER was busily preparing for the two-hundredth anniversary of the great mathematician Isaac Newton.

While the work was in full swing, Steve came in from "Science and Life." A plump citizeness trailed after him.

"Listen, Persidsky," said Steve, "this citizeness has come to see you about something. This way, please, lady. The comrade will explain to you."

Chuckling to himself, Steve left.

"Well?" asked Persidsky. "What can I do for you?"

Madam Gritsatsuyeva (it was she) fixed her yearning eyes on the reporter and silently handed him a piece of paper.

"So," said Persidsky, "knocked down by a horse . . . What about it?"

"The address," beseeched the widow, "wouldn't it be possible to have the address?"

"Whose address?"

"O. Bender's."

"How should I know it?"

"But the comrade said you would."

"I have no idea of it. Ask at the receptionist's."

"Couldn't you remember, Comrade? In yellow boots."

"I'm wearing yellow boots myself. In Moscow there are two hundred thousand people wearing yellow boots. Perhaps you'd like all their addresses? By all means. I'll leave what I'm doing and do it for you. In six months' time you'll know them all. I'm busy, Citizeness."

But the widow felt great respect for Persidsky and followed him down the corridor, rustling her starched petticoat and repeating her requests.

"That son of a bitch, Steve," thought Persidsky. "All right, then, I'll set the inventor of perpetual motion on him. That will make him jump."

"What can I do about it?" said Persidsky irritably, halting in front of the widow. "How do I know the address of Citizen O. Bender? Who am I, the horse that knocked him down? Or the cabdriver he punched in the back—in my presence?"

The widow answered with a vague rumbling from which it was only possible to decipher the words "Comrade" and "Please."

Activities in the House of the Peoples had already finished. The offices and corridors had emptied. Somewhere a typewriter was polishing off a final page.

"Sorry, madam, can't you see I'm busy?"

With these words Persidsky hid in the men's room. Ten minutes later he gaily emerged. Gritsatsuyeva was patiently rustling her petticoat at the corner of two corridors. As Persidsky approached, she began talking again.

The reporter grew furious.

"All right, auntie," he said, "I'll tell you where your Bender is. Go straight down the corridor, turn right, and then continue straight. You'll see a door. Ask Cherepennikov. He ought to know."

And, satisfied with his fabrication, Persidsky disappeared so quickly that the starched widow had no time to ask for further information. Straightening her petticoat, Madam Gritsatsuyeva went down the corridor.

The corridors of the House of the Peoples were so long and narrow that people walking down them inevitably quickened their pace. You could tell from anyone who passed how far they had come. If they walked slightly faster than normal, it meant the marathon had only just begun. Those who had already completed two or three corridors developed a fairly fast trot. And from time to time it was possible to see someone running along at full speed; he had reached the five-corridor stage. A citizen who had gone eight corridors could easily compete with a bird, racehorse or Nurmi, the world champion runner.

Turning to the right, the widow Gritsatsuyeva began running. The floor creaked.

Coming toward her at a rapid pace was a brown-haired man in a light-blue vest and crimson boots. From Ostap's face it was clear his visit to the House of the Peoples at so late an hour was necessitated by the special affairs of the concession. The technical adviser's plans had evidently not envisaged an encounter with his loved one.

At the sight of the widow, Ostap about-faced and, without looking around, went back, keeping close to the wall.

"Comrade Bender," cried the widow in delight. "Where are you going?"

The smooth operator increased his speed. So did the widow.

"Listen to me," she called.

But her words did not reach Ostap's ears. He heard the sighing and whistling of the wind. He tore down the fourth corridor and hurtled down flights of iron stairs. All he left for his loved one was an echo which repeated the staircase noises for some time.

"Thanks," muttered Ostap, sitting down on the

ground on the fifth floor. "A fine time for a rendez-vous. Who invited the passionate lady here? It's time to liquidate the Moscow branch of the concession, or else I might find that self-employed mechanic here as well."

At that moment, the widow Gritsatsuyeva, sepa-rated from Ostap by three stories, thousands of doors and dozens of corridors, wiped her hot face with the edge of her petticoat and set off again. She intended at first to find her husband as quickly as possible and have it out with him. The corridors were lit with dim lights. All the lights, corridors, and doors were the same. Then she only wanted to get away and felt terrified.

Conforming to the corridor progression, she hur-ried along at an ever increasing rate. Half an hour later it was impossible to stop her. The doors of presidiums, secretariats, union committee rooms, administration sections, and editorial offices flew open with a crash on either side of her bulky body. She upset ash trays as she went with her iron skirts. The trays rolled after her with the clatter of saucepans. Whirlwinds and whirlpools formed at the ends of the corridors. Venti-lation windows flapped. Pointing fingers stenciled on the walls dug into the poor widow.

She finally found herself on a stairway landing. It was dark, but the widow overcame her fear, ran down, and pulled at a glass door. The door was locked. The widow hurried back, but the door through which she had just come had just been locked by somebody's thoughtful hand.

In Moscow they like to lock doors.

Thousands of front entrances are boarded up from the inside, and thousands of citizens find their way into their apartments through the back door. The year

1918 has long since passed; the concept of a "raid on the apartment" has long since become something vague; the apartment house guard, organized for purposes of security, has long since vanished; traffic problems are being solved; enormous power stations are being built and very great scientific discoveries are being made, but there is no one to devote his life to studying the problem of the closed door.

Where is the man who will solve the enigma of the movie houses, theaters, and circuses?

Three thousand members of the public have ten minutes in which to enter the circus through one single doorway, half of which is closed. The remaining ten doors designed to accommodate large crowds of people are shut. Who knows why they are shut? It may be that twenty years ago a performing donkey was stolen from the circus stable and ever since the management has been walling up convenient entrances and exits in fear. Or perhaps at some time a famous queen of the air felt a draft and the closed doors are merely a repercussion of the scene she caused.

The public is allowed into theaters and movie houses in small batches, supposedly to avoid bottlenecks. It is quite easy to avoid bottlenecks; all you have to do is open the numerous exits. But instead of that the management uses force; the attendants link arms and form a living barrier, and in this way keep the public at bay for at least half an hour. While the doors, the cherished doors, closed as far back as Peter the Great, are still shut.

Fifteen thousand football fans elated by the superb play of the select Moscow team are forced to squeeze their way to the streetcar through a crack so narrow that one lightly armed warrior could hold off forty thousand barbarians supported by two battering rams.

A sports stadium does not have a roof, but it does have several exits. All that is open is a wicker gate.

You can get out only by breaking through the main gates. They are always broken after every great sporting event. But so great is the desire to keep up the sacred tradition, they are carefully repaired each time and firmly shut again.

If there is no chance of hanging a door (which happens when there is nothing on which to hang it), hidden doors of all kinds come into play:

1. Rails
2. Barriers
3. Upturned benches
4. Warning signs
5. Rope

Rails are very common in government offices.

They prevent access to the official you want to see.

The visitor walks up and down the rail like a tiger, trying to attract attention by making signs. This does not always work. The visitor may have brought a useful invention! He might only want to pay his income tax. But the rail is in the way. The unknown invention is left outside; and the tax is left unpaid.

Barriers are used on the street.

They are set up in spring on a noisy main street, supposedly to fence off the part of the sidewalk being repaired. And the noisy street instantly becomes deserted. Pedestrians filter through to their destinations along other streets. Each day they have to go an extra half-mile, but hope springs eternal. The summer passes. The leaves wither. And the barrier is still there. The repairs have not been done. And the street is deserted.

Upturned benches are used to block the entrances to gardens in the center of the Moscow squares, which on account of the disgraceful negligence of the builders have not been fitted with strong gateways.

A whole book could be written about warning signs, but that is not the intention of the authors at present.

The signs are of two types—direct and indirect:

NO ADMITTANCE

NO ADMITTANCE TO OUTSIDERS

NO ENTRY

These notices are sometimes hung on the doors of government offices visited by the public in particularly great numbers.

The indirect signs are more insidious. They do not prohibit entry; but rare is the adventurer who will risk enjoying his rights. Here they are, those shameful signs:

NO ENTRY EXCEPT ON BUSINESS

NO CONSULTATIONS

BY YOUR VISIT YOU ARE DISTURBING
A BUSY MAN

Wherever it is impossible to place rails or barriers, to overturn benches or hang up warning signs, ropes are used. They are stretched across your path according to mood, and in the most unexpected places. If they are stretched at chest level they cause no more than slight shock and nervous laughter. But when stretched at ankle level they can cripple you for life.

To hell with doors! To hell with lines outside theaters. Allow us to go in without business. We implore you to remove the barrier set up by the thoughtless apartment superintendent on the sidewalk by his door. There are the upturned benches! Put them the right side up! It is precisely at nighttime that it is so nice to sit in the gardens in the squares. The air is clear and clever thoughts come to mind.

Sitting on the landing by the locked glass door in the very center of the House of the Peoples, Madam Gritsatsuyeva contemplated her widow's lot, dozed off from time to time, and waited for morning.

The yellow light of the ceiling lamps poured onto the widow through the glass door from the illuminated corridor. The ashen morn made its way in through the window of the stairway.

It was that quiet hour when the morning is fresh and young. It was at this hour that the widow heard footsteps in the corridor. The widow jumped up and pressed against the glass. She caught a glimpse of a blue vest at the end of the corridor. The crimson boots were dusty with plaster. The flighty son of a Turkish citizen approached the glass door, brushing a speck of dust from the sleeve of his jacket.

"Bunny!" called the widow. "Bun-ny!"

She breathed on the glass with unspeakable tenderness. The glass misted over and made rainbow circles. Through the mistiness and the rainbows glimmered blue and rainbow-colored specters.

Ostap did not hear the widow's cooing. He scratched his back and turned his head anxiously. Another second and he would have been around the corner.

With a groan of "Comrade Bender," the poor wife began drumming on the window. The smooth operator turned around.

"Oh," he said, seeing he was separated from the widow by a glass door, "are you here, too?"

"Yes, here, here," uttered the widow joyfully.

"Kiss me, honey," the technical adviser invited. "We haven't seen each other for such a long time!"

The widow was in a frenzy. She hopped up and down behind the door like a finch in a cage. The petticoat which had been silent for the night began to rustle loudly. Ostap spread his arms.

"Why don't you come to me, my little hen? Your Pacific rooster is so tired after the meeting of the Junior Council of Ministers."

The widow had no imagination.

"Bunny," she called for the fifth time, "open the door, Comrade Bender."

"Hush, girl! Modesty becomes a woman. What's all the jumping about for?"

The widow was on edge.

"Why are you torturing yourself?" asked Ostap. "Who's preventing you from living?"

The widow burst into tears.

"Wipe your eyes, Citizeness. Every one of your tears is a molecule in the cosmos."

"But I've been waiting and waiting. I closed down the shop. I came for you, Comrade Bender."

"And how do you feel on the stairs? Not drafty, I hope?"

The widow slowly began to seethe like a huge monastery samovar.

"Traitor!" she spat out with a shudder.

Ostap had a little time left. He clicked his fingers and, swaying rhythmically, crooned:

> *"We all go through times*
> *When the devil's beside us,*
> *When a young woman's charms*
> *Arouse passion inside us."*

"Drop dead!" advised the widow at the end of the dance. "You stole my bracelet, a present from my husband. And why did you take the chair?"

"Now you're getting personal," Ostap observed coldly.

"You stole, you stole!" repeated the widow.

"Listen, girl. Just remember for future reference that Ostap Bender never stole anything in his life."

"Then who took the tea strainer?"

"Ah, the tea strainer! From your nonliquid fund. And you consider that theft? In that case our views on life are diametrically opposed."

"You took it," clucked the widow.

"So if a young and healthy man borrows from a provincial grandmother a kitchen utensil for which she has no need on account of poor health, he's a thief, is he? Is that what you mean?"

"Thief! Thief!"

The widow threw herself against the door. The glass rattled.

Ostap realized it was time to go.

"I've no time to kiss you," he said. "Goodbye, beloved. We've parted like ships at sea."

"Help!" screeched the widow.

But Ostap was already at the end of the corridor. He climbed onto the windowsill and dropped heavily onto the ground, moist after the night rain, and hid in the glistening playgrounds.

The widow's cries brought the watchman. He let her out, threatening to have her fined.

] CHAPTER [

: 29 :

The Author of the
"Gavriliad"

As MADAM GRITSATSUYEVA was leaving the block of offices, the more modest ranks of employees were beginning to arrive at the House of the Peoples: there were messengers, in-and-out girls, duty telephonists, young assistant accountants, and apprentices.

Among them was Nikifor Lapis, a very young man with a sheep's-head haircut and a cheeky face.

The ignorant, the stubborn, and those making their first visit to the House of the Peoples entered through the front entrance. Nikifor Lapis made his way into the building through the dispensary. At the House of the Peoples he was completely at home and knew the quickest ways to the oases where, under the leafy shade of departmental journals, royalties gushed from clear springs.

First of all, Nikifor went to the snack bar. The nickel-plated register made a musical sound and ejected three checks. Nikifor consumed some yogurt, having opened the paper-covered jar, then a cream cookie which looked like a miniature flower bed. He washed it all down with tea. Then Lapis leisurely began making the round of his possessions.

His first visit was to the editorial office of the monthly hunting magazine *Gerasim and Mumu.* Comrade Napernikov had not yet arrived, so Nikifor moved on to the *Hygroscopic Herald,* the weekly mouthpiece by which pharmaceutical workers communicated with the outside world.

"Good morning!" said Nikifor. "I've written a marvelous poem."

"What about?" asked the editor of the literary page. "On what subject? You know, Trubetskoi, our magazine . . ."

To give a more subtle definition of the essence of the *Hygroscopic Herald,* the editor gestured with his fingers.

Trubetskoi-Lapis looked at his white sailcloth pants, leaned backward, and said in a singsong voice: "The Ballad of the Gangrene."

"That's interesting," said the hygroscopic individual. "It's about time we introduced prophylaxis in popular form."

Lapis immediately began declaiming:

> *"Gavrila took to bed with gangrene.*
> *The gangrene made Gavrila sick . . ."*

The poem went on in the same heroic iambic tetrameter to relate how, through ignorance, Gavrila did not go to the pharmacist in time and died because he had not put iodine on a scratch.

"You're making progress, Trubetskoi," said the editor in approval. "But we'd like something a bit longer. Do you understand?"

He began moving his fingers, but nevertheless took the terrifying ballad, promising to pay on Tuesday.

In the magazine *Telegraphist's Week* Lapis was greeted hospitably.

"A good thing you've come, Trubetskoi. We need some verse right away. But it must be about life, life, and life. No lyrical stuff. Do you hear, Trubetskoi?

Something about the life of post-office workers, but at the same time . . . Do you get me?"

"Only yesterday I was thinking about the life of post-office workers, and I concocted the following poem. It's called 'The Last Letter.' Here it is:

> *"Gavrila had a job as postman.*
> *Gavrila took the letters around . . ."*

The story of Gavrila was contained in seventy-two lines. At the end of the poem, Gavrila, although wounded by a fascist bullet, nevertheless delivers the letter to the right address.

"Where does it take place?" they asked Lapis.

It was a legitimate question. There were no fascists in the USSR and no Gavrilas or members of the post-office union abroad.

"What's wrong?" asked Lapis. "It takes place here, of course, and the fascist is disguised."

"You know, Trubetskoi, it'd be better to write about a radio station."

"Why don't you want the postman?"

"Let's wait a bit. We'll take it conditionally."

The crestfallen Nikifor Trubetskoi-Lapis went back to *Gerasim and Mumu*. Napernikov was already at his desk. On the wall hung a greatly enlarged picture of Turgenev with a pince-nez, waders, and a double-barrel shotgun across his shoulders. Beside Napernikov stood Lapis's rival, a poet from the suburbs.

The same old story of Gavrila was begun again, but this time with a hunting twist to it. The work went under the title of "The Poacher's Prayer."

> *Gavrila lay in wait for rabbits.*
> *Gavrila shot and winged a doe . . .*

"Very good!" said the kindly Napernikov. "You have surpassed Entich himself in this poem, Trubetskoi. Only there are one or two things to be changed. The first thing is to get rid of the word 'prayer.'"

"And 'rabbit,' " said the rival.

"Why 'rabbit'?" asked Nikifor in surprise.

"It's the wrong season."

"You hear that, Trubetskoi! Change the word 'rabbit' as well."

After transformation the poem bore the title "The Poacher's Lesson" and the rabbits were changed to snipe. It then turned out that snipe were not shot in the summer either. In its final form the poem read:

> *Gavrila lay in wait for sparrows.*
> *Gavrila shot and winged a bird . . .*

After lunch in the canteen, Lapis set to work again. His white pants flashed up and down the corridor. He entered various editorial offices and sold the many-faced Gavrila.

In the *Co-operative Flute* Gavrila was submitted under the title of "The Eolean Recorder."

> *Gavrila worked behind the counter.*
> *Gavrila did a trade in flutes . . .*

The simpletons in the voluminous magazine *The Forest as It Is* bought a short poem by Lapis entitled "On the Verge." It began like this:

> *Gavrila passed through virgin forest,*
> *Hacking at the thick bamboo . . .*

The last Gavrila for that day worked in a bakery. He was found a place in the editorial office of *The Cake Worker*. The poem had the long and sad title of "On Bread, Standards of Output, and One's Sweetheart." The poem was dedicated to a mysterious Hina Chlek. The beginning was as epic as before:

> *Gavrila had a job as baker.*
> *Gavrila baked the cakes and bread . . .*

After a delicate argument, the dedication was deleted.

The saddest thing of all was that no one gave Lapis any money. Some promised to pay him on Tuesday, others said Thursday or Friday in two weeks' time. He was forced to go and borrow money from the enemy camp—the place where he was never published.

Lapis went down to the second floor and entered the office of the *Lathe*. To his misfortune he immediately bumped into Persidsky, the slogger.

"Ah!" exclaimed Persidsky, "Lapis!"

"Listen," said Nikifor, lowering his voice. "Let me have three roubles. *Gerasim and Mumu* owes me a pile of cash."

"I'll give you half a rouble. Wait a moment. I'm just coming."

And Persidsky returned with a dozen employees of the *Lathe*.

Everyone joined in the conversation.

"Well, how have you been making out?" asked Persidsky.

"I've written a marvelous poem!"

"About Gavrila? Something peasanty? 'Gavrila plowed the fields early. Gavrila just adored his plow'?"

"Not about Gavrila. That's a pot boiler," said Lapis defensively. "I wrote about the Caucasus."

"Have you ever been to the Caucasus?"

"I'm going in two weeks."

"Aren't you afraid, Lapis? There are jackals there."

"Takes more than that to frighten me. Anyway, the ones in the Caucasus aren't poisonous."

They all pricked up their ears at this reply.

"Tell me, Lapis," said Persidsky, "what do you think jackals are?"

"I know what they are. Leave me alone."

"All right, tell us then if you know."

"Well, they're sort of . . . like . . . snakes."

"Yes, of course, right as usual. You think a wild-goat's saddle is served at table together with the spurs."

"I never said that," cried Trubetskoi.

"You didn't say it, you wrote it. Napernikov told me you tried to palm off some such doggerel on *Gerasim and Mumu*, supposed to be about the everyday life of hunters. Honestly, Lapis, why do you write about things you've never seen and haven't the first idea about? Why is the peignoir in your poem 'Canton' an evening dress? Why?"

"You philistine!" said Lapis boastfully.

"Why is it that in your poem 'The Budyonny Stakes' the jockey tightens the hame strap and then gets into the coach box? Have you ever seen a hame strap?"

"Yes."

"What's it like?"

"Leave me alone. You're nuts!"

"Have you ever seen a coach box or been to the races?"

"You don't have to go everywhere!" cried Lapis. "Pushkin wrote poems about Turkey without ever having been there."

"Oh, yes. Erzerum is in Tula province, of course."

Lapis did not appreciate the sarcasm. He continued heatedly. "Pushkin wrote from material he read. He read the history of the Pugachov revolt and then wrote about it. It was Entich who told me about the races."

After this masterly defense, Persidsky dragged the resisting Lapis into the next room. The onlookers followed. On the wall hung a large newspaper clipping edged in black like an obituary notice.

"Did you write this piece for the *Captain's Bridge?*"

"Yes I did."

"I believe it was your first attempt at prose. Congratulations! 'The waves rolled across the pier and fell headlong below like a jack.' A lot of help to the *Captain's Bridge* you are! The *Bridge* won't forget you for some time!"

"What's the matter?"

"The matter is . . . do you know what a jack is?"

"Of course I know. Leave me alone."

"How do you envisage a jack? Describe it in your own words."

"It . . . sort of . . . falls."

"A jack falls. Note that, everyone. A jack falls headlong. Just a moment, Lapis, I'll bring you half a rouble. Don't let him go."

But this time, too, there was no half-rouble forthcoming. Persidsky brought back the twenty-first volume of the Brockhaus encyclopedia.

"Listen! 'Jack: a machine for lifting heavy weights. A simple jack used for lifting carriages, etc., consists of a mobile toothed bar gripped by a rod which is turned by means of a lever' . . . And here . . . 'In 1879 John Dixon set up the obelisk known as Cleopatra's Needle by means of four workers operating four hydraulic jacks.' And this instrument, in your opinion, can fall headlong? So Brockhaus has deceived humanity for fifty years? Why do you write such rubbish instead of learning? Answer!"

"I need the money."

"But you never have any. You're always trying to cadge half-roubles."

"I bought some furniture and went through my budget."

"And how much furniture did you buy? You get paid for your pot boilers as much as they're worth—a kopek."

"A kopek be damned. I bought a chair at an auction which—"

"Is sort of like a snake?"

"No, from a palace. But I had some bad luck. Yesterday when I arrived back from—"

"Hina Chlek's," cried everyone present in one voice.

"Hina! I haven't lived with Hina for years. I was returning from a discussion on Mayakovsky. I went in. The window was open. I felt at once something had happened."

"Dear, dear," said Persidsky, covering his face with

his hands. "I feel, Comrades, that Lapis's greatest masterpiece has been stolen. 'Gavrila had a job as doorman; Gavrila used to open doors.' "

"Let me finish. Absolute vandalism. Some wretches had got into the apartment and ripped open the entire chair covering. Could anyone lend me five roubles for the repairs?"

"Compose a new Gavrila for the repairs. I'll even give you the beginning. Wait a moment. Yes, I know. 'Gavrila hastened to the market, Gavrila bought a rotten chair.' Write it down quickly. You can make some money on that in the *Chest-of-Drawers Gazette*. Oh, Trubetskoi, Trubetskoi! Anyway, why are you called Trubetskoi? Why don't you choose a better name? Nikifor Dolgoruky. Or Nikifor Valois. Or, still better, Citizen Nikifor Sumarokov-Elston. If ever you manage to get some easy job, then you can write three lines for *Gerasim* right away and you have a marvelous way to save yourself. One piece of rubbish is signed Sumarokov, the second Elston, and the third Yusupov. God, you pot boiler!"

In the Columbus Theater

IPPOLIT MATVEYEVICH was slowly becoming a boot-licker. Whenever he looked at Ostap, his eyes acquired a blue lackeyish tinge.

It was so hot in Ivanopulo's room that Vorobyaninov's chairs creaked like logs in the fireplace. The smooth operator was having a nap with the light-blue vest under his head.

Ippolit Matveyevich looked out of the window. A carriage emblazoned with a coat of arms was moving along the curved side street, past the tiny Moscow gardens. The black gloss reflected the passers-by one after another, a horseguard in a brass helmet, society ladies, and fluffy white clouds. Drumming the roadway with their hoofs, the horses drew the carriage past Ippolit Matveyevich. He winced with disappointment.

The carriage bore the initials of the Moscow communal services and was being used to carry garbage; its slatted sides reflected nothing at all.

In the coachman's seat sat a fine-looking old man with a fluffy white beard. If Ippolit Matveyevich had known that this was none other than Count Alexei Bulanov, the famous hermit hussar, he would probably have hailed the old man and chatted with him about the good old days.

Count Bulanov was deeply troubled. As he whipped up the horses, he mused about the red tape which was strangling the subdepartment of sanitation, and on account of which he had not received for six months the apron he was entitled to under his contract.

"Listen," said the smooth operator suddenly. "What did they call you as a boy?"

"What do you want to know for?"

"I just want to know what to call you. I'm sick of calling you Vorobyaninov, and Ippolit Matveyevich is too stuffy. What were you called? Ipa?"

"Kisa," replied Ippolit Matveyevich with a snicker.

"That's more like it. So look, Kisa, see what's wrong with my back. It hurts between the shoulder blades."

Ostap pulled the cowboy shirt over his head. Before Kisa Vorobyaninov was revealed the broad back of a provincial Antinoüs; a back of enchanting shape but rather dirty.

"Aha! I see some redness."

Between the smooth operator's shoulders were some strangely shaped mauve bruises which reflected colors like a rainbow in oil.

"Honestly, it's the number eight," exclaimed Vorobyaninov. "First time I've ever seen a bruise like that."

"Any other number?" asked Ostap.

"There seems to be a letter P."

"I have no more questions. It's quite clear. That damned pen! You see how I suffer, Kisa, and what risks I run for your chairs. These arithmetical figures were branded on me by the huge self-falling pen with Number Eighty-six nib. I should point out to you that the damned pen fell on my back at the very moment I inserted my hands inside the chief editor's chair. But you! You can't do anything right! Who was it messed up Iznurenkov's chair so that I had to go and do your work for you? I won't even mention the auction. A fine time to go woman-chasing. It's simply bad for you at your age to do that. Look after your health. Take me, on the other hand. I got the widow's chair. I got the two Shukin chairs. It was me who finally got Iznurenkov's chair. It was me who went to the newspaper office and to Lapis's. There was only one chair that you managed to run down, and that was with the help of your holy enemy, the archbishop."

Silently walking up and down in his bare feet, the technical adviser reasoned with the submissive Kisa.

The chair which had vanished into the freight yard of October station was still a blot on the glossy schedule of the concession. The four chairs in the Columbus Theater were a sure bet, but the theater was about to make a trip down the Volga aboard the lottery ship, the *S. S. Scriabin*, and was presenting the premier of *The Marriage* that day as the last production of the season. The partners had to decide whether to stay in Moscow and look for the chair lost in the wilds of Kalanchev Square, or go on tour with the troupe. Ostap was in favor of the latter.

"Or perhaps we should split up?" he suggested. "I'll go off with the theater and you stay and find out about the chair in the freight yard."

Kisa's gray eyelashes flickered so fearfully, however, that Ostap did not bother to continue.

"Of the two birds," said Ostap, "the meatier should be chosen. Let's go together. But the expenses will be considerable. We shall need money. I have sixty roubles left. How much have you? Oh, I forgot. At your age a maiden's love is so expensive! I decree that we go together to the premier of *The Marriage*. Don't forget to wear tails. If the chairs are still there and haven't been sold to pay social-security debts, we can leave tomorrow. Remember, Vorobyaninov, we've now reached the final act of the comedy *My Mother-*

in-Law's Treasure. The *Finita la Comedia* is fast approaching, Vorobyaninov. Don't gasp, my old friend. The call of the footlights! Oh, my younger days! Oh, the smell of the wings! So many memories! So many intrigues and affairs! How talented I was in my time in the role of Hamlet! In short, the hearing is continued."

For the sake of economy they went to the theater on foot. It was still quite light, but the street lamps were already casting their lemon light. Spring was dying before everyone's eyes. Dust chased it from the squares, and a warm breeze drove it from the side streets. Old women fondled the beauty and drank tea with it at little round tables in the yards. But spring's span of life had ended and it could not reach the people. And it so much wanted to be at the Pushkin monument where the young men were already strolling about in their jazzy caps, drainpipe trousers, "dog's-delight" bow ties, and Jimmy boots.

Mauve-powdered girls circulated between the holy of holies and the Commune co-operative. The girls were swearing audibly. This was the hour when pedestrians slowed down their pace, though not because Tverskaya Street was becoming crowded. Moscow horses were no better than the Stargorod ones. They stamped their hoofs just as much on the edges of the roadway. Cyclists rode noiselessly by from their first large international match at the Young Pioneer stadium. The ice-cream man trundled along his green trolley full of May thunder, and squinted timorously at the militiaman; but the latter was chained to the spot by the flashing signal with which he regulated the traffic, and was not dangerous.

The two friends made their way through the hustle and bustle. Temptation lay in wait for them at every step. Different types of meat on skewers were being roasted in full view of the street in the tiny eating places. Hot, appetizing fumes rose up to the bright sky. The sound of string music was wafted from beer halls, small restaurants, and the "Great Silent Film" movie theater. A loud-speaker raved away at a street-car stop.

It was time to put a spurt on. The friends reached the foyer of the Columbus Theater.

Vorobyaninov rushed to the box office and read the list of seat prices. "Rather expensive, I'm afraid," he said. "Three roubles for the sixteenth row."

"How I dislike these narrow-minded provincial philistines," Ostap observed. "Where are you going? Can't you see that's the box office?"

"Where else? We won't get in without tickets."

"Kisa, you're vulgar. In every well-built theater there are two windows. Only courting couples and wealthy heirs go to the box-office window. The other citizens (they make up the majority, you may observe) go straight to the manager's window."

And, indeed, at the box-office window were only about five modestly dressed people. They may have been wealthy heirs or courting couples. At the manager's window, however, there was great activity. A colorful line had formed. Young men in fashioned jackets and trousers of the same cut (which a provincial could never have dreamed of owning) were confidently waving notes from friendly directors, actors, editors, theatrical costumers, the district militia chief, and other such persons closely connected with the theater as members of the theater and movie critics' association, the Poor Mothers' Tears society, the school council of the Experimental Circus Workshop and Fortinbras at Umslopogas. About eight people had notes from Espere Eclairovich.

Ostap barged into the line, jostled aside the Fortinbrasites, and, with a cry of "I only want some information: can't you see I haven't taken my galoshes off!" pushed his way to the window and peered inside.

The manager was working like a slave. Bright dia-

monds of perspiration irrigated his fat face. The telephone interrupted him all the time and rang with the
obstinacy of a streetcar trying to pass through the
Smolensk market.

"Hurry up and give me the note!" he shouted to
Ostap.

"Two seats," said Ostap quietly, "in the stalls."

"Who for?"

"Me."

"And who might you be to ask for seats from me?"

"Now surely you know me?"

"No, I don't."

But the stranger's gaze was so innocent and open
that the manager's hand by itself gave Ostap two seats
in the eleventh row.

"All kinds come here," said the manager, shrugging
his shoulders. "Who knows who they are? They may
be from the Ministry of Education. I seem to have
seen him at the Ministry of Education. Where could
it have been?"

And mechanically issuing passes to the lucky film
and theater critics, the manager went on quietly trying
to remember where he had seen those clear eyes before.

When all the passes had been issued and the lights
had gone down in the foyer, he remembered he had
seen them in the Taganka prison in 1922, while he was
doing time for some trivial matter.

Laughter echoed from the eleventh row where the
concessionaires were sitting. Ostap liked the musical
introduction performed by the orchestra on bottles,
Esmarch douches, saxophones, and large bass drums.
A flute whistled and the curtain went up, wafting a
breath of cool air.

To the surprise of Vorobyaninov, who was used to
the classical interpretation of *The Marriage*, Podkolesin was not on the stage. Searching around with his
eyes, he perceived some plyboard triangles hanging

from the ceiling and painted the primary colors of the spectrum. There were no doors or blue muslin windows. Beneath the multicolored triangles danced young ladies in large hats cut from black cardboard. The clinking of bottles brought forth Podkolesin, who charged into the crowd riding on Stepan's back. Podkolesin was arrayed in courtier's dress. Having dispersed the young ladies with words which were not in the play, he bawled out:

"Stepan!"

At the same time he leaped to one side and froze in a difficult pose. The Esmarch douches began to clatter.

"Stepan!" repeated Podkolesin, taking another leap.

But, since Stepan, who was standing right there in a leopard skin, did not respond, Podkolesin asked tragically:

"Why are you silent, like the League of Nations?"

"I'm obviously afraid of Chamberlain," replied Stepan, scratching his skin.

There was a general feeling that Stepan would oust Podkolesin and become the chief character in this modernized version of the play.

"Well, is the tailor making a coat?"

A leap. A blow on the Esmarch douches. Stepan stood on his hands with an effort and, still in that position, answered:

"Yes, he is."

The orchestra played a potpourri from *Madam Butterfly*. Stepan stood on his hands the whole time. His face flooded with color.

"And didn't the tailor ask what the master wanted such good cloth for?"

Stepan, who by this time was sitting in the orchestra cuddling the conductor, answered: "No, he didn't. He's not a member of the British Parliament, is he?"

"And didn't the tailor ask whether the master wished to get married?"

"The tailor asked whether the master wanted to pay alimony."

At this point the lights went out and the audience began stamping their feet. They kept up the stamping until Podkolesin's voice could be heard saying from the stage:

"Citizens! Don't be alarmed! The lights went out on purpose as part of the act. It's required for the scenic effects."

The audience gave in. The lights did not go up again until the end of the act. The drums rolled in complete darkness. A squad of soldiers dressed as hotel doormen passed by, carrying torches. Then Koch-karev arrived, apparently on a camel. This could only be judged from the following dialogue.

"Ouch, how you frightened me! And you came on a camel, too."

"Ah, so you noticed, despite the darkness. I wanted to bring you a fragrant camel-ia!"

During the intermission the concessionaires read the program.

"Do you like it?" Ippolit Matveyevich asked timidly. "Do you?"

"It's very interesting—only Stepan is rather odd."

"No, I don't like it," said Ostap. "Particularly the fact that the furniture is from some Vogopas work-shops or other. I hope those aren't our chairs adapted to a new style."

Their fears were unjustified. At the beginning of the second act all four chairs were brought onto the stage by Negroes in top hats.

The matchmaking scene aroused the greatest inter-est among the audience. At the moment Agafya Tik-honovna was coming down a rope stretched across the entire width of the theater, the terrifying orchestra let out such a noise that she nearly fell off into the audience. But she balanced perfectly on the stage. She was wearing flesh-colored tights and a derby. Main-

---

The Marriage

Text . . . N. V. Gogol

Verse . . . M. Cherchezlafemmov

Adaptation . . . I. Antiokhiisky

Musical accompaniment . . . Kh. Ivanov

Producer . . . Nich. Sestrin

Scenic effects . . . Simbievich-Sindievich

Lighting . . . Platon Plashuk. *Sound effects* . . . Galkin,
Palkin, Malkin, Chalkin, and Zalkind.

Make-up . . . Krult workshop; *wigs by* Foma Kochur

Furniture by the Fortinbras woodwork shops attached
to the Balthazar Umslopogas

Acrobatics instructress: Georgetta Tiraspolskikh

Hydraulic press operated by Fitter Mechnikov

*Program composed, imposed,
and printed by the*
KRULT FACTORY SCHOOL

---

taining her balance by means of a green parasol on
which was written "I want Podkolesin," she stepped
along the wire and everyone below immediately saw
that her feet were dirty. She leaped from the wire
straight onto a chair, whereupon the Negroes, Podkolesin, Kochkarev in a tutu, and the matchmaker in a
bus driver's uniform all turned backward somersaults.
Then they had a five-minute rest, to hide which the
lights were turned out again.

The suitors were also very comic, particularly
Yaichnitsa. In his place a large pan of fried eggs was
brought onto the stage. The sailor wore a mast with a
sail.

In vain did Starikov the merchant cry out that he was being strangled by the taxes. Agafya Tikhonovna did not like him. She married Stepan. They both dived into the fried eggs served by Podkolesin, who had turned into a footman. Kochkarev and Fekla sang ditties about Chamberlain and the payment he hoped to extort from Germany. The Esmarch douches played a hymn for the dying and the curtain came down, wafting a breath of cool air.

"I'm satisfied with the performance," said Ostap. "The chairs are intact. But we've no time to lose. If Agafya Tikhonovna is going to land on those chairs each day, they won't last very long."

Jostling and laughing, the young men in their fashioned jackets discussed the finer points of the scenic effects.

"You need some shut-eye, Kisa," said Ostap. "We have to stand in line for tickets early tomorrow morning. The theater is leaving by express for Nizhni tomorrow evening at seven. So get two seats in a hard coach to Nizhni on the Kursk railroad. We'll sit it out. It's only one night."

The next day the Columbus Theater was sitting in the buffet at Kursk station. Having taken steps to see that the scenic effects went by the same train, Simbievich-Sindievich was having a snack at one of the tables. Dipping his mustache into the beer, he asked the fitter nervously:

"The hydraulic press won't get broken on the way, will it?"

"It's not the press that's the trouble," said the fitter Mechnikov. "It's that it only works for five minutes and we have to cart it around the whole summer."

"Was it any easier with the 'time projector' from the *Ideology Powder?*"

"Of course it was. The projector was big, but not so fragile."

At the next table sat Agafya Tikhonovna, a young-

ish woman with hard, shiny legs like skittles. The
sound effects—Galkin, Palkin, Malkin, Chalkin, and
Zalkind—fussed around her.

"You didn't keep in time with me yesterday," she
complained. "I might have fallen."

"What can we do?" clamored the sound effects.
"Two douches broke."

"Do you think you can get an Esmarch douche from
abroad nowadays?" cried Galkin.

"Just try going to the State Medical Supply Office.
It's impossible to buy a thermometer, let alone an Esmarch douche," added Palkin.

"Do you play thermometers as well?" asked the girl,
horrified.

"It's not that we play thermometers," observed Zalkind, "but that the damned douches are enough to
drive you out of your mind and we have to take our
temperatures."

Nich. Sestrin, stage manager and producer, was
strolling along the platform with his wife. Podkolesin
and Kochkarev had downed three vodkas and were
wooing Georgetta Tiraspolskikh, each trying to outdo
the other.

The concessionaires had arrived two hours before
the train was due to depart and were now on their sixth
round of the garden laid out in front of the station.

Ippolit Matveyevich's head was whirling. The hunt
for the chairs was entering the last lap. Long shadows
fell on the scorching roadway. Dust settled on their
wet, sweaty faces. Cabs drove up to them and there
was a smell of gasoline. Hired vehicles set down their
passengers. Porters ran up to them and carried off the
bags, while their badges glittered in the sun. The Muse
of Travel had people by the throat.

"Let's get going as well," said Ostap.

Ippolit Matveyevich meekly consented. All of a sudden he came face to face with Bezenchuk, the undertaker.

"Bezenchuk!" he exclaimed in amazement. "How did you get here?"

Bezenchuk doffed his cap and was speechless with joy. "Mr. Vorobyaninov," he cried. "Greetings to an honored guest."

"Well, how are things?"

"Bad," answered the undertaker.

"Why is that?"

"I'm lookin' for clients. There ain't none about."

"Is the Nymph doing better than you?"

"Likely! Could they do better than me? No chance. Since your mother-in-law only 'Pierre and Constantine' croaked."

"You don't say! Did he really die?"

"He croaked, Ippolit Matveyevich. He croaked at his post. He was shavin' Leopold the chemist when he croaked. People said it was his insides that burst, but I think it was the smell of medicine from the chemist which he couldn't take."

"Dear me, dear me," muttered Ippolit Matveyevich. "So you buried him, did you?"

"I buried him. Who else could? Does the Nymph, damn 'em, give tassels?"

"You got in ahead of them, then?"

"Yes, I did, but they beat me up afterwards. Almost beat the guts out of me. The militia took me away. I was in bed for two days. I cured myself with spirits."

"You massaged yourself?"

"There's no point in massaging with it."

"But what made you come here?"

"I've brought my stock."

"What stock?"

"My own. A guard I know helped me bring it here free in the mail car. Did it as a friend."

It was only then that Ippolit Matveyevich noticed a neat pile of coffins on the ground a little way from Bezenchuk. Some had tassels, others did not. One of them Ippolit Matveyevich recognized immediately. It was the large, dusty oak coffin from Bezenchuk's shop window.

"Eight of them," said Bezenchuk smugly. "Like pickles."

"But who needs your stock here? They have plenty of their own undertakers here."

"What about the flu?"

"What flu?"

"The epidemic. Prusis told me flu was ragin' in Moscow and there was nothing to bury people in. All the coffins were used up. So I decided to put things right."

Ostap, who had been listening to the conversation with curiosity, intervened. "Listen, Dad, the flu epidemic is in Paris."

"In Paris?"

"Yes, go to Paris. You'll make money. Admittedly, there may be some trouble with the visa, but don't give up. If Briand likes you, you'll do pretty well. They'll set you up as a lifeguard undertaker at the Paris municipality. Here they have enough of their own undertakers."

Bezenchuk looked around him wildly. Despite the assurances of Prusis, there were definitely no bodies lying about; people were cheerfully moving on their feet and some were laughing.

Long after the train had carried off the concessionaires, the Columbus Theater, and various other people, Bezenchuk was still standing in a daze by his coffins. His eyes shone in the approaching darkness with an unfading light.

Part : III

MADAM PETUKHOVA'S TREASURE

A Magic Night on the Volga

THE SMOOTH OPERATOR stood with his friend and closest aid, Kisa Vorobyaninov, on the left of the passenger landing stage of the state-owned Volga River Transport System under a sign which said: "Use the rings for mooring, mind the grating, and keep clear of the wall."

Flags fluttered above the quay. Smoke as curly as a cauliflower poured from the funnels. The *S. S. Anton Rubinstein* was being loaded at pier No. 2. Dock workers dug their iron claws into bales of cotton; iron pots were stacked in a square on the quayside, which was littered with treated hides, bundles of wire, crates of sheet glass, rolls of cord for binding sheaves, millstones, two-color bony agricultural implements, wooden forks, sack-lined baskets of early cherries, and casks of herrings.

The *Scriabin* was not in, which greatly disturbed Ippolit Matveyevich.

"Why worry about it?" asked Ostap. "Suppose the *Scriabin* were here. How would you get aboard? Even if you had the money to buy a ticket with, it still wouldn't be any use. The boat doesn't take passengers."

While still on the train, Ostap had already had a

chance to talk to Mechnikov, the fitter in charge of the hydraulic press, and had found out everything. The *S. S. Scriabin* had been chartered by the Ministry of Finance and was due to sail from Nizhni to Tsaritsin, calling at every river port, and holding a government-bond lottery. A complete government department had left Moscow for the trip, including a lottery commit-tee, an office staff, a brass band, a cameraman, report-ers from the central press, and the Columbus Theater. The theater was there to perform plays which popu-larized the idea of government loans. Up to Stalingrad the Columbus Theater was on the establishment of the lottery committee, after which the theater had de-cided to tour the Caucasus and the Crimea with *The Marriage* at its own risk.

The *Scriabin* was late. A promise was given that she would leave the backwater, where last-minute prepa-rations were being made, by evening. So the whole department from Moscow set up camp on the quayside and waited to go aboard.

Tender creatures with attaché cases and catch-alls sat on the bundles of wire, guarding their Underwoods, and glancing apprehensively at the stevedores. A citi-zen with a violet imperial positioned himself on a mill-stone. On his knees was a pile of enamel plates. A curi-ous person could have read the uppermost one:

> Mutual Settlement Department

Desks with ornamental legs and other, more mod-est, desks stood on top of one another. A watchman sauntered up and down by a sealed safe. Persidsky, who was representing the *Lathe*, gazed at the fair ground through Zeiss binoculars with eightfold mag-nification.

The *S. S. Scriabin* approached, turning against the stream. Her sides were decked with plyboard sheets showing brightly colored pictures of giant-sized bonds. The ship gave a roar, imitating the sound of a mammoth, or possibly some other animal which was used in prehistoric times to replace the sound of a ship's hooter.

The finance-and-theater camp came to life. Down the slopes to the quay came the lottery employees. Platon Plashuk, a fat little man, toddled down to the ship in a cloud of dust. Galkin, Palkin, Malkin, Chalkin, and Zalkind flew out of the Raft beer hall. Dockers were already loading the safe. Georgetta Tiraspolskikh, the acrobatics instructress, hurried up the gangway with a springy walk, while Simbievich-Sindievich, still worried about the scenic effects, raised his hands, at one moment to the Kremlin heights, and at another toward the captain standing on the bridge. The cameraman carried his camera high above the heads of the crowd, and as he went he demanded a separate cabin in which to arrange a darkroom.

In the general confusion, Ippolit Matveyevich made his way over to the chairs and was about to drag one away to one side.

"Leave the chair alone!" snarled Bender. "Are you crazy? Even if we take one, the others will disappear for good. You'd do better to think of a way to get aboard the ship."

Belted with brass tubes, the band passed along the landing stage. The musicians looked with distaste at the saxophones, flexotones, beer bottles, and Esmarch douches, with which the sound effects were armed.

The lottery wheels arrived in a Ford station wagon. They were built in to a complicated device composed of six rotating cylinders with shining brass and glass. It took some time to set them up on the lower deck.

The stomping about and exchange of abuse continued until late evening.

In the lottery hall people were erecting a stage, fixing notices and slogans to the walls, arranging benches for the visitors, and joining electric leads to the lottery wheels. The desks were in the stern, and the tapping of typewriters, interspersed with laughter, could be heard from the typists' cabin. The pale man in the violet imperial walked the length of the ship, hanging his enamel plates on the relevant doors.

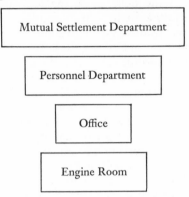

Mutual Settlement Department

Personnel Department

Office

Engine Room

To the larger plates the man with the imperial added smaller plates.

No entry except on business

No consultations

No admittance to outsiders

All inquiries at the registry

The first-class saloon had been fitted up for an exhibition of bank notes and bonds. This aroused a wave of indignation from Galkin, Palkin, Malkin, Chalkin, and Zalkind.

"Where are we going to eat?" they fretted. "And what happens if it rains?"

"This is too much," said Nich. Sestrin to his assistant. "What do you think, Seryozha? Can we do without the sound effects?"

"Lord, no, Nicholas Constantinovich. The actors are used to the rhythm now."

A fresh racket broke out. The "Five" had found that the stage manager had taken all four chairs to his cabin.

"So that's it," said the "Five" ironically. "We're supposed to rehearse sitting on our berths, while Sestrin and his wife, Gusta, who has nothing to do with our group, sit on the four chairs. Perhaps we should have brought our wives with us on this trip as well."

The lottery ship was watched malevolently from the bank by the smooth operator.

A fresh outbreak of shouting reached the concessionaires' ears.

"Why didn't you tell me before?" cried a committee member.

"How was I to know he would get sick."

"A hell of a mess we're in! Then go to the artists'-union office and insist that an artist be sent here immediately."

"How can I? It's now six o'clock. The union office closed long ago. Anyway, the ship is leaving in half an hour."

"Then you can do the painting yourself. Since you're responsible for the decorations on the ship, get out of the mess any way you like!"

Ostap was already running up the gangplank, elbowing his way through the dockers, young ladies, and idle onlookers. He was stopped at the top.

"Your pass?"

"Comrade!" roared Bender. "You! You! The little fat man! The one who needs an artist!"

Five minutes later the smooth operator was sitting in the white cabin occupied by the fat little assistant manager of the floating lottery and discussing terms.

"So we want you to do the following, Comrade," said fatty. "Paint notices, inscriptions, and complete the transparent. Our artist began the work, but got sick. We've left him at the hospital. And, of course, general supervision of the art department. Can you take that on? I warn you, incidentally, there's a great deal of work."

"Yes, I can undertake that. I've had occasion to do that kind of work before."

"And you can come along with us now?"

"That will be difficult, but I'll try."

A large and heavy burden fell from the shoulders of the assistant manager. With a feeling of relief, the fat man looked at the new artist with shining eyes.

"Your terms?" asked Ostap sharply. "Remember, I'm not from a funeral home."

"It's piece work. At union rates."

Ostap frowned, which was very hard for him.

"But free meals as well," added the tubby man hastily. "And a separate cabin."

"All right," said Ostap, "I accept. But I have a boy, an assistant, with me."

"I don't know about the boy. There are no funds for a boy. But at your own expense by all means. He can live in your cabin."

"As you like. The kid is smart. He's used to Spartan conditions."

Ostap was given a pass for himself and for the smart boy; he put the key of the cabin in his pocket and went out onto the hot deck. He felt great satisfaction as he fingered the key. It was the first time in his stormy life that he had a key and an apartment. It was only the money he lacked. But there was some right next to him in the chairs. The smooth operator walked up and down the deck with his hands in his pockets, ignoring Vorobyaninov on the bank.

At first Ippolit Matveyevich made signs; then he was even daring enough to whistle. But Bender paid no heed. Turning his back on the president of the concession, he watched with interest as the hydraulic press was lowered into the hold.

Final preparations for casting off were being made. Agafya Tikhonovna, alias Mura, ran with clattering feet from her cabin to the stern, looked at the water, loudly shared her delight with the balalaika virtuoso, and generally caused confusion among the honored officials of the lottery enterprise.

The ship gave a second hoot. At the terrifying sound the clouds moved aside. The sun turned crimson and sank below the horizon. Lamps and street lights came on in the town above. From the market in Pochayevsky Ravine there came the hoarse voices of phonographs competing for the last customers. Dismayed and lonely, Ippolit Matveyevich kept shouting something, but no one heard him. The clanking of winches drowned all other sounds.

Ostap Bender liked effects. It was only just before the third hoot, when Ippolit Matveyevich no longer doubted that he had been abandoned to the mercy of fate, that Ostap noticed him.

"What are you standing there like a coy suitor for? I thought you were aboard long ago. They're just going to raise the gangplank. Hurry up! Let this citizen board. Here's his pass."

Ippolit Matveyevich hurried aboard almost in tears.

"Is this your boy?" asked the boss suspiciously.

"That's the one," said Ostap. "If anyone says he's a girl, then I'm a Dutchman!"

The fat man glumly went away.

"Well, Kisa," declared Ostap, "we'll have to get down to work in the morning. I hope you can mix paints. And, incidentally, I'm an artist, a graduate of the Higher Art and Technical Workshops, and you're my assistant. If you don't like the idea, go back ashore at once."

Black-green foam surged up from under the stern. The ship shuddered; the cymbals clashed together, the flutes, cornets, trombones, and tubas thundered out a wonderful march, and the town, swinging around and trying to balance, shifted to the left bank. Continuing to throb, the ship moved into midstream and was soon swallowed up in the darkness. A minute later it was so far away that the lights of the town looked like sparks from a rocket that had frozen in space.

The murmuring of typewriters could still be heard, but nature and the Volga were gaining the upper hand. A coziness enveloped all those aboard the *S. S. Scriabin*. The members of the lottery committee drowsily sipped their tea. The first meeting of the union committee, held in the prow, was marked by tenderness. The warm wind breathed so heavily, the water lapped against the sides of the ship so gently, and the dark outline of the shore sped past the ship so rapidly that when the chairman of the union committee, a very positive man, opened his mouth to speak about working conditions in the unusual situation, he unexpectedly for himself and for everyone else began singing:

> *"A ship sailed down the Volga,*
> *Mother Volga, River Volga . . ."*

And the other, stern-faced members taking part in the meeting rumbled the chorus:

> *"The lilac bloo-ooms . . ."*

The resolution on the chairman's report was just not recorded. A piano began to play. Kh. Ivanov, head of the musical accompaniment, drew the most lyrical notes from the instrument. The balalaika virtuoso trailed after Murochka and, not finding any words of his own to express his love, murmured the words of the love song.

"Don't go away! Your kisses still fire me, your passionate embraces never tire me. The clouds have not awakened in the mountain passes, the distant sky has not yet faded as a pearly star."

Grasping the rail, Simbievich-Sindievich contemplated the infinite heavens. Compared with them, the scenic effects appeared a piece of disgusting vulgarity. He looked with revulsion at his hands, which had taken such an eager part in arranging the scenic effects for the classical comedy.

At the moment the languor was greatest, Galkin, Palkin, Malkin, Chalkin, and Zalkind, who were in the stern of the ship, began banging away at their surgical and brewery appliances. They were rehearsing. The mirage was instantly dispelled. Agafya Tikhonovna yawned and, ignoring the balalaika virtuoso, went to bed. The minds of the trade unionists were again full of working conditions and they dealt with the resolution. After careful consideration, Simbievich-Sindievich came to the conclusion that the production of *The Marriage* was not really so bad. An irate voice from the darkness called Georgetta Tiraspolskikh to a producer's conference. Dogs began barking in the villages and it became chilly.

Ostap lay in a first-class cabin on a leather divan, thoughtfully staring at a green canvas work belt and questioning Ippolit Matveyevich.

"Can you draw? That's a pity. Unfortunately, I can't, either."

He thought for a while and then continued.

"What about lettering? Can't do that either? Too bad. We're supposed to be artists. Well, we'll manage for a day or so before they kick us out. In the time we're here we can do everything we need to. The situation has become a bit more complicated. I've found out that the chairs are in the producer's cabin. But that's not so bad in the long run. The important thing is that we're aboard. All the chairs must be examined before they throw us off. It's too late for today. The producer's already asleep in his cabin."

: 32 :

The Shady Couple

PEOPLE WERE still asleep, but the river was as alive as in the daytime. Rafts floated up and down—huge fields of logs with little wooden houses on them. A small, vicious tug with the name *Storm Conqueror* written in a curve over the paddle cover towed along three oil barges in a line. The *Red Latvia*, a fast mail boat, came up the river. The *Scriabin* overtook a convoy of dredgers and, having measured her depth with a striped pole, began making a circle, turning against the stream.

Aboard ship people began to wake up. A weighted cord was sent flying onto the Bramino quayside. With this line the shoremen hauled over the thick end of the mooring rope. The screws began turning the opposite way and half the river was covered with seething foam. The *Scriabin* shook from the cutting strokes of the screw and sidled up to the pier. It was too early for the lottery, which did not start until ten.

Work began aboard the *Scriabin* just as it would have done on land—at nine sharp. No one changed his habits. Those who were late for work on land were late here, too, although they slept on the very premises. The field staff of the Ministry of Finance adjusted themselves to the new routine very quickly. The messengers swept out their cabins with the same lack of interest as they swept out the offices in Moscow. The cleaners took around tea, and hurried with notes from the registry to the personnel department, not a bit surprised that the latter was in the stern and the registry in the prow. In the mutual settlement cabin the abacuses clicked like castanets and the adding machine made a grinding sound. In front of the wheelhouse someone was being hauled over the coals.

Scorching his bare feet on the hot deck, the smooth operator walked round and round a long strip of bunting, painting some words on it which he kept comparing with a piece of paper: "Everyone to the lottery! Every worker should have government bonds in his pocket."

The smooth operator was doing his best, but his lack of talent was painfully obvious. The words slanted downward and, at one stage, it looked as though the cloth had been completely spoiled. Then, with the boy Kisa's help, Ostap had turned the strip inside-out and begun again. He was now more careful. Before daubing on the letters, he had made two parallel lines with string and chalk, and was now painting in the letters, cursing the innocent Vorobyaninov.

Vorobyaninov carried out his duties as boy conscientiously. He ran below for hot water, melted the glue, sneezing as he did so, poured the paints into a bucket, and looked fawningly into the exacting artist's eyes. When the slogan was dry, the concessionaires took it below and fixed it on the side.

The fat little man who had hired Ostap ran ashore to see what the new artist's work looked like from there. The letters of the words were of different sizes and slightly cockeyed, but nothing could be done about it. He had to be content.

The brass band went ashore and began blaring out

some stirring marches. The sound of the music brought the children from the whole of Bramino and, after them, the peasant men and women from the orchards. The band went on blaring until all the members of the lottery committee had gone ashore. A meeting began. From the porch steps of Korobkov's tea house came the first sounds of a report on the international situation.

The Columbus Theater goggled at the troupe from the ship. They could see the white kerchiefs of the women, who were standing hesitantly a little way from the steps, the motionless crowd of peasant men listening to the speaker, and the speaker himself, from time to time waving his hands. Then the music began again. The band turned around and marched toward the gangway, playing as it went. A crowd of people poured after it.

The lottery device mechanically threw up its combination of figures. The wheels went around, the numbers were announced, and the Bramino citizens watched and listened.

Ostap hurried down for a moment, made certain all the inmates of the ship were in the lottery hall, and ran up on deck again.

"Vorobyaninov," he whispered, "I have an urgent task for you in the art department. Stand by the entrance to the first-class corridor and sing. If anyone comes, sing louder."

The old man was aghast. "What shall I sing?"

"Whatever else it is, don't make it 'God Save the Tsar.' Something with feeling. 'The Apple' or 'A Beauty's Heart.' But I warn you, if you don't come out with your aria in time . . . This isn't the experimental theater. I'll wring your neck."

The smooth operator padded into the cherry-paneled corridor in his bare feet. For a brief moment the large mirror in the corridor reflected his figure. He read the plate on the door:

> Nich. Sestrin
>
> Producer
>
> Columbus Theater

The mirror cleared. Then the smooth operator re-appeared in it carrying a chair with curved legs. He sped along the corridor, out onto the deck, and, glancing at Ippolit Matveyevich, took the chair aloft to the wheelhouse. There was no one in the glass wheelhouse. Ostap took the chair to the prow and said warningly:

"The chair will stay here 'til nighttime. I've worked it all out. Hardly anyone comes here except us. We'll cover the chair with notices and as soon as it's dark we'll quietly take a look at its contents."

A minute later the chair was covered up with sheets of plyboard and bunting, and was no longer visible.

Ippolit Matveyevich was again seized with gold-fever.

"Why don't you take it to your cabin?" he asked impatiently. "We could open it on the spot. And if we find the jewels, we can go ashore right away and—"

"And if we don't? Then what? Where are we going to put it? Or should we perhaps take it back to Citizen Sestrin and say politely: 'Sorry we took your chair, but unfortunately we didn't find anything in it, so here it is back somewhat the worse for wear.' Is that what you'd do?"

The smooth operator was right as always. Ippolit Matveyevich only recovered from his embarrassment at the sound of the overture played on the Esmarch douches and batteries of beer bottles resounding from the deck.

The lottery operations were over for the day. The onlookers spread out on the sloping banks and, above all expectation, noisily acclaimed the Negro minstrels.

Galkin, Palkin, Malkin, Chalkin, and Zalkind kept looking up proudly as though to say: 'There, you see! And you said the popular masses would not understand. But art finds a way!'

After this the Columbus troupe gave a short variety show with singing and dancing on an improvised stage, the point of which was to demonstrate how Vavila the peasant boy won fifty thousand roubles and what came of it. The actors, who had now freed themselves from the chains of Sestrin's constructivism, acted with spirit, danced energetically, and sang in tuneful voices. The river-bank audience was thoroughly satisfied.

The second turn was the balalaika virtuoso. The river bank broke into smiles.

The balalaika was set in motion. It went flying behind the player's back and from there came the "If the master has a chain, it means he has no watch." Then it went flying up in the air and, during the short flight, gave forth quite a few difficult variations.

It was the turn of Georgetta Tiraspolskikh. She led out a herd of girls in sarafans. The concert ended with some Russian folk dances.

As the *Scriabin* made preparations to continue its voyage, as the captain talked with the engine room through the speaking tube, and the boilers blazed, heating the water, the brass band went ashore again and, to everyone's delight, began playing dances. Picturesque groups of dancers formed, full of movement. The setting sun sent down a soft, apricot light. It was an ideal moment for some movie shots. And, indeed, Polkan the cameraman emerged yawning from his cabin. Vorobyaninov, who had grown used to his part as general office boy, followed him, cautiously carrying the camera. Polkan approached the side and glared at the bank. A soldier's polka was being danced on the grass. The boys were stamping their feet as though they wanted to split the planet. The girls sailed around. The onlookers crowded the terraces and slopes. An *avant-garde* French cameraman would have found enough material here to keep him busy for three days. Polkan, however, having run his pig eyes along the bank, immediately turned around, ambled over to the committee chairman, stood him against a white wall, pushed a book into his hand, and, asking him not to move, smoothly turned the handle of his movie camera for some moments. He then led the bashful chairman aft and took him against the setting sun.

Having completed his shots, Polkan retired pompously to his cabin and locked himself in.

Once more the hooter sounded and once more the sun hid in terror. The second night fell. The steamer was ready to leave.

Ostap thought with trepidation of the coming morning. Ahead of him was the job of making a cardboard figure of a sower sowing bonds. This artistic ordeal was beyond the smooth operator. He had managed to cope with the lettering, but he had no resources left for painting a sower.

"Keep it in mind," warned the fat man, "from Vasyuki onward we are holding evening lotteries, so we can't do without the transparent."

"Don't worry at all," said Ostap, basing his hopes on that evening, rather than the next day. "You'll have the transparent."

It was a starry, windy night. The animals in the lottery arc were lulled to sleep.

The lions from the lottery committee were asleep. So were the lambs from personnel, the goats from accounts, the rabbits from mutual settlement, the hyenas and jackals from sound effects, and the pigeons from the typistry.

Only the shady couple were awake. The smooth operator emerged from his cabin after midnight. He was followed by the noiseless shadow of the faithful Kisa. They went up on deck and silently approached the

chair covered with plyboard sheets. Carefully removing the covering, Ostap stood the chair upright and,
tightening his jaw, ripped open the upholstery with a
pair of pliers and inserted his hand.

"Got it!" said Ostap in a hushed voice.

> *Letter from Fyodor*
> *written at the Value Furnished Rooms*
> *in Baku to his wife*
> *in the regional center of N.*

My dear and precious Kate,

Every hour brings us nearer our happiness. I am
writing to you from the Value Furnished Rooms, having finished all my business. The city of Baku is very
large. They say kerosene is extracted here, but you
have to go by electric train and I haven't any money.
This picturesque city is washed by the Caspian. It
really is very large in size. The heat here is awful. I
carry my coat in one hand and my jacket in the other,
and it's still too hot. My hands sweat. I keep indulging
in tea, and I've practically no money. But no harm,
my dear, we'll soon have plenty. We'll travel everywhere and settle properly in Samara, near our factory,
and we'll have liqueurs to drink. But to get to the
point.

In its geographical position and size of population
the city of Baku is considerably greater than Rostov.
But it is inferior to Kharkov in traffic. There are many
people from other parts here. Especially Armenians
and Persians. It's not far from Turkey, either, Mother.
I went to the bazaar and saw many Turkish clothes
and shawls. I wanted to buy you a present of a Mohammedan blanket, but I didn't have any money. Then
I thought that when we are rich (it's only a matter of
days) we'll be able to buy the Mohammedan blanket.

Oh, I forgot to tell you about two frightful things
that happened to me here in Baku: 1) I accidentally

dropped your brother's coat in the Caspian; and 2) I was spat on in the bazaar by a dromedary. Both these happenings greatly amazed me. Why do the authorities allow such scandalous behavior toward travelers, all the more since I had not touched the dromedary, but had actually been nice to it and tickled its nose with a twig. As for the jacket, everybody helped to fish it out and we only just managed it; it was covered with kerosene, believe it or not. Don't mention a word about it, my dearest. Is Estigneyev still having meals?

I have just read through this letter and I see I haven't had a chance to say anything. Bruns the engineer definitely works in As-Oil. But he's not here just now. He's gone to Batumi on vacation. His family is living permanently in Batumi. I spoke to some people and they said all his furniture is there in Batumi. He has a little house there, at the Green Cape—that's the name of the summer resort (expensive, I hear). It costs Rs. 15 from here to Batumi. Cable me twenty here and I'll cable you all the news from Batumi. Spread the rumor that I'm still at my aunt's deathbed in Voronezh.

> Your husband ever,
> Fedya.

P.S. While I was taking this letter to the mail box, someone stole your brother's coat from my room at the Value. I'm very grieved. A good thing it's summer. Don't say anything to your brother.

: *33* :

Expulsion from Paradise

WHILE SOME of the characters in our book were convinced that time would wait, and others that it would not, time passed in its usual way. The dusty Moscow May was followed by a dusty June. In the regional center of N., the Gos. No. 1 motor car had been standing at the corner of Staropan Square and Comrade Gubernsky Street for two days, now and then enveloping the vicinity in desperate quantities of smoke. One by one the shamefaced members of the "Sword and Plowshare" conspiracy left the Stargorod workhouse, having signed a statement that they would not leave the town. Widow Gritsatsuyeva (the passionate woman and poet's dream) returned to her grocery business and was fined only fifteen roubles for not placing the price list of soap, pepper, blueing, and other minor items in a conspicuous place—forgetfulness forgivable in a big-hearted woman.

"Got it!" said Ostap in a strangled voice. "Hold this!"

Ippolit Matveyevich took a flat wooden box into his quivering hands. Ostap continued to grope inside the chair in the darkness. A beacon flashed on the bank; a golden pencil spread across the river and swam after the ship.

"Damn it!" swore Ostap. "Nothing else."

"There m-m-must be," stammered Ippolit Matveyevich.

"Then you have a look as well."

Scarcely breathing, Vorobyaninov knelt down and thrust his arm as far as he could inside the chair. He could feel the ends of the springs between his fingers, but nothing else that was hard. There was a dry, stale smell of disturbed dust from the chair.

"Nothing?"

"No."

Ostap picked up the chair and hurled it far over the side. There was a heavy splash. Shivering in the damp night air, the concessionaires went back to their cabin filled with doubts.

"Well, at any rate we found something," said Bender.

Ippolit Matveyevich took the box from his pocket and looked at it in a daze.

"Come on, come on! What are you goggling at?"

The box was opened. On the bottom lay a copper plate, green with age, which said:

> WITH THIS CHAIR
> CRAFTSMAN
> HAMBS
> *begins a new batch of furniture*
> St. Petersburg   *1865*

Ostap read the inscription aloud.

"But where are the jewels?" asked Ippolit Matveyevich.

"You're remarkably shrewd, my dear chair hunter. As you see, there aren't any."

Vorobyaninov was pitiful to look at. His slightly sprouting mustache twitched and the lenses of his pince-nez were misty. He looked as though he was about to beat his face with his ears in desperation.

The cold, sober voice of the smooth operator had its usual magic effect. Vorobyaninov stretched his hands along the seams of his worn trousers and kept quiet.

"Shut up, sadness. Shut up, Kisa! Someday we'll have the laugh on the stupid eighth chair in which we found the silly box. Cheer up! There are three more chairs aboard; ninety-nine chances out of a hundred.

During the night a volcanic pimple erupted on the aggrieved Ippolit Matveyevich's cheek. All his sufferings, all his setbacks, and the whole ordeal of the jewel hunt seemed to be expressed in the pimple, which was tinged with mother-of-pearl, sunset cherry, and blue.

"Did you do that on purpose?" asked Ostap.

Ippolit Matveyevich sighed convulsively and went to fetch the paints, his tall figure slightly bent like a fishing rod. The transparent was begun. The concessionaires worked on the upper deck.

The third day of the voyage commenced.

It commenced with a brief clash between the brass band and the sound effects over a place to rehearse.

After breakfast, the toughs with the brass tubes and the slender knights with the Esmarch douches both made their way to the stern at the same time. Galkin managed to get to the bench first. A clarinet from the brass band came second.

"The seat's taken," said Galkin sullenly.

"Who by?" asked the clarinet ominously.

"Me, Galkin."

"Who else?"

"Palkin, Malkin, Chalkin, and Zalkind."

"Haven't you got a Yolkin as well? This is our seat."

Reinforcements were brought up on both sides. The most powerful machine in the band was the helicon, encircled three times by a brass serpent. The

French horn swayed to and fro, looking like a human ear, and the trombones were in a state of readiness for action. The sun was reflected a thousand times in their armor. The sound effects looked dark and small beside them. Here and there a bottle glinted, the enema douches glimmered faintly, and the saxophone, that outrageous take-off of a musical instrument, was pitiful to see.

"The enema battalion," said the bullying clarinet, "lays claim to this seat."

"You," said Zalkind, trying to find the most cutting expression he could, "you are the conservatives of music!"

"Don't prevent us from rehearsing."

"It's you who're preventing us. The less you rehearse on those chamber pots of yours, the nicer it sounds."

"Whether you rehearse on those samovars of yours or not makes no damn difference."

Unable to reach any agreement, both sides remained where they were and obstinately began playing their own music. The sounds that floated down the river could only have been made by a streetcar passing slowly over broken glass. The brass played the Kexholm Lifeguards' march, while the sound effects rendered a Negro dance, "An Antelope at the Source of the Zambesi." The shindy was ended by the personal intervention of the chairman of the lottery committee.

At eleven o'clock the magnum opus was completed. Walking backward, Ostap and Vorobyaninov dragged the transparent up to the bridge. The fat little man in charge ran in front with his hands in the air. By joint effort the transparent was tied to the rail. It towered above the passenger deck like a movie screen. In half an hour the electrician had laid cables to the back of the transparent and fitted up three lights inside it. All that remained was to turn the switch.

Off the starboard bow the lights of Vasyuki could already be made out through the darkness.

The chief summoned everyone to the ceremonial illumination of the transparent. Ippolit Matveyevich and the smooth operator watched the proceedings from above, standing beside the dark screen.

Every event on board was taken seriously by the floating government department. Typists, messengers, executives, the Columbus Theater, and the ship's company crowded onto the passenger deck, staring upward.

"Switch it on!" ordered the fat man.

The transparent lit up.

Ostap looked down at the crowd. Their faces were bathed in pink light.

The onlookers began laughing; then there was silence and a stern voice from below said:

"Where's the second in charge?"

The voice was so peremptory that the second in charge rushed down without counting the steps.

"Just have a look," said the voice, "and admire your work!"

"We're about to be kicked off," whispered Ostap to Ippolit Matveyevich.

And, indeed, the little fat man came flying up onto the top deck like a hawk.

"Well, how's the transparent?" asked Ostap cheekily. "Is it long enough?"

"Collect your things!" shouted the fat man.

"What's the hurry?"

"Collect your things! You're going to court! Our boss doesn't like to joke."

"Throw him out!" came the peremptory voice from below.

"But, seriously, don't you like our transparent? Isn't it really any good?"

There was no point in continuing the game. The *Scriabin* had already heaved to, and the faces of the bewildered Vasyuki citizens crowding the pier could be seen from the ship.

Payment was categorically refused. They were given five minutes to collect their things.

"Incompetent fool," said Simbievich-Sindievich as the partners walked down onto the pier. "They should have given the transparent to me to do. I would have done it so that no Meyerhold would have had a look in!"

On the quayside the concessionaires stopped and looked up. The transparent shone against the dark sky.

"Hm, yes," said Ostap, "the transparent is rather outlandish. A lousy job!"

Compared with Ostap's work, a picture drawn with the tail of an unruly donkey would have been a work of art. Instead of a sower sowing bonds, Ostap's mischievous hand had drawn a stumpy body with a sugar-loaf head and thin whiplike arms.

Behind the concessionaires the ship blazed with light and resounded with music, while in front of them, on the high bank, was the darkness of provincial midnight, the barking of a dog, and a distant accordion.

"I will sum up the situation," said Ostap lightheartedly. "Debit: not a cent of money; three chairs sailing down the river; nowhere to go; and no SPCC badge. Credit: a 1926 edition of a guidebook to the Volga (I was forced to borrow it from Monsieur Simbievich's cabin). To balance that without a deficit would be very difficult. We'll have to spend the night on the quay."

The concessionaires arranged themselves on the riverside benches. By the light of a battered kerosene lamp Ostap read the guidebook:

On the right-hand bank is the town of Vasyu-ki. The commodities des-patched from here are timber, resin, bark, and bast; consumer goods are delivered here for the region, which is fifty miles from the nearest railroad.

The town has a population of 8,ooo; it has a state-owned cardboard factory employing 320 workers, a small foundry, a brewery, and a tannery. Besides normal academic establishments, there is also a forestry school.

"The situation is more serious than I thought," observed Ostap. "It seems out of the question that we'll be able to squeeze any money out of the citizens of Vasyuki. We nevertheless need thirty roubles. First, we have to eat, and, second, we have to catch up the lottery ship and meet the Columbus Theater in Stalingrad."

Ippolit Matveyevich curled up like an old emaciated tomcat after a skirmish with a younger rival, the ebullient conqueror of roofs, penthouses, and dormer windows.

Ostap walked up and down the benches, thinking and scheming. By one o'clock a magnificent plan was ready. Bender lay down by the side of his partner and went to sleep.

The Interplanetary
Chess Tournament

A TALL, thin, elderly man in a gold pince-nez and very
dirty paint-splashed boots had been walking about the
town of Vasyuki since early morning, attaching handwritten notices to walls. The notices read:

On June 22, 1927,

a lecture entitled

A FRUITFUL OPENING IDEA

will be given at the Cardboardworker Club
by *Grossmeister* (Grand Chess Master) O. Bender
after which he will play

A SIMULTANEOUS CHESS MATCH
on 160 boards

Admission................20 kopeks
Participation..............50 kopeks
Commencement at 6 P.M. sharp
Bring your own chessboards

MANAGER: *K. Michelson*

The *Grossmeister* had not been wasting his time, either. Having rented a club for three roubles, he hurried across to the chess section, which for some reason or other was located in the corridor of the Horse-Breeding Administration.

In the chess section sat a one-eyed man reading a Panteleyev edition of one of Spielhagen's novels.

"*Grossmeister* O. Bender!" announced Bender, sitting down on the table. "I'm organizing a simultaneous chess match here."

The Vasyuki chessplayer's one eye opened as wide as its natural limits would allow.

"One moment, Comrade *Grossmeister*," he cried. "Take a seat, won't you? I'll be back in a moment."

And the one-eyed man disappeared. Ostap looked around the chess-section room. The walls were hung with photographs of racehorses; on the table lay a dusty register marked "Achievements of the Vasyuki Chess Section for 1925."

The one-eyed man returned with a dozen citizens of varying ages. They all introduced themselves in turn and respectfully shook hands with the *Grossmeister*.

"I'm on my way to Kazan," said Ostap abruptly. "Yes, yes, the match is this evening. Do come along. I'm sorry, I'm not in form at the moment. The Carlsbad tournament was tiring."

The Vasyuki chessplayers listened to him with filial love in their eyes. Ostap was inspired, felt a flood of new strength and chess ideas.

"You wouldn't believe how far chess thinking has advanced," he said. "Lasker, you know, has gone as far as trickery. It's impossible to play him any more. He blows cigar smoke over his opponents and smokes cheap cigars so that the smoke will be fouler. The chess world is greatly concerned."

The *Grossmeister* then turned to more local affairs.

"Why aren't there any new ideas about in the province? Take, for instance, your chess section. That's what it's called—the chess section. That's boring, girls! Why don't you call it something else, in true chess style? It would attract the trade-union masses into the section. For example, you could call it 'The Four Knights Chess Club,' or 'The Red Endgame,' or 'A Decline in the Standard of Play with a Gain in Pace.' That would be good. It has the right kind of sound."

The idea was successful.

"Indeed," exclaimed the citizens, "why shouldn't we rename our section 'The Four Knights Chess Club'?"

Since the chess committee was there on the spot, Ostap organized a one-minute meeting under his honorary chairmanship, and the chess section was unanimously renamed 'The Four Knights Chess Club.' Benefitting from his lessons aboard the *Scriabin*, the *Grossmeister* artistically drew four knights and the appropriate caption on a sheet of cardboard.

This important step promised the flowering of chess thought in Vasyuki.

"Chess!" said Ostap. "Do you realize what chess is? It promotes the advance of culture and also the economy. Do you realize that 'The Four Knights Chess Club,' given the right organization, could completely transform the town of Vasyuki?"

Ostap had not eaten since the day before, which accounted for his unusual eloquence.

"Yes," he cried, "chess enriches a country! If you agree to my plan, you'll soon be descending marble steps to the quay! Vasyuki will become the center of ten provinces! What did you ever hear of the town of Semmering before? Nothing! But now that miserable little town is rich and famous just because an international tournament was held there. That's why I say you should organize an international chess tournament in Vasyuki."

"How?" they all cried.

"It's a perfectly feasible plan," replied the *Gross-*

meister. "My connections and your activity are all that are required for an international tournament in Vasyuki. Just think how fine that would sound—'The 1927 International Tournament to be held in Vasyuki!' Such players as José-Raoul Capablanca, Lasker, Alekhine, Reti, Rubinstein, Tarrasch, Widmar, and Dr. Grigoryev are bound to come. What's more, I'll take part myself!"

"But what about the money?" groaned the citizens. "They would all have to be paid. Many thousands of roubles! Where would we get it?"

"A powerful hurricane takes everything into account," said Ostap. "The money will come from collections."

"And who do you think is going to pay that kind of money? The people of Vasyuki?"

"What do you mean, the people of Vasyuki? The people of Vasyuki are not going to pay money, they're going to receive it. It's all extremely simple. After all, chess enthusiasts will come from all over the world to attend a tournament with such great champions. Hundreds of thousands of people—well-to-do people—will head for Vasyuki. Naturally, the river transport will not be able to cope with such a large number of passengers. So the Ministry of Railroads will have to build a main line from Moscow to Vasyuki. That's one thing. Another is hotels and skyscrapers to accommodate the visitors. The third thing is improvement of the agriculture over a radius of five hundred miles; the visitors have to be provided with fruit, vegetables, caviar, and chocolate candy. The building for the actual tournament is the next thing. Then there's construction of garages to house motor transport for the visitors. An extra-high power radio station will have to be built to broadcast the sensational results of the tournament to the rest of the world. Now about the Vasyuki railroad. It most likely won't be able to carry all the passengers wanting to come to Vasyuki, so we will have to have a 'Greater Vasyuki' airport with regular flights by mail planes and airships to all parts of the globe, including Los Angeles and Melbourne."

Dazzling vistas unfolded before the Vasyuki chess enthusiasts. The walls of the room melted away. The rotting walls of the stud farm collapsed and in their place a thirty-story building towered into the sky. Every hall, every room, and even the lightning-fast elevators were full of people thoughtfully playing chess on malachite-encrusted boards.

Marble steps led down to the blue Volga. Ocean-going steamers were moored on the river. Cablecars communicating with the town center carried up heavy-faced foreigners, chess-playing ladies, Australian advocates of the Indian defense, Hindus in turbans, devotees of the Spanish gambit, Germans, Frenchmen, New Zealanders, inhabitants of the Amazon basin, and finally Muscovites, citizens of Leningrad and Kiev, Siberians and natives of Odessa, all envious of the citizens of Vasyuki.

Lines of cars moved in between the marble hotels. Then suddenly everything stopped. From out of the fashionable Pass Pawn hotel came the world champion Capablanca. He was surrounded by women. A militiaman dressed in special chess uniform (checked breeches and bishops in his lapels) saluted smartly. The one-eyed president of the "Four Knights Club" of Vasyuki approached the champion in a dignified manner.

The conversation between the two luminaries, conducted in English, was interrupted by the arrival by air of Dr. Grigoryev and the future world champion, Alekhine.

Cries of welcome shook the town. Capablanca glowered. At a wave of one-eye's hand, a set of marble steps was run up to the plane. Dr. Grigoryev came down, waving his hat and commenting, as he went, on a possible mistake by Capablanca in his forthcoming match with Alekhine.

Suddenly a black dot was noticed on the horizon. It approached rapidly, growing larger and larger until it finally turned into a large emerald parachute. A man with an attaché case was hanging from the harness like a huge radish.

"Here he is!" shouted one-eye. "Hooray, hooray, I recognize the great philosopher and chessplayer Dr. Lasker. He is the only person in the world who wears those green socks."

Capablanca glowered again.

The marble steps were quickly brought up for Lasker to alight on, and the cheerful ex-champion, blowing from his sleeve a speck of dust which had settled on him over Silesia, fell into the arms of one-eye. The latter put his arm around Lasker's waist and walked him over to the champion, saying:

"Make up your quarrel! On behalf of the popular masses of Vasyuki, I ask you to make up your quarrel."

Capablanca sighed loudly and, shaking hands with the veteran, said: "I always admired your idea of moving QK5 to QB3 in the Spanish gambit."

"Hooray!" exclaimed one-eye. "Simple and convincing in the style of a champion."

And the incredible crowd joined in with: "Hooray! Vivat! Banzai! Simple and convincing in the style of a champion!"

Express trains sped into the twelve Vasyuki stations, depositing ever greater crowds of chess enthusiasts.

Hardly had the sky begun to glow from the brightly lit advertisements, when a white horse was led through the streets of the town. It was the only horse left after the mechanization of the town's transportation. By special decree it had been renamed a stallion, although it had actually been a mare the whole of its life. The lovers of chess acclaimed it with palm leaves and chessboards.

"Don't worry," continued Ostap, "my scheme will guarantee the town an unprecedented boom in your production forces. Just think what will happen when the tournament is over and the visitors have left. The citizens of Moscow, crowded together on account of the housing shortage, will come flocking to your beautiful town. The capital will be automatically transferred to Vasyuki. The government will move here. Vasyuki will be renamed New Moscow, and Moscow will become Old Vasyuki. The people of Leningrad and Kharkov will gnash their teeth in fury but won't be able to do a thing about it. New Moscow will soon become the most elegant city in Europe and, soon afterward, in the whole world."

"The whole world!!!" gasped the citizens of Vasyuki in a daze.

"Yes, and, later on, in the universe. Chess thinking —which has turned a regional center into the capital of the world—will become an applied science and will invent ways of interplanetary communication. Signals will be sent from Vasyuki to Mars, Jupiter, and Neptune. Communication with Venus will be as easy as going from Rybinsk to Yaroslavl. And then who knows what may happen? In maybe eight or so years the first interplanetary chess tournament in the history of the world will be held in Vasyuki."

Ostap wiped his noble brow. He was so hungry he could have eaten a roasted knight from the chessboard.

"Ye-es," said the one-eyed man with a sigh, looking around the dusty room with an insane light in his eye, "but how are we to put the plan into effect, to lay the basis, so to say?"

They all looked at the *Grossmeister* tensely.

"As I say, in practice the plan depends entirely on your activity. I will do all the organizing myself.

There will be no actual expense, except for the cost of the telegrams."

One-eye nudged his companions. "Well?" he asked, "what do you say?"

"Let's do it, let's do it!" cried the citizens.

"How much money is needed for the . . . er . . . telegrams?"

"A mere bagatelle. A hundred roubles."

"We only have twenty-one roubles in the cash box. We realize, of course, that it is by no means enough. . . ."

But the *Grossmeister* proved to be accommodating. "All right," he said, "give me the twenty roubles."

"Will it be enough?" asked one-eye.

"It'll be enough for the initial telegrams. Later on we can start collecting contributions. Then there'll be so much money we shan't know what to do with it."

Putting the money away in his green field jacket, the *Grossmeister* reminded the gathered citizens of his lecture and simultaneous match on one hundred and sixty boards, and, taking leave of them until evening, made his way to the Cardboardworker Club to find Ippolit Matveyevich.

"I'm starving," said Vorobyaninov in a tremulous voice.

He was already sitting at the window of the box office, but had not collected one kopek; he could not even buy a hunk of bread. In front of him lay a green wire basket intended for the money. It was the kind that is used in middle-class houses to hold the cutlery.

"Listen, Vorobyaninov," said Ostap, "stop your cash transactions for an hour and come and eat at the caterers' union canteen. I'll describe the situation as we go. By the way, you need a shave and brush-up. You look like a bum. A *Grossmeister* cannot have such suspicious-looking associates."

"I haven't sold a single ticket," Ippolit Matveyevich informed him.

"Don't worry. People will come flocking in toward evening. The town has already contributed twenty roubles for the organization of an international chess tournament."

"Then why bother about the simultaneous match?" whispered his manager. "You may lose the games anyway. With twenty roubles we can now buy tickets for the ship—the *Karl Liebknecht* has just come in—travel quietly to Stalingrad and wait for the theater to arrive. We can probably open the chairs there. Then we'll be rich and the world will belong to us."

"You shouldn't say such silly things on an empty stomach. It has a bad effect on the brain. We might reach Stalingrad on twenty roubles, but what are we going to eat with? Vitamins, my dear comrade marshal, are not given away free. On the other hand, we can get thirty roubles out of the locals for the lecture and match."

"They'll slaughter us!" said Vorobyaninov.

"It's a risk, certainly. We may be manhandled a bit. But, anyway, I have a nice little plan which will save you, at least. But we can talk about that later on. Meanwhile, let's go and try the local dishes."

Toward six o'clock the *Grossmeister*, replete, freshly shaven, and smelling of eau de cologne, went into the box office of the Cardboardworker Club.

Vorobyaninov, also freshly shaven, was busily selling tickets.

"How's it going?" asked the *Grossmeister* quietly.

"Thirty have gone in and twenty have paid to play," answered his manager.

"Sixteen roubles. That's bad, that's bad!"

"What do you mean, Bender? Just look at the number of people standing in line. They're bound to beat us up."

"Don't think about it. When they hit you, you can cry. In the meantime, don't dally. Learn to do business."

An hour later there were thirty-five roubles in the cash box. The people in the clubroom were getting restless.

"Close the window and give me the money!" said Bender. "Now listen! Here's five roubles. Go down to the quay, hire a boat for a couple of hours, and wait for me by the riverside just below the warehouse. We're going for an evening boat trip. Don't worry about me. I'm in good form today."

The *Grossmeister* entered the clubroom. He felt in good spirits and knew for certain that the first move —pawn to king four—would not cause him any complications. The remaining moves were, admittedly, rather more obscure, but that did not disturb the smooth operator in the least. He had worked out a surprise plan to extract him from the most hopeless game.

The *Grossmeister* was greeted with applause. The small clubroom was decorated with colored flags left over from an evening held a week before by the life-guard rescue service. This was clear, furthermore, from the slogan on the wall:

ASSISTANCE TO DROWNING PERSONS IS IN
THE HANDS OF THOSE PERSONS THEMSELVES

Ostap bowed, stretched out his hands as though restraining the public from undeserved applause, and went up onto the dais.

"Comrades and brother chessplayers," he said in a fine speaking voice: "the subject of my lecture today is one on which I spoke, not without certain success, I may add, in Nizhni-Novgorod a week ago. The subject of my lecture is 'A Fruitful Opening Idea.'

"What, Comrades, is an opening? And what, Comrades, is an idea? An opening, Comrades, is *quasi una fantasia*. And what, Comrades, is an idea? An idea, Comrades, is a human thought molded in logical chess form. Even with insignificant forces you can master the whole of the chessboard. It all depends on each separate individual. Take, for example, the fair-haired young man sitting in the third row. Let's assume he plays well. . . ."

The fair-haired young man turned red.

"And let's suppose that the brown-haired fellow over there doesn't play as well."

Everyone turned around and looked at the brown-haired fellow.

"What do we see, Comrades? We see that the fair-haired fellow plays well and that the other one plays badly. And no amount of lecturing can change this correlation of forces unless each separate individual keeps practicing his check—I mean chess. And now, Comrades, I would like to tell you some instructive stories about our esteemed ultramodernists, Capablanca, Lasker, and Dr. Grigoryev."

Ostap told the audience a few antiquated anecdotes, gleaned in childhood from the *Blue Magazine*, and this completed the first half of the evening.

The brevity of the lecture caused certain surprise. The one-eyed man was keeping his single peeper firmly fixed on the *Grossmeister*.

The beginning of the simultaneous chess match, however, allayed the one-eyed chessplayer's growing suspicions. Together with the rest, he set up the tables along three sides of the room. Thirty enthusiasts in all took their places to play the *Grossmeister*. Many of them were in complete confusion and kept glancing at books on chess to refresh their knowledge of complicated variations, with the help of which they hoped not to have to resign before the twenty-second move, at least.

Ostap ran his eyes along the line of black chessmen surrounding him on three sides, looked at the door, and then began the game. He went up to the one-eyed man, who was sitting at the first board, and moved the king's pawn forward two squares.

One-eye immediately seized hold of his ears and began thinking hard.

A whisper passed along the line of players. "The *Grossmeister* has played pawn to king four."

Ostap did not pamper his opponents with a variety of openings. On the remaining twenty-nine boards he made the same move—pawn to king four. One after another the enthusiasts seized their heads and launched into feverish discussions. Those who were not playing followed the *Grossmeister* with their eyes. The only amateur photographer in the town was about to clamber onto a chair and light his magnesium flare when Ostap waved his arms angrily and, breaking off his drift along the boards, shouted loudly:

"Remove the photographer! He is disturbing my chess thought!"

"What would be the point of leaving a photograph of myself in this miserable town," thought Ostap to himself. "I don't much like having dealings with the militia."

Indignant hissing from the enthusiasts forced the photographer to abandon his attempt. In fact, their annoyance was so great that the photographer was actually put outside the door.

At the third move it became clear that in eighteen games the *Grossmeister* was playing a Spanish gambit. In the other twelve the blacks played the old-fashioned, though fairly reliable Philidor defense. If Ostap had known he was using such cunning gambits and countering such tested defenses, he would have been most surprised. The truth of the matter was that he was playing chess for the second time in his life.

At first the enthusiasts, and first and foremost one-eye, were terrified at the *Grossmeister's* obvious craftiness.

With singular ease, and no doubt scoffing to himself at the backwardness of the Vasyuki enthusiasts, the *Grossmeister* sacrificed pawns and other pieces left and right. He even sacrificed his queen to the brown-haired fellow whose skill had been so deprecated during the lecture. The man was horrified and about to resign; it was only with a terrific effort of will that he was able to continue.

The storm broke about five minutes later.

"Mate!" babbled the brown-haired fellow, terrified out of his wits. "You're checkmate, Comrade *Grossmeister!*"

Ostap analyzed the situation, shamefully called a rook a "castle" and pompously congratulated the fellow on his win. A hum broke out among the enthusiasts.

"Time to push off," thought Ostap, serenely wandering up and down the rows of tables and casually moving pieces about.

"You've moved the knight wrongly, Comrade *Grossmeister*," said one-eye, cringing. "The knight doesn't go like that."

"So sorry," said the *Grossmeister*, "I'm rather tired after the lecture."

During the next ten minutes the *Grossmeister* lost a further ten games.

Cries of surprise echoed through the Cardboard-worker clubroom. Conflict was near. Ostap lost fifteen games in succession, and then another three.

Only one-eye was left. At the beginning of the game he had made a large number of mistakes from nervousness and was only now bringing the game to a victorious conclusion. Unnoticed by those around, Ostap removed the black rook from the board and hid it in his pocket.

A crowd of people pressed tightly around the players.

"I had a rook on this square a moment ago," cried one-eye, looking around, "and now it's gone!"

"If it's not there now, it wasn't there at all," said Ostap, rather rudely.

"Of course it was. I remember it distinctly!"

"Of course it wasn't!"

"Where's it gone, then? Did you take it?"

"Yes, I took it."

"At which move?"

"Don't try to confuse me with your rook. If you want to resign, say so!"

"Wait a moment, Comrades, I have all the moves written down."

"Written down my foot!"

"This is disgraceful!" yelled one-eye. "Give me back the rook!"

"Come on, resign, and stop this fooling about."

"Give back my rook!"

At this point the *Grossmeister*, realizing that procrastination was the thief of time, seized a handful of chessmen and threw them in his one-eyed opponent's face.

"Comrades!" shrieked one-eye. "Look, everyone, he's hitting an amateur!"

The chessplayers of Vasyuki were taken aback.

Without wasting valuable time, Ostap hurled a chessboard at the lamp and, hitting out at jaws and faces in the ensuing darkness, ran out into the street. The Vasyuki chess enthusiasts, falling over each other, tore after him.

It was a moonlit evening. Ostap bounded along the silvery street as lightly as an angel repelled from the sinful earth. On account of the interrupted transformation of Vasyuki into the center of the world, it was not between palaces that Ostap had to run, but wooden houses with outside shutters.

The chess enthusiasts raced along behind.

"Catch the *Grossmeister!*" howled one-eye.

"Twister!" added the others.

"Jerks!" snapped back the *Grossmeister*, increasing his speed.

"Stop him!" cried the outraged chessplayers.

Ostap began running down the steps leading down to the quay. He had four hundred steps to go. Two enthusiasts, who had taken a shortcut down the hillside, were waiting for him at the bottom of the sixth flight. Ostap looked over his shoulder. The advocates of Philidor's defense were pouring down the steps like a pack of wolves. There was no way back, so Ostap kept going.

"Just wait till I get you, you bastards!" he shouted at the two-men advance party, hurtling down from the sixth flight.

The frightened troopers gasped, fell over the balustrade, and rolled down into the darkness of mounds and slopes. The path was clear.

"Stop the *Grossmeister!*" echoed shouts from above.

The pursuers clattered down the wooden steps with a noise like falling bowling balls.

Reaching the river bank, Ostap made to the right, searching with his eyes for the boat containing his faithful manager.

Ippolit Matveyevich was sitting serenely in the boat. Ostap dropped heavily into a seat and began rowing for all he was worth. A minute later a shower of stones flew in the direction of the boat, one of them hitting Ippolit Matveyevich. A yellow bruise appeared on the side of his face just above the volcanic pimple. Ippolit Matveyevich hunched his shoulders and began whimpering.

"You are a softie! They practically lynched me, but I'm perfectly happy and cheerful. And if you take the fifty roubles net profit into account, one bump on the head isn't such an unreasonable price to pay."

In the meantime, the pursuers, who had only just realized that their plans to turn Vasyuki into New Moscow had collapsed and that the *Grossmeister* was absconding with fifty vital Vasyukian roubles, piled into a barge and, with loud shouts, rowed out into midstream. Thirty people were crammed into the boat, all of whom were anxious to take a personal part in settling the score with the *Grossmeister*. The expedition was commanded by one-eye, whose single peeper shone in the night like a lighthouse.

"Stop the *Grossmeister!*" came shouts from the overloaded barge.

"We must step on it, Kisa!" said Ostap. "If they catch up with us, I won't be responsible for the state of your pince-nez."

Both boats were moving downstream. The gap between them was narrowing. Ostap was going all out.

"You won't escape, you rats!" people were shouting from the barge.

Ostap had no time to answer. His oars flashed in and out of the water, churning it up so that it came down in floods in the boat.

"Keep going!" whispered Ostap to himself.

Ippolit Matveyevich had given up hope. The larger boat was gaining on them and its long hull was already flanking them to port in an attempt to force the *Grossmeister* over to the bank. A sorry fate awaited the concessionaires. The jubilance of the chessplayers in the barge was so great that they all moved across to the side to be in a better position to attack the villainous *Grossmeister* in superior forces as soon as they drew alongside the smaller boat.

"Watch out for your pince-nez, Kisa," shouted Ostap in despair, throwing aside the oars. "The fun is about to begin."

"Gentlemen!" cried Ippolit Matveyevich in a croaking voice, "you wouldn't hit us, would you?"

"You'll see!" roared the enthusiasts, getting ready to leap into the boat.

But at that moment something happened which will outrage all honest chessplayers throughout the world. The barge keeled over and took in water on the starboard side.

"Careful!" squealed the one-eyed captain.

But it was too late. There were too many enthusiasts on one side of the Vasyuki dreadnought. As the
center of gravity shifted, the boat stopped rocking,
and, in full conformity with the laws of physics, capsized.

A concerted wailing disturbed the tranquility of the
river.

"Ooooooh!" groaned the chessplayers.

All thirty enthusiasts disappeared under the water.
They quickly came up one by one and seized hold of
the upturned boat. The last to surface was one-eye.

"You jerks!" cried Ostap in delight. "Why don't
you come and get your *Grossmeister?* If I'm not mistaken, you intended to trounce me, didn't you?"

Ostap made a circle around the shipwrecked mari-
ners.

"You realize, individuals of Vasyuki, that I could
drown you all one by one, don't you? But I'm going
to spare your lives. Live on, citizens! Only don't play
chess any more, for God's sake. You're just no good
at it, you jerks! Come on, Ippolit Matveyevich, let's
go. Goodbye, you one-eyed amateurs! I'm afraid
Vasyuki will never become a world center. I doubt
whether the masters of chess would ever visit fools
like you even if I asked them to. Goodbye, lovers
of chess thrills! Long live the 'Four Knights Chess
Club'!"

: 35 :

Et Alia

MORNING FOUND the concessionaires in sight of Chebokary. Ostap was dozing at the rudder while Ippolit Matveyevich sleepily moved the oars through the water. Both were shivering from the chilliness of the night. Pink buds blossomed in the east. Ippolit Matveyevich's pince-nez was all of a glitter. The oval lenses caught the light and alternately reflected one bank and then the other. A signal beacon from the left bank arched in the biconcave glass. The blue domes of Chebokary sailed past like ships. The garden in the east grew larger, and the buds changed into volcanoes, pouring out lava of the best candy-shop colors. Birds on the bank were causing a noisy scene. The gold nosepiece of the pince-nez flashed and dazzled the *Grossmeister*. The sun rose.

Ostap opened his eyes and stretched himself, tilting the boat and cracking his joints.

"Good morning, Kisa," he said, suppressing a yawn. "I come to bring greetings and to tell you the sun is up and is making something over there glitter with a bright, burning light . . ."

"The pier. . . ." reported Ippolit Matveyevich.

Ostap took out the guidebook and consulted it. "From all accounts it's Chebokary. I see:

'Let us note the pleasantly situated town of Chebokary.'

Do you really think it's pleasantly situated, Kisa?

'At the present time Chebokary has 7,702 inhabitants.'

Kisa! Let's give up our hunt for the jewels and increase the population to 7,704. What about it? It would be very effective. We'll open a 'Petits Chevaux' tailor's shop and from the 'Petits Chevaux' we'll have a sure income. Anyway, to continue:

> 'Founded in 1555, the town has preserved some very interesting churches. Besides the administrative institutions of the Chuvash Republic, Chebokary also has a workers' school, a Party school, a teachers' institute, two middle-grade schools, a museum, a scientific society, and a library. On the quayside and in the bazaar it is possible to see Chuvash and Cheremis nationals, distinguishable by their dress. . . .' "

But before the friends were able to reach the quay, where the Chuvash and Cheremis nationals were to be seen, their attention was caught by an object floating downstream ahead of the boat.

"The chair!" cried Ostap. "Manager! It's our chair!"

The partners rowed over to the chair. It bobbed up and down, turned over, went under, and came up farther away from the boat. Water poured freely into its slashed belly.

It was the chair opened aboard the *Scriabin*, and it as now floating slowly toward the Caspian Sea.

"Hi there, friend!" called Ostap. "Long time no see. You know, Vorobyaninov, that chair reminds me of our life. We're also floating with the stream. People push us under and we come up again, although they aren't too pleased about it. No one likes us, except for the criminal investigation department, which doesn't like us, either. Nobody has any time for us. If the chess enthusiasts had managed to drown us yesterday, the only thing left of us would have been the coroner's report. 'Both bodies lay with their feet to the southeast and their heads to the northwest. There were jagged wounds on the bodies, apparently inflicted by a blunt instrument.' The enthusiasts would have beaten us with chessboards, I imagine. That's certainly a blunt instrument. 'The first body belonged to a man of about fifty-five, dressed in a torn silk jacket, old trousers, and old boots. In the jacket pocket was an identification card bearing the name Konrad Karlovich Michelson . . .' That's what they would have written about you, Kisa."

"And what would they have written about you?" asked Ippolit Matveyevich irritably.

"Ah! They would have written something quite different about me. It would have gone like this: 'The second corpse belonged to a man of about twenty-seven years of age. He loved and suffered. He loved money and suffered from a lack of it. His head with its high forehead fringed with raven-black curls was turned toward the sun. His elegant feet, size forty-two boots, were pointing toward the northern lights. The body was dressed in immaculate white clothes, and on the breast was a gold harp encrusted with mother-of-pearl, bearing the words of the song "Farewell, New Village!" The deceased youth engaged in pokerwork, which was clear from the permit no. 86/1562, issued on 8/23/24 by the Pegasus and Parnasus craftsmen's artel, found in the pocket of his tails.' And they would bury me, Kisa, with pomp and circumstance, speeches, a band, and my gravestone would bear the inscription 'Here lies the unknown central-heating engineer and conqueror, Ostap-Suleiman-Bertha-Maria Bender Bey, whose father was a Turkish citizen who died without leaving his son, Ostap-Suleiman, a cent. The deceased's mother was a countess of independent means."

Conversing along these lines, the concessionaires nosed their way to the bank.

That evening, having increased their capital by five roubles from the sale of the Vasyuki boat, the friends went aboard the diesel ship *Uritsky* and sailed for Stalingrad, hoping to overtake the slow moving lottery ship and meet the Columbus Theater troupe in Stalingrad.

The *Scriabin* reached Stalingrad at the beginning of July. The friends met it, hiding behind crates on the quayside. Before the ship was unloaded, a lottery was held aboard and some big prizes were won.

They had to wait four hours for the chairs. First to come ashore was the theater group and then the lottery employees. Persidsky's shining face stood out among them.

As they lay in wait, the concessionaires could hear him shouting:

"Yes, I'll come to Moscow immediately. I've already sent a telegram. And do you know which one? 'Celebrating with you.' Let them guess who it's from."

Then Persidsky got into a hired car, having first inspected it thoroughly, and drove off, accompanied for some reason by shouts of "Hooray!"

As soon as the hydraulic press had been unloaded, the scenic effects were brought ashore. Darkness had already fallen by the time they unloaded the chairs. The troupe piled into five two-horse carts and, gaily shouting, went straight to the station.

"I don't think they're going to play in Stalingrad," said Ippolit Matveyevich.

Ostap was in a quandary.

"We'll have to travel with them," he decided. "But

where's the money? Let's go to the station, anyway, and see what happens."

At the station it turned out that the theater was going to Pyatigorsk via Tikhoretsk. The concessionaires only had enough money for one ticket.

"Do you know how to travel without a ticket?" Ostap asked Vorobyaninov.

"I'll try," said Vorobyaninov timidly.

"Damn you! Better not try. I'll forgive you once more. Let it be. I'll do the bilking."

Ippolit Matveyevich was bought a ticket in an un-upholstered coach and with it traveled to the station "Mineral Waters" on the North Caucasus Railroad. Trying to avoid being seen by the troupe alighting at the station (decorated with oleander shrubs in green tubs), the former marshal went to look for Ostap.

Long after the theater had left for Pyatigorsk in new little local-line coaches, Ostap was still not to be seen. He finally arrived in the evening and found Vorobyaninov completely distraught.

"Where were you?" whimpered the marshal. "I was in such a state!"

"You were in a state, and you had a ticket in your pocket! And I wasn't, I suppose! Who was kicked off the buffers of the last coach of your train? Who spent three hours waiting like an idiot for a freight train with empty mineral-water bottles? You're a swine, Citizen Marshal! Where's the theater?"

"In Pyatigorsk."

"Let's go. I managed to pick up something on the way. The net income is three roubles. It isn't much, of course, but enough for the first purchase of mineral water and railroad tickets."

Creaking like a cart, the train left for Pyatigorsk and, fifty minutes later, passing Zmeika and Besh-tau, brought the concessionaires to the foot of Mashuk.

: 36 :

A View of
the Malachite Puddle

IT WAS SUNDAY EVENING. Everything was clean and washed. Even Mashuk, overgrown with shrubbery and small clumps of trees, was carefully combed and exuded a smell of toilet water.

White pants of the most varied types flashed up and down the toy platform: there were pants made of twill, moleskin, calamanco, duck, and soft flannel. People were walking about in sandals and Apache shirts. In their heavy, dirty boots, heavy dusty trousers, heated vests and scorching jackets, the concessionaires felt very out of place. Among the great variety of gaily colored cottons in which the girls of the resort were parading themselves, the brightest and most elegant was the uniform of the stationmaster.

To the surprise of all newcomers, the stationmaster was a woman. Auburn curls peeped from under her red peaked cap with its two lines of silver braid around the band. She wore a white tunic and a white skirt.

As soon as the travelers had had a good look at the stationmaster, had read the freshly pasted notices advertising the tour of the Columbus Theater, and had drunk two five-kopek glasses of mineral water, they went into the town on the Station-Flower Garden streetcar route. They were charged ten kopeks to go into the Flower Garden.

In the Flower Garden there was a great deal of music, a large number of happy people, and very few flowers. A symphony orchestra in a white shell-like construction was playing the "Dance of the Gnats"; narzan mineral water was on sale in the Lermontov gallery, and it was also obtainable from kiosks and vendors walking around.

No one had time for the two dirty jewel-hunters.

"My, Kisa," said Ostap, "we're out of place in all this festivity."

The concessionaires spent their first night at the spa by a narzan spring.

It was only there, in Pyatigorsk, when the Columbus Theater had performed their version of *The Marriage* to an audience of astounded town-dwellers for the third time, that the partners realized the real difficulties involved in their treasure hunt. To find a way into the theater as they had planned, proved impossible. Galkin, Palkin, Malkin, Chalkin, and Zalkind slept in the wings, since their modest earnings prevented them from living in a hotel.

The days passed, and the friends were slowly reaching the end of their tether, spending their nights at the site of Lermontov's duel and subsisting by carrying the baggage of peasant tourists.

On the sixth day Ostap managed to strike up an acquaintance with Mechnikov, the fitter in charge of the hydraulic press. By this time, Mechnikov, who had no money and was forced to get rid of his daily hang-over by drinking mineral water, was in a terrible state and had been observed by Ostap to sell some of the theater props at the market. Final agreement was reached during the morning libation by a spring. The fitter called Ostap "palsie" and seemed about to consent.

"That's possible," he said. "That's always possible, palsie. It's my pleasure, palsie."

Ostap realized at once that the fitter knew his stuff. The contracting parties looked one another in the eye, embraced, slapped each other's backs and laughed politely.

"Well," said Ostap, "ten for the whole deal."

"Palsie!" exclaimed the astonished fitter, "don't make me mad. I'm a man who's suffering from the narzan."

"How much do you want then?"

"Make it fifty. After all, it's government property. I'm a man who's suffering."

"All right, accept twenty. Agreed? I see from your eyes you agree."

"Agreement is the product of complete non-objection on both sides."

"There are no flies on this one," whispered Ostap to Vorobyaninov. "Take a lesson."

"When will you bring the chairs?"

"You'll get the chairs when I get the money."

"That's fine," said Ostap without thinking.

"Money in advance," declared the fitter. "The money in the morning, the chairs in the evening; or the money in the evening, the chairs the next morning."

"What about the chairs this morning, and the money tomorrow evening," tried Ostap.

"Palsie, I'm a man who's suffering. Such conditions are revolting."

"But the point is, I won't receive my money by telegraph until tomorrow," said Ostap.

"Then we'll discuss the matter tomorrow," concluded the obstinate fitter. "And in the meantime, palsie, have a nice time at the spring. I'm off. Simbievich has me by the throat. I've no strength left. Can you expect a man to exist on mineral water?"

And resplendent in the sunlight, Mechnikov went off.

Ostap looked severely at Ippolit Matveyevich.

"The time we have," he said, "is the money we don't have. Kisa, we must decide on a career. A hundred and fifty thousand roubles, zero zero kopeks awaits us. We only need twenty roubles for the treasure to be ours. We must not be squeamish. It's sink or swim. I choose 'swim.' "

Ostap walked around Ippolit Matveyevich thoughtfully.

"Off with your jacket, Marshal," he said suddenly, "and make it snappy."

He took the jacket from the surprised Vorobyaninov, threw it on the ground, and began stamping on it with his dusty boots.

"What are you doing?" howled Vorobyaninov. "I've been wearing that jacket for fifteen years, and it's as good as new."

"Don't get excited, it soon won't be. Give me your hat. Now, sprinkle your pants with dust and pour some mineral water over them. Be quick about it."

In a few moments Ippolit Matveyevich was dirty to the point of revulsion.

"Now you're all set and have every chance of earning honest money."

"What am I supposed to do?" asked Ippolit Matveyevich tearfully.

"You know French, I hope?"

"Not very well. What I learned at school."

"Hm . . . then we'll have to operate with what you learned at school."

"Can you say in French, 'Gentlemen, I haven't eaten for six days'?"

"*M'sieu,*" began Ippolit Matveyevich, stuttering, "*m'sieu . . .* er . . . *je ne mange . . .* that's right, isn't it? *Je ne mange pas . . .* er . . . How do you say 'six'? *Un, deux, trois, quatre, cinq, six.* It's: *'Je ne mange pas six jours.'* "

"What an accent, Kisa! Anyway, what do you expect from a beggar. Of course a beggar in European Russia wouldn't speak French as well as Milerand. Right, Kisa, and how much German do you know?"

"Why all this?" exclaimed Ippolit Matveyevich.

"Because," said Ostap weightily, "you are now going to the Flower Garden, you're going to stand in the shade and beg for alms in French, German, and Russian, emphasizing the fact that you are an ex-member of the Cadet faction of the Tsarist Duma. The net profit will go to Mechnikov. Understand?"

Ippolit Matveyevich was transfigured. His chest swelled up like the Palace bridge in Leningrad, his eyes flashed fire, and his nose seemed to Ostap to be pouring forth smoke. His mustache slowly began to rise.

"Dear me," said the smooth operator, not in the least alarmed. "Just look at him! Not a man, but a dragon."

"Never," suddenly said Ippolit Matveyevich, "never had Vorobyaninov held out his hand."

"Then you can stretch out your feet, you silly old ass!" shouted Ostap. "So you've never held out your hand?"

"No, I have not."

"Spoken like a true gigolo. You've been living off me for the last three months. For three months I've been providing you with food and drink and educating you, and now you stand like a gigolo in the third position and say . . . Come off it, Comrade! You've got two choices. Either you go right away to the Flower Garden and bring back ten roubles by nightfall, or else I'm automatically removing you from the list of shareholders in the concession. I'll give you five to decide yes or no. One . . ."

"Yes," mumbled the marshal.

"In that case, repeat the words."

"*M'sieu, je ne mange pas six jours. Geben Sie mir bitte etwas Kopek für ein Stück Brot.* Give something to an ex-member of the Duma."

"Once again. Make it more heart-rending."

Ippolit Matveyevich repeated the words.

"All right. You have a latent talent for begging. Off you go. The rendezvous is at midnight by the spring. That's not for romantic reasons, mind you, but simply because people give more in the evening."

"What about you?" asked Vorobyaninov. "Where are you going?"

"Don't worry about me. As usual, I shall be where things are most difficult."

The friends went their ways.

Ostap hurried to a small stationery store, bought a book of receipts with his last ten-kopek bit, and sat on a stone block for an hour or so, numbering the receipts and scribbling something on them.

"System above all," he muttered to himself. "Every public kopek must be accounted for."

The smooth operator marched up the mountain road that led round Mashuk to the site of Lermontov's duel with Martynov, passing sanitariums and rest homes.

Constantly overtaken by buses and two-horse carriages, he arrived at the Drop.

A narrow path cut in the cliff led to a conical drop. At the end of the path was a parapet from which one could see a puddle of stinking malachite at the bottom of the Drop. This Drop is considered one of the sights of Pyatigorsk and is visited by a large number of tourists in the course of a day.

Ostap had seen at once that for a man without prejudice the Drop could be a source of income.

"What a remarkable thing," mused Ostap, "that the town has never thought of charging ten kopeks to see the Drop. It seems to be the only place where the people of Pyatigorsk allow the sight-seers in free. I will remove that blemish on the town's escutcheon and rectify the sad omission."

And Ostap acted as his reason, instinct, and the situation in hand prompted.

He stationed himself at the entrance to the Drop and, rustling the receipt book, called out from time to time.

"Buy your tickets here, citizens. Ten kopeks. Children and servicemen free. Students, five kopeks. Nonunion members, thirty kopeks!"

It was a sure bet. The citizens of Pyatigorsk never went to the Drop, and to fleece the Soviet tourists ten kopeks to see "Something" was no great difficulty. The nonunion members, of whom there were many in Pyatigorsk, were a great help.

They all trustingly passed over their ten kopeks, and one ruddy-cheeked tourist, seeing Ostap, said triumphantly to his wife:

"You see, Tanyusha, what did I tell you? And you said there was no charge to see the Drop. That couldn't have been right, could it, Comrade?"

"You're absolutely right. It would be quite impossible not to charge for entry. Ten kopeks for union members and thirty for nonmembers."

Toward evening, an excursion of militiamen from Kharkov arrived at the Drop in two wagons. Ostap was alarmed and was about to pretend to be an innocent sight-seer, but the militiamen crowded round the smooth operator so timidly that there was no way of retreat. So he shouted in a rather harsh voice:

"Union members, ten kopeks; but since representatives of the militia can be classed as students and children, they pay five kopeks."

The militiamen paid up, having tactfully inquired for what purpose the money was being collected.

"For general repairs to the Drop," answered Ostap boldly. "So that it won't drop too much."

While the smooth operator was briskly selling the

view of the malachite puddle, Ippolit Matveyevich, hunching his shoulders and wallowing in shame, stood under an acacia and, avoiding the eyes of the passers-by, mumbled his three phrases.

"*M'sieu, je ne mange pas six jours. . . . Geben Sie mir . . .*"

People not only gave little, they somehow gave unwillingly. However, by exploiting his purely Parisian pronunciation of the word *mange* and pulling at heartstrings by his desperate position as an ex-member of the Tsarist Duma, he was able to pick up three roubles in copper coins.

The gravel crunched under the feet of the holiday-makers. The orchestra played Strauss, Brahms, and Grieg with long pauses in between. The brightly colored crowds drifted past the old marshal, chattering as they went, and came back again. Lermontov's spirit hovered unseen above the citizens trying matsoni on the veranda of the buffet. There was an odor of Eau de Cologne and sulphur gas.

"Give to a former member of the Duma," mumbled the marshal.

"Tell me, were you really a member of the State Duma?" asked a voice right by Ippolit Matveyevich's ear. "And did you really attend meetings? Ah! Ah! First rate!"

Ippolit Matveyevich raised his eyes and almost fainted. Hopping about in front of him like a sparrow was Absalom Vladimirovich Iznurenkov. He had changed his brown Lodz suit for a white coat and gray trousers with a playful spotted pattern. He was in unusual spirits and from time to time jumped as much as five or six inches off the ground. Iznurenkov did not recognize Ippolit Matveyevich and continued to shower him with questions.

"Tell me, did you actually see Rodzyanko? Was Purishkevich really bald? Ah! Ah! What a subject! First rate!"

Continuing to gyrate, Iznurenkov shoved three roubles into the confused marshal's hand and ran off. But for some time afterward his thick thighs could be glimpsed in various parts of the Flower Garden, and his voice seemed to float down from the trees.

"Ah! Ah! 'Don't sing to me, my beauty, of sad Georgia.' Ah! Ah! 'They remind me of another life and a distant shore.' 'And in the morning she smiled again.' First rate!"

Ippolit Matveyevich remained standing, staring at the ground. A pity he did so. He missed a lot.

In the enchanting darkness of the Pyatigorsk night, Ellochka Shukin strolled through the park, dragging after her the submissive and newly reconciled Ernest Pavlovich. The trip to the spa was the finale of the hard battle with Vanderbilt's daughter. The proud American girl had recently set sail on a pleasure cruise to the Sandwich Isles in her own yacht.

"Hoho!" echoed through the darkness. "Great, Ernestula! Ter-r-rific!"

In the lamplit buffet sat Alchen and his wife, Sashchen. Her cheeks were still adorned with sideburns. Alchen was bashfully eating shishkebab, washing it down with Kahetinsky wine no. 2, while Sashchen, stroking her sideburns, waited for the sturgeon she had ordered.

After the liquidation of the second social-security office (everything had been sold, including the cook's cap and the slogan, "By carefully masticating your food you help society"), Alchen had decided to have a vacation and enjoy himself. Fate itself had saved the full-bellied little crook. He had decided to see the Drop that day, but did not have time. Ostap would certainly not have let him get away for less than thirty roubles.

Ippolit Matveyevich wandered off to the spring as the musicians were folding up their stands, the holiday-makers were dispersing, and the courting couples alone breathed hard in the narrow lanes of the Flower Garden.

"How much did you collect?" asked Ostap as soon as the marshal's hunched figure appeared at the spring.

"Seven roubles, twenty-nine kopeks. Three roubles in notes. The rest, copper and silver."

"For the first go—terrific! An executive's rate! You amaze me, Kisa. But what fool gave you three roubles, I'd like to know? You didn't give him change, I hope?"

"It was Iznurenkov."

"What, really? Absalom! Why, you rolling stone. Where have you rolled to! Did you talk to him? Oh, he didn't recognize you!"

"He asked all sorts of questions about the Duma. And laughed."

"There, you see, Marshal, it's not really so bad being a beggar, particularly with a moderate education and a feeble voice. And you were stubborn about it, tried to give yourself airs as though you were the Lord Privy Seal. Well, Kisochka, I haven't been wasting my time, either. Fifteen roubles. Altogether that's enough."

The next morning the fitter received his money and brought them two chairs in the evening. He claimed it was not possible to get the third chair since the sound effects were playing cards on it.

For greater security the friends climbed practically to the top of Mashuk.

Beneath, the lights of Pyatigorsk shone strong and steady. Below Pyatigorsk more feeble lights marked Goryachevodsk village. On the horizon Kislovodsk stood out from behind a mountain as two parallel dotted lines.

Ostap glanced up at the starry sky and took out the familiar pliers from his pocket.

] CHAPTER [

: *37* :

The Green Cape

ENGINEER BRUNS was sitting on the stone veranda of
his little wooden house at the Green Cape, under a
large palm, the starched leaves of which cast narrow,
pointed shadows on the back of his shaven neck, his
white shirt, and the Hambs chair from Madam
Popova's suite, on which the engineer was restlessly
awaiting his dinner.

Bruns pouted his thick, juicy lips and called in the
voice of a petulant, fat little boy:

"Mu-u-usik!"

The house was silent.

The tropical flora fawned on the engineer. Cacti
stretched out their spiky mittens toward him. Dra-
caena shrubs rustled their leaves. Banana trees and
sago palms chased the flies from his face, and the
roses with which the veranda was woven fell at his
feet.

But all in vain. Bruns was hungry. He glowered
petulantly at the mother-of-pearl bay and the distant
cape at Batumi, and called out in a singsong voice:

"Musik! Musik!"

The sound quickly died away in the moist subtropical air. There was no answer. Bruns had visions of a large golden-brown goose with sizzling, greasy skin, and, unable to control himself, yelled out:

"Musik, is the goosie ready?"

"Andrei Mikhailovich," said a woman's voice from inside, "don't keep on at me."

The engineer, who was already pouting his lips into the accustomed shape, promptly answered:

"Musik. You haven't any pity for your little hubby."

"Get out, you glutton," came the reply from inside.

The engineer did not give in, however. He was just about to continue his appeals for the goose, which had been going on unsuccessfully for two hours, when a sudden rustling made him turn round.

From the black-green clumps of bamboo there had emerged a man in torn blue tunic-shirt—belted with a shabby twisted cord with tassels—and frayed striped trousers. The stranger's kindly face was covered with ragged stubble. He was carrying his jacket in his hand.

The man approached and asked in a pleasant voice:

"Where can I find Engineer Bruns?"

"I'm Engineer Bruns," said the goose-charmer in an unexpectedly deep voice. "What can I do for you?"

The man silently fell to his knees. It was Father Fyodor.

"Have you gone crazy?" cried the engineer. "Stand up, please."

"I won't," said Father Fyodor, following the engineer with his head and gazing at him with bright eyes.

"Stand up."

"I won't."

And carefully, so that it would not hurt, Father Fyodor began beating his head against the gravel.

"Musik, come here!" shouted the frightened engineer. "Look what's happening! Please get up. I implore you."

"I won't," repeated Father Fyodor.

Musik ran out onto the veranda; she was very good at interpreting her husband's intonation.

Seeing the lady, Father Fyodor promptly crawled over to her and, bowing to her feet, rattled off:

"On you, Mother, on you, my dear, on you I lay my hopes."

Engineer Bruns thereupon turned red in the face, seized the petitioner under the arms and, straining hard, tried to lift him to his feet. Father Fyodor was crafty, however, and tucked up his legs. The disgusted Bruns dragged his extraordinary visitor into a corner and forcibly sat him in a chair (a Hambs chair, not from Vorobyaninov's house, but one belonging to Popov, the general's wife).

"I dare not sit in the presence of high-ranking persons," mumbled Father Fyodor, throwing the baker's jacket, which smelt of kerosene, across his knees.

And he made another attempt to go down on his knees.

With a pitiful cry the engineer restrained him by the shoulders.

"Musik," he said, breathing heavily, "talk to this citizen. There's been some misunderstanding."

Musik at once assumed a businesslike tone.

"In my house," she said menacingly, "kindly don't go down on anyone's knees."

"Dear lady," said Father Fyodor humbly, "Mother!"

"I'm not your mother. What do you want?"

The priest began burbling something incoherent, but apparently deeply moving. It was only after lengthy questioning that they were able to gather that he was asking them to do him a particular favor and sell him the suite of twelve chairs, one of which he was sitting on at that moment.

The engineer let go of Father Fyodor with surprise, whereupon the latter immediately plumped down on his knees again and began creeping after the engineer like a tortoise.

"But why," cried the engineer, trying to dodge Father Fyodor's long arms, "why should I sell my chairs? It's no use how much you go down on your knees like that, I just don't understand anything."

"But they're my chairs," groaned Father Fyodor.

"What do you mean, they're yours? How can they be yours? You're crazy. Musik, I see it all. This man's a crackpot."

"They're mine," repeated the priest in humiliation.

"Do you think I stole them from you, then?" asked the engineer furiously. Did I steal them? Musik, this is blackmail."

"Oh, Lord," whispered Father Fyodor.

"If I stole them from you, then take the matter to court, but don't cause pandemonium in my house. Did you hear that, Musik? How impudent can you get? They don't even let a man have his dinner in peace."

No, Father Fyodor did not want to recover "his" chairs by taking the matter to court. By no means. He knew that Engineer Bruns had not stolen them from him. Oh, no. That was the last idea he had in his mind. But the chairs had nevertheless belonged to him before the revolution, and his wife, who was on her deathbed in Voronezh, was very attached to them. It was to comply with her wishes and not on his own initiative that he had taken the liberty of finding out the whereabouts of the chairs and coming to see Citizen Bruns. Father Fyodor was not asking for charity. Oh, no. He was sufficiently well off (he owned a small candle factory in Samara) to sweeten his wife's last few minutes by buying the old chairs. He was ready to splurge and pay twenty roubles for the whole set of chairs.

"What?" cried the engineer, growing purple.

"Twenty roubles? For a splendid drawing-room suite? Musik, did you hear that? He really is a nut. Honestly he is."

"I'm not a nut, but merely complying with the wishes of my wife who sent me."

"Oh, hell!" said the engineer. "Musik, he's at it again. He's crawling around again."

"Name your price," moaned Father Fyodor, cautiously beating his head against the trunk of an Araucaria.

"Don't spoil the tree, you crazy man. Musik, I don't think he's a nut. He's simply distraught at his wife's illness. Shall we sell him the chairs and get rid of him? Otherwise, he'll crack his skull."

"And what are we going to sit on?" aked Musik.

"We'll buy some more."

"For twenty roubles?"

"Suppose I don't sell them for twenty. Suppose I don't sell them for two hundred, but supposing I do sell them for two-fifty?"

In response came the sound of a head against a tree.

"Musik, I'm fed up with this!"

The engineer went over to Father Fyodor with his mind made up and began issuing an ultimatum.

"First, step back from the palm at least three paces; second, stand up at once; third, I'll sell you the chairs for two hundred and fifty and not a kopek less."

"It's not for personal gain," chanted Father Fyodor, "but merely in compliance with my sick wife's wishes."

"Well, old boy, my wife's also sick. That's right, isn't it, Musik? Your lungs aren't in too good a state, are they? But on the strength of that I'm not asking you to . . . er . . . sell me your jacket for thirty kopeks."

"Have it for nothing," exclaimed Father Fyodor.

The engineer waved him aside in irritation and said coldly:

"Stop your tricks. I'm not going to argue with you any more. I've assessed the worth of the chairs at two hundred and fifty roubles and I'm not shifting one cent."

"Fifty," offered the priest.

"Musik," said the engineer, "call Bagration. Let him see this citizen off the premises."

"Not for personal gain. . . ."

"Bagration!"

Father Fyodor fled in terror, while the engineer went into the dining room and sat down to the goose. Bruns's favorite bird had a soothing effect on him. He began to calm down.

Just as the engineer was about to pop a goose leg into his pink mouth, having first wrapped a piece of cigarette paper around the bone, the face of Father Fyodor appeared appealingly at the window.

"Not for personal gain," said a soft voice. "Fifty-five roubles."

The engineer let out a roar without turning around. Father Fyodor disappeared.

The whole of that day Father Fyodor's figure kept appearing at different points near the house. At one moment it was seen coming out of the shade of the Cryptomeria, at another it rose from a mandarin grove; then it raced across the back yard and, fluttering, dashed toward the botanical garden.

The whole day the engineer kept calling for Musik, and complained about the crackpot and of a headache. From time to time Father Fyodor's voice could be heard echoing through the dusk.

"A hundred and eight," he called from somewhere in the sky.

A moment later his voice came from the direction of Dumbasov's house.

"A hundred and forty-one. Not for personal gain, Mr. Bruns, but merely . . ."

At length the engineer could stand it no longer; he

came out onto the veranda and, peering into the darkness, began shouting very clearly:

"Damn you. Two hundred roubles. Only leave us alone."

There was a rustle of disturbed bamboo, the sound of a soft groan and fading footsteps, then all was quiet.

Stars floundered in the bay. Fireflies chased after Father Fyodor and circled round his face, casting a greenish medicinal glow on his face.

"Now the goose is flown," muttered the engineer, going inside.

Meanwhile, Father Fyodor was speeding along the coast in the last bus in the direction of Batumi. A slight surf washed right up to the side of him; the wind blew in his face, and the bus hooted in reply to the whining jackals.

That evening Father Fyodor sent a telegram to his wife in the town of N.

GOODS FOUND STOP WIRE ME TWO HUNDRED THIRTY
STOP SELL ANYTHING STOP FEDYA

For two days he loafed about elatedly near Bruns's house, bowing to Musik in the distance, and even making the tropical distances resound with shouts of "Not for personal gain, but merely at the wishes of my wife who sent me."

Two days later the money was received together with a desperate telegram:

SOLD EVERYTHING STOP NOT A CENT LEFT
STOP KISSES AND AM WAITING STOP
EVSTIGNEYEV STILL HAVING MEALS STOP KATEY

Father Fyodor counted the money, crossed himself frenziedly, hired a cart, and drove to the Green Cape.

The weather was dull. A wind from the Turkish frontier blew across thunderclouds. The strip of blue sky became narrower and narrower. The wind was near gale force. It was forbidden to take boats to sea and to bathe. Thunder rumbled above Batumi. The gale shook the coast.

Reaching Bruns's house, Father Fyodor ordered the Adzhar driver to wait and went to fetch the furniture.

"I've brought the money," said Father Fyodor. "You ought to lower your price a bit."

"Musik," groaned the engineer, "I can't stand any more of this."

"No, no, I've brought the money," said Father Fyodor hastily, "two hundred, as you said."

"Musik, take the money and give him the chairs, and let's get it over with. I've a headache."

His life ambition was achieved. The candle factory in Samara was falling into his lap. The jewels were pouring into his pocket like seeds.

Twelve chairs were loaded into the cart one after another. They were very like Vorobyaninov's chairs, except that the covering was not flowered chintz, but rep with blue and pink stripes.

Father Fyodor was overcome with impatience. Under his shirt he had tucked a hatchet behind a twisted cord. He sat next to the driver and, constantly looking round at the chairs, drove to Batumi. The spirited horses carried Father Fyodor and his treasure down along the highway past the Finale restaurant, where the wind swept across the bamboo tables and arbors, past a tunnel that was swallowing up the last few tank cars of an oil train, past the photographer, deprived that overcast day of his usual clientele, past a sign reading "Batumi Botanical Garden," and carried him, not too quickly, along the very line of surf. At the point where the road touched the rocks, Father Fyodor was soaked with salty spray. Rebuffed by the rocks, the waves turned into waterspouts and, rising up to the sky, slowly fell back again.

The jolting and the spray from the surf whipped

Father Fyodor's troubled spirit into a frenzy. Struggling against the wind, the horses slowly approached Makhinjauri. From every side the turbid green waters hissed and swelled. Right up to Batumi the white surf swirled like the edge of a petticoat peeking from under the skirt of a slovenly woman.

"Stop!" Father Fyodor suddenly ordered the driver. "Stop, Mohammedan!"

Trembling and stumbling, he started to unload the chairs onto the deserted shore. The apathetic Adzhar received his five roubles, whipped up the horses and rode off. Making sure there was no one about, Father Fyodor carried the chairs down from the rocks onto a dry patch of sand and took out his hatchet.

For a moment he hesitated, not knowing where to start. Then, like a man walking in his sleep, he went over to the third chair and struck the back a ferocious blow with the hatchet. The chair toppled over undamaged.

"Aha!" shouted Father Fyodor. "I'll show you!"

And he flung himself on the chair as though it had been a live animal. In a trice the chair had been hacked to ribbons. Father Fyodor could not hear the sound of the hatchet against the wood, cloth covering, and springs. All other sounds were drowned by the powerful roar of the gale.

"Aha! Aha! Aha!" cried the priest, swinging from the shoulder.

One by one the chairs were put out of action. Father Fyodor's fury increased more and more. So did the fury of the gale. Some of the waves came up to his feet.

From Batumi to Sinop there was a great din. The sea raged and vented its spite on every little ship. The S. S. *Lenin* sailed toward Novorossisk with its two funnels smoking and its stern plunging low in the water. The gale roared across the Black Sea, hurling thousand-ton breakers onto the shore of Trebizond,

Yalta, Odessa, and Konstantsa. Beyond the still in the Bosporous and the Dardanelles surged the Mediterranean. Beyond the Straits of Gibraltar, the Atlantic smashed against the shores of Europe. A belt of angry water encircled the world.

And on the Batumi shore stood Father Fyodor, bathed in sweat and hacking at the final chair. A moment later it was all over. Desperation seized him. With a dazed look at the mountain of legs, backs, and springs, he turned back. The water grabbed him by the feet. He lurched forward and ran soaked to the highway. A huge wave broke on the spot where he had been a moment before and, swirling back, washed away the mutilated furniture. Father Fyodor no longer saw anything. He staggered along the highway, hunched and hugging his fist to his chest.

He went into Batumi, unable to see anything about him. His position was the most terrible thing of all. Three thousand miles from home and twenty roubles in his pocket—getting home was definitely out of the question.

Father passed the Turkish bazaar—where he was advised in the perfect whisper to buy some Coty powder, silk stockings and contraband Batumi tobacco—dragged himself to the station, and lost himself in the crowd of porters.

] CHAPTER [

: *38* :

===

Under the Clouds

THREE DAYS after the concessionaires' deal with Mechnikov the fitter, the Columbus Theater left by railroad
via Makhacha-Kala and Baku. The whole of these three
days the concessionaires, frustrated by the contents of
the two chairs opened on Mashuk, waited for Mechnikov to bring them the third of the Columbus chairs.
But the narzan-tortured fitter converted the whole of
the twenty roubles into the purchase of plain vodka
and drank himself into such a state that he was kept
locked up in the props room.

"That's Mineral Waters for you!" said Ostap, when
he heard about the theater's departure. "A useful fool,
that fitter. Catch me having dealings with theater people after this!"

Ostap became much more nervy than before. The
chances of finding the treasure had increased infinitely.

"We need money to get to Vladikavkaz," said Ostap.
"From there we'll drive by car to Tiflis along the
Georgian military highway. Glorious scenery! Magnificent views! Wonderful mountain air! And at the end
of it all—one hundred and fifty thousand roubles, zero
zero kopeks. There is some point in continuing the
hearing."

But it was not quite so easy to leave Mineral Waters. Vorobyaninov proved to have absolutely no talent for bilking the railroad, and so when all attempts to get him aboard a train had failed he had to perform again in the Flower Garden, this time as an educational district ward. This was not at all a success. Two roubles for twelve hours' hard and degrading work, though it was a large enough sum for the fare to Vladikavkaz.

At Beslan, Ostap, who was traveling without a ticket, was thrown off the train, and the smooth operator impudently ran behind it for a mile or so, shaking his fist at the innocent Ippolit Matveyevich.

Soon after, Ostap managed to jump onto a train slowly making its way to the Caucasian ridge. From his position on the steps Ostap surveyed with great curiosity the panorama of the mountain range that unfolded before him.

It was between three and four in the morning. The mountain tops were lit by dark pink sunlight. Ostap did not like the mountains.

"Too showy," he said. "Queer kind of beauty. An idiot's imagination. No use at all."

At Vladikavkaz station the passengers were met by a large open bus belonging to the Transcaucasian car-hire-and-manufacturing society, and kindly people said:

"Those traveling by the Georgian military highway will be taken into the town free."

"Hold on, Kisa," said Ostap. "We want the bus. Let them take us free."

When the bus had given him a lift to the center of the town, however, Ostap was in no hurry to put his name down for a seat in a car. Talking enthusiastically to Ippolit Matveyevich, he gazed admiringly at the view of the cloud-enveloped Table Mountain, but finding that it really was like a table, promptly retired.

They had to spend several days in Vladikavkaz.

None of their attempts to obtain money for the highway fare met with any success, nor provided them with enough money to buy their food. An attempt to make the citizens pay ten-kopek bits failed. The mountain ridge was so high and clear that it was not possible to charge for looking at it. It was visible from practically every point, and there were no other beauty spots in Vladikavkaz. There was the Terek, which flowed past the "Trek," but the town charged for entry to that without Ostap's assistance. The alms collected in two days by Ippolit Matveyevich only amounted to thirteen kopeks.

"There's only one thing to do," said Ostap. "We'll go to Tiflis on foot. We can cover the hundred miles in five days. Don't worry, Dad, the mountain view is delightful and the air is bracing . . . We only need money for bread and bologna. You can add a few Italian phrases to your vocabulary, or not, as you like; but by evening you've got to collect at least two roubles. We won't have a chance to eat today, dear chum. Alas! What bad luck!"

Early in the morning the partners crossed the little bridge across the Terek river, went around the barracks, and disappeared deep into the green valley along which ran the Georgian military highway.

"We're in luck, Kisa," said Ostap. "It rained last night so we won't have to swallow the dust. Breathe in the fresh air, Marshal. Sing something. Recite some Caucasian poetry and behave as befits the occasion."

But Ippolit Matveyevich did not sing or recite poetry. The road went uphill. The nights spent in the open air made themselves felt by pains in his side and heaviness in his legs, and the bologna made itself felt by a constant and griping indigestion. He walked along, holding in his hand a five-pound loaf of bread wrapped in newspaper, his left foot dragging slightly.

On the move again! But this time toward Tiflis; this time along the most beautiful highway in the world.

Ippolit Matveyevich could not have cared less. He did
not look around him as Ostap did. He certainly did not
notice the Terek, which now could just be heard rumbling at the bottom of the valley. It was only the ice-
capped mountain tops glistening in the sun which
somehow vaguely reminded him of a sort of cross between the sparkle of diamonds and the best brocade
coffins of Bezenchuk the undertaker.

After Balta the road entered a pass and continued as
a narrow ledge cut in the dark overhanging cliff. The
road spiraled upward, and by evening the concessionaires reached the village of Lars, about three thousand
feet above sea level.

They passed the night in a poor native hotel without
charge and were even given a glass of milk each for
delighting the owner and his guests with card tricks.

The morning was so glorious that Ippolit Matveyevich, braced by the mountain air, began to stride along
more cheerfully than the day before. Just behind Lars
rose the impressive rock wall of the Bokovoi ridge.
At this point the Terek valley closed up into a series of
narrow gorges. The scenery became more and more
somber, while the inscriptions on the cliffs grew more
frequent. At the point where the cliffs squeezed the
Terek's flow between them to the extent that the span
of the bridge was no more than ten feet, the concessionaires saw so many inscriptions on the side of the gorge
that Ostap forgot about the majestic sight of the Daryal
gorge and shouted out, trying to drown the rumble
and rushing of the Terek:

"Great people! Look at that, Marshal! Do you see it?
Just a little higher than the cloud and slightly lower
than the eagle! An inscription which says 'Nicky and
Mike, July 1914.' An unforgettable sight! Notice the
artistry with which it was done. Each letter is three
feet high, and they used oil paints. Where are you
now, Nicky and Mike?"

"Kisa," continued Ostap, "let's record ourselves for

posterity, too. I have some chalk, by the way. Honestly, I'll go up and write 'Kisa and Ossy were here.'"

And without giving it much thought, Ostap put down the supply of sausage on the wall separating the highway from the seething depths of the Terek and began clambering up the rocks. At first Ippolit Matveyevich watched the smooth operator's ascent, but then lost interest and began to survey the base of Tamara's castle, which stood on a rock like a horse's tooth.

Just at this time, about a mile away from the concessionaires, Father Fyodor entered the Daryal gorge from the direction of Tiflis. He marched along like a soldier with his eyes, as hard as diamonds, fixed ahead of him, supporting himself on a large crook.

With his last remaining money Father Fyodor had reached Tiflis and was now walking home, subsisting on charity. While crossing the Cross gap he had been bitten by an eagle. Father Fyodor hit out at the insolent bird with his crook and continued on his way.

As he went along, intermingling with the clouds, he muttered:

"Not for personal gain, but at the wishes of my wife who sent me."

The distance between the enemies narrowed. Turning a sharp bend, Father Fyodor came across an old man in a gold pince-nez.

The gorge split asunder before Father Fyodor's eyes. The Terek stopped its thousand-year-old roar.

Father Fyodor recognized Vorobyaninov. After the terrible fiasco in Batumi, after all his hopes had been dashed, this new chance of gaining riches had an extraordinary effect on the priest.

He grabbed Ippolit Matveyevich by his scraggy Adam's apple, squeezed his fingers together, and shouted hoarsely:

"What have you done with the treasure that you murdered your mother-in-law to get?"

Ippolit Matveyevich, who had not been expecting anything of this nature, said nothing, but his eyes bulged so far that they almost touched the lenses of his pince-nez.

"Speak!" ordered Father Fyodor. "Repent, you sinner!"

Vorobyaninov felt himself losing his breath.

Suddenly Father Fyodor caught sight of Bender jumping from rock to rock; the technical adviser was coming down, shouting at the top of his voice:

> *"The waves are foaming and seething*
> *As they break against the somber cliffs."*

A terrible fear gripped Father Fyodor. He continued mechanically holding the marshal by the throat, but his knees were shaking.

"Well, of all people!" cried Ostap in a friendly tone. "The rival concern."

Father Fyodor did not dally. Obeying his virtuous instinct, he grabbed the concessionaires' bread and sausage and fled.

"Hit him, Comrade Bender!" cried Ippolit Matveyevich, who was sitting on the ground recovering his breath. "Catch him! Stop him!"

Ostap began whistling and whooping.

"Wooh-wooh," he warbled, starting in pursuit. "The battle of the Pyramids or Bender goes hunting. Where are you going, Client? I can offer you a well-gutted chair."

This persecution was too much for Father Fyodor and he began climbing up a perpendicular wall of rock. He was spurred on by his heart, which was in his throat, and that itch in his heels known only to cowards. His legs moved over the granite by themselves, carrying their master aloft.

"Wooooh-woooh!" yelled Ostap from below. "Catch him!"

"He's taken our supplies," screeched Vorobyaninov, running up.

"Stop!" roared Ostap. "Stop, I tell you."

But this only lent new strength to the exhausted priest. He wove about, making several leaps, finally ending up ten feet above the highest inscription.

"Give back our sausage!" howled Ostap. "Give back the sausage, you fool, and we'll forget everything."

Father Fyodor no longer heard anything. He found himself on a flat ledge to which no man had ever climbed before. Father Fyodor was seized by a sickening dread. He realized he could never get down by himself. The cliff face dropped vertically to the highway.

He looked below. Ostap was gesticulating furiously, and the marshal's gold pince-nez glittered at the bottom of the gorge.

"I'll give back the sausage," cried Father Fyodor, "only get me down."

He could see all the movements of the concessionaires. They were running about below and, judging from their gestures, swearing like troopers.

An hour later, lying on his stomach and peering over the edge, Father Fyodor saw Bender and Vorobyaninov going off in the direction of the Cross gap.

Night fell quickly. Surrounded by pitch darkness and deafened by the infernal roar, Father Fyodor trembled and wept under the very clouds. He no longer wanted earthly treasures, he only wanted one thing—to get down onto the ground.

During the night he howled so loudly that at times the Terek was drowned, and when morning came, he fortified himself with sausage and bread and roared with demoniac laughter at the cars passing underneath. The rest of the day was spent contemplating the mountains and that heavenly body, the sun. The next night he saw the Tsaritsa Tamara. She came flying over to him from her castle and said coquettishly:

"Let's be neighbors!"

"Mother!" said Father Fyodor with feeling. "Not for personal gain . . ."

"I know, I know," observed the Tsaritsa, "but merely at the wishes of your wife who sent you."

"How did you know?" asked the astonished priest.

"I just know. Why don't you stop by, neighbor? We'll play sixty-six. What about it?"

She gave a laugh and flew off, letting off firecrackers into the night sky as she went.

The day after, Father Fyodor began preaching to the birds. For some reason he tried to sway them toward Lutheranism.

"Birds," he said in a sonorous voice, "repent your sins publicly."

On the fourth day he was pointed out to tourists from below.

"On the right we have Tamara's castle," explained the experienced guides, "and on the left is a live man, but it is not known what he lives on or how he got there."

"My, what a wild people!" exclaimed the tourists in amazement. "Children of the mountains!"

Clouds drifted by. Eagles cruised above Father Fyodor's head. The bravest of them stole the remains of the sausage and with its wing swept a pound and a half of bread into the foaming Terek.

Father Fyodor wagged his finger at the eagle and, smiling radiantly, whispered:

> *"God's bird does not know*
> *Either toil or unrest,*
> *He leisurely builds*
> *His long-lasting nest."*

The eagle looked sideways at Father Fyodor, squawked cockadoodledoo and flew away.

"Oh, eagle, you eagle, you bitch of a bird!"

Ten days later the Vladikavkaz fire brigade arrived

with suitable equipment and brought Father Fyodor down.

As they were lowering him, he clapped his hands and sang in a tuneless voice:

"*And you will be the Tsaritsa of all the world*
My livelo-ong frie-nd!"

The severe Caucasus echoed Rubinstein's setting of Lermontov's poem many times.

"Not for personal gain, but merely at the wishes . . ." Father Fyodor told the fire chief.

The cackling priest was taken on a fire ladder to the psychiatric hospital.

] CHAPTER [

: *39* :

The Earthquake

"What do you think, Marshal," said Ostap as the concessionaires approached the settlement of Sioni, "how
can we earn money in a dried-up spot like this?"

Ippolit Matveyevich said nothing. The only occupation by which he could have kept himself going was
begging, but here in the mountain spirals and ledges
there was no one to beg from.

Anyway, there was begging going on already—al-
pine begging, a special kind. Every bus and passenger
car passing through the settlement was besieged by
children who performed a few steps of a local folk
dance to the mobile audience, after which they ran
after the vehicle with shouts of:

"Give us money! Give money!"

The passengers flung five-kopek pieces at them and
continued in their way to the Cross gap.

"A noble cause," said Ostap. "No capital outlay
needed. The income is small, but in our case, valuable."

By two o'clock of the second day of their journey,
Ippolit Matveyevich had performed his first dance for
the flying passengers, under the supervision of the
smooth operator. The dance was rather like a mazurka;
the passengers, drunk with the beauty of the Caucasus,

took it for a native *lezginka* and rewarded him with three five-kopek bits. The next vehicle, which was a bus going from Tiflis to Vladikavkaz, was entertained by the smooth operator himself.

"Give me money! Give money," he shouted angrily.

The amused passengers richly rewarded his capering about, and Ostap collected thirty kopeks from the dusty road. But the Sioni children showered their competitors with stones, and, fleeing from the onslaught, the travelers made for the next village on the double, where they spent their earnings on cheese and local flat bread.

The concessionaires passed their days in this way. They spent the nights in mountain-dwellers' huts. On the fourth day they went down the hairpin bends of the highway and arrived in the Kaishaur valley. The sun was shining brightly, and the partners, who had been frozen to the bone in the Cross gap, soon warmed up again.

The Daryal cliffs, the gloom and the chill of the gap gave way to the greenery and luxury of the very deep valley. The companions passed above the Aragva river and went down into the valley, settled with people and teeming with cattle and food. There it was possible to scrounge something, earn, or simply steal. It was the Transcaucasus.

The heartened concessionaires increased their pace.

In Passanaur, in that hot and thriving settlement with two hotels and several taverns, the friends cadged some bread and lay down under the bushes opposite the hotel France with its garden and two chained-up bear cubs. They relaxed in the warmth, enjoying the tasty bread and well-earned rest.

Their rest, however, was soon disturbed by the tooting of a car horn, the slither of tires on the flinty road, and cries of merriment. The friends peeped out. Three identical new cars in a line were driving up to the hotel France. The cars stopped without any noise. Out of the first one jumped Persidsky; he was followed by "Life and the Law" smoothing down his dusty hair. Out of the other cars tumbled the members of the *Lathe* automobile club.

"A halt," cried Persidsky. "Waiter, fifteen shishke-babs!"

The sleepy figures staggered into the hotel France, and there came the bleating of a ram being dragged into the kitchen by the hind legs.

"Do you recognize that young fellow?" asked Ostap. "He's the reporter from the *Scriabin*, one of those who criticized our transparent. They've certainly arrived in style. What's it all about?"

Ostap approached the kebab guzzlers and bowed to Persidsky in the most elegant fashion.

"*Bon jour!*" said the reporter. "Where have I seen you before, dear friend? Aha! I remember. The artist from the *Scriabin*, aren't you?"

Ostap put his hand to his heart and bowed politely.

"Wait a moment, wait a moment," continued Persidsky, who had a reporter's retentive memory. "Wasn't it you who was knocked down by a carthorse in Sverdlov Square?"

"That's right. And as you so neatly expressed it, I also suffered from slight shock."

"What are you doing here? Working as an artist?"

"No, I'm on a sightseeing trip."

"On foot?"

"Yes, on foot. The experts say a car trip along the Georgian military highway is simply ridiculous."

"Not always ridiculous, my dear fellow, not always. For instance, our trip isn't exactly ridiculous. We have our own cars, I stress, our own cars, collectively owned. A direct link between Moscow and Tiflis. Gasoline hardly costs anything. Comfort and speed. Soft springs. Europe!"

"How did you come by it all?" asked Ostap enviously. "Did you win a hundred thousand?"

"Not a hundred, but we won fifty."

"Gambling?"

"With a bond belonging to the automobile club."

"I see," said Ostap, "and with the money you bought the cars."

"That's right."

"I see. Maybe you need a manager? I know a young man. He doesn't drink."

"What sort of manager?"

"Well, you know . . . general management, business advice, instruction with visual aids by the complex method . . ."

"I see what you mean. No, we don't need a manager."

"You don't?"

"Unfortunately not. Nor an artist."

"In that case let me have ten roubles."

"Avdotyin," said Persidsky, "kindly give this citizen ten roubles on my account. I don't need a receipt. This person is unaccountable."

"That's extraordinarily little," observed Ostap, "but I'll accept it. I realize the great difficulty of your position. Naturally, if you had won a hundred thousand, you probably would have loaned me a whole five roubles. But you won only fifty thousand roubles, zero kopeks. In any case, many thanks."

Bender politely raised his hat. Persidsky politely raised his hat. Bender bowed most courteously. Persidsky replied with a most courteous bow. Bender waved his hand in farewell. Persidsky, sitting at the wheel, did the same. Persidsky drove off in his splendid car into the glittering distances in the company of his gay friends, while the smooth operator was left on the dusty road with his fool of a partner.

"Did you see that swank?"

"The Transcaucasian car service or the private 'Motor' company?" asked Ippolit Matveyevich in a businesslike way; he was now thoroughly acquainted with all types of transportation on the highway. "I was just about to do a dance for them."

"You'll soon be completely dotty, my poor friend. How could it be the Transcaucasian car service? Those people have won fifty thousand roubles, Kisa. You saw yourself how happy they were and how much of that mechanical junk they had bought. When we find our money, we'll spend it more sensibly, won't we?"

And imagining what they would buy when they became rich, the friends left Passanaur. Ippolit Matveyevich vividly saw himself buying some new socks and traveling abroad. Ostap's visions were more ambitious. Something between damming the Blue Nile and opening a gaming house in Riga with branches in the other Baltic states.

The travelers reached Mtskhet, the ancient capital of Georgia, on the third day before lunch. Here the Kura river turned towards Tiflis.

In the evening they passed the Zemo-Avchal hydroelectric station. The glass, water, and electricity all shone with different-colored light. It was reflected and scattered by the fast flowing Kura.

It was there the concessionaires made friends with a peasant who gave them a lift into Tiflis in his cart; they arrived at 11 P.M., that very hour when the cool of the evening summons into the streets the citizens of the Georgian capital, limp after their sultry day.

"Not a bad little town," remarked Ostap, as they came out into Rustavelli Boulevard. "You know, Kisa . . ."

Without finishing what he was saying, Ostap suddenly darted after a citizen, caught him up after ten paces, and began an animated conversation with him.

Then he quickly returned and poked Ippolit Matveyevich in the side.

"Do you know who that is?" he whispered. "It's Citizen Kislarsky of the Odessa Roll-Moscow Bun. Let's go and see him. However paradoxical it seems, you are now the master mind and father of Russian democracy again. Don't forget to puff out your cheeks and wiggle your mustache. It's grown quite a bit, by the way. A hell of a piece of good luck. If he isn't good for fifty roubles, you can spit in my eye. Come on!"

And indeed, a short distance away from the concessionaires stood Kislarsky in a tussah-silk suit and a boater; he was a milky blue color with fright.

"I think you know each other," whispered Ostap. "This is a person close to the Emperor, the master mind and father of Russian democracy. Don't pay attention to his suit, that's part of our security measures. Take us somewhere right away. We've got to have a talk."

Kislarsky, who had come to the Caucasus to recover from his grueling experiences in Stargorod, was completely crushed. Burbling something about a recession in the roll-bun trade, Kislarsky set his old friends in a carriage with silver-plated spokes and footboards and drove them to Mount David. They went up to the top of the restaurant mountain by cablecar. Tiflis slowly disappeared into the depths in a thousand lights. The conspirators were ascending to the very stars.

At the restaurant the tables were set up on a lawn. A Caucasian band made a dull drumming noise, and a little girl did a dance between the tables of her own accord, watched happily by her parents.

"Order something," suggested Bender.

The experienced Kislarsky ordered wine, salad, and Georgian cheese.

"And something to eat," said Ostap. "If you only knew, dear Mr. Kislarsky, the things that Ippolit Matveyevich and I have had to suffer, you'd be amazed at our courage."

"There he goes again," thought Kislarsky in dismay. "Now my troubles will start all over again. Why didn't I go to the Crimea? I definitely wanted to go to the Crimea, and Henrietta advised me to go, too."

But he ordered two shishkebabs without a murmur and turned his unctuous face toward Ostap.

"Here's the point," said Ostap, looking around and lowering his voice. "They've been following us for two months and will probably ambush us tomorrow at the secret meeting place. We may have to shoot our way out."

Kislarsky's cheeks turned the color of lead.

"Under the circumstances," continued Ostap, "we're glad to meet a loyal patriot."

"Mmm . . . yes," said Ippolit Matveyevich proudly, remembering the hungry ardor with which he had danced the *lezginka* not far from Sioni.

"Yes," whispered Ostap, "we're hoping—with your aid—to defeat the enemy. I'll give you a pistol."

"There's no need," said Kislarsky firmly.

The next moment it was made clear that the chairman of the stock-exchange committee would not have the opportunity of taking part in the coming battle. He regretted it very much. He was not familiar with warfare, and it was just for this reason that he had been elected chairman of the stock-exchange committee. He was very much disappointed, but was prepared to offer financial assistance to save the life of the father of Russian democracy (he was himself an Octobrist).

"You are a true friend of society," said Ostap triumphantly, washing down the spicy kebab with sweetish Kipiani wine. "Fifty can save the master mind."

"Won't twenty save the master mind?" asked Kislarsky dolefully.

Ostap could not restrain himself and kicked Ippolit Matveyevich under the table in delight.

"I consider that haggling," said Ippolit Matveyevich, "is somewhat out of place here."

He immediately received a kick on the thigh which meant "Well done, Kisa, that's the stuff!"

It was the first time in his life that Kislarsky had heard the master mind's voice. He was so overcome

that he immediately handed over fifty roubles. Then
he paid the check and, leaving the friends at the table,
departed with the excuse that he had a headache.
Half an hour later he dispatched a telegram to his wife
in Stargorod:

> GOING TO CRIMEA AS YOU ADVISED STOP
> PREPARE BASKET JUST IN CASE

The many privations which Ostap had suffered demanded immediate compensation. That evening the
smooth operator drank himself into a stupor and practically fell out of the cablecar on the way back to the
hotel. The next day he realized a long cherished dream
and bought a heavenly gray polka-dot suit. It was hot
wearing it, but he nevertheless did so, sweating pro-
fusely. In the Tif-co-op men's shop, Vorobyaninov
was bought a white piqué suit and a yachting cap with
the gold insignia of some unknown yacht club. In this
attire Ippolit Matveyevich looked like an amateur admiral in the merchant navy. His figure straightened up
and his gait became firmer.

"Ah," said Bender, "first rate! If I were a girl, I'd
give a male beauty like you an eight per cent reduction
off my usual price. My, we can certainly get around
like this. Do you know how to get around, Kisa?"

"Comrade Bender," Vorobyaninov kept saying,
"what about the chairs? We've got to find out what
happened to the theater."

"Hoho," retorted Ostap, dancing with a chair in the
Grand Mauritian room of the hotel Orient. "Don't
tell me how to live. I'm now evil. I have money, but
I'm magnanimous. I'll give you twenty roubles and
three days to loot the city. I'm like Suvorov. . . . Loot
the city, Kisa! Enjoy yourself!"

And swaying his hips, Ostap sang in quick time:

> *"The evening bells, the evening bells,
> How many thoughts they bring. . . ."*

The friends caroused wildly for a whole week. Vorobyaninov's admiral's uniform became covered with apple-sized wine spots of different colors; on Ostap's suit the stains suffused into one large rainbow apple.

"Hi!" said Ostap on the eighth morning, so hungover that he was reading the newspaper *Dawn of the East*. "Listen, you drunken sot, to what clever people are writing in the press! Listen!

> 'THEATER NEWS
> The Moscow Columbus Theater left yesterday, Sept. 3, for a tour of Yalta, having completed its stay in Tiflis. The theater is planning to remain in the Crimea until the opening of the winter season in Moscow.' "

"What did I tell you!" said Vorobyaninov.

"What did you tell me!" snapped back Ostap.

He was nevertheless embarrassed. The careless mistake was very unpleasant. Instead of ending the treasure hunt in Tiflis, they now had to move on to the Crimean peninsula. Ostap immediately set to work. Tickets were bought to Batumi and second-class berths reserved on the *S. S. Pestel* leaving Batumi for Odessa at 11 P.M. Moscow time on September 7.

On the night of September 10, as the *Pestel* turned out to sea and set sail for Yalta without calling at Anapa on account of the gale, Ippolit Matveyevich had a dream.

He dreamed he was standing in his admiral's uniform on the balcony of his house in Stargorod, while the crowd gathered below waited for him to do something. A large crane deposited a black-spotted pig at his feet.

Tikhon the janitor appeared and, grabbing the pig by the hind legs, said:

"Durn it. Does the Nymph really provide tassels?"

Ippolit Matveyevich found a dagger in his hand. He stuck it into the pig's side, and jewels came pouring out of the large wound and rolled onto the cement floor. They jumped about and clattered more and more loudly. The noise finally became unbearable and terrifying.

Ippolit Matveyevich was wakened by the sound of waves dashing against the porthole.

They reached Yalta in calm weather on an enervating sunny morning. Having recovered from his seasickness, the marshal was standing at the prow near the ship's bell with its embossed Old Church Slavonic lettering. Gay Yalta had lined up its tiny stalls and floating restaurants along the shore. On the quayside there were waiting carriages with velvet-covered seats and linen awnings, motor cars and buses belonging to "Krymkurso" and "Crimean Driver" societies. Brick-shaped girls twirled parasols and waved kerchiefs.

The friends were the first to go ashore onto the scorching embankment. At the sight of the concessionaires, a citizen in a tussah-silk suit dived out of the crowd of people meeting the ship and idle onlookers and began walking quickly toward the exit to the dockyard. But too late. The smooth operator's eagle eye had quickly recognized the silken citizen.

"Wait a moment, Vorobyaninov," cried Ostap.

And he raced off at such a pace that he caught up the silken citizen about ten feet from the exit. He returned instantly with a hundred roubles.

"He wouldn't give me any more. Anyway, I didn't insist; otherwise he won't be able to get home."

And indeed, at that very moment Kislarsky was fleeing in a bus for Sebastopol, and from there went home to Stargorod by third class.

The concessionaires spent the whole day in the hotel sitting naked on the floor and every few moments running under the shower in the bathroom. But the water there was like warm weak tea. They could not escape from the heat. It felt as though Yalta was just about to melt and flow into the sea.

Toward eight that evening the partners struggled into their red-hot shoes, cursing all the chairs in the world, and went to the theater.

The Marriage was being shown. Exhausted by the heat, Stepan almost fell over while standing on his hands. Agafya ran along the wire, holding the parasol marked "I want Podkolesin" in her dripping hands. All she really wanted at that moment was a drink of ice water. The audience was thirsty, too. For this reason and perhaps also because the sight of Stepan gorging a pan of hot fried eggs was revolting, the performance did not go over.

The concessionaires were satisfied as soon as they saw that their chair, together with three new rococo chairs, was safe.

Hiding in one of the boxes, they patiently waited for the end of the performance, which dragged on interminably. The audience finally left and the actors hurried away to try to cool off. The theater was empty except for the shareholders in the concession. Every living thing had hurried out into the street where fresh rain was, at last, falling fast.

"Follow me, Kisa," ordered Ostap. "Just in case, we're provincials who couldn't find the exit."

They made their way onto the stage and, striking matches, though they still collided with the hydraulic press, searched the whole stage.

The smooth operator ran up a staircase into the props room.

"Up here!" he called.

Waving his arms, Vorobyaninov raced upstairs.

"Do you see?" said Ostap, lighting a match.

Through the darkness showed the corner of a Hambs chair and part of the parasol with the word "want."

"There it is! There is our past, present, and future. Light a match, Kisa, and I'll open it up."

Ostap dug into his pockets for the tools.

"Right," he said, reaching toward the chair. "Another match, Marshal."

The match flared up, and then a strange thing happened. The chair gave a jump and suddenly, before the very eyes of the amazed concessionaires, disappeared through the floor.

"Mama!" cried Vorobyaninov, and went flying over to the wall, although he had not the least desire to do so.

The window panes came out with a crash and the parasol with the words "I want Podkolesin" flew out of the window toward the sea. Ostap lay on the floor, pinned down by sheets of cardboard.

It was fourteen minutes past midnight. This was the first shock of the great Crimean earthquake of 1927.

A severe earthquake, wreaking untold disaster throughout the peninsula, had torn the treasure out of the hands of the concessionaires.

"Comrade Bender, what's happening?" cried Ippolit Matveyevich in terror.

Ostap was beside himself. The earthquake had blocked his path. It was the only time it had happened in his entire extensive practice.

"What is it?" screeched Vorobyaninov.

Screaming, ringing, and trampling feet could be heard from the street.

"We've got to get outside immediately before the wall caves in on us. Quick! Give me your hand, softie."

They raced to the door. To their surprise, the Hambs chair was lying on its back, undamaged, at the exit from the stage to the street. Growling like a dog, Ippolit Matveyevich seized it in a death-grip.

"Give me the pliers," he shouted to Bender.

"Don't be a stupid fool," gasped Ostap. "The ceiling

is just about to collapse, and you stand there going out of your mind! Let's get out quickly."

"The pliers," snarled the crazed Vorobyaninov.

"To hell with you. Perish here with your chair, then. I value my life, if you don't."

With these words Ostap ran for the door. Ippolit Matveyevich picked up the chair with a snarl and ran after him.

Hardly had they reached the middle of the street when the ground heaved sickeningly under their feet; tiles came off the roof of the theater, and the spot where the concessionaires had just been standing was strewn with the remains of the hydraulic press.

"Right, give me the chair now," said Bender coldly. "You're tired of holding it, I see."

"I won't," screeched Ippolit Matveyevich.

"What's this? Mutiny aboard? Give me the chair, do you hear?"

"It's my chair," clucked Vorobyaninov, drowning the weeping, shouting, and crashing on all sides.

"In that case, here's your reward, you old goat!"

And Ostap hit Vorobyaninov on the neck with his bronze fist.

At that moment a fire engine hurtled down the street and in the light of its head lamps Ippolit Matveyevich glimpsed such a terrifying expression on Ostap's face that he instantly obeyed and gave up the chair.

"That's better," said Ostap, regaining his breath. "The mutiny has been suppressed. Now, take the chair and follow me. You are responsible for the state of the chair. The chair must be preserved even if there are ten earthquakes. Do you understand?"

"Yes."

The whole night the concessionaires wandered about with the panic-stricken crowds, unable to decide, like everyone else, whether or not to enter the abandoned buildings, and expecting new shocks.

At dawn, when the terror had died down somewhat, Ostap selected a spot near which there was no wall likely to collapse, or people likely to interfere, and set about opening the chair.

The results of the autopsy staggered both of them. There was nothing in the chair. The effect of the ordeal of the night and morning was too much for Ippolit Matveyevich; he burst into a vicious, high-pitched cackle.

Immediately after this came the third shock. The ground heaved and swallowed up the Hambs chair; its flowered pattern smiled at the sun that was rising in a dusty sky.

Ippolit Matveyevich went down on all fours and, turning his haggard face to the dark purple disk of the sun, began howling. The smooth operator fainted while listening to him. When he regained consciousness, he saw beside him Vorobyaninov's lilac-stubble chin. Vorobyaninov was unconscious.

"At last," said Ostap, like a patient recovering from typhus, "we have a dead certainty. The last chair [at the word "chair," Ippolit Matveyevich stirred] vanished into the freight yard of the October station, but has by no means been swallowed up by the ground. What's wrong? The hearing is continued."

Bricks came crashing down nearby. A ship's siren gave a protracted wail.

The Treasure

ON A RAINY DAY in October, Ippolit Matveyevich, in his silver star-spangled vest and without a jacket, was working busily in Ivanopulo's room. He was working at the windowsill, since there still was no table in the room. The smooth operator had been commissioned to paint a large number of address plates for various housing co-operatives. The stenciling of the plates had been passed on to Vorobyaninov, while Ostap, for almost the whole of the month since their return to Moscow, had cruised round the area of the October station, looking with incredible avidity for clues to the last chair, which undoubtedly contained Madam Petukhova's jewels.

Wrinkling his brow, Ippolit Matveyevich stenciled away at the iron plates. During the six months of the jewel race he had lost certain of his habits.

At night Ippolit Matveyevich dreamed about mountain ridges adorned with weird transparents, Iznurenkov, who hovered in front of him, shaking his brown thighs, boats that capsized, people who drowned, bricks falling out of the sky, and the ground that heaved and poured smoke into his eyes.

Ostap had not observed the change in Vorobyaninov, since he was with him every day. Ippolit Matveyevich, however, had changed in a remarkable way. Even his gait was different; the expression of his eyes had become wild and his long mustache was no longer parallel to the earth's surface, but drooped almost vertically like that of an aged cat.

He had also altered inwardly. He had developed determination and cruelty, which were traits of character unknown to him before. Three episodes had gradually brought out these streaks in him: the miraculous escape from the hard fists of the Vasyuki enthusiasts, his debut in the field of begging at the Flower Garden in Pyatigorsk, and, finally, the earthquake, since which Ippolit Matveyevich had become somewhat unhinged and harbored a secret loathing for his partner.

Ippolit Matveyevich had recently been seized by the strongest suspicions. He was afraid that Ostap would open the chair without him and make off with the treasure, abandoning him to his own fate. He did not dare voice these suspicions, knowing Ostap's strong arm and iron will. Each day, as he sat at the window scraping off surplus paint with an old, jagged razor, Ippolit Matveyevich wondered. Every day he feared that Ostap would not come back and that he, a former marshal of the nobility, would die of starvation under some wet Moscow wall.

Ostap nevertheless returned each evening, though he never brought any good news. His energy and good spirits were inexhaustible. Hope never deserted him for a moment.

There was a sound of running footsteps in the corridor and someone crashed into the safe; the plywood door flew open with the ease of a page turned by the wind, and in the doorway stood the smooth operator. His clothes were soaked, and his cheeks glowed like apples. He was panting.

"Ippolit Matveyevich!" he shouted. "Ippolit Matveyevich!"

Vorobyaninov was startled. Never before had the technical adviser called him by these two names. Then he cottoned on. . . .

"It's there?" he gasped.

"You're dead right, it's there, Kisa. Damn you."

"Don't shout. Everyone will hear."

"That's right, they might hear," whispered Ostap. "It's there, Kisa, and if you want, I can show it to you right away. It's in the railroad-workers' club, a new one. It was opened yesterday. How did I find it? Was it child's play? It was singularly difficult. A stroke of genius, brilliantly carried through to the end. An ancient adventure. In a word, first rate!"

Without waiting for Ippolit Matveyevich to pull on his jacket, Ostap ran to the corridor. Vorobyaninov joined him on the landing. Excitedly shooting questions at one another, they both hurried along the wet streets to Kalanchev Square. They did not even think of taking a streetcar.

"You're dressed like a roadworker," said Ostap jubilantly. "Who goes about like that, Kisa? You must have starched underwear, silk socks, and, of course, a top hat. There's something noble about your face. Tell me, were you really a marshal of the nobility?"

Pointing out the chair, which was standing in the chess room and looked a perfectly normal Hambs chair, although it contained untold wealth, Ostap pulled Ippolit Matveyevich into the corridor. There was no one about. Ostap went up to a window that had not yet been sealed for the winter and drew back the bolts on both sets of frames.

"Through this window," he said, "we can easily get into the club at any time of the night. Remember, Kisa, the third window from the front entrance."

For a while longer the friends wandered about the

club, pretending to be railroad-union representatives, and were more and more amazed by the splendid halls and rooms.

"If I had played the match in Vasyuki," said Ostap, "sitting on a chair like this, I wouldn't have lost a single game. My enthusiasm would have prevented me. Anyway, let's go, old man. I have twenty-five roubles. We ought to have a glass of beer and relax before our nocturnal visit. The idea of beer doesn't shock you, does it, Marshal? No harm. Tomorrow you can lap up champagne in unlimited quantities."

By the time they emerged from the beer hall, Bender was thoroughly enjoying himself and made taunting remarks at the passers-by. He embraced the slightly tipsy Ippolit Matveyevich round the shoulders and said lovingly:

"You're an extremely nice old man, Kisa, but I'm not going to give you more than ten per cent. Honestly, I'm not. What would you want with all that money?"

"What do you mean, what would I want?" Ippolit Matveyevich seethed with rage.

Ostap laughed heartily and rubbed his cheek against his partner's wet sleeve.

"Well, what would you buy, Kisa? You haven't any imagination. Honestly, fifteen thousand is more than enough for you. You'll soon die, you're so old. You don't need any money at all. You know, Kisa, I don't think I'll give you anything. I don't want to spoil you. I'll take you on as a secretary, Kisula. What do you say? Forty roubles a month and all your grub. You get work clothes, tips, and social insurance. Well, is it a deal?"

Ippolit Matveyevich tore his arm free and quickly walked ahead. Jokes like that exasperated him.

Ostap caught him up at the entrance to the little pink house.

"Are you really mad at me?" asked Ostap. "I was

only joking. You'll get your three per cent. Honestly,
three per cent is all you need, Kisa."

Ippolit Matveyevich sullenly entered the room.

"Well, Kisa, take three per cent." Ostap was having
fun. "Come on, take three. Anyone else would. You
don't have any rooms to rent. It's a blessing Ivanopulo
has gone to Tver for a whole year. Anyway, come
and be my valet . . . an easy job."

Seeing that Ippolit Matveyevich could not be
baited, Ostap yawned sweetly, stretched himself, almost touching the ceiling as he filled his broad chest
with air, and said:

"Well, friend, make your pockets ready. We'll go to
the club just before dawn. That's the best time. The
watchmen are asleep having sweet dreams, for which
they get fired without severance pay. In the meantime, chum, I advise you to have a nap."

Ostap stretched himself out on the three chairs acquired from different corners of Moscow, and said, as
he dozed off:

"Or my valet . . . a decent salary. No, I was joking. . . . The hearing's continued. Things are moving,
gentlemen of the jury."

Those were the smooth operator's last words. He
fell into a deep, refreshing sleep, untroubled by
dreams.

Ippolit Matveyevich went out into the street. He
was full of desperation and cold fury. The moon
hopped about among the banks of cloud. The wet
railings of the houses glistened greasily. The flickering
gas lamps in the street were encircled by halos of
moisture. A drunk was being thrown out of the
Eagle beer hall. He began bawling. Ippolit Matveyevich frowned and went back inside. His one wish was
to finish the whole business as soon as possible.

He went into the room, looked severely at the
sleeping Ostap, wiped his pince-nez and took up the
razor from the window sill. There were still some

dried scales of oil paint on its jagged edge. He put the razor in his pocket and walked past Ostap again, without looking at him, but listening to his breathing, and then went out into the corridor. It was dark and sleepy out there. Everyone had evidently gone to bed. In the pitch darkness of the corridor Ippolit Matveyevich suddenly smiled in the most evil way and felt the skin creep on his forehead. To test this new sensation he smiled again. He suddenly remembered a pupil at school who had been able to move his ears.

Ippolit Matveyevich went as far as the stairs and listened carefully. There was no one there. From the street came the drumming of a carthorse's hoofs, intentionally loud and clear, as though someone was counting on an abacus. As stealthily as a cat, the marshal went back into the room, removed twenty-five roubles and the pair of pliers from Ostap's jacket hanging on the back of a chair, put on his own yachting cap, and again listened intently.

Ostap was sleeping quietly. His nose and lungs were working perfectly, smoothly inhaling and exhaling air. A sturdy arm hung down to the floor. Conscious of the second-long pulses in his temple, Ippolit Matveyevich slowly rolled up his right sleeve above the elbow and bound a wafer-patterned towel around his bare arm; he stepped back to the door, took the razor out of his pocket, and, gauging the position of the furniture in the room, turned the switch. The light went out, but the room was still lit by a bluish aquariumlike light from the street lamps.

"So much the better," whispered Ippolit Matveyevich.

He approached the back of the chair and, drawing back his hand with the razor, plunged the blade slantways into Ostap's throat, pulled it out, and jumped backward toward the wall. The smooth operator gave a gurgle like a kitchen sink sucking down the last water. Ippolit Matveyevich managed to avoid being splashed with blood. Wiping the wall with his jacket, he stole toward the blue door, and for a brief moment looked back at Ostap. His body had arched twice and slumped against the backs of the chairs. The light from the street moved across a black puddle forming on the floor.

"What is that puddle?" wondered Vorobyaninov. "Oh, yes, it's blood. Comrade Bender is dead."

He unwound the slightly stained towel, threw it aside, carefully put the razor on the floor, and left, closing the door quietly.

Finding himself in the street, Vorobyaninov scowled and, muttering "The jewels are all mine and not just six per cent," went off to Kalanchev Square.

Ippolit Matveyevich stopped at the third window from the front entrance to the railroad club. The mirrorlike windows of the new club shone pearl-gray in the approaching dawn. Through the damp air came the muffled voices of freight locomotives. Ippolit Matveyevich nimbly scrambled onto the ledge, pushed the frames, and silently dropped into the corridor.

Finding his way without difficulty through the gray predawn halls of the club, he reached the chess room and went over to the chair, bumping his head on a portrait of Lasker hanging on the wall. He was in no hurry. There was no point in it. No one was after him. *Grossmeister* Bender was asleep forever in the little pink house.

Ippolit Matveyevich sat down on the floor, gripped the chair between his sinewy legs, and with the coolness of a dentist began extracting the tacks, not missing a single one. His work was complete at the sixty-second tack. The English chintz and canvas lay loosely on top of the stuffing.

He had only to lift them to see the caskets, boxes, and cases containing the precious stones.

"Straight into a car," thought Ippolit Matveyevich, who had learned the facts of life from the smooth operator, "then to the station, and on to the Polish frontier. For a small gem they should get me across, then . . ."

And desiring to find out as soon as possible what would happen then, Ippolit Matveyevich pulled away the covering from the chair. Before his eyes were springs, beautiful English springs, and stuffing, wonderful prewar stuffing, the like of which you never see nowadays. But there was nothing else in the chair. Ippolit Matveyevich mechanically turned the chair inside out and sat for a whole hour clutching it between his legs and repeating in a dull voice:

"Why isn't there anything there? It can't be right. It can't be."

It was almost light when Vorobyaninov, leaving everything as it was in the chess room and forgetting the pliers and his yachting cap with the gold insignia of a nonexistent yacht club, crawled tired and heavy and unobserved through the window into the street.

"It can't be right," he kept repeating, having walked a block away. "It can't be right."

Then he returned to the club and began wandering up and down by the large windows, mouthing the words:

"It can't be right. It can't be."

From time to time he let out a shriek and seized his head, wet from the morning mist. Remembering the events of that night, he shook his disheveled gray hair. The excitement of the jewels was too much for him; he had withered in five minutes.

"There's all kinds come here!" said a voice by his ear.

He saw a watchman in canvas workclothes and poor-quality boots. He was very old and evidently friendly.

"They keep comin'," said the old man politely, tired of his nocturnal solitude. "And you, Comrade, are interested. That's right. Our club's kind of unusual."

Ippolit Matveyevich looked ruefully at the red-cheeked old man.

"Yes, sir," said the old man, "a very unusual club; there ain't no other like it."

"And what's so unusual about it?" asked Ippolit Matveyevich, trying to gather his wits.

The little old man beamed at Vorobyaninov. The story of the unusual club seemed to please him, and he liked to retell it.

"Well, it's like this," began the old man, "I've been a watchman here for more'n ten years, and nothing like that ever happened. Listen, soldier boy! Well, there used to be a club here, you know the one, for workers in the first transportation division. I used to guard it. A no-good club it was. They heated and heated and couldn't do anything. Then Comrade Krasilnikov comes to me and asks, 'Where's all that firewood going?' Did he think I was eatin' it or somethin'? Comrade Krasilnikov had a job with that club, he did. It was damp and cold. The brass band had nowhere to rehearse, and it was just awful playin' in the theater; the actors froze, they did. They asked for five years credit for a new club, but I don't know what became of it. They didn't allow the credit. Then, in the spring, Comrade Krasilnikov bought a new chair for the stage, a good soft'n."

With his whole body close to the watchman's, Ippolit Matveyevich listened. He was only half conscious, while the watchman, cackling with laughter, told how he had once clambered onto the chair to put in a new bulb and missed his footing.

"I slipped off the chair and the covering was torn off. So I look round and see bits of glass and beads on a string come pouring out."

"Beads," said Ippolit Matveyevich.

"Beads!" hooted the old man with delight. "And I look, soldier boy, and there are all sorts of little boxes. I didn't touch 'em. I went straight to Comrade Krasilni-

kov and reported it. And that's what I told the committee afterward. I didn't touch the boxes, I didn't.
And a good thing I didn't, soldier boy. Because jewelry
was found in 'em, hidden by the bourgeois. . . ."

"Where are the jewels?" cried the marshal.

"Where, where?" the watchman imitated him. "Here
they are, soldier boy, use your imagination! Here they
are."

"Where?"

"Here they are!" cried the ruddy-faced old man,
enjoying the effect. "Wipe your eyes. The club was
built with them, soldier boy. You see? It's the club.
Central heating, checkers with clocks, a buffet,
theater; you aren't allowed in without galoshes."

Ippolit Matveyevich stiffened and, without moving,
ran his eyes over the ledges.

So that was where it was, Madam Petukhova's
treasure. There. All of it. A hundred and fifty thousand roubles, zero zero kopeks, as Ostap Suleiman
Bertha Maria Bender used to say.

The jewels had turned into a solid frontage of glass
and ferroconcrete floors. Cool gymnasiums had been
made from the pearls. The diamond diadem had become a theater-auditorium with a revolving stage; the
ruby pendants had grown into chandeliers; the serpent
bracelets had been transformed into a beautiful library,
and the clasp had metamorphosed into a crèche, a
glider workshop, a chess and billiards room.

The treasure remained; it had been preserved and
had even grown. It could be touched with the hand,
though not taken away. It had gone into the service
of new people. Ippolit Matveyevich felt the granite
facing. The coldness of the stone penetrated deep into
his heart.

And he gave a cry.

It was an insane, impassioned wild cry—the cry of
a vixen shot through the body—it flew into the center

of the square, streaked under the bridge, and, rebuffed everywhere by the sounds of the waking city, began fading and died away in a moment. A marvelous autumn morning slipped from the wet roof tops into the Moscow streets. The city set off on its daily routine.

European Classics